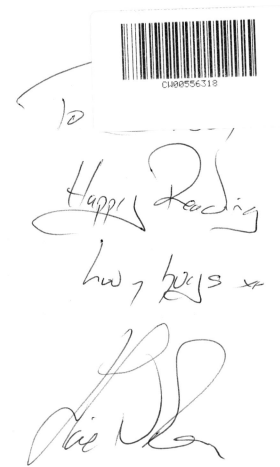
To

Happy Reading

luv, hugs xx

Of Heroes and Kings

By Elaine Nolan

Cover designed by © Paramita Bhattacharjee
www.creativeparamita.com

40 From Now Logo by © Ninja Kitten Studios

A *40 From Now* Publication
Email: 40fn@elainenolan.net

For 'Gussie' and Catherine

The two best teachers and guides

No longer in the world

But the fire ignited

In one little girl

Lives on…

And burns brighter

for having known them

Other Publications by Elaine Nolan

Evolved
> Short novel published 2014 by Pure Ice Publishing
> Soundtrack for Evolved also available on:
> Amazon, iTunes, Spotify, Deezer

Soundtrack for Of Heroes and Kings
> also available on: Amazon Mp3, iTunes, Spotify, Deezer
> (Follow links from website below)

New titles coming soon

Red Hot Summer
Evolved 2.0

To keep up to date with all new releases, please visit:
www.elainenolan.net

Table of Contents

Acknowledgements

John McInerney – Guide, Dunmore Caves, Co Kilkenny

Etain Dowling – Celtic lore, Kilkenny

Siobhan Hayden – Dungannon, Co Tyrone

Nuala Hartnell – Librarian, Athy

Teresa Kelly and Kate Lynam-Jones - Gaeilgeoirí

Marie Mannion – Coillte, Forest Manager Oughaval, Co Laois

Dominick Hartnett – Stradbally Development Group

David Delaney – Portlaoise

Louise Wills - Dublin

The Staff of Dundalk Tourist Office

Rim Aad Quinn – Carlow

Kevin Lennon – Co Dublin

Edmund Nolan – Carlow

Historical Sites & Locations

Armagh, Co Tyrone

Dundalk, Co Louth
   - the ancestral home of Cúchulainn,

Rathiddy, Knockbridge, Co Louth
   - site of Clochafarmore, Cúchulainn's Stone

Tara, Co Meath
   - site of the Lia Fáil, the Stone of Destiny

Moate of Ardscull, Athy, Co Kildare

Oughaval Woods, Stradbally, Co Laois

Arles, Co Laois

Moate of Rathvilly, Rathvilly, Co Carlow

Mount Leinster/Slievebawn, Blackstairs Mountains,
   - bordering Counties Carlow and Wexford

Prologues

I

The old man stood in the shadows, watching, as the hero of a hundred battles struggled to keep on his feet. The wind whipped the old man's cloak, but the ancient Druid paid no heed. His attention focused on the lone figure remaining on the bloodied battlefield.

With his spear as an aid, the injured warrior staggered across the dead to a tall rock nearby, scavenging for ropes, belts, anything along the way. He lashed what he found about his body and tied himself to the stone, upright and standing so that his enemies remaining at the edge of the battlefield would think him still capable of battle, and would come no closer. He heard the sound of wings flapping close by, a distinctive caw, and looked up to the darkening sky. A raven circled overhead before coming to rest upon the rock, its long beak making a play for his blood-matted hair. He jerked his head away and screamed at it, calling it a demon, an evil spirit. The bird hopped to the edge of the stone and jumped, but before reaching the ground, transformed into the most beautiful woman he'd ever seen. The wind whipped at her long red hair, her clothes, and she revelled in it, delighting in the chaos.

"You," he growled, "I should have known." She merely smiled, circling the stone and the man tied to it, stroking him across the arms and chest as she passed by. He feebly attempted to push her hand away.

"Poor Cúchulainn," she purred, her voice deep and enticing. "Forever trying to be the hero." She leaned closer and whispered in his ear. "Always choosing the lost cause, and now you've chosen your last."

"Get away from me," he growled, his breathing laboured, his body wracked with pain and injuries. He knew his end was near, but he refused to give in to her seduction, tempting as it was. He would fight her to his last, dying breath. She wouldn't win him over. He wouldn't succumb. He would die like a man. Her hand caressed his bloodied face.

"Foolish man, have it your way, but soon you will be mine. All who die come to me, sooner or later," she laughed.

He shut his eyes to her, and the laughter died away. The urge to sleep was overwhelming but he resisted its lure of peace and rest. When he opened his eyes again, the Mórrígan was gone, and only a single raven's feather remained.

II

Interpreting prophecies proved to be less a science and more an art form, oftentimes resembling the ramblings of madmen and lunatics than of sane or rational men. They came from the minds of people who saw the world with different eyes, seeing more than the ordinary person could glimpse.

The old man sifted through scraps of paper, some so delicate and seeming older than time itself. Others relatively new, but all said the same thing. Sometime in the third decade of the sixth millennium, an heir to the ancient Ard Rí, the High Kings, would be proclaimed and announced to the world.

The old man knew all of this, he'd studied the texts for years, but always hoped to glean new information every time he read them. With the year now closing on 2000, and all the fears of the millennium bug long past, what the masses didn't realise was the world already entered its sixth millennium, a world far older than Christian or Julian calendars allowed for. Only the Druids knew the true time and year, these Keepers of the Records, passed down from one High Druid to the next.

The old man sat back and sighed, confident in the knowledge that the Heir would come in his era. It now fell to him to ensure success, ensure the continuation of the line of kings. He had more planning to do, people to orchestrate, rituals to prepare for.

III

1996

She wrapped the new-born tightly in the blanket against the wintry chill and plotted her escape. They'd made her give birth on the cold earth mound just to fulfil their ridiculous prophesies but she knew her part was over; they had no further use for her. She was now a liability. She'd already tried to hide before, to escape from them, but being heavily pregnant made her easy to find, even easier to manage and control, and she hated them for it.

They gave her something to drink, to help with the labour pains, something herbal that tasted utterly vile, but as weak as she now felt following the birth, she still had enough strength to stand, to walk, to run if she needed to. They helped her to her feet, still holding her daughter close to her, trying to keep her warm, keep her safe as the child's cries pierced the frosty air.

The old man held his arms out to take the child, but she clutched her even closer, not wanting to surrender her, to give her over to the man she thought of as an evil old wizard. If she gave her daughter away then what had she left to bargain with? Only holding onto her child gave her any hope of staying alive.

It hurt to walk, but damn it, she would walk past him, would not let him see the pain she still endured, would not let him see her weakened and vulnerable. She was a Queen after all, descended from a long line of Celtic Queens; she could not afford to show any weaknesses. Not to him.

With no immediate means of escape, she complied with their demands for the moment, get in the car, get in the house. Simple instructions that she followed in uncharacteristically subdued manner. She'd let them think the birth weakened her, made her passive. She'd let them think she'd not risk her child's life, but in the early hours of the morning when the house was still and quiet, she stole away. She'd nursed the child and the baby now slept, full and contented for the moment, oblivious to the fight for freedom her mother was about to make.

Getting out of the house proved easy, no creaks or groans of doors or floorboards betrayed her. She'd parked her car at the top of the driveway, and allowed it to coast down the short hill to the gate, tapping the brakes as she pulled onto the main road, only then daring to start the engine. Her heart pounded in her chest until the lights of the village disappeared in the rear view mirror. She drove to Dublin, guessing she could hide in the city, become another single mother looking to start a new life. But her freedom was short lived. The old man found her within days, snatching the child from her arms as the others held her back, restraining her, despite her attempts to fight them off. The old man gave her that cold glare that always terrified her.

"Did you honestly think I wouldn't find you?" he growled at her, "that I would allow you to take her away from me?"

"She's not yours to take," she answered defiantly. He stepped closer to her, towering over her, intimidating her.

"Do not defy me if you wish to remain alive or ever see her again," he said before turning to leave, taking the baby with him.

"She's my child," she screamed at him. The old man paused and half turned to her, a triumphant grin on his face.

"She's mine now," he answered, laughing as her screams mingled with her baby's cry.

IV

2001

The old man found the boy in an alleyway, dressed in rags, covered in filth and dirt. And savage, to the point of being dangerous. Yet the old man remained determined, the boy was far too precious. Winning him over would take time, and a lot of patience. The wildness would have to be overcome, but then again, the old man mused, the wildness was part of who he was, what he was. It could not be erased. But if it could be harnessed then the possibilities were endless. First, he needed to gain the boy's trust.

The old man sat at a sidewalk café table. This position gave him a clear view of the alley and the paper bag he placed there. He left the bag open, hoping the scent of hot food would entice the boy out of hiding. The object wasn't to capture him. Not yet. It took a lot of researching and backtracking through records to get to this point, where he now tried to win over a feral child.

The old man thought Cúchulainn's ancient bloodline erased from the world; the original candidate killed by a bomb, and covered up as a terrorist attack. Desperation spurned him on and he returned to his carefully preserved records, and at first glance, all seemed lost, but a glimmer of hope shone through, only two generations old. The bloodline wouldn't be pure, but there it was, a remnant of the blood. This child he now attempted to win over, the only living descendant of the greatest Irish warrior.

Finding him in an American city seemed an impossible task, yet here he was and from information the old man obtained from American social services, the boy's mother died a drug user, selling her body many times to serve her habit, leaving the boy an orphan and homeless. Now, here he was. Just shy of seven years old and already a survivor. Perhaps he was the true heir after all. Time would tell.

Over the following days and weeks, the meals came regularly, the old man waiting closer each time. The boy grew more confident and bolder with this generous stranger, even being so daring as to snatch the bag from the old man's hand before diving back to his hideaway.

Until the day the old man arrived without food. The boy snarled and ran away. The next day proved better. A snarl, but he stayed. The following day, a grunt replaced the snarl. On the fourth day, he uttered his first word - "Food". The old man held out his hand and simply replied, "Come". The boy stared at him for a moment.

"I won't hurt you," the old man said. "Come with me and we will both have something to eat."

"Why?" the boy still wary of this stranger.

"I can give you a better life than the one you have now," the old man replied. "You will never be hungry again. I will send you to the best schools where you'll learn about the world, and how to succeed in it, unless you would rather stay here, picking food out of trashcans?"

The boy thought for a moment then slowly reached out to take the old man's hand.

"Trust me Setanta, and I will give you the world," he promised the boy.

Chapter 1

May 2026

Rían stepped from the train at Heuston Station, Dublin slinging her overnight bag across her shoulder. Despite being summer, an early morning chill still lingered and she zipped up her jacket. She readied her ticket for inspection. Despite the presence of automatic ticket readers, Irish Rail continued to carry out impromptu inspections, checking ID's and digital info. They had reason to be cautious. A scam concerning forged annual tickets operated for years. It was Rían's first investigative piece and her baptism of fire into journalism. Peter stood by the gate, smiling as she approached.

"Good morning, kiddo," he said.

"Hey babe, how are you this morning?" she replied. At close to 70 years old Peter blushed at being called a babe, but loving it all the same.

"Who's on your hit list today?" he asked.

"President Robertson."

"Jaysus, I remember him when he was Taoiseach *(Prime Minister)*. You'll need your wits about you interviewing that one, girl."

"He's going to need his," she replied, moving on.

"I'll be watching you. I'll let you know how you do," he said before remembering what day it was and shouted after her.

"Good luck tonight," he said and she turned around to him. "We all voted for you, so you better have that award with you tomorrow morning," he said.

She laughed, giving him a mock salute before continuing out the front of the station, towards the buses and Luas. She normally walked to work, but with an overnight bag in tow, she opted for jumping onto the next Luas, the inner city tram, that came along. At O'Connell Street, she changed to the Metro going to St Stephen's Green West.

Ireland International Media began in a little office in the Dublin suburbs and expanded aggressively, now occupying prime real estate on St Stephen's Green East, an elegant Georgian building. IIM jumped into digitalisation at the right time and now provided a service on a par with the State owned RTÉ, with radio, eFone and eNote News and Headline services to all mobile phones and handheld devices as well as providing digital TV and web editorials on a broad range of subjects. Rían Breasel fell into the 'broad range' category, focusing on the sciences, technology and her main love, the environment and all related issues. On environmental issues, she made her role, not as an eco-warrior but an advocate, using the media to highlight new technologies that would benefit everyone without harming the world. With the oil fields having dried up about 10 years previous and gas now suffering the same fate, every new development on fuel replacement interested her. Yet she also found herself thrust into politics. Not her first choice of assignments nor did she have a liking for it, but after finding her feet at IIM, discovered an aptitude for political analysis and an ability to read between the lines.

She began her career by accident, dropping out of Ancient Celtic History studies, in part out of rebellion and because at 19 years old, had no clue what she wanted to do with her life. She changed to a journalism course and found a liking and a knack for words. Her first few pieces brought her to the attention of one of the country's longer established newspapers where she fell under the wing of a veteran investigative journalist. From then on, she was hooked, but life often took funny turns, and three years ago she landed a hotly contested job with the newest media group. Now at the age of 30, on this very night she would face her biggest challenge of her career to date; a public vote of the Irish people on their media and its personalities. She'd never been a contender before, and still didn't understand why she was short-listed this time, but it was good for IIM, and IIM had been good to her.

She emerged from St Stephen's Green, jaywalking across the road, not waiting for the pedestrian lights to change. Traffic in the heart of the city was restricted to buses and taxis during the daytime so the danger was minimal. She bound up the granite steps and greeted Louise at

17

reception, picking up her messages before heading for Editorial. Later, she'd venture across the hallway to Broadcasting for the televised political programme, but before then she had a piece to get out and wanted to review her notes on the latest bio-fuel to hit the market. She'd uncovered serious flaws in their research and she doubted she would be popular when it went to print. Later that morning she arrived in the prep room, allowing the hair stylist to go through the usual routine of straightening her unruly locks while Derek fussed with her wardrobe. Her personal favourite was the well-cut pinstripe trouser suit she always wore and she didn't know why Derek got in such a tizz; the suit was her trademark. He sat down beside her, looking solemn.

"We need to talk about what you're going to wear tonight," he began, "I have a choice of two outfits, one I'm guessing you won't like but I think it's fabulous, the other I won't like, but you'll probably go for it."

"What are they?" she asked and he disappeared for a moment, returning with both outfits; one was a dress and he was well aware of her dislike of dresses. The other was trousers with a flowing wrap skirt attached and a somewhat revealing lacy top. The gown he picked would flatter her body shape with a full-length skirt that draped well.

"I'll take the dress," she said, stunning Derek. He looked at her in suspicion, but she just shrugged. "The dress. I'll go with that," she reiterated. Derek took a deep breath.

"You're sure?" he asked, unaware the IIM bosses already imposed the choice on her in the form of a strong suggestion.

"Yeah," she sighed. He left her to the rest of her prepping, partly out of fear she would change her mind. She put the dress and Derek out of her mind, returning to her notes, running through them before facing the President. She knew he'd be a tricky customer and older, more senior hands tried to counsel and caution against using her usual interview techniques. Derek handed her the last item required before going on air, a pair of clear-lens glasses, the boss's idea, thinking it would add a level of maturity and authority to her look. She took her seat and waited for the show to begin.

Chapter 2

The recently renamed New Point Depot in Dublin's East Wall hosted the Media Awards Ceremony and a number of Rían's co-workers earned nominations within their own fields. Showing a united IIM front they arrived together, emerging from the car, with Ed, her editorial boss stepping out first with the rest following. Being the most junior, in terms of age and length of service, Rían exited last and received a cheer from the waiting crowd. Embarrassed, she blushed and gave a brief wave to those watching outside the perimeter. More cars pulled up behind them and the crowd's attention turned to the latest arrival, their renewed screams drowning everything else out. The IIM team turned to have a look and Ed gasped.

"It's Seth Morand," he explained. Rían gave the man a brief glance, but other than he seemed a good-looking guy, didn't see why all the fuss. She shrugged at Ed. Her boss shook his head at her. No doubt he'd educate her and give her the low-down at some stage during the night. Ed was a notorious and unashamed namedropper, but in the media game it all counted and when it came to getting exclusives, there was no better man to secure them. Inside they sat together, again showing the united IIM team. In truth they were a good bunch of people with no falseness to the image projected, each person a valued member of IIM. The organisation themselves did their best to promote a positive staff ethos and the group photos showed genuine smiles.

After dining, the awards part kicked off and the Political Analysis and Reporting category had four contenders, with each name and title of the journalistic piece that secured their nomination called out. The cameras focused on each individual contender as their names were announced and Rían remained looking nonchalant, despite her heart pounding in her chest. Two awards already sat on their table, and being the last category, IIM's hopes of a hat-trick rested on her now, but she was up against the oldest, the more experienced and the best the business had to offer.

"And the winner is..."

A hush descended, everyone in the room holding their breath in the brief pause at this hotly contested category.

"...For the in-depth investigation into the political cover-up of electronic hospital records ... Rían Breasel," the announcer called out. IIM's table erupted, but in their midst Rían maintained her composure. She stood, and with more grace than she knew she possessed, stepped to the stage. Now for the hard part. She had no speech prepared, not expecting to win. She waited for the noise to die down, her mind racing and took a deep breath.

"A dhaoine uaisle. Is onóir mhór dom buíochas a ghlacadh libh as ucht an duais seo a bhronnadh orm anocht. Ní raibh uaim ach an fhírinne a thabhairt chun solais agus mar gheall ar seo thug sibh onóir domsa agus onóir don fhírinne. Gabhaim buíochas ó mo chroí libh. Oíche mhaith agaibh."

"(*Ladies and Gentlemen. It is with great honour that I thank you for this award tonight. All I want to do is bring truth to light and for this you've honoured me, you've honoured truth. From my heart, I thank you and good night.*)"

She stood back to tumultuous applause, smiling shyly before leaving the stage.

"Nice touch with the Gaelic," Ed commented when she returned. Before she could reply, something, or rather someone caught his attention, and he manoeuvred his way through the tables to catch up with his target, who looked about to leave.

"Mr Morand," he said and the man turned around as did the older man accompanying him. He took Ed by surprise, not expecting Morand to appear so young

"Yes?" Morand answered, his accent a soft American twang, his smile reflected in his eyes.

"Ed Delaney, of IIM," he introduced himself. "I was a client of your Dublin office." Morand accepted the pro offered handshake.

"Mr Delaney, pleasure to meet you. Congratulations to your team tonight. IIM must be very proud," Morand said, his accent growing stronger.

"Well, yes sir, we're proud of our entire team," he managed to answer. Morand gave him a puzzled look.

"You were a client up until about a year ago, I think. Is that correct?"

"Yes," Ed said, thrown off-guard and amazed to be remembered out of the thousands who availed of his company's service. "I know you have a reputation for not doing interviews, but would you consider an exclusive with IIM?"

The smile never faltered, but wariness crept into Morand's eyes.

"As you say, Mr Delaney, I don't do interviews," he replied but paused to glance past Ed to the IIM table. Ed followed his gaze. "However," Morand continued, "I might make an exception if Miss Breasel did the interviewing."

"Ah," Ed answered, "it's not her field."

Morand shrugged.

"Maybe some other time then," he replied turning to the old man waiting on him.

"Ah, Mr Morand," Ed called after him again and the young man turned around to him, a bemused expression on his face. "That won't be a problem."

"Excellent," Morand answered, his smile widening a little more. He watched Morand's eyes flicker for an instant back towards Rían before he turned away again. Morand moved gracefully through the room followed by the older man with him, whom Ed assumed to be his aide. He sighed, happy with securing the opportunity of an exclusive with one of the most elusive businessmen and bachelors in the world. Now he needed to break news of the assignment to Rían.

Chapter 3

Voting for the Northern Assembly Elections closed at 9pm. Every conceivable measure to counteract any attempt at tampering or interfering with the electronic voting systems were in place, and the results of the ballots from across the six counties were expected soon. The double-checking and systems verification now caused the delay in returning a result.

Conor Uí Neill waited with impatience at his party's constituency head office in Belfast. As the newest kid on the political block, he knew he had no right to expect any sort of a victory, but strong ambitions and high expectations drove him. Added to those qualities he also believed in the prophecies the old man read to him since he was a child. Devlin, the old man, laid a hand on his shoulder.

"Calm yourself boy," he said. "The time is almost upon us."

Chapter 4

The Liberties in Dublin underwent re-urbanisation during the previous ten or fifteen years, stealing Temple Bar's title of Dublin's trendiest area and making it one of the safest parts of the city to walk about in. Gardaí *(police)* patrolled on a regular basis, so she was taken by surprise when she was grabbed from behind. She spun around, fist at the ready to retaliate but stopped short at hitting the bedraggled old woman who clung to her. She appeared homeless, dressed in old, torn clothing, smeared in dirt, as was her face and hands.

"They will be coming for you, soon," she rasped.

"Excuse me?" Rían demanded.

"They know who you are, what you are," the old woman grabbed her arm with both her hands. Rían tried to pull loose.

"I think you're confusing me with someone else."

"No. You are the one. Be watchful, but not everything they say are lies."

"Who are they?" Rían asked trying to be patient with this woman who seemed to grow agitated by the minute.

"You will know them when they come for you."

Without warning, she released Rían and fled down a side street with more speed than Rían would have accredited to her. Rían peered down the same lane only moments later but found no sign of the raggedy old lady.

"I have an assignment for you," Ed said by way of a greeting as she arrived at her desk. "My office, now." She took her jacket off, throwing it over her chair and followed him in.

"Ever hear of Seth Morand?" he asked closing the door behind her. She sat down.

"Didn't you mention him last night?" she answered.

"Yes," he said, "car behind ours, he's the CEO of TOTAL."

23

She shrugged and shook her head. The names meant nothing to her.

"It's one of those holistic health and fitness centres," he began. "This guy owns a chain of them around the world. Started as a fitness instructor and developed his own brand of everything, from herbal remedies to the ultimate weight loss programs, all before the age of 30. He's now settled in Dublin, something about liking our country and our history. I finally got him to agree to an interview and you're doing it."

"A fitness instructor," she exclaimed. "If he's so interested in getting his story out let Darren talk to him. That's his area, not mine."

"You don't seem to realise how difficult it is getting an interview with this guy. He doesn't do them, full stop. The only way to get him to do this was agree you'd do it," he said.

"Why? Why would you do that?" she demanded.

"What? Tell him my award winning journalist won't lower her standards, can't adapt to a different genre?" he replied. He took a deep breath. "Take a scientific standpoint, do an expose on him and the company, whatever… but I can tell you whatever he and his company is doing, it's working. Don't ask me how, but it does."

"Really?"

"Yeah," Ed answered. "Do you recall all the weight I lost last year?" She nodded. "Well, you won't remember this, but the original smoking ban twenty or twenty-five years ago allowed people to continue smoking outside. Along came the total ban about ten years ago and any of us still sucking on the fags couldn't even have one just walking down the street anymore, so I decided to give them up.

"That turned out to be about as successful as a snowstorm in the Sahara. The weight piled on and I was still smoking. About 18 months ago, the wife signs me up to this guy's health centre, and now look at me, a shadow of my former self and not a ciggie in sight."

She remained sceptical.

"And the scientific bit? Were drugs involved? Have you become addicted and you now you have to sign up for his anti-drug detox?" she asked with a hint of sarcasm.

He gave her a withering glare.

"Nothing so exciting. They did a psychological profile, did a fitness regime and gave me herbal tablets to help with the cravings."

"Still not convinced," she said. "You haven't told me anything earth shattering that willpower or self-determination couldn't accomplish."

"Well, whatever this guy's secret is, it's made him a worldwide billionaire. Take this as an opportunity to stretch yourself, journalistically speaking, reach out into the realm of the unknown. You're doing the interview and that's final," he stated, leaving no more room for argument.

"Fine," she snapped and walked out of his office.

"His secretary will call you," Ed shouted after her as the door slammed shut. God! She screamed in her head. What a day!

The secretary didn't hang about, calling shortly after she sat back at her desk. The voice was male and sounded young, but divulged little in the way of personal details regarding Morand when she quizzed him. The man seemed to have a busy schedule, but cleared an entire afternoon to see her. Rían didn't know whether or not to be flattered at such attention, but she was now scheduled to meet the man himself the following day.

In the meantime, she did her research, checking him out on the web, making contact with a few of her other sources and carefully guarded contacts. Seth Morand, it seemed, was indeed a self-made man, with multiple websites devoted to him, all unofficial. He was big news in the US, being somewhat of a celebrity and a player on the social scene. Photographs of him, usually with pretty girls on his arm were abound and easily accessible on the net.

None of this superstardom endeared him to her. She was a serious journalist after all, goddamn it, not a social columnist. The only thing of interest to her was this guy's education. For a relatively young guy he held degrees in Health & Nutrition, Psychology, Business as well as qualifications in Eastern Medicine, Homeopathy and other esoteric health related areas.

Going further back into his past revealed a tougher, edgier side with him winning awards and fights in mixed martial arts tournaments, and hidden in the depths of the web, she found allegations of injured opponents, but those were unsubstantiated and she dismissed them as idle gossip.

The following afternoon she arrived at the TOTAL Dublin office in Ballsbridge, at the appointed time, surprised as he came to reception to meet her in person. As she regarded him, she surmised he followed his own fitness advice. His movements were fluid, flowing and without hesitation. He screamed of supreme confidence and self-assurance, dressed in what she guessed to be an expensive suit and tailored judging by the way it shaped and moved with him.

He was taller than she expected, and while he was certainly photogenic, he seemed more handsome in person than the pictures suggested. His smile was what radiated the most, engaging and without doubt designed to put anyone in his company at ease and as cynical and analytical as she tried to be, she understood how easily someone could succumb to his charms. She, however, was determined not to. This was a crap assignment as far as she was concerned, to which she was holding Seth Morand responsible. He greeted her warmly and led her directly to his office.

"I've read your material and leaflets," she opened with her prepared line as she sat down, "and you are not doing anything different that willpower or self-determination couldn't accomplish." She gave herself scarcely any time to glance about, to get a feel for the man from any personal possessions in the room. To her surprise, she found it sparsely decorated. Seth Morand lounged against his desk in front of her. He'd offered her water or tea as they entered, but she declined both. He, however, took a bottle of water from a mini refrigerator close to her. His company's brand she noted.

"Absolutely true," he answered enthusiastically. "But most people want a quick fix and therein lies the problem. As we both know there is no such thing. TOTAL, as I'm sure you already know stands for 'Totally Organic, Totally Active Living' and that's all I promote, simply helping my clients to set up small attainable and achievable goals, quick wins if you will, helping them to go on and improve *that* willpower, self-determination and develop a desire to keep going." He smiled again.

"And just how do you ensure these 'quick wins'?" she asked.

"Our job is to help the client work it out for themselves. They know their bodies best, what does and doesn't work, what their own strengths and weaknesses are. A lot is common sense, but it doesn't hit home until it's pointed out. All I do is point the way."

"So you rely on your clients being honest?"

He shrugged.

"Honesty *is* the best policy after all. The only ones they're hurting by lying is themselves and problems only arise when they do."

"For example?" she asked. He took a sip of water and thought for a moment before his face lit up.

"The award ceremony the other night, I noticed you were drinking champagne. Now supposing you went to loads of galas, which I'm sure a person of your standing in the media would be invited to, and other such parties, on a regular basis, maybe drinking at all of them. Now, if you came in here and signed up but lied about how much alcohol you regularly consumed, or more to the point, you lied to yourself about how much you drank, our fitness plan for you would fail, because you weren't being honest with yourself."

"But you can ensure honesty?" she asked. He chuckled.

"The body always betrays the lie," he answered.

"Meaning?"

"We all give out signals, signs that are often at odds with what we're saying. It's the art of body language."

"So you apply your psychology?" she said. He smiled. She did her homework, and it pleased him. At least she was treating this with some degree of seriousness and professionalism.

"Yes," he answered. "I use a system of standard questionnaires, carried out by trained staff and they pay close attention for body reactions or contradictions in answers. The programs, diets, fitness routines are then all created and designed for each individual."

"And the homoeopathy?" she asked.

"I adhere to one simple philosophy," he stated.

"Care to share?"

He laughed.

"It's quite simple, while you are here, attending the clinics and fitness centre, you can't take anything that alters your state of body or mind," he answered.

"Such as?"

"The usual, no drugs, alcohol, caffeine, or processed sugars," he listed off.

"So no chocolate then," she replied, a hint of sarcasm creeping in.

"Nope," he answered, "cocoa based with added sugars. All we allow are natural remedies."

"Just herbs, huh?" she said.

"Exactly," he answered, sounding victorious.

"But aren't drugs and modern medicines derived from herbs and herbal remedies? Foxglove is used in digitalis, St John's Wort in hormone replacements and other supplements. Cannabis?"

He laughed.

"Don't you scientific types ever come up with more compelling arguments than those? When's the last time you got high on...let's say, nettle tea, or overdosed on oregano or basil?"

"Overdid the tarragon on chicken once," she answered deadpan, not taking him seriously, but he either failed to notice, or chose to ignore her sardonic attitude.

"Any side effects? Rushed to the ER to have your stomach pumped? Take any counteracting medication?" he argued.

"Does indigestion tablets count, or would they contravene the no drugs rule?" she retorted. He chuckled, but didn't reply.

Complete silence reigned for a moment.

"I can go into much more detail over dinner," he said.

She stopped scribbling on her ePad and glanced up surprised, which turned into suspicion.

"Excuse me?" she said by way of reply.

"Have dinner with me, tonight," he said.

"I don't think so."

"Tomorrow night, then."

28

"You don't take no for an answer, do you?"

He chuckled.

"If I stopped after the first no, I wouldn't be where I am today. Have dinner with me," he insisted, and she noted that while his charismatic smile remained, his face now took on an expression of intensity and drive.

"Absolutely not," she refused again.

"Why not? I'm not trying to influence this interview. You'll write whatever you write. All I want to do is treat a beautiful lady to dinner."

"Do you honestly expect such cheesy lines to work?" she said, the web images of pretty girls on his arm springing to mind.

"They usually do," he answered, matter of fact.

"Not here they won't, and I don't mix work with my personal life. I'm sure someone of your social standing can appreciate that," she said.

"I don't see any harm mixing a little pleasure with business," he shot back.

"Not in my world," she answered and stood up. "I think you've given me all I need," and she left before he could raise another argument. Seth stepped out of his office after her but she was nowhere to be seen. Fergus, his secretary stood and handed him a file.

"That didn't seem too promising," he said. Seth just shrugged, taking the file from him. "As you requested, I got as much info on your latest obsession as I could," he said, "even down to dress size, as instructed." Seth scanned the pages. "You owe Derek, the studio's wardrobe guy, dinner," Fergus added.

"Me personally?" Seth asked, "or you do and I'm paying for it?"

"I'll take what's behind door number two please," Fergus replied with a cheeky grin. "You can thank him for the rest of the gossip on her too, and not much to tell. No boyfriend, or girlfriend, that anyone knows of, does a lot of charity work too."

"So do I," Seth stated.

"True, but in her case, she's discreet and it doesn't hit the headlines," Fergus replied and Seth threw him a sideways glare. "Anyway," Fergus went on, "the reader's digest version is, she rarely drinks, no drugs, likes classical music, Techno and heavy rock, runs for fun and walks the 3.5 kilometres from the train station to work and back, every day. The only dirt I found was points on her driving licence for speeding, hardly crime-stoppers stuff, but seems she likes to go a little fast in the car."

"A girl after my own heart," Seth murmured.

"Maybe a dagger in your heart judging from the way she stormed out of here," Fergus replied. Seth disappeared back into his office without another word. As the door shut, Fergus sighed. Sometimes he wondered why he bothered.

Chapter 5

Rían sat outside at the wooden picnic bench in the late evening with Lucy, her German Shepherd-Lab cross. She didn't intend relocating to Arles and so far from Rathvilly, but the views of the Carlow valley and the surrounding Dublin, Wicklow and Blackstairs Mountains made the move irresistible. Lucy sat facing her, tennis ball in her mouth, hoping Rían would play fetch, but her owner seemed intently focused on the antiquated laptop sitting on the bench. An old machine but Rían kept it running with whatever upgrades she could find. The latest machines on the market proved not to be quite as robust as she would have liked and this old one allowed her to work outside like this.

"Voice activate or manual?" the computer asked as she opened the word-processing application.

"Manual," she answered, having learned some time ago that voice-activated word processing didn't suit her 'thinking out loud' style. Trying to decipher what she said, and what she meant to say, just took too long. Now an archaic skill, manually typing remained her favourite method of composing her articles.

She paused to watch the lights of nearby Killeen village come to life, gathering her thoughts about her encounter with Seth Morand, not knowing quite what to make of him. Lucy decided to lie down on the seat, letting the ball fall to the ground, while Rían sipped herbal tea, now starting to go cold in the evening air. As the number of lights in the valley grew she snapped out of her reverie, annoyed at herself for daydreaming about Morand. She picked up Lucy's ball, throwing it down the garden with fervour. With an article to be written, she launched into it, and him, with similar vigour.

Not her finest work by any standards and she hoped Ed would decide to shelve it. Her opinions of both Morand and TOTAL were a shade away from being described as scathing, barely disguised in eloquent wording. She refused to change anything, hoping to secure the article's demise, but no such luck. Ed argued about her lack of depth, missing passion and insight, but Morand didn't give her much to go on in the way of personality, she countered, unwilling to pander to any of his egotistical wants. She concluded him to be shallow and an attention seeker. Ed put his expert hand to it, making minor adjustments before forwarding on to the printers and at the touch of a keystroke became downloadable in an instant to every handheld device and anyone in the world.

She put Seth out of her mind; more important issues overshadowed a glorified fitness instructor. The launch date of a newly developed wave generator for the Atlantic approached, and there her interest lay, wanting to be at its inauguration. That's what she wanted to be concentrating on, and tackling the so-called eco-minded politicians who delayed its construction and implementation for over two years. Back to real work, back to normal.

She finalised her travel arrangements and accommodation for the launch when a large box arrived at her desk. Suspicious, she opened a corner and tried peeking inside. None the wiser she opened the box fully. By this time, a small audience gathered. Ed, a sucker for surprises, saw the box arriving. With the lid off, she found a note atop the tissue paper. Picking it out she lifted the paper beneath to reveal a bodice, in the faintest shade of pink she'd ever seen, and below that again, a full-length skirt in the finest white silk. She opened the note to discover it was from Seth Morand. All it said was 'Gala, tomorrow night. 8pm' and signed by him. An ostentatious script, she noted. Showy, just like the man himself. Annoyed, she picked up one of her business cards and wrote 'NO' on the back, complete with exclamation mark, stapling both cards together. She folded the tissue paper back over, placed his note and her answer on top and closed the box.

"Are you mad?" Teresa exclaimed. "Tomorrow night's gala is one of the highlights of the social calendar and one of the biggest charity events in the country. Everyone who's anyone will be going. You've got to go!"

"No! I don't," Rían retorted. "And certainly not with him."

"But…" Teresa tried to explain. Rían forestalled her.

"No. I'm not going to be bought over by fancy clothes, big flashy events or just to be seen on his arm. I hate these things. There are too many people at them. Too many people I've interviewed." She returned the box to the porter.

"Please, just send it back," she said. He nodded while the others shook their heads in disbelief and dismay.

Word spread throughout the entire building and she spent the rest of the day listening to why she should be going. By early afternoon, she'd had enough and she left, also warning Ed she'd work from home the following day. Ed knew her game plan. She couldn't receive any more gifts or invitations if she wasn't around. If she thought she would be safe at home, she was mistaken. As she drove around to park at the back of the house, her heart sank. On the picnic table sat not one box, but three.

"Some guard dog you are," she said to Lucy who stood on her hind legs, front paws on the table, sniffing at the boxes. She checked the largest box, confirming it to be the one she'd returned not long ago, but with a different note this time, reading 'Pick up at your place, 6:30pm'. The man was certainly persistent. She checked the other two boxes and found they contained shoes and expensive jewellery to match.

She brought them inside and phoned directory inquiries for any courier service operating this late in the evening, disappointed to find none readily available. She'd have to wait until the morning to reach anyone. She left the boxes on the dining table and tried to banish all thoughts from her mind, but curiosity got the better of her and she succumbed to its lure. She reasoned with herself that there was no harm in trying them on. After all, how often did she get the opportunity to try on clothing this fine? To her surprise, they fitted perfectly, too perfect a fit for mere guesswork and she wondered how he knew, suspecting someone in the studio of divulging such information. The dog stared at her in amusement as she twirled and swished about.

"Well, whaddaya think?" Rían asked of her furry companion, thinking her hair would be a problem, before catching herself. No, not a problem as she wasn't going. She undressed with care and placed everything back.

The next day her usual decisive nature abandoned her and she uncharacteristically dithered about whether or not to go. She couldn't deny that Seth Morand possessed a certain presence, charisma and charm, and she could understand how women fell for it. He also laughed at resistance. 'No' became a challenge to him and she didn't want to be the subject of his intense attention. Yet she found herself wanting to see him again, annoying herself even more. With 90 minutes to go, she made up her mind, and phoned her hairdresser.

"Brian? I need help," she said and explained. As luck would have it he was free, but needed time to organise the kids and 40 minutes later arrived at her house. In less than an hour, Brian worked his magic, strawberry blond curls cascading about her face. He finished as a helicopter approached and landed in the garden, avoiding the shrubs with expert precision. Brian pushed his glasses up on his nose, and wished her luck as he gathered his things and left. Lucy growled at the helicopter, but as soon as a man stepped out, she changed to barking. Rían locked up the house, trying to quieten Lucy, bribing her with doggy treats, and approached the helicopter, where the man helped her in. He introduced himself as Danny, Mr Morand's driver. Mr Morand, he explained would be meeting her at the National Concert Hall, the Gala venue.

In Dublin, they landed atop an apartment block, Danny escorting her to the elevators and they descended to the basement to the car. A crowd gathered at the walls of the NCH to watch arrivals, and they awaited their turn to drive through the entrance. As the car drew nearer, Seth descended the steps of the Concert Hall, opening the door for her, his hand extended to help her out. Determined not to give in to him, she scowled as she took his hand and exited the car. He gave her a thorough glance.

"Wow," he whispered in her ear. "You look gorgeous," he said, wrapping her arm about his, escorting her up the steps.

"Thanks," she muttered, feeling self-conscious as they entered the building.

"Why the frown?" he asked.

"It's just... I'm not used to... I'm not comfortable in these situations," she admitted.

"You've nothing to worry about, just do what I do, smile and nod at the appropriate places. It seems to work for me," he said taking two glasses of champagne offered by a nearby waiter. He handed one to her, but she shook her head. "Have one," he said, "it'll help you relax."

"Oh really?" she asked a little sarcastically. "Doesn't this violate your 'no alcohol' rule?"

"No because you're not a client, and no breach of ethics here either, in case you're wondering."

"Maybe not for you," she threw back.

"Your article is written. Over and done with, where's the problem?" he asked amiably.

"The problem I have is your bullying tactics," she retorted. "I sent these back to you," she said, indicating the clothes. "I told you I didn't want to go. Why are you doing this?" He pulled her up short, gripping her arm and she saw a sternness to his expression.

"Did I drag you here tonight? No. Did I physically twist your arm until you gave in? No. Why am I doing this? I'm just trying to impress you enough for you to have dinner with me," he answered, glancing around to ensure no one caught their little spat. He let her go, putting his hand to the small of her back to guide her towards the buffet.

"By the way, was that your attempt at being objective?" he asked. She shot a fiery glare at him and he laughed.

"It's not my area of expertise," she fired back.

"I could tell," he retorted with amusement. She put her glass down and turned to leave. He caught hold of her arm again and gave her a questioning glance.

"Let me go," she said through gritted teeth.

"And where are you going to go, home?" he questioned. "Your last train left 40 minutes ago."

"The same way I came," she answered. He shook his head.

"Pilot was only hired for the one round trip. Sorry, sweetheart, seems you're stuck with me. Now, if you took that iron rod out of your ass and relaxed a bit, you might actually start to enjoy yourself and have a little fun. I'm not a bad guy, all I'm asking for is a chance." He released her arm. Admittedly, he did sound sincere, and damn, he turned that smile on again.

"Fine," she answered and turned to pick up her glass, taking a mouthful. Seth grinned to himself.

The night consisted of a benefit concert in the main auditorium, followed by après-concert drinks back out in both the upper balcony and the lobby, which she enjoyed. True to his word, he acted the perfect gentleman throughout. She already knew many of the other attendees, and while she hated such grand social occasions, it proved to be an enjoyable evening. She found herself glancing about for Seth only to find him doing likewise for her.

In the early hours of the morning she shyly asked him if they could leave. Puzzled by her request, she explained she felt a bit drunk and couldn't drink anymore, and if she didn't go now, she was afraid she'd do something silly. He gave a soft laugh and put his arm about her, guiding her out of the building. His car pulled up as they reached the bottom of the steps and Danny jumped out to open the rear door for them before driving to Seth's apartment. Seth helped her out of the car and into the lift, putting his arm around her to steady her. She pushed him away.

"I'm not sleeping with you," she stated, "or anything else with you, for that matter." A smile played at the corner of his lips.

"Thought never crossed my mind," he answered. She eyed him suspiciously as he led her to his apartment. His thumbprint, and a microchip embedded in his wrist, opened the door with an almost imperceptible click. He led her inside. A figure appeared at the end of the hallway and Rían stopped short.

"That's Mrs Hanson, my housekeeper," he whispered into her ear.

"You have a housekeeper?" she asked astounded. He nodded, continuing further into the apartment. She paused to take her shoes off so walking wouldn't be such a hazardous sport and followed him to the main living area, sitting down on the first sofa she reached. Seth disappeared into another room as the housekeeper regarded her with a stern expression.

"I guess you get to see this all the time, him bringing strange girls home," she said by way of making conversation and attempting to break the ice.

"No, dear," Mrs Hanson replied, "you're the first one he's ever brought back." Rían's eyebrows arched in surprise and the old lady left the room, while Seth returned with a glass in his hand. He sat down beside her, handing the glass to her. Whatever the glass contained was a strange shade of green, immediately triggering suspicion.

"Here, drink this. You'll thank me in the morning."

She sniffed the contents and made a face.

"What is it?" she asked.

"Call it my own personal recipe for a hangover cure. I know it doesn't smell great," he said. She hesitated, plucking up the courage to take a mouthful. She swallowed and grimaced, tasting worse than it smelled. She tried handing the glass back to him.

"Don't be such a baby. Take another mouthful," he advised, looking so sincere that she believed him and tried a second helping, but no way would she take a third. He took the glass from her this time.

"I'll show you to the guest bedroom. If you need a hand getting out of those clothes, I'd be more than happy to oblige," he said. She gave him a tight smile.

"Nice try, but I think I can manage, thanks," she replied and followed him down the hallway.

Chapter 6

The soft click of a door woke her and she opened her eyes, finding Mrs Hanson leaving a tray on the dresser. The old woman left without a word and Rían sat up, stretching, surprised to feel refreshed instead of hung over. Seth's miracle cure sure seemed to work. Breakfast consisted of toast and a smoothie, no doubt another of his recipes. She also spotted clothes on the dresser chair; jeans in her size, a tee shirt and a cashmere jumper, appearing to be a little too large for her. She got a hint of cologne and guessed the garment belonged to Seth. A pair of casual trainers completed the ensemble. She took a quick shower, eating breakfast as she dressed.

She left the room and wandered down the hallway towards music. She hadn't paid much attention to the place last night but it opened out into a vast space, and she found Seth at the opposite end, a short staff in his hand and a look of intense concentration on his face. Sweat glistened on his body as he worked through kata's and other martial art forms she recognised. He wore traditional loose pants and stepped barefooted across the width of the room as he spun the staff, putting both the weapon and his body through its paces. Her initial assessment of him proved accurate as she scrutinised his well-defined and bare torso, shimmering with perspiration. She stepped closer, making as little sound as possible so as not to disturb his concentration. He registered her movement from the corner of his eye as she neared, and he stopped, breathing hard.

"Morning. Did you sleep ok?" he asked. She nodded. "How's the head?" he then asked, already guessing the answer.

"Grand," she replied. "Thanks for the change of clothes. Your jumper?" she asked in return, eying up his collection of practice weapons, neatly arranged on a rack by the edge of his workout area. She picked out a bokken, a wooden practice sword.

"Yeah. Now I get to meet you again when you have to return it," he grinned.

"I could always post it back," she answered.

"You wouldn't take that chance and risk having me popping up at any time," he said. She smirked, confirming his guess that she'd been thinking that. She spun the sword, with a flick of her wrist. His grin turned to a questioning frown.

"You know how to use that?" he asked.

"A little," she answered in a modest tone. "A few basic moves," she added.

"Okay, show me what you've got," he said, and she heard the confidence and superiority in his voice. She hesitated for a moment, thinking.

"Em, yeah, okay," she said. With the point of the sword on the floor, she drew a semi-circle around her, a dividing line between them. She noticed the smile on his face slipped a little. She'd just challenged him and now found himself unsure of his opponent. Seth caught a faint smile on her face, but her eyes narrowed somewhat. He gripped the staff at its midway point while she waited patiently for him to make the first move. He didn't disappoint, striking at her with surprising speed. The blow would have bruised her calf if she hadn't blocked it with the sword. She retaliated with similar speed stepping inside the staff's reach while fending off another blow and elbowed him in the ribs. He grunted and stepped out of her reach, spinning the staff and attempting an up stroke, catching her on the arm, and stinging, he thought smugly, if he went by the grimace on her face. They both stepped outside the other's reach.

"A few basic moves, huh?" he questioned.

"Okay, a couple of lessons," she conceded, and reacted quicker than he expected to his next attack, while she counterattacked without warning. They continued in similar fashion. Neither gave the other a moment's rest as they parried and deflected each other's blows. Her strength surprised him, as did her sometimes dirty tactics, such as trying to step on his bare feet and landing a left hook to his cheek. If she wanted to play like that he'd be more than happy to oblige, but she ducked under what would have been a nasty knock to the jaw. She started to perspire from the effort and she knew he wasn't being gentle, but damn, it was good to knock the smug smile from his face.

They had different fighting styles and she noted his weaknesses, in particular, where he left himself a little too open when he swung in from his right. She waited until the next time he feigned to the left and dropped to her knees sliding on the wooden floor, sword point up. She caught him in the midriff with the sword point while she grabbed his staff from overhead. The wooden point was just sharp enough to cause the barest pinprick of blood on his skin. The smile was definitely gone now, with surprise replacing disbelief. And that too, was damn good to see. He stepped back and released the staff she was still holding. She stood up and twirled his weapon.

"I didn't know you could do that," he said, watching her warily, catching his breath.

"This is what happens when you rely on other people for information," she shot back, also breathing heavily. "They don't know everything either."

"Where did you learn to fight?" he asked.

"Various places," she answered, placing the weapons on the floor.

"Explains why you don't have any particular style, except to fight dirty," he accused her, stepping closer to her. She suppressed a laugh at his sulking but he did his damnest to hide it.

"A girl's gotta do...," she said by way of explanation, but she didn't get to finish as he took her head in his hands and pulled her close, kissing her deeply. She placed her hands on his chest, feeling his heart pounding. She pushed him, hard, and he backed away.

"I am not one of your conquests," she growled at him and turned on her heel and left. Unable to move himself, he let her leave, stunned, and annoyed, and a mixture of everything else. No one ever bested him like that, nor rejected him so completely. Fergus was right; she was an obsession since that first night he'd seen her. Last night he'd been on his best behaviour, hoping, no, anticipating his gentlemanly ways would be enough to win her over only to find she'd whooped his ass this morning.

He shook himself out of his reverie and his brooding and his smile returned. The wooing of Rían would have to take a different route.

"A little tougher than you expected?" Mrs Hanson asked, suppressing a smile of her own. She came out to investigate the commotion and now disappeared back into the kitchen, smirking to herself.

Rían walked to Heuston train station, and while she didn't have her wallet or commuter ticket on her, her thumbprint and the info on the chip in her wrist would be enough to ensure she got on the train. Peter stood at the gate scanning tickets and he let her on without a problem. His greeting was as cheerful as always and it helped put a smile back on her face, but she sank back into brooding on the 45-minute journey home.

The old woman's bizarre warning came to mind and it rattled her, more than she cared to admit, and she'd remained edgy since it happened. She now replayed it, questions about whom she had to be wary of. Was it Seth Morand? Why did he infuriate her so much? Unable to provide any alternative to the old woman's warning, she arrived at the only logical conclusion; the old lady was a complete nutcase, but Rían's instincts hummed uneasily.

She hailed a taxi from outside the train station at Carlow, but when she got back to the house, she found a small bouquet of flowers lying on the picnic table, with a note. She ignored them while she reached for the spare key in order to retrieve her cash card to pay the driver. When he left, she opened the note, which contained only one word, 'sorry'. Boy, this guy worked fast. No point in letting the flowers suffer she thought and took them inside and into water.

"You're fired," she said to Lucy on the way in. "Your guard-dogging days are over, fur ball!"

Chapter 7

The weekend arrived with no further communication from Morand and late Saturday evening, when the day turned cooler for the dog, she decided to go for a run. The forest, her usual haunt, would be quieter at that time, with less people likely to be around, leisurely strollers or otherwise. She dressed in her running gear and drove the 10 minutes to Oughaval Wood, on the outskirts of Stradbally, parking in the inner car park, letting an excited Lucy out from the back seat. She set her music player, securing the earphones in her ears and Millennium Trance, a techno revival group, blasted out. She didn't bother with a leash on Lucy who bound forward, stopping abruptly at the first grassy mound to take a sniff. Rían passed the barrier and took the red and green trail, heading straight on.

Run by Coillte, a semi-State body, the forest operated on a financial basis and as with most of their forests, opened Oughaval to the public, maintaining walkways and trails through the woods. The trail she took suited her running needs better, with a steadier rise. Having warmed up by a brisk walk to the top, the trail then swept to the right before descending at a fast pace into a hollow followed by another similar rise on the other side. She started to jog at the beginning of the decline and Lucy dutifully lobbed alongside her. She discovered the dog made a great training buddy, with the odd exception where the pooch decided to have more fun criss-crossing in front of Rían's feet. She continued on, following the middle forest trail while Lucy stopped every now and again to sniff in the grass along the way or investigate noises in the deep hollow on their left, never letting Rían get too far ahead or out of sight. They reached another junction of two trails, in the hollow known as Mass Rock. Rían pulled up short at seeing two men standing at the Rock, calling Lucy to her, putting her leash on. She didn't pay any particular attention to them other than to keep Lucy on a short lead, attempting to reign in the dog's natural curiosity, but a sudden jerk from the dog found Rían yanked sideways as Lucy pulled in their direction. One of them hunkered down to greet the dog. Only then did Rían pay them any notice and her face hardened when she recognised one.

"And I thought you couldn't be led astray," Seth Morand said as he scratched Lucy behind the ears. She turned the volume down on the music player and caught her breath.

"Depends on who's doing the leading," she retorted, trying to pull Lucy away. She glanced at the other man from under the rim of her baseball cap. He appeared much older than Seth, and she recalled seeing him and Seth speaking to each other at the Gala. Seth straightened up and she noticed a difference in him, wondering if the old man's presence had anything to do with it. His cockiness was cooled somewhat.

"Are you on the way back out?" he asked.

"No," she answered, "only getting started," and she turned to go.

"Why don't you two go on and I'll make my own way back," the old man said. "I don't fancy my chances with this hill." He pointed to the steep rise with his stout walking stick.

"Mind if I join you?" Seth asked.

"Yes, I do," she replied, not caring to hide her dislike and turned to go. She exited the hollow at speed, sprinting up the rise. Lucy sprang up along beside her. Seth watched her method of ascent and followed suit.

The hill soon levelled out and by the time Seth reached the top Rían had put a lot of ground between them. He continued sprinting to catch up, while she jogged down the wide tree lined avenue until reaching another junction. Turning right would bring them back to the car park but Rían turned left and slowed to a fast walk, aiming for the next hill. Seth caught up with her and Lucy darted ahead of them both. Rían checked him out from the corner of her eye.

"I'm sorry about the other morning," he said.

"Yeah, I got the note," she replied.

"I meant no offence in any way. You caught me completely off guard," he sounded genuine and she glanced at him. Gone was the cheesy, charismatic smile. He seemed to act more naturally and less like a man who got everything his own way.

"Not much point in training if you can't adapt to a given situation," she shot back.

"I don't think adapting was my problem. Underestimating my opponent was. That, and believing her when she claimed to have limited skills," he answered. She smirked.

"I'm going to program that hill into the machines, maybe get this place on the virtual screens," he said.

"Virtual screens?" she asked, her curiosity piqued. He laughed.

"You don't go to a gym much, do you?" he said.

"I have a dog," she said by way of an explanation. "With two or three walks a day, who needs a gym?"

"A fair point. However, the city doesn't provide the opportunity to experience places like this. It's the hottest new thing, the virtual outdoors only indoors, in an air conditioned booth with a surround screen, playing any walk or run you want."

She shook her head in disbelief.

"So, did your researcher tell you about this place?" she asked.

"Didn't know about this place until today," he answered.

"If you're not stalking me, what brings you here?" she asked.

"The old guy," Seth answered. Rían remained silent, giving him the opportunity to expand but he remained quiet and reticent.

"Family?" she asked and he shook his head. "Business associate?" she pressed.

"Acquaintance," he finally answered.

"Hmm, the plot thickens," she said. "So does this old man have a name?"

"Why the interest in him?" Seth countered.

"Just curious," she answered.

"Professional or personal?"

"Maybe a little of both," she replied. "Anyone who can switch off that arrogance of yours is going to pique my interest." He gave her a scathing look. "Is he local?" she pressed.

"Ardscull," he finally gave her an answer.

"The Moate?" she asked. "That's an historic site. I didn't think anyone could get planning permission up there."

"He has friends in the right places," he said.

"Hmm, sounds like there's a story there," she said.

"A bigger story than my apparent narcissistic need to be in the public eye?" he shot back, referring to her article. It sounded like she'd hit a nerve. This was definitely not the same person she'd interviewed or met at the Gala and she wondered just how much influence this old man exerted over him.

"So who is he?" she pressed again.

"You don't give up, do you?" he said and she gave him a look of surprise, considering the source.

"No one's making you stay if you don't like the line of questioning," she shot back and he laughed softly at her.

"Brehon McCormac," he answered. She gave him a quizzical side-glance.

"An odd name," she said and he looked surprised.

"What, McCormac?"

"No, his first name, Brehon," she answered.

"Why?" he asked. She frowned and hesitated a moment.

"It's an old name, ancient in fact, but that was the name of the legal system of the ancient Celts," she answered.

"I guess that makes sense," he said.

"Meaning?"

"He's em… a High Druid," he told her. She stopped and looked at him.

"A Druid?" she asked and Seth nodded. "Is that why you don't do interviews? Allegations of Druidic cults could ruin a man's business reputation," she said.

"Do you ever stop being a reporter?" he shot back.

"No," she answered matter-of-factly. "So are you … a Druid?"

"No," he answered.

"Are you in a cult?" she asked and he laughed again.

"No."

"Is your company a front for a secret worldwide cult?" she pressed.

"Yes," he said, "we're secretly trying to convert the entire world to Celtic Druidism. You found me out. Happy now?"

She scowled at his flippant attitude, knowing he toyed with her.

"Can I print that?"

"Can you afford the libel?"

Without another word, she resumed running and he chuckled to himself before following, but the effort of keeping up with her began to take its toll. She slowed again to a walk, allowing him to catch his breath.

"As the proclaimed lord of the fitness world, you're not exactly a shining example of stamina, are you?" she said.

"I'll admit I've slipped a bit, and haven't had the time to run since I moved here. Besides, I prefer to chase beautiful women. It's better sport," he answered. She gave him a haughty look before a sly smile appeared.

"I'd better make it worth the effort then," she said and took off up the hill at a fast pace. Seth swore using language he wouldn't normally use in polite company but broke into a jog, and as she slowed to a walk, he pulled on his reserves to catch up.

Through the trees, the setting sun glowed, a red fireball in the sky, illuminating the forest in a fiery radiance and he stopped to take in the view.

"Still want to programme this place?" she asked. Still out of breath, he could only shrug. The next and last hill wouldn't be so bad, she promised, coaxing him into a gentle jog back to the car park.

Lucy led the way back to the car. Seth searched around and muttered under his staggered breath as Rían poured water into a dish for the dog, drinking deeply from the bottle herself. She handed the bottle to Seth only to see confusion and consternation on his face.

"What's wrong?" she asked.

"The old man's not the most patient of people. Looks like I've been abandoned," he answered taking the bottle from her.

"Don't all you billionaire types have personal chauffeurs available on demand? Don't you even have a bodyguard? After all, you *do* hit like a girl?" she threw at him.

46

"No, some of us have managed to successfully integrate into regular society, live normal lives. I drove to Ardscull myself, all on my own," he answered back, "and the old guy drove us here. I didn't expect to be running into you and then being deserted, so I didn't even bring a phone." She deliberated for a moment.

"I'll drop you back," she said.

"I didn't plan this, if that's what you're thinking," he answered.

"Never said you did, and I certainly don't think you planned on me whooping your ass again." He grinned, but it wasn't his ass he thought of, having checked hers out as he ran along behind her. He leaned forward, taking deep breaths as Rían took a towel and sweater out of the car.

"I can't believe I'm this bent out of shape," he confessed.

"Don't worry," she said drying her face and neck, "I won't charge for the assessment, or the personal tour." She put her sweater on and stretched her legs. "I'm going home first to drop Lucy back and shower. You can stay here and I'll pick you up, or I can leave you in Ballylynan and do likewise, or..."

"I'll behave myself," he promised, "what's the Irish phrase...'too bollixed' to try anything?"

She nodded and grinned.

"I'll drop you to Ardscull and that's all. Don't invite me in; I won't be staying, not for dinner, cup of tea, coffee, anything."

"You got yourself a deal. Is this your car?" he asked not believing his eyes as he stared at the 2004 registered Nissan 350Z roadster sports car.

"Yeah, why?" she said.

"These are really rare now, almost a collector's item, you were lucky to find one in such good condition, this looks near perfect," he answered, finding a new lease of life now that something piqued his interest.

"It *is* perfect," she answered, "and I didn't find it, my folks gave it to me. My dad bought it as a birthday gift for mum when they were originally launched. She drove it up until about 5 years ago, then transferred ownership to me. It doesn't have most of today's standard stuff like auto-indicators; they're still on manual, as is the gearbox. Not long after they got it, they converted it from a petrol engine to a bio-fuel one and replaced the original battery with lithium power cells about seven or eight years ago, when batteries became impossible to get."

"So no speed de-limiters either," he concluded, knowing cars weren't installed with an auto-speed module until the mid '15's.

"Nope and limited GPS for navigation only which makes speed tracking harder but more fun to drive," she allowed herself a grin.

"So the question becomes not how did you get caught for speeding twice, but how you only got caught twice?" he joked and she frowned at him. "Your speeding violations are a matter of public record," he defended himself, "it's accessible to anyone."

"You want to walk to Ardscull?" she challenged. He grinned and hung his head looking up at her with his best puppy-dog eyes. For the first time since meeting him, she laughed at him.

"Get in," she commanded.

He remained quiet on the short journey back. That surprised her, but he used the time to observe her driving, using the antiquated gearing system with ease. He even resisted the urge to comment on the 'Slow' road markings that she seemed to disregard. Further on they came to a series of chicanes, where she threw the car into the corners at speed, gearing up and down like a rally driver. They passed the village's name sign and she eased off the accelerator, letting the car slow down by itself. Unlike more modern cars, the Nissan didn't come fitted with an automatic speed de-limiter that would start slowing the car down once it passed the speed sign. GPS modules had been systematically installed on all the speed signs in the country that interacted with a car's electronic control and reduced power to the engine. As the sports car predated the de-limiter's inception, driver discretion was still required. Rían turned on her indicator, braking hard and turning left into the drive and along by the house. The view struck him first, and it awed him. Her large garden sloped away revealing the Carlow valley below and beyond. In the distance the mountains were crystal clear in the light of the setting sun, displaying the deepest purple hue.

"No wonder you commute," he said, "with a view like this to come home to." She smiled and un-harnessed Lucy. The dog jumped out and picked up one of her favourite toys lying close by returning to Seth and tapping him with her paw until he paid her some attention. He made a grab for the toy but she moved away playing her much-loved game of 'grab-my-toy, if-you-can'. After a couple more attempts, Seth gave up but followed the dog to the edge of the lawn.

"What mountains are they?" he asked. Rían walked up beside him.

"Straight ahead are the Wicklow Mountains, to the left are the Dublin Mountains," she answered, pointing to them, "the Blackstairs Mountains are to the right. Beyond that lies Wexford. You can even see Ardscull from here." She pointed to it. "There, the rise with the thick clump of trees," she said. He nodded.

She left him to the view and walked back to the house, unlocking the patio doors and disarming the security system. He sat down at the picnic table, Lucy sitting at his heel, toy still in her mouth. Rían reappeared with a bowl and a large glass. The bowl she placed on the ground, laden with food for the dog, the glass she handed to Seth. He sampled its contents.

"Strawberry shake, extra protein?" he asked.

"Summer fruit smoothie, no protein and tastes a hell of a lot better than your concoctions," she answered. He smirked, leading her to suspect the nasty stuff didn't need to be in the shake he'd given her after all. "I'm going for a shower, won't be long." He just nodded and turned back to the view.

He grew up in a city, bright lights, bustling sounds and constant motion. Sitting here felt like being on another planet, a peaceful and serene one with hardly a sound. Before long the sound of her moving about the house, a clicking on wood, knocked him from his reverie and he moved to the door, peering in. Rían stood at the breakfast bar, leaning over the worktop. She focused on the computerised glass inserted into the counter-top, unaware of how much her ass stuck out, or of how shapely he found it now clothed in the leather pants she wore. A suitably tight fit too, he thought in approval. She gave him the briefest of glances before returning to the screen. From the console, she set the timers for various lights about the house and the heat to come on before she expected to be home. She remotely opened the garage door and started the ignition in her other car.

"For someone with a hi-tech house you have an out-dated security system," he commented.

"It may be out-dated by today's standards, but it's far more secure than the modern stuff."

"Really?" he said, not believing her, but continuing to check out her behind.

"Computers will always be vulnerable to hacking, despite every security measure you put in place. You'll always get some smart arse that sees a challenge as an invitation." For a split second she glanced at him before going on. "But you try getting past a 7-bolt locking system. This is one of those times where I'll take old, tried and trusted over technology." He didn't have an answer for her, so he changed the subject.

"A little dressy for playing chauffeur," he commented. She straightened up and he took in her full ensemble, including her pseudo-rock chick, high-heeled, biker boots, and a midnight blue camisole with matching long-sleeved top

"Contrary to popular belief, I *do* have a social life," she countered.

"And your hair's curly again, same as the other night, you do that often? You normally have it straight, don't you?".

A smile played on her lips.

"You really need to sack your researcher," she answered. "For the record, the curls are all me. The studio thought straight hair would give me more of a mature look when I first started. Same with the glasses, before you ask, they're a prop, I don't need them. Anyway, time to go."

She ushered him out of the house, while she reset the alarm and turned the key in her so-called antiquated lock. She directed him to the garage and Seth heard a car motor running, a more modern car for regular journeys, she explained as she led him to her black, year old Audi A4. Seth chuckled to himself.

"Mine's dark blue."

"You surprise me. I had you pegged for a flashier, sportier car like a Porsche."

"You seem to have a bad opinion of me."

"It may be bad, but I dare say it's accurate," she shot back.

Ardscull was sixteen kilometres away, and they returned the way they came, at a more sedate pace, he noted. This car was speed compliant, even if the driver wasn't and the chicanes didn't have the same rallying quality this time around. They drove through the village of Ballylynan, continuing on to Athy. Being a weekend evening, the town was already lively, the revelry in full swing as she passed straight through it, continuing without stopping, with Ardscull another five kilometres the other side of the town. Seth warned the entrance would be difficult to spot and she slowed down, following his directions and she never would have found the gates if he hadn't pointed them out. The high gates seemed made of wrought iron and without having to pause or announce themselves, they swung open. Rían took her time driving through the narrow entrance and crept up the winding tree-lined drive. Small lights about a metre from the ground, and spaced about two or three metres apart, added limited illumination along the way. At the top she found a large gravelled area in front of the house, which seemed to be busy, judging by the number of cars already parked. Seth neither seemed surprised nor offered any comment. The front door opened as they approached and the old man appeared, silhouetted against the interior lighting before the exterior lights came on exposing him. He'd changed from casual to formal and as she manoeuvred the car around to face the way out, he stepped out towards them. She eased to a stop and Seth seemed strangely subdued.

"Thanks," he said opening the car door to get out.

"No problem," she answered getting ready to pull away again. The old man reached the car as Seth got out. They exchanged a quiet word, too low for Rían to make out. She wanted Seth to close the door so she could go, but the old guy put his head in instead. He gave her a broad grin that chilled her.

"Ms Breasel, thank you very much for bringing Seth back," he said, sounding as though she returned his lost puppy. He spoke in a deep, cultured tone, with an accent too indistinct to make out.

"You're welcome," she answered with more grace than she felt.

"I'm having a little get-together with friends tonight, won't you join us?" he asked. She glanced at Seth standing a little behind the man but couldn't read any emotion or expression from him.

"No, thank you," she replied, "I have some place to be and I'm already running late."

"Tomorrow then, you'll come for Sunday lunch. My way of apologising for putting you out of your way," he said.

"Again, no thanks and no apology necessary," she replied, revving the car a little to hint at leaving.

"How are my dear friends Moira and Ciarán these days? I'll admit I've been remiss in keeping contact with them," he said, and her eyes narrowed in suspicion. "I believe they're on vacation at the moment, in Peru?" he asked. How did he know her parents? She couldn't recall ever meeting this man before.

"They're fine, as far as I know" she replied. The old guy sensed her unease and distrust of him.

"They've just left Cusco and the Sacred Valley. Have they climbed Huayna Picchu yet?" he asked letting her know he was privy to their travel plans.

"I haven't heard. They didn't bring any means of communication with them so I don't get regular updates," she answered.

"Ah, the good old days," he answered. "Your parents always did fly in the face of convention." Seth frowned but said nothing. His gaze shifted back to Rían. "Until tomorrow," the old man said, "lunch will be about 2pm, I look forward to your company then, my dear." Not allowing her the chance to raise another objection he closed the car door and walked back towards the house. Seth gave a brief wave before following, but he stopped the old man as he reached the front door. Seth squared up him

"What the hell was that about? You know her already?" he demanded. The old man glared at him.

"Do not dare to question me, boy," he growled at the younger man. Seth stood his ground.

"When you told me to get to know her, I didn't expect you to ditch me in the woods with her," he threw back.

"It has all worked out the way it should," the old man replied.

"Meaning?" Seth demanded.

"Don't push me on this. The time is not right for you to know."

"So you're using me to get to her?" Seth asked, growing angrier.

"Boy, we are all only a means to an end," the old guy snapped back. Rían studied the two men standing in the doorway and guessed strong words were being exchanged until they both turned and stared at her. Startled, she hit the accelerator harder that she meant to, sending the front wheels into a spin before getting a grip and moving off.

McCormac re-entered the house, bring the argument to an abrupt end.

Seth turned back towards the drive, trying to make out the taillights of Rían's car through the trees before following the old man in.

Chapter 8

The telephone woke her the next morning, and she disabled the video-view option, not allowing anyone to view her in a bedraggled state. Neither did she recognise the number calling her, but indicated the call originated from the Athy area.

"Hello," she answered, all traces of sleepiness gone.

"Good morning, Ms Breasel," an unfamiliar male voice replied. "This is Mr McCormac's private secretary."

"Who?" she asked, now sitting up.

"Mr Brehon McCormac. You returned Mr Morand to Mr McCormac's residence last night," the secretary explained. "I'm phoning to finalise arrangements for lunch today, and to inquire as to any dietary requirements you may have."

"Nothing to finalise as I won't be attending," she said. The secretary paused, and Rían thought she heard a faint gasp.

"Oh," he answered, "Mr McCormac will be most displeased."

"Convey my apologies," she said and hung up, flopping onto the pillows and pulling the duvet back over her head. The peace was short-lived as the phone rang again soon after. She checked the caller-id. Persistent, she thought and hesitated before answering.

"Rían, my dear." Not the secretary this time, but the old man, and she took an instant dislike to the way he said 'my dear', sounding condescending and superior, and he used her name as though he knew her. "My dear, I simply won't take no for an answer," he continued, and in a fleeting thought, she wondered if he was responsible for the same attribute in Seth.

"I have other arrangements," she said by way of an excuse.

"Nonsense, I won't hear of it," he answered. She closed her eyes and pressed her fingers on her forehead, hitting pressure points to ease the tension, and knowing what the next ploy would be.

"I can have my secretary pick you up," McCormac said. She no longer wondered where Seth Morand got his pushiness. She knew she wouldn't win this one either, and a bubble of resentment grew at the thoughts of being bullied and manipulated in this way.

"No, I can drive myself," she answered.

"Excellent," he answered, "and I've taken the liberty of ordering a seafood dish for you. Moira tells me you don't eat red meat." Anger coursed through her. Her mother told him?

"I shall expect you about 2 o'clock then, my dear," he said. The line disconnected before she could answer and a roar of frustration and anger escaped her, causing Lucy to raise her head from the end of the bed, her ears flat, whining in sympathy.

She showered, and dressed in jeans, with a fitted black shirt. She had to power dress during the week, weekends were for getting casual, and being dragged by the scruff of the neck to a la-de-dah lunch wouldn't change that. Ever the journalist, she searched on the internet for anything on this guy before leaving the house, but she came up empty handed, no mention of him at all. As Seth pointed out to her the night before, the public domain contained every conceivable scrap of information on everyone, but not this guy, setting her journalistic antenna tingling again.

She arrived at Ardscull a few minutes late, a minor hold-up in Athy screwing up her timing, but again, the gates opened automatically upon her arrival and in daylight, she sped up the drive much faster than the night before. Three cars sat at the entrance, and assumed the blue A4 to be Seth's, meaning he was still here. The front door opened by the time she parked and got out.

"Good afternoon, Ms Breasel," the man at the door said and she recognised the voice as McCormac's secretary. "You are just in time, Chef is ready to serve," he said. She stared at him in disbelief. Who were these people, with chefs, secretaries and housekeepers? Such existence and servitude died out in the last millennium. Someone calling her name distracted her and she turned to the direction of the sound. Seth seemed surprised.

"You came," he said.

"I don't think I had much choice," she shot back, feeling a twinge of regret for her sharpness when she saw the look of concern on his face.

"Mr Morand will show you the way, Ms Breasel," the secretary said and Seth broke his stare to look at him before nodding.

"Sure, this way," he said putting his hand to the small of her back to guide her along, leading her through the house. He held a door open for her and she found herself in the dining room.

The old man grinned upon seeing her, a fixed smile she noted, that never reached his eyes. She sensed a tingle at the back of her neck and felt uneasy.

"Welcome Rían," he said offering a hand. She took it, but while his handshake was firm, it felt cold to the touch and he held her hand a little too long for her liking. Seth followed her in, closing the door behind him.

"Let me introduce you to my other lunch guests," he said turning to them. The two women present looked as alike as chalk and cheese. The tall blond, dressed in a fitted red silk top and loose elegant black pants he introduced as Cíanna, her handshake soft and delicate. Naoise, the other woman, had a strong grip but only a single shake of her hand. Blessed with freckles and a flowing mass of curly red hair, she was the poster girl for the ideal Irish colleen. She dressed in a similar fashion to Rían; jeans and a white tee shirt, a tattoo snaked from under the sleeve on her left arm. Both women seemed to be of similar age to Rían.

"And Seth you already know. Come, sit," he said as they took their seat, Rían noting how he orchestrated the seating arrangements. With himself at the head, Seth sat on his left while he placed her on the right and opposite Seth. Cíanna sat beside Rían and Naoise beside Seth. Seth bristled at the arrangement, but remained silent.

"Rían works for Ireland International Media as a journalist, and hosts their political review show mid-week," McCormac explained to the others but to Rían it seemed they already knew. Her distrust of McCormac grew with each passing moment. For someone she only just met, he appeared to be well versed and knowledgeable about her.

"Isn't that the same media group that interviewed you not long ago?" Cíanna asked.

"Why, yes of course," McCormac answered with a grin. "A Susan Harvey? I believe she's a colleague of yours."

Rían nodded.

"She's the Religious Affairs Correspondent," she answered, and thanked the young waiter who placed a laden plate in front of her.

"A pleasant, knowledgeable young lady," McCormac said. "She seemed interested in all the current religious revivals that appear to be occurring. I also got the impression she takes us 'fringe elements' seriously."

"She's more open to the so-called fringe elements than to the mainstream religions," Rían answered.

"Do explain, please," McCormac said.

"She's big into Wicca, but she's open minded on the subject, believes all roads lead to the one source," Rían answered, conscious of all attention focused on her. Away from the studio, the attention made her uncomfortable, as did the topic.

"Hmm, interesting," McCormac said. Rían glanced at Seth who stayed uncharacteristically quiet but interested in the conversation. He gave her a quick smile.

"And what do you believe in?" the old man pried. She hesitated, sensing something more to the question, something deeper. She shrugged.

"I believe in the physical world, in physics and in the power of nature," she answered.

"Such as the Wave-Generator in the Atlantic? I believe you'll be covering its inauguration. I must say, I'm rather looking forward to your take on the whole thing," he said. That took her a little by surprise.

"My take on it? I can tell you that now," she answered.

"By all means," he said.

"Simple. We've finally learned to harness the power of nature without destroying it, using its force to enhance our lives instead of creating a man-made source with the potential to destroy life," she answered.

"Didn't the ancient Celts adhere to a similar philosophy?" Naoise asked.

"Yes," Rían answered. "As did most indigenous tribes around the world."

"But the Celts were far more advanced," Cíanna commented from beside her.

"Is that so?" Rían asked.

"Yeah." To her surprise, Seth answered. "They were superior iron workers, well in advance of most other cultures. They created weapons using meteorite ore long before anyone else discovered how to, making swords that were pretty much indestructible."

"Only a man would view an ancient civilisation's success in terms of the weapons they made," Naoise shot at him.

"Their weapons made them superior," he countered. Rían sensed a strong and unfriendly rivalry between these two. She glanced at the old man who seemed to be enjoying the open discussion.

"Naoise's right, Seth. The Celts were more than just their weapons," Cíanna interrupted them both.

"For example?" McCormac said, stirring it up some more. "Rían?"

She shrugged.

"You all seem more knowledgeable on this subject than I," she said. McCormac scrutinised her for a moment before moving on.

"Cíanna?" he asked.

"If I said Newgrange, we all know I'd be wrong," Cíanna replied. "Honour made the Celts a force to be reckoned with, honour to the Clan, their families, their friends. They were also knowledgeable in solar and lunar cycles and how they related to the land."

The old man nodded, as though praising a child.

"Why is Newgrange wrong?" Seth asked. "Isn't it supposed to be a perfect example of engineering on the solar cycle?"

"It is," Rían answered, when no one else would. "But Newgrange is about five thousand five hundred years old."

"And?" he asked.

"Newgrange is Stone-age, it predated the Celts by about three thousand years," she answered. The old man regarded her for a moment and when he seemed satisfied with what he found, decided on a change of topic.

"My dear, I have some wonderful and colourful tales to tell of your father…" he began, and dominated the conversation for the rest of the meal as he regaled her with her father's exploits as a young man. While she had no doubts most of the high jinks ascribed him could be true for the most part, she got the impression McCormac was trying to put her at her ease and impress upon her the extent of his involvement with her folks, and how much he had their confidences.

After dessert and coffee, he suggested retiring to his study for a more intimate conversation alone with her. The others he left outside to their own devices and amusement. She noted how they acquiesced to him like obedient little children. A rude shock awaited him if he expected her to be as submissive as the others.

"Scotch?" he offered but she shook her head and looked about his study. "Are you sure?" She gave the same answer and he poured only a single glass.

"Seth tells me you're a Druid," she said, picking up and examining some of the various ornaments on the shelves. Her curiosity in his trinkets amused him, and while he loathed anyone touching these precious objects, he sensed she was testing his reaction to her doing so.

"I am," he answered, swirling his scotch slowly. "But the concept is not new to you either." She glanced sideways at him, her eyebrow flickering upwards for a second, her telltale giveaway sign. She slowly turned around to face him, folding her arms across her.

"I've no idea what you're talking about," she lied, but she wasn't convincing.

"Don't play games with me, child," he said. "Your parents brought you up in our tradition, in the ancient ways. You were taught much more than the basics, you were taught our rituals and ways. In fact, up until about 10 or 12 years ago you were a regular practitioner. For some reason you stopped when you left school and went to college. For some unknown reason you then gave up your Celtic studies, turned your back on everything, your upbringing, your history. You delved into other religions, other philosophies, tested out other beliefs. I'm not admonishing you for opening your mind and broadening your education but I thought you'd return to us after your spiritual experimentation. Now it seems you don't adhere to any of them." He regarded her with care, changing emotions skimming across her face until she settled for glaring at him.

"Is that why I'm here? For you to re-ignite my faith?" she demanded. He smiled, a cold, calculating smile.

"Not quite," he answered, "but everything is related."

"What do you mean?" she asked.

"Your passion for history, your environmental and scientific endeavours, your spirit for the honourable causes, your sense of honour, your history, it's all a part of who you are. All a part of *what* you are," he said.

"Which is?" she asked.

"You are the direct descendant of the last of the Ard Rí of Ireland," he said. She stared at him incredulously before laughing. He wasn't amused. She shook her head, composing herself.

"Read a little too much Dan Brown, haven't we," she replied. "You're probably big into conspiracy theories as well. Watch X-file re-runs much?"

He slammed his glass onto the side table and stood up, glaring at her. Pulling himself to his full height, he towered over her, but she stood up to his intimidation tactics.

"You insolent child," he roared at her. Her expression hardened. She may be insolent, and proud of it, but how dare he call her a child. "Don't you comprehend the magnitude of what you are a part of?"

"Obviously not," she retorted and he stepped back from her.

"No, of course you wouldn't." He seemed to be talking to himself, but regarded her the way a scientist would view a fascinating specimen. He sat back down and took a sip of his scotch.

"Sit," he ordered in a somewhat gentler tone. She hesitated for a moment, the urge to get the hell out growing by the minute. She did as requested, sinking into the deep leather seat.

"Your lineage can be traced back as far as 1315 AD, to the last Ard Rí, the High King, Edubard a Briuis," he began. "Even before then, Breasal Boidhiobhadb, from whom your family name is derived from, was High King at about 200 BC. Since a Briuis, the order of Druids to which I belong, have preserved his blood-line throughout the centuries, ensuring its continuation from generation to generation."

"Not to throw you from your well-rehearsed little speech," she interrupted, "there's a minor problem with your little scenario."

"Which is?" he asked in an almost bored tone.

"There is no right of succession in this country, there never was, so all this descendant crap is a load of bollocks. High Kings were elected from the provincial Kings, who were elected from the Clan leaders," she said. A smile played at the corner of his lips. "The 'Flight of the Earls' episode also puts paid to any sovereignty issues when the most likely nobles to succeed left this country in 1607. In fact, if you want to get down to the nitty-gritty of all this shit, then anyone born in this country, who can trace their family history back far enough, can make a claim."

"So you do remember your history, little one."

"You are not making a Pretender out of me."

"Child, we've prepared you from the moment you were born, with no part of your life left to chance. You were taught the correct history of your people, not the piffle the education system churns out. You were immersed in histories of the Tuatha de Danann, the Milesians and the Celts. This is who you are. Why won't you accept it?" he demanded.

"Because it's a load of shite," she said. "This country has been a republic, a free state since 1922. It answers to no King. Or Queen for that matter." He held his hand up to her, forestalling any more of her arguments or use of crude language

"Silence," he told her, in a tone that brooked no further argument.

"You were born in Ráth Bhaile, or Rathvilly to use the English, at the site of Crimthan, the King of Leinster around 440 AD. Like Crimthan, you were born on the Moate. You came into this world on the 31st night of October, at Samhain, Halloween, New Year's Eve in the ancient Celtic tradition. Not only were you born on the eve of a new year, but also of a new millennium according to the ancient calendar. You were conceived at Imbolc, the 1st of February in the Rites of Spring. Centuries of planning are in your birth."

"I suppose you're going to tell me there's a prophecy," she threw at him. Anger rose in him again before he caught it.

"Of course there is, my dear. All of these things have been prophesied. We have been guiding you, teaching you, protecting you for the past 30 years, advancing your career in the last five, helping you prepare for public life and leadership. We have controlled your entire life," he stated.

"As you pointed out, I gave all this crap up ten years ago. I've been watching out for myself ever since. Nobody held my hand and I didn't need anyone's help. Everything I have achieved I earned on my own," she said.

"I beg to differ," he answered. "Did you think it sheer luck you escaped the fate of other more notable journalists who investigated the criminal underworld? Luck and beneficence you secured a sought after position on TV? You were put into the public eye and you won the public over. You were guided into politics and political analysis so that you would better understand how to govern this country. You were born to rule, and by all that is sacred to me child, that is what you are going to do. You have no idea how hard we have worked to bring you to this point, how hard we have protected you throughout the years. You were almost lost to us once, but by the fortune of the Gods, you are still alive today."

"What the hell are you talking about?" she demanded.

"I am referring to your narrow escape when a bomb exploded just outside of Heuston station, about three years ago, and on the train you regularly travelled on. If memory serves me, you missed the train by mere seconds. Providence spared you."

"That was a terrorist attack," she said, remembering all too well the shock wave from the blast and the searing heat that the newer bombs generated. Every life was lost in the targeted carriage, the carriage she normally sat in, as well as the carriages on either side.

"Covered up as a terrorist attack, but if you recall, no group ever claimed responsibility, despite the growing number of them," he answered. "Prior to that was your little mugging incident."

"Nothing more than a thug trying to intimidate me, make me back off my investigation," she said.

"Is that what you think?" he asked. "The poor fellow got a nasty shock to discover you're more than capable of defending yourself. Unfortunately he didn't survive long enough for to be apprehended by the authorities." She looked at him, alarmed at what he implied. "No. We had nothing to do with his demise. Those who sent him to eliminate you made sure he wouldn't be in a position to either identify them, or reveal their intentions."

"Who are *they*?" she challenged.

"*They* are all who fear you, fear who you are and what you are. From cults who may think you are their anti-Christ, the beginning of their end, to those in power who would see you as a threat."

She shook her head and pulled herself out of the seat.

"I'm not listening to any more of this. Whatever fantasy is going on in your little brain, I am not a part of it, nor am I willing to be," she told him. His eyes narrowed.

"You are a fool, child. Insolent and a fool. I fear we've left you unguided for too long," he said.

Without being drawn any further into another argument with him, she slammed the door behind her.

Chapter 9

The old man rattled her, and she hated him, still considering him crazy and in a dangerous way. Despite the heat of the day, she felt cold and trembled, shaking in part from anger. So her lack of faith concerned him? Her faith, or lack thereof, was a private and personal issue, she thought, growing more infuriated. The old woman's words came back to her. "They will be coming for you," she said. "You will know them when they come for you." What happened today couldn't be mere coincidence. Is this what she meant? She was descended from High Kings? It was the most ridiculous notion she'd ever heard. As the old man pointed out, the last High King reigned until 1315 although, if memory served, a number of other sources claimed the High Kingship ended with Rory O'Connor about 150 years earlier, over a millennium ago and half again. No, impossible and un-provable.

With the release of the controversial Dan Brown book two decades before, an investigation followed, revealing the Vatican did possess proof. All this attention on the church resulted in a revival of people's faith. The backlash the church feared never materialised. Instead, vocations began to increase again, and the phenomenon wasn't confined to the Catholicism either. All the Christian-based religions confirmed record attendances. People needed something to cling to and believe in, especially in the midst of economic crisis and turmoil. This situation with the Ard Rí would be impossible to prove, unless they possessed the body of the last High King, well preserved, and stashed away somewhere.

The sound of a car slowing and turning into her drive shook her from her thoughts. Lucy wagged her tail, but considering she allowed complete strangers to leave flowers and clothes, her discretion wasn't reliable right now. She turned around not surprised to find Seth. He walked to her and straddled the bench to sit facing her.

"You left without saying goodbye."

She just shrugged, not wanting to say anything, not to him.

"Want to talk about it?" he asked but she shook her head, not trusting that McCormac hadn't sent him to try winning her back, to reason with her.

"He doesn't know I'm here," he said, sensing her distrust, and seemed genuinely concerned. "He didn't hurt you, did he?"

"Would an assault on my spiritual sensibilities count?"

He smirked.

"He can be a devious old bastard at the best of times. I don't know why he insisted on having you to lunch but I'm guessing there's a druidic connection."

She frowned at him.

"Why would you assume that?"

"That conversation at lunch was by design, to tease out how much you knew, how much we all know about this stuff. It's his version of a pop-quiz, but, as discreet as your landscaping is you have an oak grove at the bottom of your garden and an effigy of the Horned Man hanging over your door. You know a lot more about this stuff than you've let on."

"Okay, you got me, I'm part of a worldwide Celtic conspiracy," she said sarcastically.

"Cool, we should consolidate our efforts then," he answered laughing, but she didn't share his humour.

"If he's such a bastard, why stay with him? What hold does he have over you?"

He stood up and took a few steps away from her, pausing before turning back to face her.

"Sometimes there are obligations we have to honour."

"Honour is one thing, but not to personal detriment."

"It isn't that simple. You asked me yesterday about him, my relationship with him."

"You have … a relationship with him?" she asked, thinking of all the women usually hanging out of him.

"Not that kind of relationship," he said, sounding annoyed.

"So what is he to you?"

"He's... sort-of a father figure, a mentor for me. He's been a major influence on my life, all my life."

"In what way?"

He shrugged and seemed to struggle with an answer, seemed to struggle with trusting her.

"He … found me … when I was a child."

"Found you? What about your parents?"

He hesitated for a moment.

"My mother died when I was about five or six, I don't even remember her. According to the old man, she had a drug problem and died of an overdose. Never knew my father, it's doubtful I ever had one. Now you know why I don't do interviews, none of this is public knowledge".

"But something like this would add to your success story?"

"Would it? Why draw attention to it? It would only put my entire life under scrutiny, including the people in my life."

"Like who? McCormac?"

"Not just him," he answered. "I have parents, people who took me in, fostered me when the old man asked them to. They lost their own son a couple of months earlier to some form of leukaemia, about the same age as me, and it was never made public. I became their son then, stepped into his life."

"Sounds like a perfect match," she said and he laughed softly.

"Hardly, I was the child from hell," he answered and she raised an eyebrow as much as to say 'gee, what a surprise'. "But the old guy knocked some manners into me."

"Not enough," she said. "So is this the reason you're so driven, you think you have to prove yourself to the world?"

"Whoa, talk about deep," he threw back.

"You're not the only one to dabble in psychology."

He turned away again, seeming deep in thought before turning back to her, frowning.

"I don't even know why I'm telling you all of this, you're probably the worst person to be talking to," he said. "You're a journalist," he added when he saw her glaring.

"Don't worry, I've no evidence to back it up, and I couldn't afford the libel."

He laughed and sat back down.

"You're one complex woman Rían Breasel. You speak fluent Irish, you fight like a hellion, you probably know more about Celtic history and druidism than Naoise does, and the old man's itching to get his hands on you. Who are you?"

"After everything you've just told me, I could ask you the same question."

"Oh, you reckon there's more to me than being, and I quote, 'a glorified fitness instructor'? I liked that one, it was one of your nicer descriptions of me," he said, again referring to her article.

"You didn't exactly give me much to go on," she countered.

"You didn't exactly give me much of a chance."

He glanced at his watch. "I gotta go, I'm heading back to Dublin but I'd like to see you again. Can I call you?" he asked and after a pause, she nodded.

He left and in that moment an idea, an action plan came to mind, so simple, so obvious and damn near impossible.

She needed to find the raggedy old woman.

The task proved harder than anticipated. The following morning she used her list of contacts, getting in touch with anyone who might help, but without a name to look for, the task seemed impossible. Rían returned to the place where she'd first encountered the woman and talked to the locals, but no one recalled ever seeing her. Under the guise of doing an article on the current wave of homelessness in the city, she contacted the various shelters throughout the capital. Female homelessness, while not rare, was less common than their male counterparts were and should be easier to find. While the shelters had a few older women on their records, none matched the brief description Rían gave them. By the middle of the week, she started to lose faith and hope. The Internet yielded no answers either. The only lead, and vague at that, led her to a mental health institution on the outskirts of the city, which sounded plausible considering the woman's apparent state, with one slight problem. The woman in question, a patient of the hospital and matching Rían's description, had disappeared. Her source had scant details, no forwarding address, and no family details, with the bills paid for by an American corporation, which turned out to be only a holding company upon further investigation. None of this put her at ease but it remained the only definite lead. That a holding company paid the bills raised her suspicions enough to probe deeper.

Later that evening a taxi took her to Killiney, one of the affluent suburbs of Dublin, and dropped her off at the hospital. This late in the evening, most, if not all, of the administration staff was gone. That left nurses and orderlies to deal with, and the occasional intern. The main door opened before she even stepped out of the taxi.

"You the one here about our runaway?" he called across at her. His lack of professionalism and indiscretion annoyed her, but she nodded as she walked towards him. "My friend says you're a very concerned ... niece," he went on, pausing for effect on her role.

"We're all very worried about her," Rían answered, keeping to her cover story.

He led her to a room on the top floor, one of the more secure wings, her guide informed her, and she wondered how the woman managed to escape. He unlocked the door and allowed her to step in. She gave the room a quick sweeping glance, noting the single, narrow bed bolted to the floor in the far corner from her and behind the door, a sink and toilet unit were built into the wall. No privacy here, she thought. The walls seemed to be covered in strangely designed wallpaper, but on closer inspection of the closest wall to her, discovered it to be writing of some sort, indistinct scribblings but her heart skipped a beat. The orderly pushed past her into the room.

"Your aunt's a complete loon," he said, indicating the walls. "Every time we clean these up, she starts all over again with this crap." Rían said nothing but reached out to touch them, her fingers tracing a line and she stepped further into the room, surveying the wall in front of her.

"Hey, you look like you can read this shit," he said.

"I can," she admitted.

"What the hell is it then?" he asked. "No one here has a clue what it is, what it means, or why she keeps writing it."

Rían gave the rest of the room a thorough look before answering.

"It's ancient writing," she said, scanning through rune symbols, old Viking script and Celtic Ogham.

"Huh," he answered.

"Any objections if I take a copy of this?" she asked, pulling her phone from her pocket not asking, just saying the words as a matter of courtesy. He just shrugged and she started scanning, taking her time, making sure she got everything. As she caught snatches of words, the growing sinking sensation jumped into hyper drive, and she wondered if trying to find this woman was such a good idea anymore.

"You done?" he asked as she did a quick 360 around the room, making sure she hadn't missed anything. He checked his watch in an overt and obvious gesture.

"Yeah, all done," she answered, taking the hint and leaving.

Chapter 10

True to his word, Seth called and dropped by during the early part of the week. Away from Ardscull, the well-dressed and smooth moving Seth she first encountered returned, but the arrogance seemed a little tempered. He brought her a power smoothie for lunch the day he came to her office and she challenged him on this, demanding to know if his concept of taking her to dinner involved something like a broccoli shake. He laughed before admitting he'd put some in her drink the night of the gala, and laughed more at the face she made recalling the vile taste.

He didn't try prying any further into the weekend's affair at Ardscull, nor did he enquire into her current investigation. What he did ask about was her plans on getting to the Wave Generator the following week. She regarded him with suspicion until he explained about his invitation to attend the inauguration and subsequent celebrations, and offered to accompany her, if she found the arrangement agreeable. He promised to fit in with her plans. This turnaround in him surprised her. No bullying, no pushiness and she found herself uploading a copy of her itinerary onto his e-organiser, which he dropped into his inside jacket pocket without reading. Admittedly, she started warming to him, but the events of the weekend left her wary.

By Thursday evening, she'd made no further progress in finding the old woman. She boarded the last train home, busy with late evening shoppers, but she managed to get a double seat to herself despite the volume of passengers, and she pulled the hardcopies of the Runic and Ogham scribblings from her backpack. At every opportunity, she scanned through them, trying to figure them out, having a considerable proportion deciphered already. McCormac was correct about her when he said she'd remembered most of her lessons, but who could forget a Vegvisir, the runic compass or a Valnott, the death knot. These symbols only appeared a small number of times on the printouts, but for the most part the old form of Irish Gaelic rambled on about a lost child and the Ard Rí. When she returned home after her visit to that room she realised she still didn't have a name to put to the woman. Not like her to forget little details like that, but the room threw her off her game, unsettled her.

The light began to fade as the train reached Carlow with night almost upon her by the time she left the 24-hour supermarket with groceries, and drove home. The stretch of road before Ballickmoyler widened and as she spotted movement ahead on the hard shoulder she manoeuvred the car out to the white line in order to give the figure a wider berth, but something about the person made Rían slow up and give more than a cursory glance. The figure appeared bedraggled, dressed in tatters, and a woman. Checking her rear-view mirror for anyone driving behind, Rían pulled back in, gearing down in rapid succession, bringing the car to a stop. Halting further away than she intended she threw the car into reverse, stopping a bit away from the person. She jumped out and ran towards the woman. Seeing someone running towards her, the old woman panicked, turned and began to run in the opposite direction. Rían caught up and caught hold of the older woman who screamed and tried to pull away, lashing out at her attacker, but Rían deflected most of them with ease while trying to talk to her. Finally realising who grabbed her, the woman took Rían's head in her hands.

"Found you," she whispered to Rían repeatedly.

"Yeah, you did," Rían reassured her. "I'm going to take you home." The woman panicked again.

"Not home," she screeched and grabbed fistfuls of her own hair. "They hurt me at home. Bad place, bad place. Not home."

Rían held her by the shoulders.

"No, my home," she said trying to reassure her. "My home is safe. They can't hurt you there."

"Promise? No bad?"

"No bad, just you and me," Rían said. The older woman burst into tears, collapsing onto the ground and hugging herself. She started rocking and chanting to herself, repeating 'found you'. Rían struggled to get her upright and into the back of the car. The seatbelt freaked her out and against better judgement Rían left it off. With home only another 5 minutes away, she could take the risk. Back at the house, she guided the older woman inside.

"Do you have a name?" Rían asked and the woman had to think, all the time tapping the side of her head.

"Marianne," she answered and Rían smiled. The moment of lucidity seemed to last and Marianne started to become distressed again at realising her dishevelled state.

"How about a bath and some clean clothes?" Rían asked.

"Bath? Get clean? I like clean. Clean is good," she mumbled and followed Rían to the bathroom and while the water filled the tub, allowed Rían to undress her. Rían guessed her to be about the same size as her, a little thinner, but her own clothes should fit. She helped Marianne into the bath and sponged her back but Marianne began slipping back into herself. She started to rock in the water, muttering and repeating herself, growing more audible.

"Took my baby. Away. Away. Took her out of my arms. Snatched her. Took her away from me. My baby. My little girl. Gave her away. Gave my baby away. Now they want her again. Want to take her again." Marianne snapped out of her trance, grabbed Rían's arm with surprising strength, and searched in her eyes.

"They took you from me. You were ordained, you were special to them and I tried to stop them, tried to protect you from them. But they were stronger and they took you. I tried to run away with you, but they caught us. Locked me away. Gave me drugs to forget you, to forget my baby. How could I forget about my little girl? How could I forget about my own child? I had to warn you, had to find you, to warn you. I ran away to find you. They used me to have you, to have their heir."

Rían pulled away, backing up until she hit the wall, a tightness growing in her chest and she sat on the floor, stunned and shocked, staring at this woman. She wanted to find this woman, to find the truth, but this? What she implied was… impossible, insane. She validated what McCormac said, but she also implied she was… Rían pulled herself from the floor and caught hold of the woman.

"Who are you?" she demanded.

"Your mother," she answered.

"No, you can't be." Rían let her go and slumped back to the floor, her mind racing. She pulled herself together long enough to help Marianne out of the bath. Cleaner, Rían made out the woman's features, noting the similarities to her own, the shape of the eyes, the nose. But they were also similar to the woman she called mother for all of her life. She helped Marianne into clean clothes and made some chicken soup for the both of them. Marianne seemed to be growing more alert and coherent with each spoonful, maybe because she felt safe, Rían reasoned, while she herself didn't. Not anymore.

"I ran away before," Marianne began, "I always run away, when I can. I try to find you. I found you before." Rían looked at her questioningly. "You were seven years old. You ran away too. You ran to the woods in Rathvilly. Are they still there?" she asked. Rían shook her head. They'd been cut down years ago for a housing development. "I made tea at a little fire I started," Marianne went on and a memory hit Rían.

"You made me tea," she said, stunned.

"You ran away from them," Marianne said with glee, "just like I did."

"I was sick of studying, of learning all the ancient laws. They wouldn't allow me to play with the other kids. I had to learn about Tír na nÓg and all the other fairy tales," Rían said, remembering slamming the door as she ran out. Remembered tearing her dress on a fence she climbed over. God, how she hated dresses, was made wear them all the time.

"I ran away again at 14. Stayed away for longer that time. They found me in Blessington a week later," she told Marianne and the older woman chuckled.

"Would love to have seen their faces, their precious one missing, gone from their hands," she said. Rían didn't share her mirth as she remembered the punishments that followed.

"It wasn't pretty," Rían confirmed. "We argued for days. I didn't want to learn that stuff anymore." Rían shook her head. "And I don't want this again; I gave all this nonsense up a long time ago." Marianne grabbed hold of her.

"Not nonsense. Real. All souls return from the other realm, the Otherworld. The Tuatha de Danann, Tír na nÓg, all real," Marianne spoke with more clarity than she possessed all night, with more passion and conviction. To Rían's eyes, she believed all this, but Rían remained unconvinced.

"You need proof?" she said, "about me?"

Rían shrugged, not knowing what to say.

"DNA," Marianne said.

"What?" Rían asked.

"It will prove to you who I am, who you are."

Rían thought about it, and knew she was correct, with DNA analysis now a common and quick procedure, but at this hour of the night, she wondered if she should set about doing something now, while this woman, who claimed to be her mother seemed to be remaining lucid for the moment. Who knew what her mental state would be like if left until the morning?

Rían made some calls, giving a concocted story to explain the urgency. The closest hospital to her with such a service was Waterford Regional, an hour's drive away. Due to the number of cases passing through every day, the testing lab now operated 24/7 and if she got there tonight, she'd have the results by morning. The drive took less than an hour, and the car beeped at her on a number of occasions regarding her speed, which she ignored. While driving above the limit, she also stayed under the upper leeway threshold.

Sam, her given contact, met her at the entrance and ushered her and Marianne past the Emergency department, up to the lab. Rían stepped into the room and stopped short. She put a hand back to stop Marianne from following, using the door to shield the older woman.

"Rían?" Cíanna said in surprise. "Is everything ok?" Rían stared at her, dressed in green surgical scrubs.

"You're a doctor?" Rían asked, stunned. Cíanna smiled.

"Yes, on accident and emergency rotation. What brings you to the DNA lab?"

"A story I'm working on," Rían lied.

"Nothing sinister, I hope," Cíanna answered "Well, I'd better get back. An unidentified DOA came in, I hoped I'd find him in the DNA database," Cíanna said by way of explanation. "Let me know if you find anything," she asked the technician, who nodded in reply. Cíanna left, but not before giving her a strange glance and upon exiting the lab she found the older woman waiting outside and scrutinised her as she exited. Rían's heart raced, and wondered how long before the old man found out. She pulled Marianne inside and kept an eye on Cíanna as she disappeared down a side corridor.

"I don't think we have much time," Rían said, not offering an explanation, not wanting to frighten Marianne any more.

"They're going to find me again, and take me away, aren't they?" she said.

"Not if I have anything to do about it," Rían assured her. Sam spoke in low tones to the technician who seemed reluctant to help but who agreed. Sam disappeared to get a doctor.

Rían frowned when she spotted a syringe.

"I thought DNA only needed a swab?"

"Not for a full chromosomal analysis. Needs blood," he answered.

Fear grew and she wondered if she'd taken the best course of action when the door reopened and a strange man entered, dressed in scrubs and displaying a stunning set of teeth. Rían made a grab for Marianne, but she never reached her. Grabbed from behind she felt a sting in her neck followed by a burning, yet icy, sensation as the contents of the syringe surged through her system. Her breathing grew staggered and her legs gave way. She heard Marianne screaming as though from a distance. Rían dropped to her knees on the floor as the door re-opened, and Cíanna re-entered. No soft smiles this time, only a cold, hard glare. Then complete blackness overcame her.

Chapter 11

Rían's eyes flickered opened and she stretched, her body feeling stiff and sore. Taking some time she realised she was home and in her own bed. Marianne. Rían threw off the covers and leaped out of bed, and searched from room to room, but found no sign of the woman. The only evidence Rían found were her clothes, tattered and torn, on the floor of the utility room, beside the laundry basket. The bowls from the soup the previous night were cleared away; everything neat as a pin. She went to the bathroom and using the mirror, checked out the site of an ache on her neck and found a circular mark from the pressure syringe below her right ear.

Anger and adrenaline coursed through her as she put a plan of action together. She grabbed keys, surprised to find the security system still armed. Whoever returned her home probably hoped to convince her she'd been dreaming, she surmised and wondered if her parents supplied the alarm code. After all, they supplied other information to the old man. Her parents. She still thought of them as that. Now she couldn't be sure. Not any more. But that was going to be her first port of call. Their home. Her home. The place where she grew up.

Her car sat in the drive, also returned, the keys left on the countertop. She grabbed them on her way out and drove into Carlow, continuing on to Rathvilly. It was months since she'd been here, and with the exception of summer blooms, nothing much changed. She entered the house, disabling the alarm similar to her own, her dad having installed them both. Was he her dad? She put the question out of her mind and concentrated on the task at hand. She needed evidence, a shred of proof that the old woman told the truth. In the safe, she found what she was looking for, her birth certificate. She'd never needed it before. They organised her passport, her ID, which was on the chip in her wrist. Everything had been controlled. She had been controlled. She unfolded the paper and read the details of her life. She held the undeniable truth in her hands, in black and white, on a proper paper trail. Her mother's name was in fact Marianne, with her maiden name the same as Moira's. None of this made sense, unless...

She put the papers back, shut the safe and relocked the house. Instead of driving off, she walked instead to the Moate, only a 5-minute walk away. Compared to Ardscull, Rathvilly's Moate was tiny in size and tucked in at the next crossroads, with two slender granite stones less than a metre high providing the entrance to the site. She climbed up to them and stepped through, circling left, climbing the mound, using the limbs of the few trees to pull herself up. She never came here to hide, being too exposed, but she always came here to sit and think, to get a better perspective on things. She climbed to the top and did a 360-degree turn. Where trees didn't obstruct her view, she had an almost complete circle of scenery of the surrounding vale and the mountains beyond them.

Sensing movement behind her, she turned, finding McCormac standing behind her, leaning on a walking stick. She regarded him with suspicion. She didn't hear him approaching, or climbing, he seemed to have simply ... appeared. She looked down to the road and found no sign of any car either. So how the hell did he get up here without a sound?

"Why are you making this difficult on yourself?" he asked, his tone gentle.

"Have I ever been any other way?"

He smirked.

"No, not really."

"Marianne?" she demanded and he sighed.

"What we did, we did for your own good, for your protection," he answered. "I presume by now you know she's your natural mother?" .

She nodded.

"Unfortunately, she proved to be too ... unstable, unreliable as a mother. For your own safety we took you from her for fear she'd harm you, even kill you. After all, she almost smothered you once."

"And the people I call parents?"

"Family," he answered, "Moira is in fact your aunt, sister to Marianne. Your father is, well, your father. Moira stepped in to take care of you and things happened, as things tend to do. They fell in love and married." He paused, giving her time to take it all in. "Marianne is still a danger to you," he added referring to the previous night. "We had to get you out safely."

"By drugging me?"

"A precaution, for their protection," he answered and she raised her eyebrows at him. "You've turned into quite the little warrior. Seth's been training for years, was taught by the finest Masters I could find. He's won every competition he's ever entered, until he fought you. You're the only one to defeat him."

"Dirty tactics," she admitted.

"In battle there is no such thing as dirty tactics, only tactics that win and tactics that lose. Do you get ríastrad?"

"The ... what?"

"In ancient times, warriors, in the heat of battle entered into a form of battle frenzy or fervour. I have no direct translation, but I think the modern term would be 'in the zone'," he said.

She didn't answer, her expression said it all and he laughed.

"So, you do. Tell me if I'm correct. Time slows down for you. You notice your opponent's movements in the minutiae of details. You see the slightest quiver of hesitation or intent. You can anticipate their next move before even they themselves are aware of it?" The hardening of her expression answered him. "That is why they drugged you, for their own safety. Ríastrad would have come on you while you tried to defend Marianne," he added.

"Where is she now?" Rían asked.

"We've taken care of her. She will no longer be a danger to herself, or to you." His answer had a tone of finality and she didn't press any further. "Now will you accept your destiny?"

"Based on what evidence? Your word and the word of an insane woman?" she threw back at him. "Where's the empirical proof of your claim?"

"The proof lies not in the past, my little one, but in the near future."

"Meaning?"

"Consider it an experiment, your empirical proof of who you are."

"Which is?"

"A ritual, just a ritual. If you are the true heir the stone will call out," he answered.

She looked at him, stunned.

"You're talking about the Lia Fáil," she said. "But that's just a fairy tale, and besides, the English took the real stone over 400 years ago."

His smug grin grew.

"A fallacy, the Scottish Coronation Stone was taken, and the Lia Fáil is more than a mere fairy tale. If I am wrong, then nothing will happen. If that is the case, I will be gone from your life."

At last, she thought, the first piece of sense he made since meeting him. And if that's what it took to get rid of the old coot once and for all, maybe it was worth it. She said nothing and turned to go.

"We'll speak again on this," he said, and she turned to face him. To her surprise and unease, he disappeared.

Chapter 12

The phone inside Seth's jacket pocket shook and he took it out, checking the caller display. Sighing, he excused himself from the meeting and stood in the lobby outside the boardroom, facing the wall of windows overlooking the city. He hit the call-answer button and heard the old man's voice.

"Come to Ardscull tonight," he said. "It's time we talked." The call ended abruptly and without having to say a word, Seth put the phone back into his jacket pocket. He remained standing in front of the windows, hands in his pockets, lost in thought. When he came out of his brooding, he checked the time; calculating his arrival time if he left now. Being a Friday evening, the later he left his departure the longer it would take, so he decided go there and then. He had clothes at the old man's house and therefore no reason to return to his apartment first. He drove into work himself this morning, as though anticipating something to happen.

Even leaving when he did, the journey still took 2 hours, with the biggest time delay getting out of the city. The old man waited for him in his study, immersed in a book, barely acknowledging his presence when he stepped into the room. Seth unbuttoned his jacket, loosened his tie and sat in the deep leather chair he'd always hated.

"You wanted to know about my interest in Rían," the old man said. Seth looked at him, with a bored expression on his face, but he waited the old man out.

"Rían Breasel is of vital importance," McCormac went on, giving him a brief explanation.

"What does this have to do with me?" Seth asked when the old man finished.

"It's what you've been training for. Since the dawn of time your duty has always been, and will always be, to defend and protect the heir," the old man answered.

"A bit overdramatic, don't you think," Seth commented dryly. "As for being her bodyguard, she is more than capable of taking care of herself. And I don't think she's the sort of girl to agree to have one, especially not me."

"That's not the point," the old man snapped at him and Seth chuckled, a defiant glint in his eyes.

"So that's what happened last Sunday when she stormed out. She's not as accepting of this as we are, is she? And now you want me to watch her without her realising we're watching over her," he said.

"Hmm," he old man mused, "sometimes you do show some semblance of the intellect of your namesake, however, you're not ready."

Seth's eyes narrowed at the implied insult, and the tiny muscles in his cheeks quivered as he clenched his jaw, but he said nothing, sensing something was going on that he wouldn't like. He may have given the impression in public that he deferred to the old man, but things were quite the opposite in private. The old man did his best to knock manners, and other lessons, into the younger one, but that never stopped Seth from questioning him every step of the way. With sudden realisation, he recognised the same trait in Rían, suddenly understanding how alike they were after all.

"You need to know who Setanta is, boy. You need to remember."

"I already remember," Seth retorted.

"Fool," the old man growled at him, "your memories are incomplete and without them you can never be the champion he was." Seth sighed, not liking where this led, knowing the old man was goading him. "You need to complete and restore the link to the past."

"Is that why you summoned me here tonight?" Seth answered. "And conveniently there's a new moon, just perfect for opening the doors to the Otherworld."

The old man just smiled and it chilled Seth to the bone.

His instincts proved right; he didn't like this at all. He always hated these rituals, if for no other reason than they left him weak for days. The pain he blocked out, the memories were harder to do, but over time, he'd learned how to dull those too.

At the back of the house at Ardscull, in the recesses of the garden, the old man built his ritual chamber. A modern take on the ancient burial mounds like Newgrange, this one seemed built into the ground, covered by a mound of grassy earth, and only one, single entrance to come and go by. Subtle lighting, recessed into the ceiling and walls, illuminated the interior, and the walls themselves contained an odd mix of herbs and potions and digital technology.

Under normal conditions, he'd be completely nude for these things, but usually no one else would be involved other than the old man. Tonight, a sheet preserved his modesty from Cíanna and Naoise as they stood by the old man in the chamber. Seth stared at a fixed point on the far wall as the trio went through the prescribed preparations. Being indoors, the others opted for normal clothing, no robes, no hooded cloaks, ancient druidism adapted to fit in with modern times. The old man handed a small bowl to Naoise who walked around the solid stone altar to Seth. She ceremoniously handed the bowl to him.

"For those who seek the truth. For those who seek the light," she intoned.

"I seek the truth. I seek the light," he muttered in response and took the bowl, hesitating before drinking. It tasted vile, as these potions always did, and for a fleeting moment, he smiled as he pictured Rían's reaction to the bowl's contents. Naoise took the bowl back and returned to the old man. Both women returned to him, taking an arm each and walked him to the altar. Didn't the old man trust him to go through with this, he thought angrily? He didn't need to be chaperoned like a novice. He sat on the stone, swinging his legs up, grateful for the sheet covering his ass, protecting him from the cold stone altar.

Cíanna put her hand to his chest and pushed him down until he lay prone. She took both of his arms and raised them over his head. This was new, he thought before realising his hands were now bound and secured to the stone above his head. While he concentrated on Cíanna, he failed to realise Naoise performed a similar operation at his feet. Firmly secured to the stone, he tested his bonds and found no give in them, and he fought a rising panic, trying to stay calm. Cíanna then placed a digital heart monitor over his heart and another device further down on the other side of his chest.

The herbs in the potion kicked in, and his heart began pounding in his ears. As the old man approached the altar, Cíanna put a small wooden rod between Seth's teeth and closed his mouth. Fuck, he thought in alarm, panic winning the battle inside him, just how bad would this be? His eyes widened in fear as the old man raised a dagger in both hands, then plunged it into Seth, who screamed.

The boy Setanta, so the legend went, had the strength of an ox, ran faster than a horse and jumped higher than a bird. But that was only the legend. The stories often neglected to mention having the courage of a lion. By the age of five, he levelled a troop of older boys on a hurling playing field, single-handedly, with only a hurley to defend himself. As if he needed to defend himself. None of the other boys came close to matching the little boy. He had his first taste of battle, of victory, and of ríastrad.

At seven years old came his legendary killing of Culann's guard dog, and his subsequent promise to take the place of the hound for a year until Culann trained a replacement, thus earning him his hero name, Cúchulainn, Hound of Culann. At seventeen he stood alone against the army of Maeve and Ailill, stood against the might of Connacht, defending Ulster against every champion and warrior Maeve threw at him and slaying in the process, Cailitin whose clan would be Cúchulainn's eventual downfall. He trained on the Isle of Skye, his training oftentimes brutal and at nineteen, he killed his best friend from Skye, forced to do so in single combat to the death. He wept at Ferdia's death.

He sired a son, not of his wife Emer's womb, but from another's. A boy as bold and as brazen as his father. Unfortunately, like his father, he refused to yield to his opponent. Even more unfortunate, Cúchulainn also failed to recognise his own child and killed him in single combat. That memory burned deeper than all the others did. However, there were bright moments. He fell in love and wooed a fair and fiery maiden called Emer, and her love saved and protected him from times of illness, mortal danger and despair. His downfall and death eventually came through wizardry, treachery and revenge and at twenty-seven, he died bravely, tying himself upright, dying a hero's death, on his feet.

Seth's body convulsed at the memory of Cúchulainn's death throes. His body suffered too and Cíanna did what she could to staunch the blood flowing from his wounds. Every wound Cúchulainn ever sustained, every knife cut, every stab wound, including the final killing one, now crisscrossed Seth's body. An alarm sounded from the preparation table behind Cíanna.

"His heart's gone into arrest," she said to the old man. "He's dying." Her fingers tapped on the laptop's keys and she hit the enter key. Seth convulsed again as an electrical charge from the digital monitor surged into his heart. The heart-monitor console display on the screen flat-lined. She programmed a higher charge and a second, stronger electrical charge surged through his body. The console showed a blip, erratic at first, but soon gained momentum and a steady sinus rhythm established itself. She turned back to her patient to attend to his wounds, but they'd already begun to heal themselves, red, angry scars puckering his skin. As a trained physician, Cíanna knew what she saw was impossible, but the ancient part of her accepted it without question.

Seth opened his eyes, not wanting to awaken from the darkness, for in the blackness lay peace and forgetfulness. His body was wracked with pain, hurting even to move. He turned his head and found he was in his room in the old man's house. He wasn't alone; Cíanna sat nearby, reading. At hearing him stir, she moved to him, checking his pulse, his pupils, his wounds. Most of them now seemed years old, but were still tender to touch, the memory of them still fresh in his mind. One still worried her, the last one that appeared, Cúchulainn's fatal one and she changed the dressing again. The wound the old man inflicted also seemed to be healing well.

"What time is it?" he said, his throat burning and raw. Cíanna picked up a pressure syringe and he tried to move away from her, but couldn't.

"Relax," she said, "this is for the pain, and a sedative. You need to rest. And it's after midday, Sunday."

"What? I've been out almost two days?"

"Hope you didn't stand anyone up last night," she said. "The old man wanted to talk to you when you woke, but I don't think you're able for that at the moment. This should give you about another 4 hours rest. After that, you're on your own."

He nodded consent and she put the needle to his skin, and he grunted as she released the drugs into his system.

"They should start to kick in in about 5 or 10 minutes, and you need to eat when you wake up. Your body's been through hell. Give it plenty of rest and take the time to heal. As for the memories, just let them come. Trust me on this; fighting them will only make things worse."

"How would you know?" he asked in a whisper. With the barest of smiles, she undid the next button of her shirt revealing the tops of her breasts and her finger traced the line of a scar on her breastbone, similar to the one the old man inflicted on him.

"Remember, give yourself time to heal, so no picking fights. Especially not with anyone who can beat your ass," she said laughing. He groaned in disgust. Did everyone know? She pulled the covers back over him and picking up her book, left him in peace.

He closed his eyes, waiting for the sedative to kick in, waiting for the memories to come. She lied, they didn't come, they hit him with a bang. A crushing blow would have been a better description. He rolled over and buried his face in the pillows, stifling his screams and his tears. Then, mercifully, the sedative kicked in.

Cíanna's assessment of when he'd wake up was accurate. When he opened his eyes, again he found hot food left on the dresser. He raised himself up, still weak, but guessing the painkillers were still working. He was stiff and he stood, stretching the stiffness out of his arms and back. He stood in front of the mirror and surveyed the damage from Friday night, his anger growing with every scar he found. This never happened before, never a mark left before. These looked years old, the lines white and silvery on his tanned skin, some of them quite long. They crisscrossed his back and most of his torso. He looked battle-scarred. He was battle scarred he thought without humour. Not even his face escaped as he spotted a line on his forehead just below his hairline. One on his thigh was star-shaped. Spear, he thought, remembering how it happened. Damn that old bastard, he thought angrily and turned away from the mirror. He took some clothes out of the wardrobe and started to dress.

He couldn't continue to put off the old man any longer and he left the sanctuary of his room. He was again back in his study and Seth eased himself into the seat this time, glaring at the old man, who seemed oblivious and uncaring of the younger man's discomfort.

"Well, how much do you remember?" he demanded.

"Everything," Seth said. Another memory hit him. "You were there when I died. I mean, when he died."

"Don't be ridiculous boy," the old man answered, "that would make me two thousand years old, more, and that would be impossible." Seth eyed him with suspicion and pulled himself back out of the chair to leave.

"What plans have you with Rían this week?" the old man asked and Seth glared at him, wondering how he'd found out.

"I'm accompanying her to Galway," he answered.

"Watch her well," the old man warned.

Seth gave him a withering glare.

"That's about all I'm capable of doing at the moment."

The old man stood, towering over Seth. Another bullying tactic Seth was used to and he stared rebelliously back.

"Remember who you are," the old man growled to him. "You are the living embodiment and direct descendent of this country's greatest hero. You are Setanta, you are Cúchulainn. Never forget that."

"How could I forget," Seth answered still feeling the scars burning on his body.

"Good," the old man's answer was gruff. "Your priority and duty now is to protect the heir. She is all that matters. Nothing else must distract you in this task. Not even your feelings for her."

"Any feelings you think I have for her will not interfere."

"Good," the old man said again and dismissed him.

Chapter 13

Returning to work the following week, Rían picked up her messages from reception as she arrived on Monday, surprised to find one from Seth, accompanied by a single white rose. His note said he'd booked his train ticket and would meet her at the station the following morning. The first Waterford train arrived into Heuston about 8:40am with the Galway train due to leave at 9:30am, giving her enough time to grab a coffee and her ticket, but when she went to the reservation office, found Seth picked them up, leaving a message where he could be found. She entered the lounge, located alongside platform one, and found him sitting on a sofa at the end of the room, cup in his hand, lost in thought. He gave a start as she sat opposite him and his hard expression softened when he registered her. He looked ... haunted.

"You collected my ticket," she said and he smiled.

"Made sense to pick them both up when I got here," he answered. She studied his face. Something was amiss.

"You ok?" she asked. He nodded and smiled, but lacked his usual dynamism.

"Tired," he said by way of explanation.

"You mean, you actually work?" she said and he smirked, sipping from his cup.

"No, just another wild weekend," he answered. With 10 minutes before departure, they left the lounge.

"Either you're not planning to stay, or you're going to live in those clothes for the next few days," she said, noticing he had no bags. He took her carry-case and laughed.

"Sent my luggage on ahead," he answered. Truth be told, he hadn't the strength to carry his bags, and struggled with Rían's small case. They walked up the platform, and as she stopped to board the business class carriage, Seth caught hold of her arm and led her further up the train, to first class. She frowned at him.

"We got upgraded," he explained and shrugged, trying to imply he was innocent. As soon as they settled in, the train left the station and much to her surprise, Seth fell asleep in the seat opposite her. She took out her ePad and worked for a while, but paused every now and again to scrutinise him while he slept. He seemed so vulnerable, she thought, and boyish. She noticed a scar on his forehead, and couldn't remember seeing one before. The journey took a little over two hours and he awoke as the train shuddered to a halt in Galway, looking disorientated for a brief moment.

"You must have had one hell of a wild weekend," she commented as he wiped sleep from his eyes but he still seemed tired.

"You have no idea," he answered.

Danny, his driver stood by the station exit, waiting for them and she gave Seth a glare. So much for going along with her schedule. Inside the car, he opened the folder Danny left for him, containing among other things, their hotel reservations and room key cards, having already been checked in by Danny. From the hotel's underground car park, they went directly to their rooms via the lift and when the elevator doors opened Seth strode out and crossed the lobby to the door opposite, using the keycard to enter. Rían followed him into the suite of rooms, clearly unhappy.

"Penthouse?" she asked and he nodded. "You agreed to fit in with my plans," she said, her anger and frustration rising. He shrugged.

"I did, I only made a few minor adjustments," he answered. "We still took the train, didn't we?"

"After we got conveniently upgraded; a penthouse suite and first class seats are not minor adjustments," she argued.

"You still have your own room, what's the big deal?" he argued back.

"You're doing it again," she accused.

"Doing what?

"Taking over, taking total control."

"Oh, that," he said, taking his jacket off. Weariness crept back into his voice, and he threw himself in to an armchair, but glanced about for his bags. "I suppose that means you're going to turn down the dress I got you for the launch party tomorrow night," he added. She bristled with anger.

"Were you born this much of a control freak, or did you take lessons?" she said. He laughed.

"A little from column A, a little from column B," he answered, and she threw her eyes to the heavens, giving up. He laughed to himself.

"Which one's my room?" she asked.

"Ladies choice," he answered, and she affected a dramatic gasp.

"You're giving me a choice?"

"Fine," he answered and stood up, "I'll take this one," and he pointed to one of the doors. Picking up his bags he grinned at her before disappearing into his chosen room.

A ferry transferred the guests and press alike to the purpose-built power station off the coast of the Aran Islands for the launch scheduled for 3pm, and she welcomed the break from him, the Press and VIP guests occupying different areas of the boat. After a brief tour of the installation, the groups assembled in the public gallery, and the countdown began. While most watched the timer, Rían's eyes were fixed on the generator out in the ocean, as the machine kicked into gear and the power spiked before settling into a constant energy stream. Then came the press release, and Rían stepped to the fore.

"Minister, isn't it ironic that you're here today, taking some of the credit when five years ago, as the appointed Minister for Economic Initiative, you originally shelved this project?"

"Eh, the technology wasn't available at that time."

"And Minister, what about the more recent allegations that, once initiated under your current portfolio, the project not only went considerably over budget, but that a government memo, signed by you, allowed for the transfer of additional exchequer funds to keep the project going, with the main contractors having either family or political connections to you, personal connections?" The room fell silent following her allegations.

Seth stood at the side of the room, watching her with avid interest. And she questioned his aggressive tactics? After a brief pause, the Minister's press officer stepped in, announcing an inquiry into the matter with a statement issuing soon after. The Minister cut his end of the press conference short, allowing the scientists and engineers to take centre stage. Rían sat back continuing to take notes but with a triumphant smirk, Seth noted.

Returning to Galway Seth disembarked first and waited for her by the car. He shook his head at her as she neared.

"You have some nerve questioning my methods and actions."

"What are you talking about?" she asked, confused and he gave her a scornful laugh.

"Hmm, the words pot, kettle and black come to mind." He opened the car door for her.

"What?"

He pushed her in, not being gentle about it and sat in beside her.

"Do you ever watch yourself doing these interviews? Personally, after my interview with you, I think I got off lightly."

"What the hell are you talking about?"

He turned to face her.

"You … are ruthless," he answered.

Realisation finally dawned on her.

"You mean the press conference?"

"No, the side show at Disney World. Of course the press conference."

She smirked.

"It's just politics."

He sat back in the seat again.

"Danny, remind me never to go into politics," he said.

Danny glanced at them in the rear-view mirror.

"Will do, Mr Morand."

Rían glared at both men.

She sequestered herself in her room for the rest of the day, using the time to type up her article. Seth checked in on her a few times, enquiring if she needed anything, but she rebuffed all his offers, until late in the evening when he strode in. He grabbed her by the arm, and before she could raise a protest, hauled her out of her room without saying a word.

"What the hell are you playing at?" she demanded when he let her go. He pushed her towards the balcony.

"You haven't taken a break or eaten all day, so resorting to my charming ways or as you like to call them, 'my bullying tactics', I took the liberty of ordering. Hungry?"

"Yeah, a little," she admitted and surveyed the table. He held her chair as she sat down, poured her a glass of wine before taking to his own seat.

"I knew I'd get you to have dinner with me," he said and she gave him a half-hearted glare

"I'm still not sleeping with you."

"Maybe I don't want to sleep with you."

"Oh, so now I'm not good enough to sleep with."

"Oh no, I've seen what you can do with a weapon and with words, and frankly sweetheart, I don't think I'd feel safe."

Ready with a retort, she caught the mischievous glint in his eye and knew he was teasing her.

"So what's the story with this politician you hammered today?" he asked, and once she realised he was genuinely interested, began to tell him about it. With the help of good food and another glass of wine, she started to relax, her grumpiness and ill temper disappearing, and he made surprisingly good company. After dinner, they moved to the lounge seat and continued talking, but the evening grew colder as darkness fell. He disappeared for a moment, returning with a blanket, which he wrapped around himself, but sat behind her, wrapping his arms and the blanket around her. She stiffened and resisted in his arms.

"Just trying to keep you warm," he said.

"Couldn't get a second blanket, no?" she asked.

"They're all out," he said, "I thought we could use the body thermo-whatsits. You did physics at school, you know what I'm talking about."

"Oh, yeah, did an in-depth analysis of thermo-whatsits for final exams," she answered. His arms enclosed tighter about her as she relaxed, allowing herself to lean into him and they sat in silence for a while, watching the sea and the boats in the distance. He reached for his glass, shifting position in the seat and his hand came to rest at the back of her neck, which he began to gently stroke.

"Does that work where the cheesy lines don't?" she asked smartly, enjoying the pressure of his thumb, but wouldn't admit it.

"I wouldn't know, never needed an alternative strategy before, besides, you have a knot … right there," he went on, pressing in and making her wince. "Get a lot of headaches?"

"I do now, but don't tell me, you have a program perfectly suited to help."

"Of course, but I'd have to give you the once over, check for other hot-spots."

She half turned to face him.

"You don't give up, do you?"

"Never," he whispered and leaned forward to kiss her. She resisted initially but her body loosened and relaxed against him, returning his kiss. He pulled away.

"You're not a conquest," he said. She regarded him for a moment.

"So what am I then?" she asked. He smiled.

"Probably the biggest challenge I've ever faced," he confessed.

"You're only saying that because I whooped your ass."

He grabbed hers in response, knocking her off balance and he grunted in pain as she fell forward onto him. She righted herself but looked alarmed. He looked down to what caught her attention and found blood soaking his shirt. She pulled his shirt up and gasped at his torso, knowing the scars were not there the last time she saw his bared chest.

"Was this part of your weekend?" she asked, pressing a napkin against his open wound.

"Told you it was wild," he answered through gritted teeth. She disappeared for a moment, returning with the first aid kit she always carried when travelling.

"What the hell happened?" she asked, but he remained silent as she cleaned and bandaged his wound. She sat back when she'd finished.

"You going to tell me what happened?"

"Why? You don't believe in any of this stuff."

"This has something to do with McCormac, doesn't it?"

"Who else?"

"What was it, some druidic ritual?"

"Just a ritual."

"Do all his rituals involve bodily mutilation?"

He heard fear in her voice.

"Not usually. It's never happened before."

"Before?"

"It's a long and complicated story," he admitted, "and definitely not something I want in the public domain, as I imagine you wouldn't want his claim about you to get out."

She stood up and backed away from him.

"You know about that?" she demanded and he nodded. "How long have you known?"

"Only since the weekend. Looks like I was way out with the Druidic connection. I thought that maybe you were a high priestess, or something like that, I'd never have guessed a Queen. I guess that's why he wanted me to get to know you."

She backed more away from him, her anger flaring again.

"All of this has been a ploy, an attempt to win me over?" she demanded. He stood, unsteady on his feet.

"It's not like that," he argued back. "Yes, he used me to get to you, but from the moment I saw you at the awards ceremony, I've wanted …"

"Wanted what?"

"You," he admitted.

She said nothing for a while, conflicting emotions raging through her.

"I saw you", he went on, "for the first time on your political show maybe a year ago, the old man was watching it, insisted I watch it as well. At the time two words came to mind about you, and they were 'high maintenance'." He held his hand up to forestall an angry retort. "By that, I mean someone who I'd have to work hard at in order to maintain her interest in me."

"Not your type?" she said angrily and he chuckled.

"Oh, on the contrary, so my type," he answered. "It's no fun if it's too easy. But I watched you, and you're a force to be reckoned with. At the time, you wouldn't let the poor guy deflect the line of questioning and as well versed as I was in dealing with the media, I have to admit, I learned a lot just from watching you. I starting watching you then every time you were on, organised my schedule around it and then at the awards ..." he paused again, thinking, "I don't think you realised how you appeared that night. You were majestic, you were regal, everything the old man says you are, but I didn't know that at the time. You had a grace that most people never achieve in their lifetime. You had such a presence on that stage. You spoke with authority, in Irish and while I didn't understand all of it, it sounded beautiful and you ... just ... shone. And from that moment I wanted ... you."

"You reckon you have to work at getting my interest?"

"What do you think I've been trying to do?"

"Oh, you *were* trying?"

He laughed, softly, knowing she taunted him.

"It doesn't really matter now," he said.

"Why not?"

"Now, I have a duty to perform and that's to protect you, and however much I want you, I can't let how I feel about you get in the way," he answered.

"Why? Because the old man says so?" she asked and he nodded. "You always do what he says?"

"I usually fight it, but eventually..."

"Huh, didn't peg you for a guy who gave in easily."

"I don't, hence the knocks he gave me over the years."

She took a drink to calm herself, to take the time to mull things over.

"So *who* are you? Who are *you* supposed to be?"

"What if I told you Seth was shortened from Setanta?"

She looked at him incredulously.

"What, Cúchulainn? You're a descendant of Cúchulainn?"

"It's a little more complicated that just being a descendant. I am him. I can sense him inside me."

She shook her head, trying to stifle a derisive laugh as she turned away, her mind racing.

"This isn't bullshit," he added quietly. "Look at my body. You know these scars weren't here two weeks ago." She looked at the scars again.

"But how?"

"Every time he did these rituals on me, he added a little bit more, more memories, more sensations, more…"

"More Cúchulainn?"

He nodded.

"Yeah. I could feel that part getting stronger each time, it's always been a part of me, of who I was. Only this time, it came with all the scars."

"It also explains the string of women," she said sarcastically and he laughed, but it hurt.

"You really do have a bad opinion of me and no, it's not accurate, not completely," he answered.

"Oh, you didn't inherit that bit?" she shot back. He held his tongue, biting back a snippy reply. "So you believe it? All of it?" she asked.

"I don't think I've ever not believed, or ever doubted that I'm who he says I am. Even after what happened at the weekend, I don't feel any different. I have a lot more memories that I know aren't mine and the scars are attached to those, but yeah, I guess I do believe," he answered.

"But how can you be so sure?" she pressed.

"I don't think a spirit or a soul can reconnect to someone without a prior connection," he said. "There has to be a link of some sort, like through a bloodline. I know too much about Setanta's life, details not in any books or stories I've read. Is it possible he picked me from the streets because of my vulnerability or desperation? Yeah, sure it's possible, but I don't believe that, and if I'm wrong, you can be damn sure someone is going to pay for what I went through at the weekend."

"And his claim about me?"

"I've no reason to doubt him."

"Descendant of Setanta, huh?" she said.

He held his arms out.

"In the flesh."

"No wonder you don't do interviews. Something like this would seriously cramp your reputation," she said and reached out, pressing on his wound. He grunted and winced.

"A lot of good you're going to be as a bodyguard," she said.

He caught hold of her hand and pulled her close.

"It'll heal," he murmured, and kissed her.

He awoke the following morning on the sofa, with Rían lying asleep in his arms. They continued talking late into the night, returning indoors as the temperature dropped. He eased himself up doing his best not to wake her. She stirred but stayed asleep and he returned to his own room and showered, checking under the dressing she applied to his wound. To his amazement, it appeared almost healed, although still red and angry. With a scheduled meeting in his Galway office, he had no option but to leave her, ignoring the old man's instructions. Some things were unavoidable in the real world and he left her to sleep. He returned a short while later, finding her out on the balcony, working away in the summer's sun, the remnants of breakfast on the table.

Danny drove them into the city centre, and they spent the day wandering about, having a relaxed late lunch in the pedestrianized area. Given recent events, she was amazed how normal it seemed. Likewise for Seth. He found it normal in a strange way, rarely taking days off midweek and always in the company of McCormac or the other two women when he did. Danny drove them back to the hotel, and as the party to celebrate the new generator was held there, Danny had the night off. Back at the suite, Seth unwrapped the dress he'd chosen for her, strapless and full length in midnight blue.

"It's pretty," she conceded, "do you always pick out what your date should wear?"

He regarded her for a moment, trying to figure out where she was going with the question, but he shook his head.

"No, my dates usually know how to dress for these occasions," he answered smartly, "but you hide yourself in clothes. You wear that pin-striped suit when you interview because it's a masculine costume, perfect for being aggressive and authoritative. A dress is all about re-connecting with your feminine side and promoting your best features."

"Don't you ever get tired of all this psychology crap?" she threw back a little defensively and he knew he'd hit a nerve.

"With you I don't think that would be possible," he shot back humorously, sending her to get dressed. Re-emerging, she found him fiddling with his cuff links as he waited for her.

They entered the function. Rían recognised some of the other attendees, striking up a conversation and to his surprise, it was in Irish. While he had a few words of Gaelic, they spoke too fast for him.

"I'll get us something to drink," he said into her ear and she gave him a brief nod. He wandered off towards the bar, returning with two glasses when a hand grabbed him on the arm.

"You were foolish to come here, boy," the stranger said in a low tone at Seth. Seth's face hardened. "Connacht is not safe for the likes of you. Cúchulainn should've known better. Old enemies are coming. You'd best heed the signs." Seth tried to pull his arm away.

"What enemies?" Seth demanded.

"The ones who would see you dead, boy," he chuckled, releasing him and walked away. He disappeared into the crowd. Seth searched the room for Rían, cold fear rising as he failed to locate her. He spun around only to find her standing behind him.

"You ok?" she asked.

"I am now," he replied, his smile half coming back, but not reaching his eyes. He handed her a glass while scanning the crowd.

"What's wrong?" she asked. He shook his head. As much as he tried to relax, he couldn't, and a short while later he used his wound as an excuse for them to leave the party.

He spent the rest of the evening sitting out on the balcony alone, staring out at the ocean. His mind raced. Was he really Cúchulainn, the ancient hero? And what of these old enemies?

Rían left him to his brooding, but he wished she would stay with him, startled by how strong he felt about her, torn between his desire for her and the duty the old man placed on him. Would getting involved with her be putting her life in jeopardy? Would these old enemies use her to get to him, harm her? His mind spun in a thousand different directions.

A glass appeared in front of his eyes, amber liquid inside.

"You look like you could use this," she said as he took the glass, swirling the contents before knocking it back in one go, grimacing as it burned his throat.

"That bad huh?"

"The whiskey or what's going on in my head?"

"Either," she answered, sitting next to him. "Want to talk about it?"

"Not sure where to start."

"Has this anything to do with what happened downstairs?"

"You saw that?"

She nodded.

"You don't think I'd let my bodyguard get that much out of my sight, did you?" she replied and he smirked before slipping back into seriousness again.

"That man you saw downstairs said Cúchulainn's enemies were coming. I don't want you caught up in that. I don't want you getting hurt because of it."

"And being proclaimed Ard Rí isn't going to bring its own set of problems or enemies. Tell you what, we'll join forces, stand side by side against them, after I teach you how to defend yourself a little better."

"I can't believe you're being this flippant about it,"

"Because I don't believe in any of this, remember? I'm not making light of your beliefs but I don't want to fight with you over this."

"Everything's changed," he said. "I've changed. As much as I hate to admit it, I can sense him, Cúchulainn, trying to take over. You've changed, become important, but in the wrong way that matters to me."

"And what way is that?" she asked. He seemed to struggle for words.

"I want you so badly it hurts," he admitted.

"Bet you say that to all the women," she answered.

"No, just the ones I'm supposed to protect," he shot back. She grabbed his hand and pulled him out of his seat.

"Come on tough guy, brooding doesn't suit you."

"Why? What else did you have in mind?" he asked and a sly grin spread across her face.

"Well, for starters, I can't get the zip undone on this dress. I've been trying for the past hour to get out of the damned thing," she answered. He chuckled as he reached his arms around her and she let the dress fall, a deliberate accident, before gathering it and holding it modestly to her body.

"No underwear", he commented.

"You didn't give me any *to* wear", she countered.

Ignoring the raging argument in his mind, he kissed her.

"Now what?" he asked and she raised a questioning eyebrow at him.

"Some descendant of Cúchulainn's you are if you don't know by now", she answered smartly.

Chapter 14

Ulster

Conor Uí Neill sat in his new office in Stormont, never doubting his victory in the polls, taking his position as Premier in his stride. Devlin followed his political victory with the Rite of Kingship, crowning him King of Ulster, a brief step towards becoming Ard Rí. In addition, as a descendant from the original Uí Neill High Kings, the Ard Rí was his destiny, his right.

"Any word on that bitch?" Conor growled at Devlin, who took up the post of his senior advisor.

"Our brethren on the mainland made contact with us," he answered, "and they are taking care of the matter."

"When?" Conor demanded.

"Soon," the older man answered.

"And the whelp?" Conor asked. Devlin signed.

"McCormac appears to have restored Cúchulainn within the American," he answered.

"An American," Conor spat. "A desecration of the old ways."

"The American is as much a Celt as you or I," Devlin said. "It is his birth right. He is of Celtic Blood."

"Can we use that to our advantage?" Conor asked.

"Be patient boy," the old man counselled. "Everything will unfold in time."

Chapter 15

Rían woke with a start, locating the faint beeping that woke her, finding it came from Seth's phone. She reached across him to stop the chime and as she moved, his arms tightened around her.

"Morning," he murmured.

"Hi," she answered softly, smiling at him. He looked to be dozing off again and she stroked a strand of hair from his forehead, tracing her finger along the scar, wondering if it was one of his recently acquired ones. Sighing, he opened his eyes and looked at her.

"Hungry?" he asked.

"For food or...?" she replied and he gave her a squeeze.

"You're incorrigible," he accused her.

"One of my more endearing traits," she answered. He grunted, throwing her off with ease. He stood and she appraised his full form as he stretched, pulling the scars on his back taut. He ordered breakfast for them before showering and when he emerged from the bathroom, Rían was gone. He stuck his head out of his room just long enough to hear her showering in her own room.

Danny dropped them back to the station after breakfast, handing Seth his ePad and helping Rían with her luggage. Seth stayed awake this time, working away, while Rían dozed off instead. Every now and again, he watched her. All the arguments in his head were gone. The voices now quiet. No admonishing, and no regrets, which surprised him. He always enjoyed the thrill of the chase more than the actual capture, but this time something changed. The rules changed without telling him. Rían hadn't succumbed to him, not given in to him. Last night she was his equal, but as still as much a challenge as ever. If anything, he was the one who yielded to her. The sudden revelation startled him, confused him.

Another car awaited him when they arrived at Heuston and he offered to drop her off at her office, but she was catching the next train to Carlow, and after checking the departures board found it was leaving from one of the outer platforms 20 minutes later. She stepped onto to the travellator, Seth only a step behind her, and he put his arms around her.

"Stay with me tonight" he said. She smiled and shook her head.

"I can't," she said

"Okay then, tomorrow's Friday so no doubt I'll get a summons to Ardscull, I could pick you up from work and you could keep me company on the way," he said giving her his best boyish look. She laughed at him.

"You never give up, do you?" she said and he shook his head.

"Hmmm. Now who said they wouldn't have dinner with me and wouldn't sleep with me? And did I give up, did I lose faith? Admit it, I growing on you, you're definitely warming to me," he said, squeezing her in his arms.

"Fine, you can pick me up," she said. They stepped off the travellator onto terra firma and walked the rest of the way to the platform. As they reached the gate, he caught her by the arm pulling her back towards him and he kissed her again.

"Promise me you'll be careful," he said pulling away from her, concern starting to creep into his voice and she gave him a lopsided smile.

"No more than usual," she answered, and not the response he was looking for. "I'll be careful," she conceded.

"Let me know when you get home," he said.

"I will," she said. "Ever the bodyguard. If you're so concerned, why are you letting me out of your sight?"

"I can't avoid it at the moment, why do you think I want you to stay with me," he answered. Before she had a chance to give him a smart answer, her phone rang interrupting them. The number displayed as unknown and she hesitated before answering.

"Rían," the old man said and she clenched her jaw as she recognised his voice. "Come to Ardscull tomorrow night. I'll arrange for Seth to pick you up." Without waiting for a reply or objection from her, he hung up, and Seth looked at her questioningly.

"Did you have anything to do with this?" she demanded.

"Do with what?" he asked, confused.

"You're bringing me to the old man tomorrow night," she told him. At that instant, Seth's phone rang.

He came to a stop in front of the old man's house. He didn't recognise the other car parked in the drive, but Rían did, and her face hardened.

"Great. My parents," she answered flatly. "Now what?"

"You don't sound too happy," he said. "Want me to stay with you?" She gave him a half-hearted smile.

"My big tough bodyguard, huh? No, this is one battle I need to face on my own," she answered. The old man met them at the door as they entered the house, and without a word pointed towards the drawing room. They headed in that direction, but the old man grabbed a hold of Seth, stopping him from following her. Rían glanced back and caught the concern on his face but she gave him the barest shake of her head before continuing on. The old man caught the look between them and pulled Seth back.

"What did I tell you about your duty?" he demanded of the younger man. Before Seth could answer the old man walked away, heading for his study and Seth knew he had to follow. He did so reluctantly. As he entered the room McCormac threw the paper on the table in front of him, and before picking it up Seth knew what angered the old man. While not unusual for his picture to be in the social sections, this one caught him up close and personal with Rían, and it required little interpretation.

"Very cosy," the old man commented in a snide tone.

"You're the one who told me to get close to her," Seth shot back.

"Did something happen between the two of you?"

"Like what?" Seth replied, stalling.

"Don't play games with me boy," the old man said, his tone low and menacing.

"No," Seth answered, hiding the lie.

"If something has, and you've allowed your emotions to cloud your judgment, you have put her life in danger," McCormac said. Thinking of the warning he got in Galway, of old enemies coming for him, he mentally kicked himself but stayed silent, revealing nothing to the old man. Too angry to argue, he left the study without a word. The old man watched him go. Perhaps he'd been too hasty in restoring Cúchulainn in full within Seth. After all, Cúchulainn's womanising ways were almost as legendary as his heroic feats, and Seth, once socially schooled and rehabilitated from the street urchin he was, never lacked the ability to charm any woman, and they all fell for that charm. If they became lovers, it could put everything he worked towards and achieved in jeopardy.

Rían entered the drawing room.

"What are you doing here?" she demanded defiantly.

"McCormac sent word for us to come home," her father simply answered.

"For what?" she asked. Ciarán indicated for her to sit and she did so reluctantly.

"It's almost time, to go to Temair," he answered.

"To Tara, to the Lia Fáil," she stated and he nodded.

"Why didn't you tell me?" she said, feeling her anger rising.

"Honey, we didn't tell you before now for your own good," Moira answered.

"Rían, we couldn't tell you," Ciarán said calmly. "If it got out, if you'd said anything to anyone about who you were, even jokingly, your life would have been in danger, and we didn't want that to happen. We were just trying to protect you."

"So what the old man told me, you're saying it's all true?" Rían demanded. Ciarán nodded. "So years of ramming Celtic history down my throat, telling me all about honouring my duties, my obligations, it was all leading to this? To ruling?" She looked from one to the other, her father and the woman she thought of as her mother. "What if I don't want this? What if I refuse to go through with it?" she demanded.

"Now you're being selfish," her mother threw at her.

"Selfish? You're the one who's lied to me about who you were all these years. Do you honestly expect me to just roll over and give in, let this happen?" Rían growled. Ciarán stepped in between the two of them as he'd done countless times over the years.

"Honey, you're right, we should've told you before now, and you should've heard it from us, not the old man," he said, "but, the time never seemed right, you dropped out of your college course and we didn't hear from McCormac for so long, honestly, there didn't seem to be a need to tell you." She sat back in thought, and sighed.

"I don't want to do this," she answered.

"None of us have a choice, honey," he said.

"So when is all this going to happen?" she asked.

"Alban Heruin" the old man said, entering the room.

"Summer Solstice," Rían answered, "longest day of the year."

"You remember more than you let on," he answered her in a somewhat patronizing manner, "and you're correct, you will be Ard Rí at the lighting of the Solstice fires, which is a week from tonight. For your own safety, you will stay here until then." Rían got to her feet.

"I don't bloody think so," she replied unable to contain her anger any longer.

"You don't have a choice in this child, stay or risk dying."

"I'll take the risk," she said and stormed out of the room.

Finding herself back at the main door, she went out and crossed the drive to the lawn beyond. Putting her hands on the back of the bench, she leaned over and took deep breaths, trying to calm down. She heard the door opening, but refused to turn around until Seth gave a roar. Startled, she glanced behind her, seeing a dark figure fast approaching. She threw herself to the ground as a flash of steel shone where she'd been standing, and kicked out at the stranger. He moved quickly out of her reach. She rolled over and scooted under the garden seat, but her assailant anticipated her move and aimed for her head. She reacted in time and the knife stabbed the ground. She kicked out again and when he put himself out of her reach, she rolled backwards and stood up. Behind her attacker, she saw Seth closing in on them. With a hand on the back of the bench, he leaped over the seat to join the fray just as Rían ducked to avoid another swipe. The attacker changed direction midway and the knife caught her on the arm. She fell back onto the ground, blood flowing from her wound, but she scrambled back, putting more ground between them. She caught a glint of steel in Seth's hand as he launched an attack on her assailant, cold fury on his face. Even being taller than Seth, the stranger was no match for him as he moved in fluid motions, blocking each attack before plunging his own dagger into his opponent, twisting the blade and her assailant fell to the ground.

Seth spun around to her. Blood smeared his hands and streaked his shirt, but he appeared to be unscathed. The ferocity in which he fought frightened her, but her anger at her assailant outweighed her fear of Seth.

"Who was that ?" she demanded as Seth knelt down and pulled the mask off, quickly searching the body, but only found military issued tags.

"An English agent," the old man answered from behind them with Ciarán and Moira running towards them, and Seth nodded, handing the tags to him. The old man helped her up from the ground. "They know who you are now."

"But why come after me? I'm not a threat," she argued.

"Yes, you are," he replied. "The English monarchy is in turmoil at the moment, brother against brother and not only are they fighting themselves, they are also fighting republicanism."

"What has that got to do with me?"

"You are their newest and oldest threat. You are probably the rightful heir of the entire British Isles, which were once Celtic nations, don't forget. The Anglo-Saxons tried to wipe out the Celtic Kings but the Druids protected and hid the High King and his family, and we have ensured the success and survival of each descendant. We made you who you are, moulded you and when the time is right you will rule, with more than enough to support you within the Dáil and Seanad. That kind of power will always be a threat to those who can never possess it. And no one has ever conquered the Celts. They have been beaten, subjugated, served under enemy control, but the true spirit of the Celt has never been broken. That is why they will always fear you. And in that, you are their greatest threat, an ancient foe that cannot be overcome. Now will you accept who you are?"

"And if I don't?" she challenged.

"Whether you do or do not, they will never stop coming for you, never stop trying to kill you. Whether you do or don't, you will always be a threat," he argued with her. Moira stepped in.

"This needs to be taken care of," she said trying to staunch the bleeding on Rían's arm. "You can argue this with her later, but I'm not having her bleed to death first. Is Cíanna here?"

"Not yet, but she's on her way," he answered.

Rían sat in sulky silence as Cíanna stitched her wound, her touch light and delicate.

"How did you know he was English?" she asked McCormac.

"I only heard a few hours ago of the possibility of an attempt on you," he answered.

"Nice of you to share," she said.

"Would you have listened?" he asked.

"Probably not," Ciarán answered for her, knowing his daughter well.

McCormac wouldn't allow her to leave the grounds, sending Seth and Cíanna to her house for clothing while he showed her to her room, issuing a warning, while she had unrestricted access to anywhere in the house, outside was off limits unless either himself, Seth or Naoise were with her. He refused to leave until she agreed to his demands but he knew she wouldn't heed his warnings, would test the boundaries of her confinement. He'd left Rían too long to her own devices and she'd grown far too independent. Not that independence was a new concept for her, she always had a rebellious streak. Sometimes she took after Marianne too much. He'd have to warn the others to be vigilant with her. He left her to settle in, retiring to his study to ponder on the best course of action to take with her.

There was a soft tap on the door and she opened it, finding Seth on the other side. He stepped in and he handed a holdall to her.

"Hey, no fair. Your room's bigger than mine," he joked.

"The Royal suite, only right seeing as I'm about to be proclaimed High King," she answered sarcastically. He put his arms around her, pushing her back onto the bed.

All rooms with the exception of his study contained surveillance cameras, and the old man fixed his attention on the display screen, at one image in particular among the many tiled pictures, the view of Seth entering Rían's room. His worst fears were confirmed as he watched them, knowing the boy lied to him about their relationship. The old man knew him too well, but perhaps he underestimated Rían in this. From his vantage point he saw it was Seth who surrendered and succumbed to her, she didn't give herself in wanton abandon, but remained in control. Seth wasn't one to give his heart away but in this instance he seemed altogether far too fond of the girl. Damn that child, he thought. None of the other Ard Rí gave him this much trouble. His only consolation came from the knowledge that she had the potential to become a great Ard Rí, if that temper of hers could be curbed, if she would listen to counsel and wasn't so damned headstrong. But he was secure in the knowledge that she held onto most of her training, remembered her lessons and when the time came, knew she would have a greater appreciation for her destiny.

The problem of her relationship with Seth remained. This changed everything, interfered with the plans he made. Or would they? Perhaps not, he thought, but it required a skilful hand to rearrange and manoeuvre the players into their correct places, and would significantly change Seth's role in all this.

Chapter 16

Naoise promised to show her the gym and called for her early the next morning. Using the bedroom door, Rían hid Seth's sleeping form, not allowing the other woman to know she hadn't been alone. The gym was enormous, a high ceiling, wooden flooring and plenty of windows ensuring lots of light. Mats were stacked up along one wall along with strike pads and a freestanding punch bag.

"Want to work with the pads?" Naoise asked.

"Sure, if you think you're able," Rían answered and the other woman selected a large strike pad and a narrow, shorter one to go along her arm.

"I think I can handle it," Naoise said. "I taught martial arts and kickboxing." Rían was surprised and impressed.

"Really? By that I take it you don't teach anymore," she said.

"I still teach the odd time, but I manage the European sports therapy division in TOTAL," Naoise answered.

"As in Seth's company?" Rían asked and Naoise shrugged.

"Don't ask, long story," she answered positioning the strike pads and called out combinations to her as Rían struck at the pads, taking it easy at first until Naoise chided her for her lack of effort, offering her hints and minor corrections on her technique. After a long series and combination of punches and kicks together, Rían ended with a backspin, hitting the pad with the back of her fist. Naoise laughed and Rían stopped, frowning at her, perspiration trickling down her face.

"No wonder he lost to you," she said, still laughing. "He's so caught up with fighting fair and with honour he'd never expect something as nasty as a spinning back-fist."

"I didn't try that on him. A left hook was enough," Rían answered, grinning. Naoise dropped the pads back and handed her a towel. Rían wiped the sweat from her face and neck and turned around, sensing someone else in the room. She found Seth standing in the doorway, leaning against the frame and glowering at Naoise.

"I can take over from here," he said to her, stepping into the room.

"No, its fine," she replied, standing close to Rían, helping her take her gloves off and deliberately taking her time. It only served to antagonise Seth even more.

"Go," he said in a low voice.

"Do this again tomorrow?" she asked Rían.

"Yeah, sure," Rían answered, and watched in puzzlement as Naoise strolled out of the room.

"Now what?" she asked of him as she dried herself off. He lobbed a waster, a wooden practice sword, at her and she caught it by the grip.

"You're defending needs a little work," he commented.

"Oh yeah?" she answered and he was surprised at how she was taking his comment. "This is coming from the guy who leaves his right side open when he does a horizontal left-to-right cut?"

"No I don't," he answered defensively.

"Eh, yeah, you do," she said matter-of-factly. "How do you think I was able to get in under your strike the last time?" The news didn't help to improve his mood. "It's no big deal," she went on, "you learned the proper, traditional ways. I did some Mu-Thai kickboxing, some Bujikan, and a lot of self-defence stuff. I learned to spot weakness and use them to my advantage." He swung his sword at her, which she blocked with ease, flowing into a strike of her own, designed to prove the point to him. As anticipated, he moved to cut from his left and she changed stroke midway, swung the weapon around and slapping him in the ribs with the flat of the sword.

"Ok, point taken," he admitted.

"We can do a little work on that if you like," she said cheekily and he gave her a withering glare, taking a swing at her, which she again deflected.

"So what is up with you this morning? I can't have left you in that bad a mood," she said, and a grin played at the corners of his mouth.

"It's not you," he answered, stepping in for a close strike, but she closed the gap even further limiting his attack.

"Ah, Naoise then, you two seem fond of each other," she said, "so what's the story there?"

"We lived together for a while," he answered and she arched an eyebrow in surprise at him.

"She was your girlfriend? Explains the animosity."

"No! I was about eight, not long civilised when the old man brought her home to where I was fostered," he began, making a low sweep from the right. "Being a bit older than me she thought she could take over, tried to bully me."

"So what happened?" she asked, wary as a grin spread across his face.

"I punched her," he answered, stopping to laugh at the memory. "Landed her flat on her ass. I got into so much trouble, but I didn't care. After that, she made it her personal mission to make my life as miserable as possible and every year she'd come back for summer vacation, the entire summer vacation. Since that first year everything with her has been a competition between us, martial arts, school, my girlfriends." He took another sideswipe at her and she jumped out of the way before his words registered and she stopped short.

"Your ... girlfriends?" she asked and he nodded.

"That's why I never brought girls home," he said and attacked again. "And she's doing it again."

She stopped.

"What? You think she's hitting on me?" she asked incredulously.

"Of course. What else do you think she was doing here?" he demanded. Rían shook her head.

"We had a training session. We will have another training session tomorrow, just like I'm having a training session with you. I'm not sleeping with her," she argued.

"Yeah, that's what you told me and look what happened," he argued back. She laughed at him.

"Honestly, she's not my type," she answered, "and she must've really hit a nerve with you, I'd never suspect you were this insecure."

"I'm not insecure," he growled back, renewing his attack.

From his study, the old man focused on the scene in the gym, observing Rían's fighting skills first with Naoise and now with Seth and while he confessed to knowing little about physical combat, recognised the fluid movements of a practiced fighter.

"She's good," Naoise said from behind him.

"So beating him the first time wasn't a fluke then?" he asked.

"No," she admitted. "I'd say they were evenly matched." On the screen Seth landed on his back, Rían having swept his feet from under him, and now stood with her sword point resting at his throat.

"Evenly matched, you said?"

Chapter 17

Seth found her in the old man's study, flicking through the pages of an old book and more stacked around her.

"Will you please let me know when you're going to disappear," he said.

"That would defeat the purpose of disappearing," she answered, not looking up from her book. They were alone together for the first time in days and he risked kissing her, but she lacked passion and he guessed the old man annoyed her again.

"What are you doing in here?" he asked.

"I'm trying to find out anything I can about this ritual, what to expect. I don't want to walk blindly into this," she said.

"Need a hand? I do have some experience in the ritual department," he said.

"Really?"

"Only in theory."

"What? Didn't they do practical ritual-making in college?"

"We did some experiments, like sacrificing virgins, but I haven't done one of those in years," he answered as deadpan as he could manage but couldn't contain himself and burst out laughing. "I struggled trying to remember all my Celtic history."

"How did you ever make it in the business world?"

"Just a different battlefield, with numbers instead of swords, and numbers I have a head for."

"And you consider yourself Celtic?"

"Sweetheart, I'm second generation American. To the best of my knowledge, my family, my original family, emigrated from Ireland, back in the mid 1980's, so yeah, I consider myself Celtic. I had the old guy teaching me all this stuff. My foster parents were strong believers, deeply spiritual people, and raised me in the old ways and old beliefs. We celebrated Imbolc, Lughnasada, it's always been part of my life."

"It was part of mine too. My parents used to do this, but I hated it, I had no interest. Not in any religion."

"But this isn't about religion, it's about spirituality."

"Meaning?"

"It's about being a decent human being, helping others where you can, how you can."

"If it's about helping others, how can you justify the profits you make?" she threw back at him. He sat forward, bristling at her questioning. Gods, she was in a foul humour.

"I'm not in it for the profit. It just happens to be a by-product for what I do."

"Wealth is a by-product?"

"Yeah. Sometimes it is."

"So you do what you do purely to help others?"

"Yeah, I do. God! Now I know how that politician felt. I really did get off lightly when you interviewed me."

She just shrugged and he hunkered down in front of her but found her expression unreadable. He reined his temper in.

"What's wrong?" he asked, more gently.

"I don't think I can do this, I don't want to do this. This isn't real. None of it means anything. To me, he's a delusional old man, living in this fantasy world, and we're all pandering to him, sustaining his fantasy. I can't help thinking this is all some sort of a con or a scam and I'm just so afraid that you're a part of it," she finally revealed her innermost thoughts.

"I'm not," he answered. "And if it is some sort of a scam, then you can be damned sure someone is going to pay for what I went through."

After five days, the house arrest became too much for Rían. The forecasted rain fell as scheduled, but she sensed a gap in the downpour and stole from the study, feeling a mild sense of satisfaction as she left by a side door, reaching the trees without an alarm sounding. Leaving the grounds by the narrow walking gate, she headed for the Moate of Ardscull, less than two minutes' walk away. She paused at the entrance of the Moate to read the information on the display console, surprised to find

114

a long and chequered history attached to the place and a connection to a High King, however long ago. No wonder the old man settled here, she thought. She herself passed this place many times but never stopped to investigate before and now, looking in, felt a pull she couldn't explain. Climbing the three steps, she entered the outer ring, following the dirt trail that led away from the entrance and towards the central mound that rose sharply to a height of about twenty-six or twenty-seven metres. She walked the circumference of the lower trail, returning to the start before backtracking to a point where an upward trail seemed manageable, and began to climb. At the top, a second ridge encircled the inner hollow, overgrown with vegetation and trees. At this height, the wind pulled at her hair and drops from the overhead trees splattered to the ground. She took a deep breath, smelling the freshness that always accompanied rain, and relished the freedom.

At the house, the old man entered the study, expecting to find her and annoyed to discover her gone. A quick scan through the cameras also failed to find her and fear now tempered his annoyance. Damn that child, he thought. Naoise and Seth both returned from their respective searches, Seth smug in the knowledge that Naoise slipped up and allowed Rían to escape.

"She's not on the grounds," he reported to the old man.

"Then where the hell is she?" he demanded. Seth pulled out his handheld device.

"In Galway, I set this to detect the signal from her chip. I can find her via GPS" he said before swearing. "She's off the grounds," he told them.

"What?" the old man roared.

"She's at the Moate, and moving around inside," Seth said.

"Go," the old man ordered.

At one point through the trees, from the top of the ridge, Rían spotted the entrance to the old man's house with Naoise and Seth leaving by the main gates, and watched them making their way along the road. In truth, she expected them sooner and guessed by the way Seth checked something in his hand he tracked her via her chip. Seth reached her first and presumed Naoise stayed in the lower part.

"What do you think you're doing?" he asked harshly.

"Getting some fresh air, stretching my legs," she answered.

"Why didn't you tell one of us?" he demanded.

"Bring my royal entourage? I don't think so," she retorted and saw his face harden. "I'm not doing this to spite you. I've had people constantly around me for the last five days, I needed a break. I needed space. Can't you understand that?" He softened a little.

"Yeah, I can, but sometimes we don't have the luxury of this kind of freedom, and right now, you don't," he answered, taking hold of her injured arm and squeezing. "Or do you need to be reminded of what happened the last time you stormed off alone?" Even though her wound healed faster than she could explain, it still hurt under his pressure and she pulled away from his grasp. She pushed past him and descended the mound, meeting Naoise at the bottom.

"You going to scold me too?" she demanded.

"No point. Not like you're going to listen," Naoise replied. They heard rustling up ahead and Seth jumped the last two metres to land in front of her, a knife appearing in his hand. Naoise also reacted, pushing Rían behind her. The old man appeared at the top of the lower ridge and glared at the three of them.

"It's well you picked this place to come to," he said to Rían. "This is an ancient site, with enough power to draw on for protection, if the need arose, but power here comes at a price." He paused and looked up at the central mound. "The Earth here has tasted too much blood and that is the price she now asks," he said in almost a whisper. "Now, back to the house, at once," he snapped, as though speaking to disobedient children.

Chapter 18

If she thought her previous concept of house arrest hard to bear, the next two days became intolerable to her, unable to move about without someone by her side. On the last day, the old man sat with her and outlined the sequence of events for that night, his knowledge and history so detailed and vivid that if she didn't known better, she'd have sworn he'd been present when these rituals originally took place. He then left her alone, completely alone, for the first time since her little disappearing act and she relished the solitude, the peace, the quiet. She closed her eyes and sighed. Was she doing the right thing? Would this nonsense be over tonight? By the gods, she hoped so. She desperately wanted to return to her own life, and have the old man fulfil his promise to never bother her again. She opened her eyes and they once again rested on the dark green robe he left for her to wear, putting it on at the last minute. The old man came for her again, leading her from the study to the helicopter waiting on the lawn. The mode of transport surprised her, having given little thought to the actual logistics of getting to Tara, about 100 kilometres away. The rotors already started to spin and the growing downwind pulled at her robe and hair. The old man let her in first and she found Cíanna and Naoise already seated inside. McCormac followed quickly on her heels, indicating she sit between the two women. Seth was the last in, running from the house to catch up with them, and sat beside the old man. Before the helicopter took off, the old man handed Rían an ornate cup.

"You need to drink this," he said. A fleeting frown crossed Seth's face, which did nothing to assure her or ease the growing doubts. She hesitated before bringing the cup to her lips, but paused to inhale its warm and spicy scent. She took a sip.

"Drink," he said again, adding a softer please at the end. "It will make everything go much easier." She took a mouthful and slowly swallowed before taking another drink. She finished the cup and handed it back to him. She sat back in the seat as the helicopter whisked her to her fate, becoming tired and warm and as the minutes passed, the tiredness grew. It seemed she barely closed her eyes when Naoise's hand on her shoulder woke her up.

"We're here," she said helping her stand. Cíanna was already out and helped her step down, but she struggled to stand. The wind whipped at her and even in her drowsy state, she knew it wasn't coming from the rotors.

"Windy," she murmured.

"There's a storm coming," Cíanna said glancing at the darkening sky. "Are you ready?"

Rían nodded. The two women led her up towards the little church and she thought they would get out of this wind, but the women continued on to the old standing stones, with two hooded men standing by them.

"Who wishes to pass?" one intoned.

"One who seeks to find her destiny," Naoise answered.

"Is she worthy?" the second man asked.

"Only the Lia Fáil, the Stone of Destiny, can decide," Cíanna answered. One of the men turned and led the way, while the other waited for them to pass, then followed them. Under normal circumstances, a swing gate was employed at the entrance to the site, but removed for tonight and the little procession moved into the open plain. Thunder rumbled in the distance as the procession made its way in. The going was slow and bumpy, crossing the rises and hollows of the barrows as they made their way to the stone. Once, the mighty stone towered over men, but over time, and a number of minor relocations, it now sat in the centre of the largest mound and about 1.5 metres tall, just tall enough to reach to Rían's chin. Naoise turned Rían around, pushing her back against the stone and Cíanna bound her hands behind her, her arms around the stone. The old man towered over her and she looked up at him.

"Are you ready, child?" he asked, almost grandfatherly. She nodded, her tongue refusing to cooperate. He smiled. "It will be over soon," he said and turned away from her. In the growing darkness, she thought she saw her parents in the circle of people around her. She tried to shake her head awake, but it only added to the disorientation. The old man tapped his staff on the ground three times and intoned:

"Ó Neamh go talamh *(From Heaven to Earth)*

Ó beatha go bás, go beatha arís *(From Life to Death and Life again)*

An spiorad iománaithe, *(The Spirit made whole)*

An talamh inchollaithe, *(The Land made flesh)*

Neamh agus talamh aontaithe, *(Heaven and Earth become one)*

Gach a bhfuil sean athnuaite, *(The old becomes new)*

Éirinn aontaithe *(Eire becomes one)*"

Seth watched with interest. Having always been on the receiving end of the old man's rituals, this was his first time to witness one. Thunder continued to crash overhead without any rain. The old man repeated the passage twice more, and his voice grew to a roar as he raised his hands and staff to the sky, unfazed by the peculiar thunderstorm. Lightning streaked across the sky, with thunder barely missing a beat. The old man roared once more and a bolt of lightning struck the Lia Fáil, lingering unnaturally long for lightning and a ringing echoed into the air. Seth gasped sharply. The stone sounded. He thought Rían screamed and started to run to her, but he felt a hand on his shoulder and turned to find Naoise holding him, shaking her head. He turned his attention back to Rían, now slumped against the stone and appeared to be unconscious.

"It is done, she is Ard Rí," the old man announced and walked towards her. Four others followed the old man, and as he cut the binds holding her to the stone, she fell forward into their arms. They laid her on the ground as the old man took a dagger from his robes, placing it against her sternum. Seth gave a roar and started towards the old man. This wasn't supposed to be part of the ritual. He found himself knocked to the ground. Angered, he jumped up and threw a punch at his assailant, pushing him effortlessly aside. He got a few steps closer before being tackled again, and he fell. He kicked out at the assailants and struggled to get up. Others gathered around him, some pinning him down, more behind him, holding him back. Naoise crouched beside him and held a small knife to his throat.

"Not the time to play hero," she said to him.

119

"What are you doing to her?" he demanded.

"Stop struggling and see," she answered. Still restrained, he craned his neck to catch sight of the continuing action. The old man made a cut into her breastbone and spoke in a low tone, but Seth could make out the words as the old man began to chant again.

"Ón dorchadas glaoím ar d'anam *(From the darkness, I call your Spirit)*
Isteach sa solas, isteach beatha *(Into the light, into life)*"

Rían's body convulsed, her back arching, but the four druids held a limb each, restraining her movements until the convulsion ended, and she went limp again. The old man stood up.

"We are done," he said to the others, and they carefully lifted her from the ground. Cíanna stepped over to him.

"I'll leave her to you and Naoise to prepare," he said, and Cíanna bowed her head in acquiescence.

"And Seth?" she asked.

"I still need him, but I want him quiet on the way back," he answered. Cíanna turned and nodded to Naoise, who in turn gave Seth a maniacal grin before delivering a powerful right hook to his head.

Opening his eyes made little difference, darkness continued to envelope him, only now his head hurt like hell. Who'd have thought the woman could punch that hard. As his eyes adjusted to the gloom dots of faint glows began to register, too small and soft to be of use, but the scents gave the location away, and he knew he was in the old man's ritual chamber at Ardscull. He stood, still disorientated from the blow, and cautiously reached out to steady himself, not wanting to touch or disturb any of the vials of potions dotted about the place. He steadied his breathing, shutting the headache out and re-orientated himself, sensing where the stone altar and the door were. He made his way to the door, knowing he'd find the control pad for the lighting and pressed buttons until the subtle lights embedded in the walls began to glow. He tried the door handle, not surprised to find it locked, but with luck, the old man hadn't thought to restrict his access. He put his thumb to the pad in the wall and the door opened with a soft click. He eased it open just enough to peep through, finding it was dawn, and no one about. He hesitated leaving and turned to glance about the chamber, surprised to find a figure resting on the stone. He went to it, slowly peeling back the cloth to find Rían beneath. He called her name, but she didn't stir. He gently shook her but to no avail. He couldn't leave her there, not to the old man's devices. Carefully lifting her into his arms, he carried her out of the chamber, making his way around the side of the house to the drive and to his relief found his car still there. She still hadn't stirred and he gently placed her on the ground while he opened the door and lifted her in. At a loss as to where to go, he decided on her home, a familiar place for when she woke. He took off slowly, no screeching or spinning of wheels, no dash to freedom. The gates opened automatically at the end of the drive and only when he reached the road did he take off at speed. He lifted her sleeping form from the car and brought her inside, and she woke as he lowered her on the bed. She held onto him.

"Stay with me" she said, staring at him with sleepy eyes. He smiled.

"Of course," he said and leaned over to kiss her. She caught hold of his tee shirt with surprising strength as she kissed him back, pulling him towards her. He drew back but her grip held him close. "Rían, I don't think..." he tried to protest, but her lips stopped any more words getting out and he surrendered to her.

He opened his eyes not recognising where he was, but recognising the still sleeping body curled into his. Not surprising considering the passion, the almost primal force with which she'd made love to him during the morning. He softly kissed her shoulder but she remained asleep. He got up and dressed, leaving her still sleeping and headed for the kitchen. He was starving, not having eaten since the previous day, and no doubt she would be hungry too when she awoke. He checked the fridge and larder, not surprised to find barely enough essentials to make something decent to eat. He heard soft footfalls and sensed Rían behind him, the sheet wrapped around her.

"Hungry?" he asked, and she stood behind him as he set about his culinary task.

"Yes, but not for food," she replied huskily, nipping his shoulder aggressively.

"You're insatiable, woman," he replied, hiding his discomfort at her biting. She laughed, softly, but something unsettled him, triggering a distant memory, triggering one of Cúchulainn's memories. His body stiffened and he spun around, a small knife in his hand, which he brought level with her throat.

"What's wrong, Setanta," she purred. He searched her eyes and his expression hardened as he realised he wasn't talking to Rían. Realisation hit him, and hit him hard. The old man's second ritual, he brought back... No! That was impossible, it had to be, but this woman before him wasn't Rían. In body yes, but in spirit... The old man brought back the one woman in history Setanta loathed, despised. He returned his sworn mortal enemy.

The old man returned the Mórrígan.

Seth applied more pressure on the knife at her throat, and she backed up a step, giving him room to manoeuvre, and he stepped away, making his way around the breakfast bar to the door not daring to turn his back on her. She watched him with a malevolent glint in her eyes and took a slow, deliberate step towards him. He understood now. The old man used him, allowed them to escape so that he could complete the embodiment ceremony when they made love. He was responsible for the Mórrígan being here. How could he have been so stupid, he thought as he fled.

Chapter19

Devlin lowered his tired arms and the misty figures he materialised from the lake evaporated. Beside him, Conor seethed after witnessing the Ceremony of Kings at Tara. Something in the mist caught the old man's eye, and he re-conjured the scene again, watching McCormac's latest act. The mist swirled, distorting the view somewhat, but McCormac's actions were unmistakable. He returned a Spirit to the physical world. The question now was who, and Devlin had his suspicions. If these proved correct... He shuddered, not wanting to think about the consequences.

"The bitch has no right," Conor growled.

"You heard the Stone, as we all did," the old man beside him replied. "She is Ard Rí, but it doesn't mean you can't contest the claim. Something else happened tonight, which may have greater implications than just naming her Ard Rí."

"What is it?" Conor demanded.

"We may have a greater, more powerful enemy to face than just the girl," Devlin answered. "I have to consult with others before I know for certain."

"Who?" Conor insisted, and for the first time in his life, he saw the old man's calm composure slipping and fear coming through.

"I won't answer until I know for certain," Devlin answered, "so don't ask me again." He turned and walked away from the lake, deep in thought and deeply troubled.

Chapter 20

She watched him backing out of the house and barely contained her laughter as Cúchulainn, the hero, fled before her. She heard him leave by some noisy contraption and knew she should know the name of the chariot, but it escaped her. A new sensation for her, as was the body she now found herself in. She wandered back to the bedroom where she woke up, and standing in front of the mirror, dropped the sheet she'd used to cover this body and surveyed the reflection. It was shorter than her usual form with smaller breasts, and the hips a little more rounded, but overall a fit and strong body. It would have to do if this was the body she'd been returned to.

She turned and scanned the room, opening a set of doors and found clothes. She browsed through them until finding something she liked and dressed leisurely in black leather pants and a black shirt. A chime, a strange ringing, distracted her and she searched about the room trying to locate the source of the sound. She found the small noisy device and read the words that appeared in the lighted area and pressed the button underneath the word 'Freagra' (Answer). The head of a man came into view, startling her somewhat.

"An Mór Ríon (Great Queen)," the old man said in Irish.

"Shea? (Yes?)" she answered.

"An bhfuil tú i do aonar? (Are you alone?)" he asked.

"Shea, d'imigh Setanta as an tí (Yes, Setanta left the house)," she told him.

"Fan ansin, táim ag teacht (Stay there, I'm on the way)," he said and the image of him disappeared, the screen going blank. She turned the object in her hand over but the talking picture wasn't at the back either. She shook the device but to no avail, the picture didn't return and she tossed the thing onto the bed. This was a strange world she'd returned to.

A short while later a noise outside, a rumbling on stone and a door closing, distracted her investigation of the house and she met the old man in the kitchen.

"An Mórgacht *(Highness),*" he said.

"Where am I?" the Mórrígan asked. While she still looked like Rían, the voice was somewhat lower and slightly more accented than how Rían normally spoke.

"In the ancient lands of General Lughdaidh Laighis, now known as County Laois, the Queen's County," he answered.

"When am I?" she then asked.

"2026," he replied and she shook her head, astounded.

"That's almost 600 years since I last returned, why so long?" she demanded.

"It wasn't possible before now," he answered.

"And why in this fashion?" she said angrily. "Why did you wait until the Ceremony of Kings? Instead of a rebirth, I have been ... inserted into someone else's fully-grown body. I should have been reborn, should have been allowed to grow and learn about this world, not be thrust into it."

"My apologies, Great Queen, but the Ceremony of Kings was the only opportunity I had," he explained. "What of her now, her spirit?" he asked.

"She's contained, for now. I haven't had an opportunity to speak with her myself, but I will soon," she said.

"Then I must warn you, she can be a little tempestuous at the best of times," he advised her and she smiled.

"Good. I expect nothing less of one of my descendants," she answered. "What of my sisters?"

"Both Badb and Nemain returned to this world without incident and await your arrival, if you'll allow me to take you to them," he said and ushered her out of the house. He held the car door open for her and helped her in. In truth, he expected the Mórrígan to be angrier, furious in fact. The Ceremony of Kings wasn't the ideal time to return her to this world, but he felt justified in his actions. Marianne ran away soon after

Rían's birth, taking nearly five days to find her. And Rían, well, Rían was just as stubborn and determined to do things her own way. He had no doubts that both the Mórrígan and Rían had similar temperaments, but which one would prevail? The Mórrígan obviously had the upper hand for the moment, and he wondered how long it would last. He suspected Rían wouldn't give in easily.

The car drove up to his house and the door opened before it came to a stop. Both Naoise and Cíanna came forward as she alighted from the car and they embraced her.

"Nemain," the Mórrígan recognised her.

"I'm called Naoise in this time," she answered.

"And Badb," the Mórrígan named the other woman.

"Cíanna now," she answered, "conas atá tú? *(how are you?)*"

"Tá ocras agus tuirseoch orm *(I'm hungry and tired),*" the Mórrígan said. Cíanna took her by the hand.

"We've food and a bed ready for you," she said.

"What happened to Seth?" Naoise asked. The Mórrígan grinned.

"He fled as soon as he realised who I was, and what happened," she answered.

"Some hero," Naoise muttered.

"I'm not complaining. He held a knife to my throat so I'm rather glad he left without slitting it open. It would have been an awful waste of a journey," the Mórrígan said.

"Agus isteach an leaba, cén chaoi a raibh sé? *(And in bed, how was he?)*" Naoise asked.

The Mórrígan's widening grin more than enough of an answer.

"Why do you ask sister, haven't you taken him yet?" she asked.

"Naoise prefers to antagonise him, rather than make love to him," Cíanna answered as they entered the house.

Chapter 21

Devlin stood at the edge of the circle drawn on the floor. Twelve other men completed the Conclave, and they too stood in their places. A mixture from most religions, they stood united in their horror and indignation at McCormac's actions, for they too saw the signs or heard what happened. Not everyone believed though, some expressed disbelief, doubting what they heard and however reluctantly they were to participate, they now agreed to take part in finding answers. Devlin tapped his staff on the stone floor of the room three times. Another man, three men away from him, and at the southern point on the circle, repeated the action, the men at the west and northern points followed suit.

"The circle is complete," Devlin said and began the incantation.

"An doras a oscailte *(Open a doorway)*

An bealach a oscailt *(Open a way)*

Spiorad tar amach *(A Spirit come forth)*

Isteach an domhan a fear *(Into this mortal world)*"

From the large bowl of salt water in the centre of them all, a mist began to appear and rise. Startled, one of the men started to back away.

"Keep the circle," Devlin growled at him. "Break the circle and you break the spell." The offender stepped back into line.

"I'm not comfortable with this, Devlin," he said in response. Devlin turned to glare at him. Bloody Christians, he thought, all talk but no stomach for what had to be done.

"None of us are comfortable with this," Devlin retorted, "but it's the only way to get answers." The mist continued to grow, spiralling upwards without spreading out, spinning faster as it grew taller than the tallest man in the room. Each man held his breath, each hiding their fear from the others, each having their own reasons to fear the Mórrígan's return. From the mist, a form took shape and a female face stared at them, the rest of the mist forming an almost transparent, shimmering body.

"Are you the Guardian?" one man asked, a Catholic priest, and Devlin glowered at him. The misty figure turned to face him.

"There are no guardians to this world," she answered, her voice soft and distant. "We have no need of sentinels, only those whom we invite can ever find and enter Tír na nÓg. Why have you called me forth to answer childish questions?" She tilted her head as she stared at the priest. He involuntarily made the sign of the cross, which appeared to puzzle her.

"Bean uasal *(Gentle lady)*, forgive us," Devlin taking control again. She turned to him. "We called you for a more important matter. A spirit was brought into this world last night."

"Yes," she confirmed. "Our Great Queen departed our world for yours." Devlin felt a sinking feeling and heard someone gasp.

"So it's true. the Mórrígan has returned?" he asked. She nodded. "How do we return your Queen to you?" and she seemed puzzled by the question.

"Why do you wish to return her?" she asked. The question threw him.

"She doesn't belong here, we should return her to her own time," he answered. She shook her head and smiled.

"Foolish man," she said. "She has waited a long time to return to your world." Seeing the look of growing horror on his face, she laughed again. "We, the Tuatha de Danann, do not confine ourselves to our own worlds. We care greatly about this land, this was our land, and these are our people. It was never our intention to withdraw completely, to abandon everything we fought for. We rest and sleep in our own time and place, but when we awake, we come forth. We have always done so and will continue to do so. Why would the Great Queen be different?"

"But the manner of her return is not natural," Devlin argued.

"True," she conceded. "It has thrown all the realms out of balance."

"How can this balance be restored?" Devlin asked, seeing an opening.

"In time all will find its proper rhythm," her answer was cryptic, and not the one he sought.

"And if I wished to help this process, what could I do to restore the balance?" Devlin persisted. The mist wavered before reforming.

"The Great Queen would need to be returned to our world," she answered. "Her Spirit must be released from its mortal body."

"The girl would have to die," he said and she nodded. This caused a murmur from the others, and she turned to regard them all in turn before returning to Devlin, looking less substantial as time went on and Devlin knew time was running out. This ritual had a time limit, the Spirits could only be brought into this world like this for only a short time before returning. He had more questions and knew he was on borrowed time now.

"Of the girl, of the mortal body the Mórrígan now resides, what is her significance, her role in all of this?" he asked.

"The girl is of her blood and of the blood of kings."

"The girl is a descendant?" he answered. She nodded her misty body fading.

"And what of Nemain and Badb?" knowing this would be his last question.

"Both left our world a long time ago," she answered.

"Bean uasal, go raibh maith agat *(Gentle Lady, thank you)*," he said to her. She inclined her head and the mist dissipated.

As at the start, so it must be at the end, and he tapped the stone floor three times with his staff. Unlike the opening of the circle, the releasing of the circle now went anticlockwise, with the man at the north point following him in tapping the stone, west and south following.

"The circle is undone," he told the assembly, annoyed to hear numerous sighs of relief. The priest turned to him.

"What did she mean, there is no guardian. In all of the world's mythology there is a guardian. The Greeks and Romans had Pluto, the Vikings had Hel. Even we Christians have St Peter guarding the gates of Heaven. It was a logical question," he argued.

"Logical, yes," agreed Devlin, "but the Tuatha de Danann are a different race of people. As she said, the other worlds and realms of the Tuatha were always difficult to find. After they withdrew from the mortal world, they retreated to hillocks, to faery forts. Suspected sites of the Sidhe, the Tuatha, the Faery Folk, were always treated with respect and superstition by the natives, people gave them a wide berth. Combine that with the Sidhe's reputation for a nasty revenge on any trespasser and you then have a culture of fear and awe. What need do they have for a guardian? Anyone unlucky enough to find the Sidhe and enter their world, were dealt with in a harsh and brutal manner." Silence hung in the room as those who never heard this information digested it, and for those who had, having dismissed this knowledge as nonsense from childhood, now found themselves struggling to reconcile their beliefs, this knowledge now in direct conflict with their own individual religions and faiths. The moment of stunned, shocked silence was brief before disorder broke out.

Devlin stepped away and sat, trying to shut out some of the commotion. For the most part, the members of the Christian faiths appeared to be taking this news better than others, but they too seemed shaken by what they just witnessed. Most present were reluctant to use the other realm's original name of Tír na nÓg, or land of youth, synonymous with fairy tales and mythology. But this was no fairy tale, the myths and legends were real. The spirit that greeted them confirmed their worst fears. The Mórrígan had returned and the girl was one of her descendants.

The issue of descendent was important. Devlin knew any of the spirits could return to this mortal world, with the normal route through rebirth where the soul became part of the new body, usually at the moment of conception. Failing that, the next logical time would be at the actual birth. The child would grow and learn as any child did, all the time retaining a link to Tír na nÓg. They wouldn't know who they were in their previous lives, but there would always be something magical about them, something special. Now the rules changed. The Mórrígan was returned in full force, with full knowledge and power into a body with a direct link to the past through her bloodline. Not only was this unheard of, but it was one of those unwritten laws expressly forbidding it from happening. Had the Mórrígan returned and inhabited a body that wasn't a descendant, then the Mórrígan's power would have been considerably reduced. If that had been the case, she wouldn't have been able to conjure so much as a sneeze.

"The only answer is death," one voice sounded louder than the rest, and advocated the assassination of the Mórrígan from the outset. Devlin looked up.

"That will be difficult to achieve," he said quietly and the din in the room lessened.

"Why?" the Presbyterian minister demanded. "She is now in a mortal body and mortal bodies can be killed."

"She will be more sensitive to her surroundings, shifts in energies. She'll sense any attack on her, and you are all forgetting, or perhaps you don't understand what's going on. She is not alone. The Trinity has been returned, reunited. McCormac hid it from everyone," Devlin answered.

"What do you mean by the Trinity here?" the Rabbi asked.

"The Mórrígan is one of three Goddesses, sisters in the symbolic sense, but still…" he answered. Combined, history has shown them to be the most evil, most destructive force, ever. They decided the fates of men in battles, incited wars and revelled in the slaughter. Badb is the ancient word for vulture, and Nemain means frenzy. However powerful the Mórrígan is in her own right, with her sisters they will be almost unstoppable, the horror unimaginable."

"Blasphemy," the others spat. "The Trinity is God the Almighty, Christ and the Holy Spirit. Who ever heard of women described as gods?" Devlin pressed at his temples trying to alleviate the thumping from behind his eyes. Bloody Christians, he thought bitterly again.

"The Trinity is not just the preserve of your faiths, it has been in existence since the dawn of time, as have female deities," Devlin explained. "The Trinity exists in Hindu as Brahma, Vishnu and Shiva, the ancient Greeks had Zeus, Poseidon and Hades. Then there are the three fates, the three Harpies. Don't you understand, everything in this world works in three's, even the concept of the past, the present and the future is a Trinity. In this case we are dealing with a culture almost as old as time itself, and incredibly diverse. The Celtic beliefs consist of multiple Trinities. It began with Eirn, Banba and Folda the original names for the island, and then came the Mórrígan, Badb and Nemain. And do not underestimate these women. Celtic women were as fierce, if not more so, than their men."

"What are you saying Devlin, we cannot fight them?"

"They can be fought, but will require a concerted effort from everyone here," Devlin answered. The Anglican minister stood up.

"In that case, Druid, I must tell you that His Majesty, King William has ordered an assassination," he said.

"Yes, we know about that," Devlin said, "and they failed."

"No, this is another attempt," the minister answered, "but His Majesty has revoked protocols and ordered this threat to be eliminated by whatever means necessary." Devlin shook his head.

"You've just condemned more of your country men to death," he replied matter-of-factly. "Gentlemen, fighting amongst ourselves will not resolve this. We need to work together, so please take your seats, we're going to be here for a while."

Chapter 22

Seth drove. At first, he instinctively turned for Ardscull but realised his error when he got to Athy, averting at the last roundabout towards Dublin. His apartment would only be a temporary port of call, to pick up some clothes before he went on his way again. The problem was where to go. He had no safe haven to run to. He never needed one, never expected the need for one, and now he had nowhere to go. He could always go back to Ardscull, face the old man, confront him, but what would that achieve, he argued with himself. No, he couldn't return there. He slammed the heel of his hand on the steering wheel in temper.

Mrs Hanson wasn't in the apartment when he got back, which was probably just as well, he mused darkly, or she would have taken the brunt of his temper. Not since his youth had he felt this angry, this enraged and in truth, its intensity scared him a little. He threw clothes into a holdall and left, deciding against taking his car again. He could be tracked too easily, if indeed the old man was looking for him. Hiring another car was also out of the question. Technology limited him, limited his options. He could leave the country, but go where? Home to the States? The old man had people there too. And what of Rían? What about her, a voice snarled in his head. She was no longer Rían, the voice argued. She was now the Mórrígan, the Battle Queen, and the greatest living evil to ever walk the Earth.

Night fell by the time he made his way into the heart of the city and O'Connell Street teemed with life. The Irish, for the most part, had a relaxed attitude towards celebrities and other notable people and left them well enough alone. But his face was printed recently in a number of social journals and while technology limited him, being recognised and photographed limited him even more, especially when he was a frequent patron of the high-end clubs located nearby. He pulled his baseball cap down low on his head to shield his face. He needed to get off this street, and fast. From O'Connell Street he had a number of choices, with Bus

Árus, the central bus depot located at the end of Abbey Street, and Connolly rail station just beyond that, on Amien Street. In the opposite direction, Heuston train station lay three kilometres away. The last alternative was the underground Metro to the airport. Was leaving the country really an option, he wondered. No, he decided, he couldn't leave Rían. He headed east, down Lower Abbey Street, towards the bus depot and after a quick glance at the departures board found the next bus out of the city left for Dundalk. It seemed as good a choice as any, he supposed, wondering why it felt familiar to him.

He got a ticket from the driver and took a seat near the back, away from other passengers. He threw his holdall into the storage bay overhead and sat by the window, sitting back, watching the city pass by. He thought about Rían and the events of the previous night, knowing he should have suspected something when the old man gave her that cup to drink from, never suspecting the old man had another agenda. Naoise obviously knew about the second ritual, as had most of the others, judging by the number he tried to fight off. Some great warrior he turned out to be. His thoughts returned to Rían. From his own experiences, he knew the Mórrígan couldn't take over her. He guessed it would be similar to Cúchulainn being inside his head, but would Rían be strong enough to stand up to the Mórrígan? If she couldn't then there was no hope at all.

He reached Dundalk late in the night and found a place to stay close to the bus stop, a small hotel in the centre of town that didn't look for identification and never questioned him on his method of payment, using a pre-paid cash card. His own credit cards would pinpoint him as soon as he used them. The hotel itself was a world away from what he was used to, small with no room service, but had a decent bed and a shower. It would do for a few days until he figured out his next move. Exhausted, he fell asleep without undressing as soon as he sat on the bed and lay back. The strain from the past 24 hours finally catching up on him.

He awoke with a start, a cold sweat trickling down the small of his back and he tried to steady his breathing. Light filtered through the blinds and he checked the time, finding he'd slept less than four hours. The dream was still vivid and he shuddered involuntarily, still reeling from the sense of helplessness, dreaming he was back in Chicago, no longer eight years old but unable to fend for himself as they came for him. He rolled over, pulling the bed covers over him, trying to stop the shivering, but sleep refused to return. He lay on the bed for a while, listening to the sounds of life stirring outside, beginning with the birds and growing to a crescendo with traffic.

Giving up on sleep, he got up and stood by the window, a roadside view, and further out, beyond the town, the Cooley Mountains loomed, large and dark. Yet they felt familiar and comforting. He knew the sensation came from Cúchulainn's memories, he'd never been here before. He undressed and showered, taking his time, turning the water up as hot as he could bear. He skipped breakfast, his stomach in turmoil and leaving the sanctuary of his room and the hotel, he took a walk through the town, noting street names and its layout, getting his bearings. It was bigger than expected and busy with businesses opening up for the day, and life went on. Had he really expected the world to come shuddering to a stop with the return of the Mórrígan? Just because his own little world crashed about his head didn't mean the rest of the world wouldn't carry on regardless.

He found himself back at his hotel and took the lift up to his floor. Stepping out onto the landing, he surveyed both approaching corridors. Something caught his eye and suspicion arose. A plain white envelope sat on the floor by his door. He looked about him but the corridors either side were empty. He opened the door to his room and looked inside before stepping in, finding it as he left it and he picked up the envelope. His name was neatly handwritten on the other side and he felt a stirring of panic. Someone knew he was here, despite giving a false name when he checked in.

He let the door close behind him, locking it before sitting on the bed. He ripped the envelope open and pulled out a white card. The note, also handwritten, not typed, the script small, neat and legible, only containing an address and a time; the corner of Clanbrassil Street and Crowe Street at 11 o'clock. He checked his watch and found only two hours to go, two hours to find this place and develop an attack or defensive strategy.

135

From his bag he unwrapped a number of knives he'd packed, set about securing them about his body, knowing he'd be walking into a trap, and not willing to do so unarmed. His early morning scouting paid off and he found the corner without a problem, right in the centre of town but he continued across the road, all senses on high alert and scanned the area for anyone watching for him. Circling around the next block, he approached the corner from a different angle and already an escape strategy formed in his mind, should the need arise.

As the appointed time drew near, he approached the corner, watchful for any sign of an attack. As he got closer to the meeting point, another man appeared from the adjacent street and stood at the corner. Seth stopped. The other man seemed not much taller than him, appeared to be a bit older, with dark, neatly cropped hair, sporting a goatee and well dressed, wearing a three-piece suit despite the growing heat of the midsummer's day. His stance was relaxed and Seth immediately assessed him as a low threat. A quick sweeping glance about the junction revealed a different story and he spotted a number of men dotted about at various points including behind him, their attention firmly focused on the two of them.

"Mr Morand, glad you could make our little meeting," the stranger said stepping towards him, a hand extended. "Conor Uí Neill," he introduced himself. Seth ignored the outstretched hand and Conor just shrugged, letting his hand fall.

"You're the self-appointed King of Ulster," Seth said, recognising the name.

"It's no worse than proclaiming your little bitch as High King. At least my claim is legitimate and of the Uí Neill bloodline, all the way back to Conchobar mac Nessa," he said, the name of the ancient Ulster King stirring more memories within Seth, but he remained silent. "You're a popular man, Mr Morand, seems everyone's looking for you at the moment. Fortunately, we found you first," Conor went on.

"How?" Seth demanded.

"Technology," Conor answered and reached inside his jacket. Seth took a step back and his hand instinctively went for one of his knives before he caught himself. Conor caught the defensive gesture and a smile played at the corner of his mouth. "I have something for you. Call it a gift. A gesture of good faith," and he took something from his inside pocket. "Which wrist is your chip in?" he asked. The damn chip, Seth thought angrily. Damned by technology and he mentally kicked himself for not thinking of it. No wonder Uí Neill found him so easily. How far behind was the old man? Conor held out his hand showing him a thick leather strap about two cm wide, with an intricate Celtic design and scrollwork.

"What is it?" Seth demanded.

"Which hand?" Conor asked again.

"Left," Seth answered, taking another step back as Conor reached for his arm.

"Relax man, I'm not the enemy here. I'm probably the only friend you have right now. This…" he held up the strap, "is going to save your life. It contains an electronic disrupter that'll distort and scramble your chip's signal, and hide you from that old sorcerer of yours." Seth weighed it up. It would certainly be an advantage, but at what cost?

"That means you wouldn't be able to find me either," he countered.

"A small price to pay in the battle against great evil," Conor answered. Seth thought for a moment before holding his arm out, accepting it and allowed Conor to secure the bracelet on him. Conor saw the tip of the hilt of the small blade at his wrist.

"You have nothing to fear from me, Mr Morand. I'm not your enemy," he said.

"So what do you want?" Seth asked.

"To offer you sanctuary from the old man and that witch," Conor answered. "Why else would you come to Dún Dealgan? To Dundalk?" He spread his arms wide to indicate the town. "This is the ancestral home of Cúchulainn, your home. You were drawn here."

"I don't know what the hell you're talking about, but I don't need your help," Seth said and turned to walk away, hiding his confusion from Uí Neill. He just got the next available bus out of the city, didn't he? No, it was pure co-incidence he'd ended up here.

"And just how far do you think you'll get with the Mórrígan on your tail?" Conor asked, matter of fact. Seth hesitated a moment before taking another step. "I know what the old man did, how they used you," Conor said after him. "All I want is for us to work together."

"Work together, how?" Seth asked.

"To kill that bitch," Conor answered

"I can't do that," Seth said.

"She's no longer the woman you think she is. The old man broke honour by bringing the Mórrígan back, broke your honour when he used you to do his dirty work," Conor reasoned with him.

"I still can't help you," Seth was adamant.

"So you'll turn your back on your family?" Conor asked.

"What?" Seth asked cautiously. "I don't have any family."

"I beg to differ, man. You were fostered," Conor said. Seth stiffened, the details of his fosterage were never made public. "In the old times, fostering was akin to having your own family and it came with the same honour obligations," Conor told him.

"And?" Seth demanded.

"We're brothers, man, well, foster-brothers," Conor told him. Seth shook his head.

"Bollocks," he said but Conor just smiled.

"Your foster mother is Emer McNally. She married Donal Morand, whose name you took. My mother's name is Deirdre McNally married to Mark Uí Neill, who was my father. Emer and Deirdre are sisters. That makes you my cousin by adoption, but you were fostered, and that makes you my brother. And the bonds of foster are stronger and carry more honour, brother." Seth shook his head, not believing a word, not wanting to believe.

"I'm not your brother, fostered or not," Seth growled at him.

"Fair enough, but as Cúchulainn you also have certain obligations to Ulster," Conor changed tact.

"And I'm not Cúchulainn," Seth's answered hotly, turning to go again. Conor sighed.

"I'd hoped we'd reason this out, brother, but you're forcing my hand. I didn't want to resort to this," he said and Seth glared back.

"Resort to what? Have your goons attack me, capture me, torture me?" he demanded. Conor laughed.

"Nothing so melodramatic or heroic," he answered. "As the descendant of Ulster's Champion and a child of Ulster, I put a geis on you Seth Morand, in the name of Ulster and charge you with her defence," he said pronouncing the curse as 'guesh'. Seth stifled a laugh and shook his head, began to walk away, thinking that maybe he would be better off leaving the country after all. This was getting just too bizarre. These people really were nuts.

Then it hit him. Slowly at first, starting with a tightening in his chest, his breathing becoming restricted. He thought someone had a hand on him, pushing him down but found no one there as he looked. The weight continued to grow, threatening to buckle him, force him to the ground.

"What the hell have you done?" he growled at Conor.

"Do you understand the concept of geasa?" Conor asked.

"It's a taboo, a superstition," Seth answered through gritted teeth, starting to sweat from fighting this invisible and oppressive force.

"That's the common use for it," Conor answered. "Cúchulainn's taboo was of course he couldn't eat dog meat, especially after taking the place of a dog for a year. Most of the time geasas were used as superstitions in order to protect the Kings from making fools of themselves or from getting themselves killed. I think the modern version of the concept is Protocols. But geasa can be so much more. They can be used as a curse, or to put an obligation on someone."

"You think you can force me to do what you ask?" Seth demanded, gasping for air and beads of sweat appearing on his forehead. Conor shook his head.

"No, not my will, but whatever is necessary to defend Ulster. You did so almost two thousand years ago and the time will come to defend her again, and of course, defend me as King of Ulster, brother," Conor answered coldly. Conor gave the barest gesture to one of his men. "You're tied to me now. It's a bit like a marriage, 'until death us do part'."

"That can be arranged," Seth snarled, pulling a blade from under his shirt and moved in to attack Conor, but a blinding, searing pain exploded inside his head and he fell to his knees. A car pulled up alongside them at the edge of the footpath as Conor grabbed a handful of hair, yanking Seth's head up and Seth stared at cold, hard eyes.

"I probably should have warned you about that, but then again, from talking with Emer, she says you always had to learn things the hard way," Conor said and let him go. "Get into the car, Seth," he said. Seth refused to move and two men grabbed him from behind, hauling him to his feet and pushed him toward the car. He got in, sitting beside Conor, who, much to his surprise, handed him his knife back.

"You're not going to try that again, are you, brother?" Conor asked.

"No," Seth answered taking the blade from him without any more pain reoccurring, but his breathing was still laboured.

"Relax. The more you fight the geis, the harder it gets to breathe and the heavier it feels," Conor advised, a hint of sympathy returning to his voice. Seth sat back, not wanting to surrender, but he knew he had no choice. His thoughts turned dark. So he couldn't kill Conor, and as Conor said, they were now tied to each other until death. A possible solution ran through his head. If he couldn't kill Conor, could he kill himself? Or would the geis prevent that as well. There was always one way to find out, but could he end his own life? He was a warrior, had been trained to fight all his life, not give up like this, but he saw no other way out. And what if Conor was correct about Rían? If so, then he had nothing left to live for.

"Where are we going?" he asked. Conor smiled.

"Not far. There's something I think you should see," Conor answered. As promised, the drive was only a short one and their convoy of three cars pulled up onto the side of the road. Getting out of their car, Seth felt a strange sensation, one of apprehension and uneasiness. Conor crossed the road to an opening in the wall opposite the cars. He stepped over and waited. With a push from one of Conor's men, Seth followed, but his unease grew as he saw the stone standing at the centre of the field.

"Where are we?" he demanded.

"Just outside Knockbridge," Conor answered, but the name meant nothing to Seth or to Cúchulainn inside his head. The feelings came from Cúchulainn, and in the back of his mind, he knew he should know this place. Conor walked up the gentle slope of the field ahead of him, aiming for the stone and Seth followed behind him with the help of another push. The stone was immense, standing about three metres tall and angled slightly, with a rippled effect etched by the wind that blew constantly across the hilltop. It slightly ruffled his hair and despite the heat from the midday sun, he felt chilled, adding to his unease. Seth circled the stone, staring up at it, fear growing.

"This is Clochafarmore, in the Field of Slaughter" Conor told him, pronouncing it as clock-a-far-more. "The Stone of the Big Man," he translated. Seth glanced at him before realisation hit him.

"This is where he died," he said. "This is the stone he tied himself to." From the back of his mind got a sense of defiance from Cúchulainn, the ultimate last stand and he knew the hero would do the same all over again. Seth reached out his hand and stopped a hair's breadth from touching it, the stone of his ancestor, his stone. His fingers made contact with the ancient rock, and memories came flooding back from Cúchulainn. They hit him like a bolt of lightning and he cried out, falling against the stone. At his death, Cúchulainn's blood and life force flowed into the stone, and it now flooded back into Seth. He fell to his knees, clinging to the stone as he felt the power surging through him. As the last bolt hit, he felt the scar on his chest burning and cried out before he lost consciousness and fell to the ground.

Conor suspected Cúchulainn's power still resided in the stone, and only his descendant could unleash it. He signalled to his men who now approached and ordered Seth put into the car. The American would need careful watching, but the geis should hold him and as Cúchulainn, he would understand the nature of his geis better.

Chapter 23

Rían awoke, her eyes fluttering open before coming into focus, and looked about the unfamiliar room where she found herself. It was large and ornately furnished, and she lay on a large bed. She sat up, still disorientated, and tried to figure where she was, but no answers came. She got up, wavering a little, unsteady on her feet. What was the last thing she remembered? Thinking back was like wading through mist, but she recalled the old man giving her something to drink, something that made her drowsy. She barely remembered landing at Tara, but she thought she remembered hearing a loud bang that startled and frightened her and left her feeling cold and numb. Maybe it was from standing in the wind, at least she could remember that much. What happened after that remained a complete mystery.

She looked about the room, and with a sudden realisation and growing fear, found no door. There was a large array of windows at the opposite end of the room to her, but no door. How in hell had she gotten here? More importantly, how the hell was she going to get out? Her head throbbed, as much from the dehydration as from the quandary she found herself in and she felt thirsty, needing something to drink. As she scanned the room again, she found a jug of iced water on the dresser, condensation covering the glass and the ice chinking. She felt uneasy and could have sworn the jug wasn't there moments earlier. She walked over to the dresser and poured herself a glass, sipping the cold water slowly, surprised to realise she didn't feel hungry when it was at least 24 hours since she last ate. Taking her glass with her, she went to the windows. Expecting to see scenery of the grounds of the house she was in, the reality of what she saw both shocked and stunned her. She dropped her glass as she pressed herself up against the window, shouting. The glass smashed on the wooden floor, pieces scattering about her feet, but she paid no heed. From the windows, she looked at Cíanna and Naoise, only they appeared huge, almost giant-like. She pounded on the glass and shouted their names, but they didn't hear her. She turned back towards the room, her eyes scanning it, searching for something to break the glass. She spotted a large porcelain washbowl, and grabbing it from its stand, hurled it at one of the windows. To her horror, it rebounded from the glass back towards her, and barely jumped out of its way before it crashed to the floor, smashing to pieces. She managed to turn her face away but not before a piece of debris nicked her just above the eye. When she reopened her eyes to survey the damage and pick the pieces up, the bowl no longer lay in fragments on the floor. It was back in its original place, on its stand, intact, where she first found it. She stared at it in disbelief. No way should that have happened, no way it could have happened. She turned to look at the glass she dropped, and it too, was whole again. This had to be a dream, she concluded. It was the only explanation. She felt awake, but she had to be dreaming, so the question was how she was going to wake herself up and get out of this place?

She returned to the window and tried shouting again to Cíanna until her voice grew hoarse. It seemed to be starting to work, Cíanna frowned and asked what was wrong. Then Rían felt the strangest sensation. She felt words coming from her.

"She's awake. Leave us while we talk," she heard herself say. At least it sounded like her. From the window she watched both of the other women leave the room, and on closer inspection, she recognised it as within the old man's house. She sensed someone behind her. She had never seen this woman before, but she seemed oddly familiar. She was tall, much taller than Rían, with long flowing red hair, tied back from her face. She was dressed in what Rían guessed to be some form of battle gear, a leather breastplate laced at the sides, long leather cuffs laced up at her wrists. Silver bands circled both upper arms and a torque sat at her throat. Her body and face had a hardness, a toughness. They stared at each other for a few moments before the strange woman broke the silence.

"You slept for a long time, child," she said, her voice low and deep, "I was beginning to fear my return caused you some damage."

"Your return? Just who the hell are you? What is going on? Where am I?" Rían demanded. The woman smiled, but her eyes seemed like ice.

"I have many names, I've been called Machá, Marú, an Mór Ríon" she said and paused when realisation crossed Rían's face.

"The Mórrígan," Rían gasped.

"That's how I am generally known," she answered. Rían shook her head. While she never doubted the historical existence of the Great Queen, she always believed the scholar's versions that the Mórrígan was an amalgamation of a number of powerful women in Celtic history and lore, but now that theory seemed defunct. She really did exist, or did she? Maybe this was all just a dream.

"This is no dream, child," the Mórrígan said, as though reading her thoughts, "and you are where you've always been." Too cryptic for Rían, she stared at the older woman in bewilderment and the Mórrígan sighed sharply. She'd never been known for her patience. "We two, here now, are only essences of who we are, we're spirits, or souls. I have no physical body in this world in which to reside in. The Sean Fhear (*old man*) didn't perform the ritual for my return at your conception or birth and you were allowed to grow and develop your own spirit, independent of mine. Now, we have two spirits residing in the same body."

"It won't be a problem when you leave," Rían shot back.

"It's not so simple, child," the Mórrígan answered. "In order for a spirit to be released, the physical body must die. You must die, only then will we both be free."

"I don't have a problem with that," Rían answered and the Mórrígan backhanded a slap across her face with lightning speed, sending Rían reeling back.

"Don't be a fool, little one. By the ancient geis, an Ard Rí cannot take their own life. It is forbidden for you to do so and you would also be dishonouring your obligations to your people," the Mórrígan answered. Rían touched her lip and pulled her hand away to reveal blood. Rage bubbled within her and she threw a punch at the older woman, a right uppercut, catching her on the jaw, but the Great Queen merely grunted as it landed, and grabbed Rían by the throat in return, propelling her across the room. Rían crashed into the end post of the bed, cracking her head.

"Heed me well," the Mórrígan growled at her. "You and I will work together. You have knowledge of this world I do not possess and if you do not aid me, I will have no difficulty in killing you. And if I kill you here, only your spirit ceases to exist and this body becomes mine."

Within the blink of an eye, she disappeared. No loud bangs, no dramatic gestures or conjuring, no shimmering of the air. Rían eased herself up to sit against the bedpost. The Mórrígan? Dear God, what was the old man thinking, bringing her back? A number of things ran through her head simultaneously. Firstly, Seth's belief that only a spirit could return into a body it was connected to, by blood. Did that mean the Mórrígan was one of her ancestors? But the Mórrígan existed at the beginning of time. How could anyone trace a bloodline back that far? And Ard Rí? The Mórrígan told her of her obligations as Ard Rí. Did that mean the stone sounded, that she had been proclaimed? Was that the noise that startled her? But at least she knew where she was. She was still in her own mind, trapped in her head, while the Mórrígan had control over the rest of her, over her body, her actions, her movements, over what she did and said.

To the casual observer, Rían seemed asleep on the sofa, the only oddity being a trickle of blood from her lip, but as she opened her eyes, coldness in her look made it clear the Mórrígan was back in control. The bloody lip surprised her and caused her concern. That wasn't supposed to happen, but meant any injury inflicted on the spirit would be transferred to the body, meaning she would be unable to carry out her threat on Rían. She suspected this would be the case, the manner of her return made everything unstable, and the old rules no longer applied. She stood up and wiped the blood from her mouth, and hoped Rían didn't learn the Mórrígan's threat carried no weight. As she passed the fireplace, she looked at her reflection in the mirror above the mantelpiece. The face of Rían stared back at her, the same defiant little face she just encountered.

By the gods, that child had spirit and mettle to dare strike back at her. In a way, it was a small comfort to her that a fragment of her own spirit, her essence, survived throughout the generations. While the face started to become familiar, this body wasn't and she felt ungainly as she moved. It was annoying to have lost her poise and grace, but she knew that would only come with time and practice. She felt the urge to burn off some of her anger, and she left the room for the training hall Naoise showed her the previous night. She felt agreement from Rían. So, the little one was aware of her thoughts also. Perhaps she should consider putting a barrier in place to shield Rían.

"Put up a barrier and I won't help you," Rían said to her defiantly.

"Do I need to win you over then, little one?" the Mórrígan asked. "There is so much I can teach you, if we work together."

"Like what?" Rían demanded and the Mórrígan sensed doubt and scepticism coming from her.

"You do not believe me, child?" she asked.

"It's not a matter of believing you, it's a matter of trusting you," Rían answered rebelliously and the Mórrígan laughed.

"I give you my word, from one Queen to another. Help me understand this world, and I will help you understand the universe."

"How?" Rían asked.

"Do you always ask this many questions?"

"Yes."

"The universe is made up of energy, little one, but that energy can be manipulated, can be moulded and shaped. This is what I can teach you."

"You're talking about magic," Rían said with contempt. "There's no such thing."

"Really?" the Mórrígan mocked. "Then explain my presence."

"I'm having some sort of psychotic, schizophrenic episode," Rían concluded. At this stage, it was the only explanation.

"Schizophrenic?" the Mórrígan asked.

"A mental disease," Rían answered. "Multiple personality disorder. You're not really here, you're a figment of my imagination, a delusion I've lost myself in." She sensed anger rising within her body as the Mórrígan's fury grew.

"You insolent child," the Mórrígan roared at her. "This is no delusion, no figment of the imagination." Rían just shrugged. That damn child was testing her, she realised and stopped and laughed. Yes, she would make a fine Ard Rí. "Enough. Show me what this body can do," she said.

She picked up a long and short sword and practiced a few slow strokes, getting a feel for the body, for how it moved, moving steadily faster as she gained her sense of balance, and from the windows of her room, Rían watched, noting the variations on her own techniques.

The old man found her in the training room, barefooted and moving with intense purpose, fully focused on her actions, so intent that she failed to notice him. He found it difficult to talk to her since her arrival, having sequestered herself with her sisters, and they guarded her jealously. Early in the morning, he knocked on the door of her room, only to be greeted by a half-dressed Cíanna. A quick glimpse into the room revealed the Great Queen asleep beside Naoise and he presumed the three women spent the night together. Not unusual, he knew. In ancient times, men and women more often than not, kept their own company. While there were never any indications of the kind of relationships that society in the past four or five hundred years frowned on, disapproved of and tried to oppress, it wasn't unusual for the Celts to find comfort and affection within the arms and body of someone of their own sex. Naoise never hid her preferences for other women, especially when it gave her the opportunity to flirt and seduce the women Seth had an interest in.

Now, she was alone for the first time since her arrival and he wasn't about to relinquish this opportunity to speak with her. Watching her, in Rían's form, he could tell she had yet to find balance in this new body, but that was slowly changing. He watched her practice a combination of attack and blocking strokes, recognising the fluid movements of a trained warrior, knowing she found the odd lapses in balance frustrating. He took a step closer and a floorboard creaked under his foot. She spun around, fury etched in her face and weapons at the ready. Her stance relaxed when she saw him but was slow to lower her swords, her stare cold and hard as she regarded him.

"Forgive the interruption," he said. She returned the swords to their stands.

"You go by the name Brehon in this time," she said. "How strange you take the name for Law, of Judgement, the name for the rules that governed our time and existence, while at the same time you flaunt those very laws. Do you consider yourself the law in this time, the supreme puppet master and governance of everyone?" Her voice cut like ice as she spoke.

"No, Mistress, only taken as a whimsy at the time, but it is my duty to uphold the ancient rules and laws where I can. I took an Oath, and have been bound to that," he answered.

"But you are only a Druid, old man, do not forget that. You may stand above men, even above Kings. But you do not stand above the Gods," she said, and even though she spoke softly he detected a dangerous edge. He gave her a brief nod of submission.

"What are those?" she asked, referring to the wrapped items in his hands. He held them out to her.

"These have been cared for throughout the centuries, awaiting your return," he said, holding them out to her. She unwrapped the longest item, carefully lifting the material to reveal a large sword. She pulled the blade from this scabbard and a smile played on her lips.

"How?" she asked.

"The druids who found it a thousand years ago, recognised it as belonging to you," he answered.

"But it's still perfect," she said.

"Our people were excellent sword smiths, knew how to make them strong enough to survive the ages. We know it's not Claíomh Solus," he said.

"The Sword of Light was never mine, that belonged to Lugh and then to Cúchulainn. But this one has power of its own, not as powerful as Claíomh Solus, but it's powerful enough," she told him. "And the other item?" she asked. He unwrapped that one for her.

"Your original breastplate. The leather has been treated and re-treated over time, and the brass buckles replaced perhaps a millennium ago. I took the liberty of replacing those with titanium," he said. The word titanium meant nothing to her and from the back of her mind Rían tried to explain, but all she understood was that it was some sort of durable metal. She put the sword back in its scabbard and reached out to touch the hardened leather.

"This couldn't have survived the centuries. It looks as good as the last time I wore it," she said incredulously.

"I found it in Tír na nÓg, it hasn't been in this world long enough for time to ravage it. In the Otherworld, it's only been a short time since you did wear it," he answered. He held it out to her.

"I also need to speak with you," he said. She remained silent but the coldness returned to her face. He paused for a moment. "Rí Uí Neill requests a meeting," he told her.

"An Uí Neill as King? Of Uladh *(Ulster)* I presume?" she asked and he nodded. "He wishes to contest our claim to the Ard Rí?" He nodded again. "Arrange it."

She took the sword and breastplate with her as she left, leaving him alone in the training room and he sighed.

Chapter 24

"Welcome back to the land of the living, brother," Conor said as Seth opened his eyes. He looked across the room to the Ulster King and eased himself up, shaking his head to try dislodging the fuzziness that remained.

"Where am I?" he demanded.

"Emain Macha," Conor answered. "Not the real one, of course, they turned that into a national monument and park. But we're not far from it. I called this house and the grounds Emain Macha. A fitting name, don't you think?" Seth didn't care either way.

"How long have I been out?" he asked.

"Three days," Conor answered. "I was starting to get a bit worried." Seth shook his head in disbelief, getting out of bed and standing up. He caught Conor staring at his scars but did nothing to hide them, not caring what the man thought. He scratched at the dense growth of stubble on his chin.

"How do you feel?" Conor asked, but Seth was suspicious.

"Fine," he answered cautiously.

"I'm concerned because you banged your head off that stone," Conor tried to sound anxious, but Seth detected the insincerity.

"Why the fuck don't you ask what's really on your mind?" Seth growled at him. "You want to know if I've turned into him, into Cúchulainn." Conor allowed himself a smirk.

"Have you?"

"I don't feel that much different. I still want to smash your smug little face in, that hasn't changed,"

Conor's cheeks coloured in anger.

"Remember what happened the last time."

"I haven't forgotten," Seth answered coldly. He picked up his clothes, somewhat surprised to find his holdall close by and disappeared into the bathroom. He took his time under the hot shower and when he was about to shave he paused, considering his options.

When he re-emerged refreshed, dressed and sporting a goatee not dissimilar to Conor's, Conor was gone. The three-day rest was good for him, he felt stronger, more refreshed than he had in weeks. Oddly, he had no sense of Cúchulainn within him, no separate entity sending him thoughts and emotions and yet he felt complete, whole. The stone, he thought. It must've completed what the old man started. He and Cúchulainn became one, became whole. But, as he told Conor, he didn't feel any different. His sense-of-self was whole and intact.

He threw open the door and found a man at the other side. Startled, the guard brought his gun up, taking a defensive posture. Seth regarded him with scorn, but Conor more so. What the hell was the man thinking, using guns? The modern armament was of no interest to him, but gave him a measure of the man he was dealing with. Conor wasn't going to stick to the ancient and honourable rules. The man had no honour, Seth concluded, but succeeded in binding Seth to his obligations. He pushed past and headed for the stairs, the guard followed close behind. The house wasn't as large as the one at Ardscull and he found Conor in the kitchen.

"Hungry, brother?" he asked.

"A little," Seth admitted and Conor turned to a little portly lady.

"I'm afraid we don't do anything as fancy as your high-power shakes," he said sarcastically to Seth who ignored the insult and checked the pot the woman was stirring.

"Just some good old fashioned stew," she told him.

"That'll be fine," he answered and she filled a bowl for him. Thanking her, he sat at the table. He noticed the bowl she gave Conor wasn't so generous and the man didn't even have the courtesy to thank her. Seth was starting to get a fuller picture of this man who considered himself Ulster's King, and the view wasn't a pleasant one. Another man entered the room.

"Well?" Conor snapped.

Seth regarded man at the end of the table with interest. He was much older than either himself or Conor, reminding him of McCormac.

"They've agreed to a meeting," this old man said. Conor caught Seth watching him.

"This is Devlin, my Druid," he explained and Devlin saw Seth's posture stiffen.

"And you lad, must be Setanta," Devlin said.

"It was shortened to Seth a long time ago. I don't go by that name anymore," he answered. "And what meeting?" he asked. Conor gave him a cold look, not knowing how much to trust him with yet. Devlin too, also held his peace.

"I'm meeting that witch of yours," Conor said and Seth shrugged.

"Good luck. I hope you know what you're letting yourself in for."

"Why don't you tell me?"

Seth laughed and shook his head.

"I wouldn't want to spoil the surprise," he answered humorously but with a hint of malice. Whether it was Rían or the Mórrígan Conor was meeting, the man wouldn't have an easy time, with either of them. Without finishing his food, he stood up. The little portly cook looked worried.

"Was anything wrong with dinner?" she asked, concerned. He smiled and gave her shoulder a gentle squeeze.

"No Fleur, sweetheart," he answered, having heard another member of the kitchen staff call her by name. To his surprise, she blushed. "It was good. I've just lost my appetite." He turned to Conor. "Am I under house arrest, or can I leave? If we're this close to Emain Macha, it means we're close to Armagh. I'd like to see the city."

"Will you return to us, brother?" Conor asked, sitting back.

"Like I have a choice."

"I'll have someone drive you in and show you around."

"Don't you trust me?".

"It's not a matter of trust, brother, I'm concerned for your safety."

"I'm in Ulster, it can't get much safer for me," Seth argued back, not believing him, and wishing the asshole would stop calling him 'brother'.

"If you want to go to Armagh, those are the terms."

Chapter 25

The car made its way through the centre of Belfast, Naoise sitting up front with the driver. The Mórrígan and the old man sat at the back.

"This is madness," McCormac said to her.

"How so?" she asked. "You think Uí Neill is going to harm me? He wouldn't dare. He's a politician and more likely to bore me to death than attack me." She smiled but he caught the dangerous glint in her eyes.

"I think you should reconsider and allow Naoise to accompany you," he said and she shook her head.

"To bring her would be seen as a sign of weakness, that I feared him, that I saw him as a threat," she replied as the car pulled up to the designated hotel and McCormac got out before the driver turned off the engine. He offered a hand to her, helping her out and she took a step before suddenly stopping and turned, scanning the buildings opposite.

"What is it?" McCormac asked. She shook her head, unable to explain what she sensed, but she felt … something. She turned back and strode up the steps, entering the lobby. McCormac recognised Devlin and sneered.

"Causing trouble again Devlin?" he said.

"Of course," Devlin replied, "but then again, I learned from the best." The Mórrígan raised an eyebrow at McCormac, but said nothing.

"An Mór Ríon," Devlin acknowledged her, "Conor is waiting for you inside." He indicated the restaurant behind him. McCormac stepped forward first but Devlin stepped in front of him.

"Only her," he said, "and Great Queen, no weapons, please."

"Of course, Druid Devlin," she answered, honouring him by using his title and from under the back of her shirt she pulled a large dagger from its scabbard, spinning it in her hand before handing it to McCormac, hilt first, surprising him.

"I'm afraid, highness, I must insist you allow these men to confirm there are no others," he said, almost apologetically as two men closed in on them, scanners at the ready. She gave him a cold, hard stare and he involuntarily took a step back before she held her arms out to allow the search.

"How unfortunate, Druid, we weren't afforded the same courtesy," she said quietly, but there was no mistaking the menacing tone.

"I give you my word, Conor is unarmed," he tried to assure her.

"And the word of a Druid means what these days?" she asked.

"We still adhere to our Oaths and the ancient Laws. My word is truth," he said, almost humbly. The men completed their sweep of her body and gave the all clear.

She lowered her arms and swept past the group, pausing only for the door to be opened for her. McCormac remained outside, hiding his anxiety. Devlin turned to him.

"What were you thinking, bringing her back, meddling with the Great Spirits?" he demanded. McCormac gave him the barest of smiles.

"What a pity you weren't this inquisitive when you were my student," he answered. "If you'd remained faithful you would have been a part of it."

"But I am a part of it," Devlin retorted.

"No, you are not," McCormac growled back. "You are interfering and meddling as a child does. You proclaimed an Uí Neill as King and you hope to advance yourself by making him Ard Rí."

"Isn't that what you've done, throwing that girl into the position," Devlin argued.

"You were a fool when you were my student, boy, and you're still a fool," McCormac answered. "The Lia Fáil sounded. She is who she is."

"But the Mórrígan?" Devlin practically screamed at him. McCormac remained calm.

"It was her time to return," he answered and sat on the nearest sofa. Frustrated, Devlin was unsure of his next move. Damn, why did that man always affect him that way? But he had one more ace up his sleeve that he guessed the old man didn't know about.

Inside the restaurant, the lighting was dim, but not so dim that she couldn't see clearly into the corners of the room as she walked in. Conor sat at a table at the end, making her walk the length of the room. She knew it for the ploy it was and keeping her eyes fixed on him, she slowed to a stroll, swaying slightly. She noticed his eyes lowering, fixing on her hips and she smirked to herself, thinking how little men changed in all the millennia. Throw in a heaving bosom and their brains turned to mush. As she reached the table, he remained seated, refusing to stand to honour her or at the least acknowledge her as his equal. She held her temper at this insult and pulled a chair out to sit down.

"Are you Rían or the Mórrígan?" he demanded as she sat.

"I am both, and we are one," she replied cryptically.

"Then you know you've defied Brehon law. You weren't proclaimed Queen for any province. Your claim to the High Kingship is void."

"And yet the Stone sounded," she answered, sitting back in the chair.

"I am the rightful heir," Conor declared. "I claim that right from my father, and from his father."

"You are so concerned with Brehon law that you neglect the obvious flaw in your argument," she said calmly.

"And what is that?" he demanded.

"The Bloodline comes through the mother's side, not the father's. It is the way it has always been, and always will be. To claim from your father goes against the laws you declare to hold to. I'm surprised your Druid even permitted you to claim kingship of Ulster," she answered.

"Brehon law forbids a woman," he retorted.

"Nonsense," she answered pleasantly, her continuing calmness only fuelling his anger. "There is recorded evidence that Maeve was Ard Rí for eight years in 661BC and co-ruled with her husband Cimbaeth for seven years before that. If you're going to argue on points of law and precedence, it would have been in your best interests to research this matter before coming here. All you are doing is showing your ignorance, little man. As for being a woman, get with the 21st century. Women can now do anything we like without a man to hinder us. In fact, it's almost like the old ways, when men and women were equals, before the Romans and

155

Christianity, and their narrow-minded philosophises, destroyed our society.

"Unlike you however, I can claim birth right. From the Leinster King, and the last Ard Rí, twenty-two generations of offspring have all been women. The line has been kept pure and intact. My line."

Conor seethed. She'd hit a nerve. He was unaware of Maeve, as he was unaware of Rían's lineage. Devlin told him none of this.

"We will go to war over this," he threatened her and much to his annoyance she shrugged. He stood up to go.

"So be it," she replied. "I'd hoped our meeting would show you the error of your ways, but obviously not." She stood also, squaring up to him. "And it's been such a long time since I've had a good battle, I am eager for a decent fight. I hope you fight better than you can argue your case, little man." He turned and stormed off, disappearing into the lobby.

McCormac entered the room and she sat back down, the old man taking the seat Conor vacated.

"He's not withdrawing?" he asked and she smiled slyly at him.

"He is arrogant and reckless, and unfortunately he is also fully convinced that it is his right. He wishes to fight for it, and a fight he'll get," she answered.

"Then we have a problem if we go to war," he said quietly. "It seems we've lost Cúchulainn," he answered.

"What do you mean, lost him?" she demanded coldly.

"I've just learned from Devlin that Conor placed a geis on Seth, and as Cúchulainn, he is honour bound to defend Ulster, if you go to war," he told her.

"A geis?" she smirked, "Conor is grasping at straws. He's using geasa as an obligation then and not as a prohibition?" The old man nodded. She slowly shook her head, thinking.

"You left Seth in the new world too long old man," she said to him.

"I had no choice," he defended himself. "It was pure luck to find him when I did. If they found him first, they would have claimed him for Ulster."

"Yet now they have him anyway," the Mórrígan said harshly.

"But his heart is not with them."

"Yet he will stand with them."

"I did what I could with him, taught him what he needed to know, taught him our ways," he reasoned and she sighed.

"If we have to stand against him then so be it. There is nothing new in that anyway," she said.

"His allegiances may be divided because of Rían," the old man suggested.

"Perhaps," she conceded. "But perhaps this, bringing me back and into her form, is too much of a betrayal for him."

"If he is their Champion it would be wise if you did not go against him," he advised. "If I recall, Cúchulainn injured you the last time you fought."

"I remember," she replied tersely, "but that was against Cúchulainn. How much has he taken over the boy?" For the first time she saw doubt in the old man.

"In truth, I don't know," he admitted. "I've been infusing Cúchulainn's spirit into him since he was a child, there was never a hint he wasn't becoming part of Seth, but … sometimes I wondered how much Cúchulainn was taking hold."

"So perhaps it is not Cúchulainn I would be facing then," she replied. The old man shrugged. He couldn't answer her, and that troubled him, but not as much as it troubled her.

As they left the hotel, she had the same sensation and this time she recognised it, knowing it came from Rían. Seth was somewhere nearby and Rían sensed him. But how, the Mórrígan wondered. How could the child be aware of him? Strong emotion surrounded Rían and that disturbed and troubled the Mórrígan. She opened herself to the elements and sought him out, sought his energy signature and found him in the building across the road. With her strength returning, she noted with satisfaction that she could pinpoint his exact location in the building opposite. She knew he was standing at a window, watching her. But his energy flow differed from how Rían remembered it and the energy flow differed from how the Mórrígan herself remembered Cúchulainn's, but she found traces of both in the man. So they have become one, she thought grimly. Their car pulled up at the kerbside, but she hesitated before getting in, watching the window where she knew him to be.

"What's wrong?" the old man asked, concerned.

"He's nearby," she answered.

"Who?" he asked.

"The boy. But, he is also Cúchulainn, I sense them both together," she answered. She could tap into Rían's memories now, and knew the depth of her feelings for Seth. Interesting, she thought, wanting to speak with the child, find out what she was up to, but it would have to wait. For the moment, she kept her own counsel, not wanting the old man to know everything.

Chapter 26

Seth watched her leaving the hotel, a little startled when she stopped and looked up towards the window where he was standing. She couldn't have known he was there, could she? But then again, he still thought of her as Rían, part of him expected it to be her. Conor entered the room.

"Has she left yet?" he asked.

"Just leaving now," Seth answered. Conor stood beside him and looked out the window at them.

"Bitch," he growled.

"Went well then?" he asked sarcastically.

"She refused to give up her claim. I've told her I'll go to war."

"You just told the Mórrígan you wanted a war?" Seth demanded incredulously. "Are you insane? You're giving her the very thing she delights in, revels in. War is her realm, her domain."

"It's not going to be a problem," Conor said.

"Oh really?" Seth sneered, but felt a chill as Conor grinned at him.

"As my Champion, you'll be the one facing her," he said.

Chapter 27

Life went on and she watched as some of the senior managers from IIM arrived at Ardscull to declare their allegiances to her as Ard Rí, pay homage to her as the Mórrígan. Rían kept her fury in check, knowing the Mórrígan sensed it, and laughed every time. So this was what the old man meant when he told her how they'd shaped and moulded her life.

Day by day, Rían's sense of the Mórrígan grew stronger and it took a while to realise and understand what she felt, this tingling sensation every time the Mórrígan did what she called opening herself to the elements, the universal energy. The concept was completely foreign to Rían. As far as she was concerned, it was all hocus-pocus, airy-fairy nonsense. So why did it feel so real, how could she sense it as strongly as she did? She had no answer. No logical answer.

In the meantime, she saw and sensed how the Mórrígan protected herself whenever she projected her spirit outward by creating a sphere of energy around herself, charging it with positive and negative energies. She used the basic tenets of physics, Rían surmised, yet she experimented and copied the Mórrígan, slowly and carefully, without drawing attention to herself.

The process was slow and difficult for her, overcoming her complete scepticism being the greatest obstacle, but she did it, though not quite sure how. The Mórrígan sensed something before the meeting in Belfast, and while she was preoccupied with Conor, Rían opened herself and reached out, guessing Seth wouldn't be too far away. It came as a bit of a shock to her to find him, but not half as much as it had to the Mórrígan, and Rían quickly withdrew, tightening that sphere around her. Damn, she thought. She'd exposed what she was doing, but surprisingly the Mórrígan didn't appear in her room to question her.

What she needed was a book, something to explain what was going on, describe what to do, but there was one minor problem with that request, the Celts never wrote anything down. By the time such record keeping became fashionable, most of the Celtic way of life had transformed, changed by other influences and cultures. She needed a guide, someone to show her what to do, teach her to control this. Should she ask the Mórrígan, confide in her? Nah! Rían completely dismissed that notion, afraid that if she did, the Mórrígan would completely take over, usurp what little power Rían did have. Even if the Mórrígan didn't do that, but helped her as she promised, could Rían be sure the other woman wouldn't try to control it, and her? Rían knew she was probably putting herself in even more danger by experimenting the way she was, but what other choice did she have, really?

Fed up with her confinement, she put as much effort and energy as she could into getting free of her surroundings. Not really knowing what to expect, or what she was doing for that matter, she pushed it out, releasing all the want, and desire like an explosion. She felt a rush of air around her and her vision blurred. As the sensation passed, as abruptly as it began, she fell to the ground, dizzy. But at least she was out of her damned room.

She looked around her, finding herself at a lakeside, a dense forest a bit behind her. She looked up at the clear blue sky and the hot sun as it beamed down, glinting off the water. She sat up, dusting the dirt from her hands and surveyed her surroundings, noting how quiet it was, how peaceful. The water lapping at the shore was barely a whisper.

From the side of the lake she spotted a figure, a woman, coming towards her. As she got closer Rían stood, and she stopped beside Rían, looking down at her.

"You need to return, a leanbh *(child)*. She knows you are gone and she will come looking for you. Learn to shield yourself and leave a trace of yourself behind, then return to me. We will talk then," the lady said.

"But where am I?" Rían asked.

"You are in Tír na mBéo, the Land of Life, the Land of the Living," she answered.

"Tír na mBéo?" Rían asked. "Not Tír na nÓg?"

The woman shook her head.

"There are many Tír's or lands within the Otherworld, seventeen to be exact, and you have landed yourself in only one of them."

"How do I leave a trace of myself behind?" Rían then asked.

The woman smiled and stroked her face.

"When you know how, you will be ready to return to me," she said.

Rían felt herself falling backwards, a reversal of the sensation to get to the other land. She wasn't doing it this time, too exhausted to attempt that again. She landed on her arse on the floor of her room, breathless, stunned and confused. In what seemed like an instant later, the Mórrígan appeared before her, looking furious, but Rían thought she also detected something else. The word fear came to mind, but she dismissed that notion. The woman wasn't capable of that emotion. The older woman looked about suspiciously.

"What have you done?" she demanded of Rían.

"Nothing," Rían answered, and put up a barrier, imagining it as a solid brick wall, knowing the Mórrígan would otherwise know and sense what she was trying to hide.

"Why are you sitting on the floor?" the Mórrígan asked suspiciously.

"Practicing my dance moves," Rían shot back, bracing herself for a physical retaliation from the older woman. Surprisingly, none came.

Rían sensed apprehension in her, could feel the Great Queen pushing against her barrier, but while the Mórrígan pushed, she also left her own self unguarded, not considering Rían much of a threat to her. Gazing up at her, Rían saw the strangest thing, what looked like delicate silver threads flowing from the other woman. Rían blinked a few times, thinking perhaps it was a delayed reaction from her journey to the lake and back, but the threads remained, seeming to pulsate. Looking beyond them, she saw a nimbus of silvery light surrounding the Mórrígan, like an energy field around her body. Whatever it was, Rían thought annoyed, the bitch was trying to find an opening into her, trying to probe into her thoughts, causing Rían a dilemma. How could she retaliate without revealing or exposing what she could do? The simple answer was she couldn't. Retaliation would have to wait until she could better control this.

She had a thought and tried it out, trying to be as subtle and as gentle as she could. She allowed one of the Mórrígan's tendrils to attach to her, to take hold while she built up a feeling of fear and awe towards the older woman. She imagined them to be like bubbles, floating up to the attached thread. They affixed themselves to the Mórrígan's link to her and as the emotions pulsated back towards her, Rían imagined her own thread dragged along in the wake of the bubbles, establishing a two-way connection. Emotions from the Mórrígan slammed into Rían and she gasped, covering it with a cough.

The Mórrígan remained suspicious but continued to remain unaware of what Rían did. She gave a cursory sweeping glance about the room. With a final glare for Rían, she abruptly left without another word, severing all connections.

Rían relaxed and breathed a heavy sigh of relief. Now she understood what the woman by the lake was talking about. Exposed, the Mórrígan inadvertently revealed much of herself to Rían. The woman was afraid. Afraid of Rían and that fear stemmed from the complete sense of loss of her and Rían knew it happened the moment she left this room, left this realm.

And left this body? Had she actually done it, she wondered? Was this why she needed to leave a trace of herself behind? A part of herself that the Mórrígan could sense and not panic about her disappearing? She moved to the bed, curling up, asleep by the time her head hit the pillow.

The Mórrígan blinked awake.

"Everything alright?" Cíanna asked from the seat opposite her.

"I'm not sure," the Mórrígan confided in her. "The child is up to something, but somehow she has learned to close herself to me and I cannot see."

"Well, it was inevitable," Cíanna conceded.

"In what way?" the Mórrígan asked, taken a little aback.

"Listening to the old man, he said she was a very precocious child and even with my own limited experience with her, she's very astute. She watches everything, questions everything. I wouldn't be in the least bit surprised if she was learning from you," Cíanna answered.

"But why hide it from me?"

"Would you trust you, given your reputation?" Cíanna asked

"No. I suppose not. I know she has ability, I can sense power within her, but she needs to be guided," the Mórrígan answered.

"So just be careful what you show her," Cíanna advised.

"My little sister. Always the calm voice of reason, despite what the history books say," she said.

"With you and Nemain around, one of us has to be," Cíanna answered humorously.

Chapter 28

Seth took to practicing with Conor's men as they trained each morning. If nothing else, it alleviated the boredom and gave him something to do, gave him a sense of purpose. He trained with intensity, channelling his fury and rage into strengthening his body. Knowing of Seth's history in martial arts, Conor demanded fighting and swordplay lessons from him, much to Seth's annoyance. Conor's skills were limited and his technique amounted to barely more than hacking with a sword, in Seth's opinion.

It began badly, Conor insisting on engaging in a one-on-one mini-battle, despite Seth's advice to go back to basics. After multiple bruises, welts and as much humiliation as he could suffer, Conor gave in. For Seth, it took very little effort to deflect obvious blows, defend himself, and overpower the other man, Ulster Premier or not. King or not.

They returned to basics and to Seth's surprise, Conor turned out to be a quick learner. Not necessarily a good student though, and after a few sessions, Seth suspected Conor knew more than he let on, just lapsed into bad habits and methods. Not un-correctable, but it seemed to require more effort on Seth's part than on Conor's. It was in the middle of one of these early morning sessions when his mobile rang. Seth recognised the number and answered it, surprised.

"Yeah," he said to the caller and Conor looked at him puzzled.

"Can we talk?" the old man asked. Seth gave Conor a sideways glance.

"Sure, where?" he answered.

"To the first mountain we climbed up when you arrived here," McCormac answered cryptically. "Tomorrow?"

"Sure," Seth answered, "at the same time." He disconnected the call.

"Planning on going somewhere, brother?" Conor asked.

"Yes," he answered bluntly.

"Without my permission?" Conor challenged. Seth stepped closer to him until they faced each other.

"Some things you can't control," Seth growled at him.

"I forbid it. I order you to stay here," Conor answered back and Seth sneered at him.

"Your life is not in any danger, so ordering me is not going to work," he answered. "I thought you knew how this geasa thing worked and I now know it's not to be at your constant beck and call. I'm leaving, I'll be back tomorrow night. It's as simple as that."

"I can have them stop you," Conor said, nodding to two of his guards. Seth regarded them, and his captor, with utter contempt. As they stepped closer, Seth spun around, delivering a roundhouse kick to the chest of the closest man, landing him on the floor metres away. The second man was a little more ready for an attack, but he made the mistake of taking a swipe at Seth's head. Seth side-stepped him, pushing the man's arm aside, but grabbed his head as he brought his knee up and impacted with his jaw. Unconscious, the man fell to the floor. Seth spun back to face Conor, who had a rethink, knowing he wouldn't win, knowing he had no way of stopping Seth if the man was determined enough. He was Cúchulainn after all, and if the legends were anything to go by, nothing short of sorcery ever stopped or slowed the hero down. From the set look on Seth's face he knew his Champion was determined enough to risk life and limb, a risk Conor couldn't afford to take. He pulled his car key from the pocket of his jacket and tossed it to Seth.

"Take my car. It's faster," he said to a stunned Seth, "but if you run I will find you."

"I'll be back tomorrow night," Seth answered, calmer than he felt, suspicious of Conor's motives and sudden change of mind. Seth didn't question it, just left the room.

Conor's personal car, not the one he used for official business, was a sporty little number and Seth smirked at what Rían would have said were she to see him in it. The drive, he knew, would be a long one, knowing Conor could track him every kilometre of the way anyhow via GPS. From Armagh, he took the M1 motorway all the way to Dublin. He kept to the speed limits, not wanting to draw undue attention to himself. The car itself was more than enough to have the Garda Traffic Corp on his tail on more than one occasion. At Dublin, he exited the M1 for the M50, joining the early evening queue. Traffic continued to flow until getting closer to the city centre, where it came to a virtual standstill as he hit the start of rush-hour traffic. He continued on the M50 until it ended and became the M11 and headed for Wexford, but an hour and a half later turned off just before Enniscorthy, onto the N80 for Bunclody. Stiff and tired from driving he stopped in Bunclody town, his final destination not far away, but he had at least eight hours before his rendezvous with the old man. He checked into a hotel, no pretence this time, no need to hide. Anyone who was interested enough or who needed to find him now could.

From the window of his hotel room he saw the 'Welcome to Carlow' tourist sign, and knew he was less than a hundred metres from the county line. The place he would be heading for later was kilometres away but still on the Carlow-Wexford border. He went to sleep, tired from the drive, but he slept fitfully and awoke a number of times during the night with a start. When the alarm on his phone rang, he'd been awake for some time. He arose and showered, leaving the hotel while it was still dark. If the hotel staff thought it odd he checked out at that hour of the morning, they never said, just wished him a pleasant journey. A nice thought he mused darkly, knowing this meeting wouldn't be a pleasant one, but curiosity burned in him. What did the old man want?

He headed towards Carlow but took the left turn after passing the county sign, the Blackstairs Mountains his destination, the mountain range that divided Carlow and Wexford, and the same range that Rían had a view of from her house. While Mount Leinster was the tallest mountain within that range, it wasn't the first one he and the old man hiked up. He drove at an easy pace, watchful for road signs and relying on the on-board GPS to help guide him up the hillside. The road wound its way up, twisting and turning sharply at times, narrowing the higher he ascended. The sky brightened with dawn, making the going a bit easier, and as he drove over a cattle grid remembered he needed to be more careful from here on up. The road now wound along the edge of the mountain and one wrong move would see him hurtling down the mountainside. He eased off on the accelerator, taking his time around the final bend. The road opened out at the base of Mount Leinster and Slievebawn, and he parked in front of the Nine Stones.

The old man tried to impress upon him the importance of the Stones on his first visit here, shortly after his move to the country, and in hindsight Seth knew he should've paid more attention to the old man, the Stones having something to do with the inauguration of the Leinster Kings. But Seth's mind had been on other matters at the time. Perhaps if he'd fully understood the man's obsession with kings he wouldn't have found himself in his current predicament. He stopped the engine and got out, standing by the Stones, watching as the dawning sunlight crept up behind Mount Leinster. He waited until it grew lighter before beginning the climb of Slievebawn, the White Mountain.

The mountain had three stages to it, the first section a relatively gentle slope to walk up, with stone outcroppings marking the end. Then the going got a little steeper, white stones protruding from the ground becoming more common the higher he went until he reached the top of the second rise. From here on the ground would be softer and boggy and a number of times he had to take a side leap to avoid the soggy ground, the ancient part of him annoyed at the effort it took to leap across them, the younger part thinking he needed to get back to plyometric training.

The top levelled out and he reached a mound of stones. Beyond them sat four boulder-sized white rocks, grouped together, the ones that gave the mountain its name and he stood atop one. From here, he had an almost 300-degree view of the Wexford valley on one side and Carlow on the other.

The sun continued to rise behind Mount Leinster, the windmills from the nearby wind farm silhouetted against the morning light. The wind stirred his hair, and it whistled faintly at this height, as he regained his breath from the climb. He felt a sense of elation here, felt a sense of strength. For the first time in a while, he felt a sense of peace.

Then the old man appeared.

Chapter 29

The Mórrígan awoke with a start, alone in her room, both Naoise and Cíanna gone, but as she reached out with her senses, felt them nearby. That wasn't what woke her. Something else was amiss, out of balance and she dressed quickly. From a stand by the door, she grabbed her long sword on the way out, and ran down the stairs to where the other two were, finding them in the kitchen.

"What is it?" Naoise asked startled.

"We have to get out of here, out of this house. Now," the Mórrígan insisted. "Where is the old man?"

"He left to meet Seth. Why?" Cíanna answered.

The Mórrígan frowned.

"Can't you sense them?" she demanded, and Naoise and Cíanna looked at each other puzzled. "There's a battalion advancing on us right now. Neither of you can sense them?" she asked incredulously. They both shook their heads, but didn't delay another moment, just followed her out, Naoise taking a minor detour to grab weapons for herself and Cíanna. Leaving by a side door, they kept low, making their way to the trees and crouched down.

"How many are we talking about?" Naoise asked and the Mórrígan looked at them both curiously.

"How is it you can't sense them?" she demanded. Naoise shrugged.

"It's obviously not a skill or ability we have in this time," Cíanna concluded. The Mórrígan sighed impatiently.

"I sense about fifty. Open yourselves to me," she said and again Naoise and Cíanna exchanged glances.

The Mórrígan put a hand to each of their heads and opened herself to them, finding their essences, their spirits and joined them together. She heard their shocked gasps, but she now felt complete. She let them go and Cíanna panted for breath, struggling with what happened but Naoise recovered quicker and looked about her, understanding what her sister said.

"They don't know we've made it out of the house," she said in a savage whisper, about to stand, but the Mórrígan grabbed her.

"Don't be foolish, sister. We have the element of surprise, but we need to choose our battleground wisely," she told her. They looked at each other and as one knew where to go, and they crept along through the trees, the Mórrígan sensitive to every variance in energy, sensing every disturbance and the other two felt what she felt. Just like old times, the Mórrígan mused, and heard Naoise chuckling softly in agreement, felt her agreement. Cíanna concerned her, as she continued to struggle with the bond. She gave Cíanna's shoulder a gentle squeeze and felt begrudging acceptance in return.

"I'll be fine," Cíanna said. "I just need time to adjust to having you in my head."

They made it to the gate only to find it guarded. Not heavily, and the guards at the gate were not as attentive as they should have been, not expecting an attack. The women easily dispatched the two inside the gate, dragging their bodies into the bushes to hide them.

The two remaining outside the gate stood with their backs to them, more concerned with any visitors approaching than anyone attempting to leave. They too were easily overpowered and given quick deaths. Keeping to the wall the three made their way to the Moate where they would make their stand.

Chapter 30

Seth sensed the old man nearby before hearing him.

"It was late October when we first came here," the old man commented. Seth barely glanced at him, but continued staring out over the valley. "How're they treating you, boy?"

Seth regarded him coldly before jumping down from the rocks.

"They don't treat me like a school kid, but I guess that's not how you mean," he shot back.

"I see you've made the papers again," McCormac went on, "though you don't seem to be enjoying the headlines this time around." Seth shrugged. He'd been dragged to Belfast with Conor a number of times, and their appearance together caused write ups, and rumour mongering in the papers. Conor milked their association, and the publicity for all it was worth, but Seth would have been happier remaining in the background, for once. He'd never been shy of that sort of thing, his foster parents being leading socialites, his foster father a prominent businessman in the States. From a young age, Seth had been exposed to the public eye, learned how to use it, play to it, but he certainly wasn't naive about its power, either constructively or destructively. One of his foster father's tenets was never conduct business in private that couldn't withstand scrutiny in public. It was sound advice and one Seth adhered to. This business of mixing with politics was always a dangerous one. McCormac held his hand out, palm facing the younger man before pulling back.

"So it's true, your Becoming is complete. She said you were one."

"She?" Seth demanded. "The Mórrígan or Rían?"

"Does it matter?" the old man challenged, and Seth's face hardened even more. The old man involuntarily took a step back, sensing the fury and rage in the boy, yet with a grim satisfaction to know he had become Cúchulainn, and if he needed further proof of Cúchulainn's presence, the facial hair was more than evidence enough. Seth preferred being clean-shaven but Cúchulainn always felt the need to sport a short beard. Being

171

the youngest of all of Ulster's warriors, he took much joking about his boyish face and his age that, as soon as the hairs started to sprout, he let it grow as a testament to being a man. Seth experimented in his early twenties, but complained that it itched too much and that lasted all of a week. Now, the neatly trimmed beard, combined with the fiery glare, gave him an almost demonic look.

"You used me to bring her back," Seth roared at him.

"I told you your feelings for Rían would be detrimental."

"Detrimental?" Seth exploded.

"You didn't have the same reservations when I restored Cúchulainn."

"Cúchulainn wasn't about war and destruction."

"It was all he lived for, all you lived for. Would you deny that, deny what you've always referred to as your killer instincts?" McCormac replied.

Seth backed off.

"That's completely different."

"How so?" McCormac countered. "I've watched you ruthlessly eliminate competitors, both in sports and in business. What makes you so different from the one you despise so much? The answer, boy, is there is no difference. Is that why you've always hated her? Because she has always been your equal? And yet you, as Cúchulainn could only be semi-immortal, relying on your fame and your heroic deeds to keep your name alive."

He saw the rage bubbling within the younger man. Seth, as a child, had a short temper but learned to control it over the years, growing into a level and cool headed man, but with Cúchulainn, now that was a different matter, a different man. Cúchulainn's anger had always been quick, his vengeance swift, but would Seth's coolness tone down the ancient hero's fire? Seth turned away.

"Is this the only reason you wanted this meeting, to antagonise me?" he demanded.

172

"No lad, it wasn't, but I needed to know who you are now," McCormac answered. "I know about the geis Uí Neill put on you. How tightly does it bind you?" Seth sighed and relaxed his stance.

"I'm bound to it with my life. If he were in any danger right now, I'd feel compelled to go to him straight away."

"That tight?" McCormac said and Seth nodded.

"Can you remove it?" Seth asked and his shoulders dropped as the old man shook his head.

"Only the one who imposed it can lift it from you or, depending on the complexity of the geis, it could be lifted upon their death."

"And I can't kill him," Seth answered. "I already tried that one. I'm bound to him and I'm bound to Ulster."

"Now, that is a problem," McCormac said. "Even if Uí Neill dies, you're still tied to Ulster." Seth nodded. "Return to Ardscull with me, perhaps we can find a way around it." Seth shook his head.

"I can't. I gave my word I'd return," he answered. McCormac suddenly turned away, facing the other direction.

"The girls are in danger," he said more to himself, but Seth heard him. McCormac turned back to him. "Did you have anything to do with this? Was this your idea, distract me while others attack them?" Seth looked at him bewildered.

"What the hell are you talking about?"

"You had nothing to do with this?"

"Do with what?" Seth asked. The old man turned and moved away to leave, but just as he was about to disappear, Seth ran forward and grabbed hold of him. The air distorted around him and he closed his eyes against the wave of nausea that hit him.

Chapter 31

Seth waited for the wave of nausea to pass before opening his eyes again and found he still clung to the old man, who glared at him, tried to pull free from his grasp. Seth let him go and looked around, finding himself back at the Moate. From the trees and the upper mound he heard roars, the sounds of fighting and he instinctively leaped into action. The old man shook his head, musing to himself. Cúchulainn had definitely returned. There was no doubt about it as he watched Seth making his way up the mound, a long dagger appearing in his hand.

A number of assailants put themselves into his path, but as he told Seth at the top of Slievebawn, the killer instinct within him took over, and he eliminated his attackers in a cold and clinical manner as he made his way upward. Seth reached the top of the mound and found the three women fighting together as one, as though they practiced together all their lives. Rían's hair was free and he saw her pushing dishevelled curls from her face. She stiffened and glanced in his direction giving him a cautious look before turning her attention back to her assailants.

The three were surrounded by a larger circle of warriors and Seth recognised some of them as Conor's men, but not all. The old man's words made sense to him now. He thought Seth set this up, thought him capable of such treachery. He jumped into the fray and attacked the attackers from behind, throwing disarray into the ranks. He picked another weapon up from the ground and fought two-handed, working his way in as the women fought their way out.

Bodies lay strewn about the Moate, blood seeping into the ground, and in the end, there was no sound, no groaning from the wounded. There was none. Silence reigned on the hilltop.

Rían moved forward, moving seductively towards him, and pushed him against a tree, one that sat precariously close to the edge of the mound, with a long drop down if he wasn't careful about his movements.

She pinned him to the tree with her body and kissed him before he could stop her or say a word.

"I knew you'd come back to me," she said softly when she broke away and he gasped for air. He looked into her eyes and pushed her away with force, conscious of Naoise and Cíanna also standing either side of her.

"I came for Rían," he said. The woman in Rían's body cocked her head to the side and grinned.

"I'm afraid she's not here at the moment, can I take a message?" she asked, but the sarcasm was unmistakable. The old man made it to the top of the mound.

"What happened?" he demanded.

"They came as soon as you left this morning," Naoise answered. Seth saw the suspicious look the old man gave him, but he remained silent. "The Mórrígan sensed them so they didn't take us unawares. We got out of the house and made our way here," Naoise went on but the old man didn't seem assured. The Mórrígan regarded him curiously.

"He had nothing to do with it," she said, inclining her head towards Seth. "I know that's what you suspect." The old man's face hardened, and Seth wondered why, but sensed a power struggle going on here and for once, it wasn't the old man who had the upper hand. As if sensing his thoughts, the Mórrígan turned to him and smirked. With lightning speed, she swung her sword up and he found the point of it at his throat. He pushed himself back against the tree as far as it would allow, but the point bit in.

"Why did you come back?" she asked of him, stepping closer to him, putting more pressure on the sword point, easing her body against him again. He slapped her hand away, moving his head out of the sword's way, but the blade scratched him.

"I don't know why I came," he admitted.

"You thought you could save her," the Mórrígan answered, sensing his emotions. She stepped away, re-sheathing her sword. "Foolish, but admirable," she added. "Go back to Uí Neill. Tell him his ambush failed."

"There's no way he could have known?" Seth argued with her, but he thought about how quickly Conor gave in to him. Had he planned this all along?

"Uí Neill didn't plan this," the old man interrupted and everyone's attention turned to him. "This was Devlin's work."

"I agree," Seth added, not caring whether his opinion mattered or not. "Some of them were Conor's men, but the rest I don't recognise. Who are they?" he asked the old man, and everyone regarded him coolly. He shrugged at them. "What? I can't ask now?"

"You ran away," the Mórrígan spoke in a voice like ice. "You abandoned your obligations here. What gives you the right to ask? Or are you trying to play a game with both sides?"

"I don't play games. A part of you once knew that," he growled.

"That part was beguiled by you, but no longer. Even she's not impressed you abandoned us so easily," the Mórrígan shot back.

"Enough," the old man roared at them. "Devlin didn't act alone in this. He had help, from England, and other sources. This was a concerted effort to eliminate you." He looked directly at the Mórrígan. "He and others will continue in their attempts to return you to your own realm."

"This is my realm now," she growled at him and Seth saw the old man's features harden. Her ferocious look turned back to him. "Have you come to your senses and returned to us?" she demanded of him. He shook his head.

"You know about the geis, and I am bound to that. I gave my word I'd return," he answered. He felt a chill as the three women regarded him with equal expressions.

"Perhaps you can instil some of that sense of honour into Uí Neill."

"I'm doing my best," he answered.

"Return him back to where you found him," the Mórrígan said to the old man. "He is of no use to us here, and the less he knows of us from now on, the better," she said. The old man's jaw set but he said nothing. After a moment's pause, he stepped forward and took hold of Seth.

"Are you ready lad?" he asked and Seth just nodded before the wave of nausea returned.

For Rían it was like watching a film, but with added sensations. Every move the Mórrígan made, she felt it. Every thought, she sensed, and every time the Mórrígan opened herself to the elements, Rían felt a prickling on her skin, as like static electricity. She saw the Mórrígan joining with Naoise and Cíanna, watched as the three Spirits connected to each other, the other two now like ghosts in her head. Just bloody great, she thought sourly. More walls and barriers to put up to protect and shield herself, but it soon became clear that no further protection would be required. Neither Naoise nor Cíanna had any power here. Neither of them had any abilities in this area. All this magic stuff came from the Mórrígan, but somehow she could use their Spirits and accentuate her own power. Both Naoise and Cíanna, by default, gained some of this, but only by remaining connected to the Mórrígan.

For a while, the Great Queen regularly reached out to them, more to assure herself of the connection, almost as if she didn't trust the links to remain, but the connections were stable, and the checks became less frequent. Realisation dawned on Rían and she sat back, thinking it all out logically. She could sense the other two women, but it wasn't as if she could read their minds or anything. Strong emotions or any definite thoughts projected outwards by either of them she could sense, otherwise there wasn't much to it. Was this how the Mórrígan sensed her? Was this the presence she felt? Rían now knew what she had to do. She needed to create another ghost, just like Naoise and Cíanna. She needed to create a ghost version of herself.

She was also intrigued, and worried about the sudden appearance of Seth coming to their aid. He came for her, did he? Why did he feel different? From the Mórrígan, she sensed so much more about him. She felt his anger, and such anger at that. His arrogance was gone but it seemed to be replaced by ... defiance was the only word she could think of. His confidence hadn't been shaken, but that too was different. Seth had, after all, ran out of the house when he realised what happened.

That memory she got from the Mórrígan, and while Rían understood he did so more for self-preservation than from cowardice, it hurt her feelings. He abandoned her. From her vantage point, she was also in a position to see and experience the Mórrígan's side of this, and that was strangely in turmoil. The woman was torn between her strong desire for him, and wanting to put a dagger through his heart. Was that reserved for Seth, or Cúchulainn? Or both?

She watched as Seth disappeared from view but the old man remained, looking tired and weary and they set about removing the bodies strewn about the Moate. It wouldn't do to have an innocent walker happen upon them and as tired as he was, he set about this task, but felt the Mórrígan's hand on his shoulder and she joined her energy to his, working together. The Mórrígan sensed fear of her within him and smiled to herself. The power he sensed from her almost overwhelmed him and he found himself fighting not to lose himself in that seemingly endless pool of energy. How had she become so strong? He suspected the answer lay not with the Mórrígan, but with Rían. Had he missed something when she was growing up, overlooked something?

One by one, they moved the bodies to a different realm, and in truth he couldn't even begin to guess where, the Mórrígan had full control and kept that information from him, much to his annoyance. Later in the day, having returned to the house, the Mórrígan retired for the evening, exhausted from the day's exertions. She visited with Rían to check on how the child fared, hoping to catch Rían unawares. Her efforts were in vain, Rían kept a rein on her emotions and revealed nothing to the Great Queen.

Later, much later, Rían sat still, trying to practice her meditation techniques, focusing on her breathing and quietening her racing mind. She needed complete and full concentration for this. She opened herself to the elements, to the universal energy, felt it prickling on her skin. The more power she drew the more the prickling sensation grew, becoming almost painful.

Conscious of drawing on too much energy, and drawing the Mórrígan's attention to her, she eased off but fixed in her mind what she wanted to do. She needed a version of herself, an anchor, but not necessarily an interactive one. Besides, that was beyond her skills and knowledge at present. She needed a mirror image of herself and she focused on every detail, every outline. She closed her eyes and put her will into it, feeling a shift in the energy around her but also a drain on her own energy.

Opening her eyes, she saw herself. She gasped, as did her replica. Rían reached out as she had with Naoise and Cíanna, and felt this other presence before her. It felt real and substantial and she hoped it would be enough to keep the Mórrígan at bay. Satisfied with her work so far she sat back. Now she needed to get herself back to the lake in Tír na mBéo.

She fixed the image of that place, and the woman in her mind. As with the last task, she put all her energy and will into it and after a moment's hesitation, she felt a similar sensation of moving forward. She landed at the lakeshore again, with a little more grace than the first time. Nearby sat the same woman Rían met. The woman regarded her with a cool gaze, a bemused eyebrow arched at her.

"That was sooner than I expected, a leanbh *(child)*," she said as she stood and walked towards her. She placed her hands on Rían's head and a smile appeared. "And yet you have achieved the task I set you. Gráinne is ainm dom agús táim do eolaí, do mhúinteoir ar an áit seo. *(My name is Gráinne and I will be your guide, your teacher in this place)*."

Chapter 32

Seth found himself back at the Nine Stones, back by the car, with no sign of the old man. He leaned forward, fighting the nausea, and vowed never to ask the old man to move him from one place to another again, or to hold onto him when he did. But that was the least of his worries, his primary concern now was how to deal with Conor and Devlin upon his return. Whoever orchestrated the attack on the Mórrígan wouldn't have anticipated his appearance at the top of the Moate, nor his participation in helping her survive. Why had he done that, he wondered. He fought for the Mórrígan, which was insane. She was the last person in the world he would have jumped into a battle to save. However, she was still Rían, and in that tiny detail lay the difference.

He paused for a moment. Was she, though? The Mórrígan seemed in total control and Devlin was correct when he said the triune was restored. Naoise and Cíanna completed the threesome. And he just helped them. He knew he should have guessed about Naoise and Cíanna. He grew up with them after all, and as much as Naoise antagonised him and fought with him, he couldn't bring himself to kill her. Was that what the old man hoped for, childhood loyalty? It had stronger bonds on him than Conor's claim of fosterage. Did the old man also know of the possible connection to Conor when he placed Seth into the care of the Morand's? Too many questions, he thought, with very few answers. When he felt stronger, he got back into the car, taking a drink of water, washing the bitter metallic taste from his mouth, then drove back down the mountainside

He arrived back in Armagh late in the afternoon and re-entered the house, heading to the kitchen for one of Fleur's culinary concoctions, finding himself hungry after the non-stop drive. He discovered Conor was in Belfast, in an extended parliamentary session that expected to go on well into the evening. Good, Seth thought, fewer questions to answer,

"I take it boy, they're all dead," Devlin asked him from the kitchen doorway. Seth stiffened before facing the Druid.

"Who?" he asked, but he was too tired from the battle and the drive to make it sound convincing. He expected an outburst, but Devlin shook his head and entered the room, sitting at the large table.

"No games, boy, I know you were there. You weren't supposed to be, but somehow…" he answered as Seth rubbed his tired eyes and sighed. "There may be a geis on you, but that doesn't stop you from playing games with us," Devlin added and jumped, startled, as Seth's fists slammed onto the table.

"My integrity or my loyalties have never been called into question before. It's no secret how I feel about Conor, but I am honour-bound, which is more than I can say about him," he roared at the older man. "And that's twice today I've been accused of playing games."

"They obviously fear you as much as I do," Devlin answered

"Fear me?" Seth asked, almost laughing. "I'm practically a prisoner here and I've been betrayed by those I grew up with and thought I could trust. I'm not the one playing games." Devlin regarded him for a moment before nodding.

"Sit lad, have something to eat with me," he said, "Fleur, what's on the menu tonight?"

"Nothing too fancy, seafood chowder and some pasta," she answered, stepping forward. She put her hand to Seth's head and he looked at her puzzled as tension melted away. She turned to Devlin.

"It's as I told you," she said to the older man, "He's lonely here, and feeling lost, but he can be trusted and confided in."

Seth's jaw dropped.

"Who the hell are you?" he asked in whispered tones.

"I'm just the cook, dear," she answered and Devlin laughed.

"You're the one who says we can trust him," Devlin answered. Fleur sighed and took her hand away from Seth's head, stretching both hands out into the room, palms up and closed her eyes as each hand moved away from each other in an arc. She opened her eyes and took the other chair beside Seth.

"The room is sealed, we can talk freely," she said. "Devlin and I were once students of McCormac. Of course he wasn't always called McCormac, but that's the name he uses now."

"Why are you telling me this?" Seth asked.

"Why shouldn't we?" she countered. "You were a student of his as well"

"But that's different. I'm not a Druid. I have no abilities in that area. I'm…" he struggled for words to define who or what he was.

"You're a lost little boy right now," she teased, and laughed as he glared at her. "You're struggling with your duty, your obligations, but at the same time you're struggling to find out who you are, who you've been." Seth searched her eyes, looking for any hint of something, malice, deceit, anything he could fight against, but he found kindness and sincerity instead. "I helped McCormac trace back through the records to find you. You weren't an easy child to find either," she went on. "And now, you've become Cúchulainn, and in that too you're lost. You as Seth, are now, what, almost thirty-two years old?" she asked and he nodded.

"Cúchulainn died at twenty-seven," Devlin took up the explanation. "He doesn't know what it means to be a thirty-something. This is unchartered territory, for both of you. "But I'm curious to know why he wanted to meet with you."

"He said he needed to know who I was now, wanted me to go with him to Ardscull to figure out the geis, figure a way around it, but then he sensed the attack," he admitted.

"Did he ask you to go with him?" Devlin asked. Seth shook his head.

"He thought I had something to do with it, thought I planned it," he answered, but they heard the anger in his voice.

"The timing was unfortunate, that's all," Devlin said. "But you were still there," Seth regarded him for a moment before nodding.

"The old man was about to leave and I grabbed hold of him," he admitted. Fleur smirked beside him.

"Ever the hero," she said. "I dare say you found it an experience worth repeating," and laughed at his sour face. She patted his hand in a grandmotherly fashion. "If it's any consolation, Devlin was sick for days after his first experience." The older man gave her a disgusted look before turning back to Seth.

"So answer my question boy, are they all dead?" he asked, giving Seth a penetrating look. Seth nodded. "Some by your hand, I dare say," Devlin said, and again Seth said nothing, only nodded. "It's alright lad, I dare say you only did what you felt you had to. And this was foretold."

"What do you mean foretold?" Seth asked.

"Part of the prophesy McCormac is working from," Fleur began, "makes some mention to old enemies uniting, of fighting together."

"You fought with her? Together?" Devlin asked and Seth nodded.

"Cúchulainn and the Mórrígan battling side by side, and not against each other, for once," Fleur said. "So it's begun."

"What has?" Seth asked looking at each of them.

"The final battle of the Tuatha," Devlin's answer in almost a whisper. Fleur balled up her towel, and threw it at him.

"You always have to make everything sound so melodramatic," she rebuked. "We don't know for sure, and you're frightening the boy." Seth gave her a flat stare, but he knew a final battle was coming. There always was, but between whom? He suspected he was one of the prime candidates.

"If it's any consolation, I'm not welcome back there," Seth said.

"No consolation, but a comfort," Fleur said, taking hold of his hand. "But know you have a home here."

The next morning he felt more refreshed and relaxed than he had in ages. Fleur's cooking did wonders, not to mention placing her hands on his head again and alleviating all the tension. While it remained unsaid, it was implied Fleur wished to remain the matronly little old cook. Any abilities other than culinary were not to be shared. Too many secrets, Seth thought. Everyone had too many damned secrets. He dressed in sweats, planning on running a few laps about the grounds and bound down the stairs.

Trusting the geis to keep Seth in line, Conor no longer felt the need to post a guard at his door, or appoint someone to follow him about the place. After all, hadn't he proven he could be trusted by returning? Didn't they know where his allegiances now lay? He suspected Conor and Devlin talked about him last night, but he hadn't stuck around to find out. Exhausted, he retired early, falling into a deep sleep. This morning the King was taking a lie in, compensating for the late schedule of the previous night, releasing Seth from his lesson and improving Seth's temper on this fine summer morning.

He began with a slow jog to warm up before lengthening his stride and quickening his pace. Rían was right about getting back into running, the wind feeling good on his face as he went, leaving all thoughts behind. As he passed by the edge of the lawn, a small, fist-sized ball rolled across his path. He slowed and scooped it up, throwing it back towards the three men in the centre of the lawn without breaking his stride. He heard his name called, or more to the point heard the term 'Yank'. From training with them in the mornings, he had an amicable friendship with most of the men, but not all. He slowed as they approached and stood in his path, armed with hurleys.

"I heard you used to play," one said.

"Used to," Seth answered, "but not for years."

"From what I heard, Cúchulainn was a legendary player."

"So the stories say," Seth replied.

"How about it then, hero."

"No thanks," Seth answered, but at the back of his mind he itched to play. He knew where that came from, but he didn't want to give into the ancient part of him. He made himself move away, starting back into a jog.

"The stories never said anything about our hero being such a coward," the first man threw at him and Seth stopped, knowing they were trying to goad him into playing.

"If I thought you wanted to just play and not retaliate for what happened the other morning, then sure, I'll play," Seth answered and caught the hurley they tossed to him.

His grip tightened and loosened on the top of the handle as he got a feel for the weight of the ash. He inspected it for any obvious flaws or cracks, but it seemed playable. He shifted the hurley to his right hand, but what he said was true, it was years since he'd played. There'd been a strong Irish community in Chicago and he'd had plenty of opportunities to play as a kid, encouraged by the old man and his foster folks.

The men put together a makeshift goalpost using a soccer net, although the traditional goalposts were in the form of an 'H', but it was still better than nothing.

"Are you using points?" Seth asked and the men looked at each other before shrugging.

"Yeah, sure, if you think you can get close enough to get it over the bar," the first antagonist answered and a cold, mischievous grin spread across Seth's face.

"Seeing as I'm at the disadvantage of three against one, how about you let me have the first shot," he dared them. The main man of the trio shrugged again and tossed the sliotar *(ball)* to him. He stopped the ball with the bas of the hurley, the flat rounded end, and caught it on the flat of the bas. The three men backed up a few steps and took up a staggered defending formation, trying to narrow Seth's striking options, not expecting him to be able to gain much distance. Seth tossed the sliotar into the air and adopted the locking position on the hurley, griping the handle two-handed and struck the ball as it descended again. The force with which he hit it surprised and shocked his opponents, driving it the length of the lawn and into the net. He ran between them, shouldering the main antagonist out of his way, knocking him to the ground. The remaining two reacted quickly, trying to trip him with their hurleys but he took a leap-dive over them, landing into a roll, and back on his feet again. God, he loved this game. He retrieved the sliotar and turned to face them again, finding all three back on their feet.

A shout from one drew attention, but Seth ignored it until a fourth man stepped onto the grass, ready to play. He struck the ball again, sending it soaring into the air and as his opponents looked up, he barrelled through them, using his own hurley to clip an ankle or two before catching the sliotar again in his hand and running with it, taking no more than the four steps the rules of hurling allowed. He spun around and threw the ball in the air, striking again at the goal, and scoring.

185

He reined his cockiness in, knowing the dangers of giving into it, knowing it would cause him to slip up and get him hammered against the now increasing number of men on the grass. Four became six, then eight and he grinned to himself. Now things started to get interesting. They had possession of the ball this time, passing it forward. They surged towards him and he braced himself for the onslaught, hurley at the ready for defence, using the very top and the heel of it to inflict as much damage as they tried to bestow upon him. He broke through and snatched the ball from the air, swinging the hurley about him, giving himself space to play and launched the ball again at the goal, scoring again.

Eight opponents became twelve and they struggled to score against one man. And on it went, ducking to avoid a jab to the head as he ran with the sliotar, or elbowing an opponent out of his way. Thinking of how he admonished Rían for using dirty tactics, he laughed to himself. No one else knew of the joke in his mind and assumed he laughed at them. With that, the twelve-man team made a combined and concerted effort to overwhelm him. But to no avail. He swung the hurley at knees, ankles, heads, whatever got in the way, while he managed to avoid getting too bruised or beaten up. Caught up in the exhilaration of the game, Seth failed to notice the audience gathering at the edge of the lawn.

Conor stood watching in rapt awe, Devlin beside him looking grim and solemn. Seth's antics even managed to pull Fleur away from her beloved kitchen and she stood beside Devlin, glancing at the old man for his reaction. Flooring the last remaining man on the field, Seth lifted the sliotar from the ground and sent it sailing under the bar and into the net, making it a magnanimous defeat of Conor's men.

His breathing was heavy but not laboured as he surveyed the damage with satisfaction, and tossed the hurley back at his original taunter before leaving the lawn. Damn, but that felt good, he thought to himself.

"Was there ever a doubt?" Fleur asked Devlin so softly no one else heard her.

"Not any more," Devlin whispered back, watching the mischievous grin set on Seth's face.

Devlin caught up with him as he walked away from the lawn, but remained silent as he walked alongside him. Seth stopped.

"What?" he demanded. Devlin shook his head.

"No point in talking to you, boy, you're still in ríastrad," he said and saw the fire blazing in Seth's eyes.

"You make it sound like it's a bad thing," Seth accused him.

"Do you even realise what you've done?" Devlin asked.

"I had a game of hurling," he answered.

"You played like Cúchulainn," Devlin told him.

"Maybe that's because I am him," Seth retorted. Devlin caught hold of his arm.

"You just floored twelve men who were bigger, stronger and heavier than you and you barely sustained a scratch," Devlin said. "Do not lose yourself Seth." The younger man's glare was intense but Devlin stood his ground, the issue far too important to back down on.

"Isn't this supposed to happen?" Seth challenged. "Isn't this who you want me to become?" Devlin shook his head.

"No. I certainly don't," he answered. "The Cúchulainn I knew of was an insufferable boast, with too much fire in his blood, and whose ultimate goal was to secure his place in the history books for being a hero. You're not that man, Seth. You act out of honour but he acted out of a need for glory. Don't let yourself become him." Seething, Seth yanked his arm out of the older man's grasp and stormed away, but three or four steps later he stopped and turned back to face Devlin.

"What the hell am I supposed to do?" he demanded. "Be him, don't be him. All you people are pulling me in so many different directions, I don't even know who I am anymore."

"I'm not trying to tell you one way or the other, Seth," Devlin answered, keeping his composure. "All I can do is offer guidance."

"So what am I? Who am I?" Seth demanded.

"You are Seth Morand," Devlin replied, "descendant of Setanta, but only a descendant. You are not him, nor do you have to be, if you don't want to be."

"So why tell me not to be him?" Seth challenged.

"Because I like Seth, I never liked Cúchulainn," Devlin answered. Seth's eyes blazed brighter and hotter for a moment before the fire in them cooled. His stance changed, relaxed a little.

"You were there? You knew him?" Seth asked. Devlin chuckled and walked on.

"I wouldn't exactly say that," he answered as he passed Seth. Seth was about to ask but Conor approached him and slapped him on the back.

"I don't know whether to be proud or annoyed at you," he said.

"Really? Why is that?" Seth asked.

"Well, for a start, you put twelve of my men out of action, but now I know you're worth at least that number, if not more," Conor answered. Seth wouldn't even dignify that with a response and started to walk away.

"That's twice you've walked away from me," Conor accused.

"Get used to it," Seth threw back without stopping.

Enraged, Conor turned away, with such speed and force from temper, that he failed to notice Fleur approaching from behind at a slow pace, and he collided with her, knocking her to the ground.

"For God's sake woman," he roared at her, "watch where you're going." He turned from her and found himself face to face with Seth, who grabbed him by the throat, single-handed and squeezed. Conor, struggling to breathe, wrestled with Seth's hand, but to no avail.

"How dare you speak to her like that," Seth said, his voice low and threatening. "How dare you speak to anyone in that manner. For a so-called King you have little respect for the people who support you and your claim. If I were you, I'd give some serious thought to an attitude adjustment."

Conor's face turned a fitting shade of crimson and not just because of Seth's grip. Seth let him go with an almighty push, sending him staggering backwards, gasping for air.

"How did you...?" he tried to say.

"Why didn't I fall to my knees in agony?" Seth finished for him and Conor nodded. "Because it's not my intention to kill or hurt you," Seth answered in a calm and cold voice, giving Conor a thin smile to match.

Paying him no further heed Seth knelt down to help Fleur up, gently gripping her under her arm to help her stand.

"Are you ok?" he asked, concerned, and she nodded, but it soon became obvious she wasn't. Her hip took a bang on impact, and walking back to the house would be slow and painful. Seth scooped her up in his arms, and carried her back despite her admonishing and protestations. Devlin looked on in amusement.

"Is this Seth or Cúchulainn?" he asked as they passed.

"A little from column A, a little from column B," Seth replied. Refusing to listen to her, he carried her to her room, placing her on her bed.

"Why do you stay here, with him?" he asked her.

"Because this is my home now. Where else would I go?" she countered.

"You've no family?" he asked and her smile was slow in coming, showing a hint of sadness when it did.

"I did, once, a daughter, but..." she trailed off. Seth remained quiet. "I knew your mother once," she started again and he looked at her in surprise. No one ever talked to him about her.

"I'm guessing she was an almighty terror," he answered, half joking, but stopped at her solemn face. She shook her head and patted the bed, indicating for him to sit.

"She was the quietest, sweetest waif of a child," she answered. "You look like her, did you know that?" He shook his head. "The likeness is incredible. Mind you, she never had a goatee," she joked, adding some levity to the conversation. She reached out her hand and touched his cheek.

"What happened to her? All I've ever known about her was that she was a drug addict, that she died of an overdose," he said and she sighed.

"She was driven to it, by others. She wasn't strong enough to withstand the pressures on her, her obligations. She was a timid and quiet child. Eventually she couldn't take the pressure anymore, sought any means to cope, to escape, to alleviate the burden. Drugs were all too easily available back then. Dealers had no conscience about who they sold their poison to and in a very short time she became addicted."

"What was her name?" he asked, curiosity burning within him. For the first time in his life, he had the opportunity to learn who he was, where he came from.

"Alana," she answered and he gave a little sigh. Now he had a name and starting to get a better picture than the image of a down-and-out.

"Then what happened?" he asked.

"She ran away. She would have been about fourteen, maybe fifteen years old at the time. Got herself pregnant and had you just before her sixteenth birthday. Having you gave her a new sense of purpose, something outside of herself to focus on, but it didn't last for long. Her spirit was just too fragile. She ran away again when you were about four, I think. Took you with her. Perhaps she thought she was saving the both of you. Who knows? I only hope she's at peace now." Seth remained quiet, taking it all in, his history, his life. While the old man never spoke of her, claiming to have no knowledge about her, Seth suspected otherwise but always allowed the matter to be dropped. In any event, the picture he painted of her was never a flattering one. Now she was a real person.

"I think I have some pictures of her about somewhere," Fleur added. "I could try finding them for you, if you like." Something felt odd to him.

"Why would you have pictures?" he asked.

"She was under my care, for a little while," she answered. He thought about it before nodding.

"I'd like that," he said. Her sad smile returned and he sat back. Did he really want to know any more, know what she looked like? He had no memories of her whatsoever, no sense of her. She hadn't even been a ghost in his life.

"She'd be proud of you," she added and he blushed. A strange sensation for him and he didn't know why. Why would thinking his mother, his real mother, being proud of him give him this sense of ... this feeling of ... completion?

"You're a good lad, Seth Morand," Fleur told him and he smirked.

"I dare say there's a few who'd disagree," he said, laughing softly.

190

"But I'll bet that never stopped you," she replied. He laughed louder.

"Never," he agreed.

"And a ladies' man, by all accounts," she scolded playfully.

"But always a perfect gentleman," he bantered with her.

"Hmm," she replied.

"Thank you," he said as he got up and left, pausing at the door for a final glance. As the door closed, she lay back against the pillows and she covered her face with her hands. Memories and emotions, locked away for the better part of forty years, came flooding back and tears poured out.

Chapter 33

"Why does everyone call me child the whole time?" Rían asked, exasperated. Gráinne laughed beside her.

"Because you are, little one," Gráinne answered in what Rían came to realise was her usual quiet tone. "We are all children of the universe. You, of all people can understand this. In the greater scheme of the cosmos, we are only the latest arrivals amongst the stars. But we of the Tuatha de Danann have also lived for eons."

"So, I seem like a child to you," Rían finished. Gráinne's smile widened. "And the old man?" Rían asked, and a frown flittered across Gráinne's face.

"He is not of the Tuatha de Danann, nor is he Milesian. He is a Celt, of sorts, descendant from a mystic tribe."

"Mystics? I don't remember ever reading about them," Rían said.

"You wouldn't," Gráinne answered. "They are a different race from us, but to make it more difficult to explain, they are also not entirely separate from us either. It is possible for someone to be born with the ability to be a Mystic. Some think that perhaps they are direct descendants from the great and wise Dagda himself, the father of our people and the Mórrígan, the Mother of all." Gráinne paused at seeing Rían's frown.

"The great Evil Queen herself?" Rían asked. Gráinne seemed shocked.

"It appears your history has not been kind to her," she answered.

"Yeah, probably not," Rían conceded. "All the stories describe her as the bringer of savage destruction and mayhem."

"Let's not be naïve here either," Gráinne answered. "She's very good at that too, but as a Goddess, she is also about life, birth, fertility. She is a triune Goddess, the maiden, the mother and the old crone. She symbolises all stages of our lives, but she also fought for what she believed in, defended her people, her children. Your stories of her have been distorted over the years, influenced by a group of people who tried to suppress women's status and power." She paused at seeing Rían's bemused expression. "Do not look so surprised a leanbh, just because we do not inhabit your world does not mean we have no interest or knowledge of it. We return to it, from time to time, and there are always a number of us there, whether through a rebirth, or just to visit briefly. And while we have an interest, we do not interfere, we do not meddle in the lives of mortals."

"Oh really?" Rían asked. "Then why has my life been turned upside down?"

"Because you are different. You are a High Queen amongst Queens. You are a child of the Mórrígan and you are her. You belong in our Realms, and in your own world. A child such as you, while not unique, is rare, one who can live in, unite and connect with all the Realms."

Rían smirked.

"That probably explains why everyone freaked out whenever I ran away as a child," she said.

"Freaked out?" Gráinne questioned.

"Got a bit upset," Rían explained.

"Child, if they were only a bit upset with you, then you got off lightly. But truly, you are her child. The Mórrígan also never abided much by the rules imposed upon her." Gráinne stroked her cheek. "The likeness is incredible."

"I'm not as tall," Rían commented and Gráinne shook her head.

"The physical similarities or dissimilarities do not matter. It is with the spirit where you are both the same. I dare say you have a temper to match hers." Rían shrugged sheepishly. "You also have the potential to be as strong as her." Rían shook her head.

"I don't think so. I've seen what she can do, sensed the kind of power she wields. I could never control that kind of energy," she said.

"Do not underestimate yourself, a leanbh. Look at what you've learned so far, the power you can already manipulate, and in so short a time," Gráinne answered.

"Sometimes I feel like I should know this already. Maybe if I kept up my studies at the time," she confessed.

"Little one, none of this can be learned from a book. All things work out as it is meant to be," Gráinne answered. "This is now your time to learn. You are open to the power, and the possibilities around you. Allow yourself the time and the patience."

Rían thought about it for a moment.

"If I can connect with all of the Realms, does that make me one of these Mystics as well?" she asked.

"Only time can tell, child. There's a lot more to it than just the ability to move within the Realms, and you would need someone other than I to teach you," Gráinne answered.

"Someone like the old man?" Rían asked.

"Perhaps. He would be a better judge of your abilities in that area," Gráinne conceded and Rían sighed. So much for running away from him and his teachings.

She arrived back at her room, much surprised to find the Mórrígan waiting for her. The other woman sat in a chair, facing the windows, staring out. Rían glanced at the figure on the bed, finding the image of herself still there. Not sure what to do, Rían knew she needed to make the image disappear, before the Mórrígan saw them both. Within the safety of her barrier, she built up enough energy to recall her form back into herself, visualising it as snatching the energy back and she lowered her defences, carrying out her task, noting with satisfaction that it worked first time, and exactly how she planned. Maybe she was starting to get the hang of this thing. Sensing a sudden shift in energies, the Mórrígan sat forward, and turned around. At her piercing stare, Rían slammed the barrier back into place and gritted her teeth.

"What do you want?" Rían demanded, and the Mórrígan glared at her while standing up. "You have my body, access to my knowledge and my memories, what the hell more do you want?" Rían continued, matching the Mórrígan's glare. The older woman stepped closer, towering over Rían, but her anger grew as Rían adopted a bored and indifferent attitude in response.

"What are you hiding from me?" she demanded, her voice low and menacing.

"What could I possibly be hiding from you, oh Great Queen?" Rían snapped back and saw the Mórrígan's hand clenching, but to her surprise, the fist relaxed. Rían smirked, unable to contain herself but that disappeared as the Mórrígan's hand tightened about her throat.

"Don't play games with me child," she growled at her.

"Wouldn't dream of it," Rían managed to answer despite the grip on her. Rían maintained a reign on her fear and reasoned with herself, that this woman wouldn't risk harming her, couldn't risk losing control of her. From her conversation with Gráinne and from the link with the Mórrígan, Rían knew the other woman couldn't harm her, much less kill her. That knowledge helped her overcome the rising panic. Sensing her scare tactics were not working, the Mórrígan released her, and stepped back, furious.

"Do you think you can learn everything you need to know from watching me?" she asked of Rían, who saw the nimbus of light suddenly flaring around the woman, but it disappeared just as quickly. "Your boy came to save us," the Mórrígan said, changing the subject. Suspicious of where she was going with this, Rían remained quiet. "He's not the man you think he is."

"Nor is he the one you think he's become," Rían countered.

"He is Cúchulainn."

"Unlike you, Cúchulainn had a very short life," Rían argued back.

"Meaning?"

"Seth's older than Cúchulainn, and he's not the same hothead."

"Your feelings for him are too strong. When the time comes, those feelings will get us killed." She saw a frown cross Rían's face. "Sooner or later, we are going to have to face him in battle."

"Battle?" Rían said. "I have no intentions of fighting him."

"Do you think you'll have a choice?" the Mórrígan countered. "You can be assured that he'll have no such qualms about fighting us."

"Fighting you," Rían threw back at her. "I'm not going to help you."

"Really? You would allow him to kill you?" the Mórrígan retorted, seeing the confusion on the younger woman's face.

"Seth wouldn't do that," she said, and the Mórrígan laughed at her.

"He will because he thinks it's me he's fighting, and he will because he is also Cúchulainn," she argued back. The enormity of the other woman's words hit Rían.

"Does it have to come to a battle?" Rían asked. The Mórrígan softened her stance.

"I'm afraid it does. It is inevitable and has always been this way, every time Cúchulainn and I have returned to this Realm," she answered.

"But why?" Rían demanded. "And why drag us into your little war?"

"I didn't drag you, child. You were always going to be a part of it, as was he, because of who you both are."

"Ard Rí?"

"It is who you are after all," the Mórrígan gloated. "Accept your destiny a leanbh, accept who you are. Accept what you are." Rían clenched her jaw, biting her tongue. Sensing she wasn't intimidating the child, the Mórrígan departed, returning to the external world. Rían heaved a sigh of relief. She'd had the narrowest of escapes, and she knew it, but guessed the woman didn't believe a single word. Exhausted from jetting in and out of realms, and from the effort of reintegrating her copy back in, she sat in the chair vacated by the Mórrígan, and fell asleep.

Because of their closeness, she felt the child's exhaustion, felt the moment she fell back asleep. She reappeared back into the room and watched the sleeping form of Rían. She reached out to touch the girl, to connect with her, but hit that damned barrier the child erected, tingling her fingertips.

So, she'd learned to shield herself, had she? It gave the Mórrígan pause, and creating another chair, she sat down opposite the girl, opening herself and tentatively reached out to the child's barrier. Not that the Mórrígan ever did anything tentatively. She could be gentle, even tender if necessary, but her life only ever consisted of war, strife and battles. Not all of them started by her hand either.

Oftentimes she'd been reborn into times of strife, times of great unrest, where her natural leadership secured her a place at the forefront when the fighting began, or when a leader and strategist was needed. She now sat back, watched her sleeping descendant, and smirked to herself, a sense of pride in Rían, the result of millennia of offspring. Her Spirit, her essence, hadn't diminished in all that time.

She allowed her energy to surround the child, trying to blend her own with Rían's, surprised to find the child's barrier rock solid. The Mórrígan's eyes narrowed in brief annoyance, but tried again, softly pushing against the barrier, but found more and more resistance. Damn, where did the child learn that? Giving up on a direct assault, she relaxed and allowed her energy to sit on Rían's barrier, sensing the energy, the power beneath it, surprised at its strength, leaving her to wonder, how strong the younger woman was. She remained until Rían began to stir and returned to the external world. She considered leaving a thread, a connection to the child, but decided against it, guessing Rían would find it and she needed to gain the child's trust. That trust would be of vital importance in the days and months to come, if the prophecies were anything to go by.

Rían awoke with a start, regarding the second chair in her room with suspicion. She couldn't recall it being there before, but she pushed it to the back of her mind. She stood and stretched, thinking back on her original problem, and wondered how to get around the Mórrígan again and back to Tír na mBéo. She'd spent the past five days and nights in that Realm, but knew only a short time passed here, probably only hours. Gráinne tried to explain it as best she could, but all Rían could think of was a Star Trek analogy of an inter-dimensional time warp, complete science fiction but it sounded good, almost rational. The subject arose when Rían became anxious about returning as night descended upon them by the lake, but Gráinne reassured her, explaining the time anomaly. The following four days turned into an intense crash course in working with this energy, or as Gráinne called it, 'magic'. That term didn't sit well with Rían.

They started with the basics first, barriers and protection, shocking Rían to find out how fragile the Spirit was. Tough in a lot of aspects, and strong when emotions and manipulating energies were involved, but at its very essence, its very core, it was a fragile and delicate thing. Then came the rules and Rían put it into physics terms, taking the basic tenet that energy was neither created nor destroyed, but changed from one form to another. For the most part Gráinne agreed with her, and that's when the debate started. While the underlying energy of an object could not be destroyed, the item itself could and would, be altered destructively if one weren't careful. Great care, Gráinne stressed, and great restraint was required. It wouldn't do to just alter energy flows indiscriminately, but they could be bent and nudged without causing widespread chaos or destruction.

Learning that control took her days, frustrating her to the point where she thought she would go insane. Gráinne started with protection, not allowing her to progress until it became second nature to her. Creating a protective sphere about her had been easy, and even Gráinne marvelled at the speed she learned, but warned against learning too much too soon. If Rían overreached herself, she could burn herself out with too much energy coursing through her, or worse, destroy herself. The words of warning were not lost on her, but after the first thrill of lighting a candle, she found it difficult not to want to expand her knowledge and power even more.

Once she got the hang of it, how to control it, Gráinne allowed her to return to her own Realm for a rest, secure in the knowledge that the child wouldn't kill herself, or anyone else for that matter. But why make her leave a trace of herself and find a way back in the first place, Rían asked. A test, Gráinne replied, to prove not only that her arrival in Tír na mBéo wasn't a fluke, pure luck, but that she had the strength, determination and ability to reason the problem out for herself, and belief in that ability.

Now, Rían wanted to get past the Mórrígan again. Gráinne mentioned something in passing that caught Rían's attention, a minor detail of the Mórrígan not having complete control of Rían's physical body, but Rían had surrendered unquestioningly. At discovering this, anger flared, and the lesson Rían worked on, burst into flames. That, too, Gráinne turned into a lesson on the importance of control. Emotions had to be put aside. Was this why the Mórrígan was always portrayed as cold and dispassionate? More than likely, Gráinne replied, for the kind of power the Mórrígan wielded, great control was required. Yet Rían saw the other side of the Great Queen, the unrestrained passion, the fiery Spirit and Gráinne smiled at her, asking whom it reminded her. Realising she wasn't much different, Rían laughed.

So Rían had control then, did she? But how to reassert herself and not alert the Mórrígan to her actions? How to keep the woman thinking nothing was amiss and control still within her grasp? Rían sat back down in the chair and stared out the window, trying to formulate a plan.

She thought about the meditation techniques Gráinne taught her, the tensing and relaxation of muscles, and she wondered if this was the way to go to reconnect to her own body. Looking at her hand, she clenched it into a fist, feeling the muscles in her arm contracting and tightening, and focused her attention on repeating the same action on a bigger scale. She opened herself, reaching out for her physical self and tried to repeat the same action. To her surprise and satisfaction, it worked. She sensed the pain of it from the Mórrígan, as a sharp dart travelled down her arm to her fingertips, causing her to cry out. To Rían it seemed like a mild tingle, a prickling on her skin. Anger flared within her, and she wanted to strike back at the Mórrígan, deliver a nasty blow to her, and Rían unleashed what she hoped would cause a headache.

She tumbled from the chair as a blinding pain erupted in her head, behind her eyes, burning them and was unconscious by the time she hit the floor.

Chapter 34

Devlin took him up to the library, located at the top of the house and taking up the entire length of the attic, with rows of books, spanning a vast array of subjects.

"What are these prophesies you and the old man keep going on about?" Seth asked, watching the older man as he pulled out a large volume and laid it on the nearest table, leafing through the pages.

"Here it is lad," he said turning the book towards Seth, who scanned the two pages, but to Seth's sense of order and clinical neatness, the writings seemed chaotic, disjointed and disorganised.

"How do you make sense of any of this?" he asked in disbelief.

"Years of practice," Devlin said pointing to a short paragraph. "It begins here with the lines 'Born at the birthplace of Kings, at the waning of the year, when the veil of time and the barrier between the worlds grows thin.' Now Conor was born on the mound of Emain Macha. What about your girl?"

"From what the old man said, she was born on the Moate of Rathvilly, on the eve of the Celtic new year, the thirty-first of October," Seth answered.

"Rathvilly Moate, eh? Allegedly the birthplace of the last Leinster King. Conor was also born on the last day of October," Devlin said. "So we now have two who begin to fit the bill, identical birthdays, although Conor is older by six years."

"But the Lia Fáil sounded," Seth told him. Devlin nodded.

"I know, I saw, I heard too," he admitted.

"How...?" Devlin held his hand up to forestall him.

"Of course I wasn't there. But there are other means and methods of seeing these things boy," he said.

"So how can you still doubt the old man's claim about Rían," Seth argued.

"Because the old man would know how to manipulate the Stone," Devlin countered. Seth shook his head.

"He's good, but he's not that good," Seth answered. "Do you honestly think he has the ability to decide someone's fate?"

"Not only the ability, but the capability," Devlin answered. Seth shook his head again.

"The Stone is supposed to be impervious to that kind of manipulation. For centuries, it's been used to declare the rightful King or Queen. Why would you doubt it now?" he asked. Devlin paused and gave him a penetrating stare before a smile cracked on his face.

"A good point, young man," he conceded. He returned to his book. "Right, here's something interesting, it says a hero shall be reborn and rise again to stand with the King. That boy, I can only imagine refers to you."

"But the old man was engineering it so that I stood on her side," Seth said. Devlin's finger moved over the rest of the words.

"Here's the bit we were discussing the other day. Ancient enemies shall unite and in battle fight as one, but old rivalries are born anew'. You and the Mórrígan both fought together on the Moate of Ardscull, but as for old rivalries perhaps that means you will be rivals again."

"What is this intense rivalry between Cúchulainn and the Mórrígan?" Seth asked.

"I don't know lad. Don't you? Don't you have a sense of it, of why?" Devlin countered.

"I haven't a clue. All I feel is this intense hatred of her. I don't know where it comes from, or why, but it feels like an almost overwhelming rage. The old man thinks it has something to do with her and Cúchulainn being equals, but Cúchulainn could never be completely immortal," Seth answered. Devlin laughed.

"The old man always did have his head rammed so far up his own arse," he said and Seth chuckled. No one ever spoke of the old man in such irreverent terms before. Devlin went on, scanning the pages, pointing to another paragraph written in a scrawl in one corner. "Here it makes mention of the return of ancient and great Spirits. I think we can agree that bit has already happened, although I have to admit, I never once considered the Mórrígan would be one of the great and ancient ones to be returned to this world. "

"I'd have thought she would have been sent to hell for eternity," Seth commented and Devlin frowned at him.

"I thought the old man taught you Celtic history?"

"Yeah, but it doesn't mean I remember it all. Why?"

"There's no such place as hell in Celtic lore," Devlin answered. "The closest you get is a place called Dun Scáith, or Fortress of Shadows, not a bad or evil place, but it seems to be where shady figures or the lost end up. The Mórrígan certainly wouldn't end up there. Now this bit is interesting. It says not only is it the return of ancient spirits, but of an ancient power. Has your girl got this, the power? I know Conor certainly doesn't, but then again are we talking about power in terms of magic, or in Conor's case, political power?" Seth shook his head.

"Not that I know of. Within her work she's got a certain amount of influence, but as for magic, I don't think so. She's opposed to the notion of it, thinks there's a scientific explanation for it," Seth answered.

"Hmm," the older man mused to himself. "Interesting, to be that strongly opposed to something. We deny certain parts of ourselves that we don't want to admit to."

"Whoa! Are you trying to tell me she has magical abilities?" Seth asked.

"All I'm saying is not to discount the possibility," Devlin replied. "I only sensed the Mórrígan when we met in Belfast, so I can't say one way or another, but if your girl is as opposed to the concept as you say, and she hides herself in science to explain everything, perhaps she's denying her own abilities to herself." Seth broke into laughter.

"She is going to freak out if she does," he said. Devlin didn't share his mirth.

"So long as that outburst doesn't involve the use of magic or a loss of control, we should be alright," he said.

"What do you mean?" Seth asked sobering up.

"If she does have this power or ability and she can't control it, she could release it destructively, maybe even killing herself in the process," he answered.

"That's obviously a worst case scenario," Seth commented and Devlin nodded. "I don't think that will happen," he went on. "She calls me a control freak, but she's just as bad."

"Humph," Devlin answered. "Let's hope so."

"So Rían is still there, somewhere?" Seth asked.

"I couldn't say lad," Devlin answered, "but it's possible, especially if she's as stubborn as you say."

"Stubborn doesn't even begin to describe her," Seth replied.

"Then you've nothing to worry about," Devlin said with a grin.

"So you and Fleur studied this with the old man?" Seth started. Devlin closed the book and returned it to its slot on the shelf.

"I wouldn't quite say that," Devlin answered scanning the shelf and taking down a few more books. "We tried, but he's not the most patient of people, nor the most instructive, as I'm sure you discovered, and he keeps too many secrets."

Seth smirked.

"Fleur mentioned something about having a daughter," he said, giving Devlin a sideways glance.

"Alana? That's one very sad story," Devlin answered without looking up from his books, not noticing as Seth stiffened.

Seth closed the kitchen door behind him. Fleur heard the soft click but didn't turn around. She didn't need to, she had a sense of him already.

"What is it, boy?" she asked, surprising him somewhat.

"Why didn't you tell me who you were?" he demanded.

"Would you have believed me?" she countered. "No, you wouldn't have, so what would have been the point?" she answered for him. "I dare say you've struggled with the idea of belonging all of your life, but with everything you've been though, your own scepticism would have left you doubting the truth, had I told you."

"What about Devlin? Is he my grandfather?"

"Oh, were that true, it would make life so much simpler, but no."

"And my father?" he asked. She shook her head.

"We never found out who he was," she answered. "It would be better for the both of us if no one else knows you are my grandson, especially Conor. He'd only use that knowledge to manipulate us." He nodded in agreement.

"And Devlin? I presume he knows," he said.

"Some of it, but not this. I'm guessing he let something slip and you've figured this out for yourself," she said.

"He told me your daughter's name," he admitted.

"Let me be the one to tell him. He'll be upset I didn't share this secret with him, before now. He'll get over it," she said.

"And who is my grandfather?" he asked. She shook her head.

"Ask no questions boy, and I'll tell you no lies," she answered, holding up her hand to forestall the argument she knew was building. "A girl's got to keep some secrets to herself. And don't even think of throwing the question at me when I'll least expect it. I'll not tell you now, and I won't tell you then." He sighed and smiled.

"Fine. At least I now know where some of my stubbornness comes from," he answered and broke into a laugh at her look of indignation.

"I wouldn't be such a smart arse boy. I may be an old woman, but I could put you across my knee and teach you a lesson or two," she told him. He gave her his 'yeah, right' look with a sardonic grin, but that grin disappeared from his face as a pressure grew around him, making him feel as though he was being squeezed. It only lasted a few moments, but the unpleasant sensation remained.

"Point taken," he conceded.

"Now off with you," she said. "I've dinner to make ready and I don't have all day to stand about chatting. We'll talk about this again." He nodded and she smiled as she watched him go. The veil and web of lies and deception were now starting to unravel she thought, and was quite happy about it.

Chapter 35

"What happened?" Cíanna asked as the Mórrígan came around, but she refused to let the woman sit up until she checked her over. Finding nothing wrong, she helped her up.

"I don't know," the Mórrígan answered,

"Did Rían have anything to do with this?" Cíanna asked.

"No. I don't think so," the Mórrígan replied. "She's as stunned as I am."

"Was it an attack of some sort?" Cíanna continued to quiz her. Again, the Mórrígan shook her head.

"This doesn't seem like an attack," she said.

"What then?" Cíanna pressed.

"I need some fresh air," she replied. "And I need to get out of this house for a little while. Find Naoise, and the three of us can go to that forest the child is fond of." There was no need to find the other woman. She burst in through the door.

"What the hell happened?" she demanded. "It felt like an explosion in my head."

"You should've been on this end of it then," the Mórrígan retorted.

"I think you're right, we need some air. I'll drive," Cíanna volunteered.

"Don't we need to tell the old man?" Naoise asked, but felt hostility from the Mórrígan and Cíanna. "I guess not," she murmured and followed the other two.

Rían found herself on the floor, and God, how her head hurt. Her pride took the bigger hit, knowing she knocked herself out, acting recklessly, with no protection, no barrier, no restraint and no control after five days of having control and precaution drummed into her. Sitting up, she felt a sharp tingling in her body. That was one way to learn to keep emotions out of the process, she thought sourly, a hard way to learn it.

Drained and exhausted, she could only sit and watch as the three left Ardscull for Oughaval.

Rían was surprised at the intensity of the hostility directed at the old man. She knew the Mórrígan harboured resentment towards him regarding the way she'd been brought back into this world, but there was something more to it. At Oughaval, they took the long uphill path and, although the day was hot and heavy, it was cool in the woodland shade, despite no breeze. They reached the top of the next rise and ensured they were alone before any conversation began.

"What is this resentment you have for the old man?" Naoise demanded. The other two regarded her, before the Mórrígan broke the silence.

"He broke all laws to bring me back. By right, he should have waited for the next in line, for the birth of Rían's child," she said.

"That would have been too late for us, we'd be old women by then," Naoise answered.

"You could have been my senior advisors," the Mórrígan said, laughing at Naoise's unimpressed look. "My dowdy aunts," she called them, laughing loudly, and Cíanna thumped her on the arm in disgust.

"But you haven't explained this ... animosity," Naoise pressed her. "We've known him longer, so maybe we're blind to some of his failings."

"And you accept what he says without question," the Mórrígan answered.

"Not always," Naoise replied.

"Almost always," Cíanna conceded, "And it's because we've known him for so long. For the most part we've accepted what he's said, but he hasn't always been right. Remember how he opposed me going to college, to my becoming a doctor?" Naoise nodded.

"I always thought it strange, Badb the Vulture wanting to become Badb the Healer," she said, and Cíanna smiled as memories came back to her.

"He said I was Badb, born to destroy, that I wasn't Dian Cecht *(Celtic God of Healing)*, or one of his descendants," Cíanna answered. "But both my parents in this time are doctors, are healers. It was already in my blood." The Mórrígan stepped away, taking in the view of the valley.

"These are gentler times, sisters," she said, "and in this time we don't have to go to war. It would be nice to know peace, occasionally. But the old man has interfered too much. He risked too much to bring me back and now, all is in turmoil. The Realms are unbalanced. He has too much control, and yet everything is out of control." She sighed. "Perhaps this is our purpose here this time, to restore order to the chaos."

"That'll make a change for us," Cíanna commented. "Don't we usually cause the chaos?"

The Mórrígan gave her a bemused look.

"Usually, but why stick to old habits? Do you not remember our lessons of old, to always do what the enemy least expects?"

"Is the old man our enemy?" Naoise asked and the others felt the wave of worry coming from her.

"You trust him too much, sister," the Mórrígan answered, "when he should not be trusted at all. He has other plans for us, and not all of them will be to our liking, or in our best interests. Take care what you say to him." Both woman felt the conflict within Naoise.

"He's been like a father to me," Naoise admitted, and the Mórrígan placed her hands on her shoulders.

"He used you, as he's used us all, and would use us again. Even Seth hasn't escaped his manipulations," she said. At the mention of him, she felt surprise from the others. "What?" she shrugged. "I can't say his name now? He's no less a part of this than we are. He's been used as much as we have. The old man elevated himself on the wings of Seth's financial success, would have done the same with Rían, if she'd allowed him to control her life. And despite not wanting you to become a doctor, it hasn't prevented him from using your skills when the need arose."

"You admire Rían, don't you?" Naoise said surprised, and felt guarded emotion from Cíanna.

The Mórrígan smiled.

"She's stubborn, strong-willed and determined, temperamental and a hot head," she replied.

"Not in the least like anyone we know," Cíanna answered.

"She is of my line to the core, but Rían steers her own course, and has the wisdom to accept when she cannot change her path," the Mórrígan said.

"That's the part I have my doubts about, as you know," Cíanna replied, feeling Naoise's surprise. This was the first she'd heard of it, and she felt anger and hurt that they hadn't confided in her.

"I'm sorry Nemain, I couldn't tell you until ..." the Mórrígan began. Naoise pulled away from her.

"Until you knew where my loyalties lay?" she roared at her. "You thought I would tell the old man everything?" They felt her anger, but the Mórrígan stood her ground with her, opening up more of herself for Naoise to see. Naoise stopped as realisation hit her. "Rían has the same power as you, and you were afraid I'd let something slip to him."

The Mórrígan nodded.

"He is already envious of the power I have, and I have no doubts that he would control that power, if he could," she answered, the others aware of her anger rising. "That's why I am cautious with him, my sister. He is dangerous, not just to me, but to us all. Should he discover Rían's power, he'll find a way to control her, and then control me. And no man has ever, and will never, rule me," she finished vehemently.

Naoise thought upon her words and knew them to be true. While the old man was a strong influence upon her life as a child, rescuing her from a certain life of poverty, misery and a possible early grave, she never questioned his decisions even when she felt they were wrong. Her own story wasn't that much different from Seth's but she always felt she had more to prove to the old man than Seth did. He was the old man's little golden boy, and that rising star climbed to great heights. Perhaps if she'd stood her ground more, as Seth had, she would have made similar achievements, but she always acquiesced in the hopes the old man would choose her first, would want her first, for once.

Now, not even her Spirit sisters confided in her, and it hurt to find how much they hid from her. She clenched her jaw, willing the sting of tears away. The Mórrígan caught hold of her, aware of every emotion raging in turmoil within her, and wrapped her arms around her.

"I will never doubt you again, sister," she whispered into her ear, "but you must trust me on this."

"You have my unswerving loyalty. You always did," Naoise answered, and the Mórrígan could hear the heat of restrained anger in her voice. She broke the embrace but her hands held Naoise's face.

"I know," she answered, "but these are dangerous times also. Far more dangerous than if we were going to war. At least then we'd know who our enemies were. This time may be gentler, but the danger is hidden and insidious, causing us to doubt those whom we hold dear. I trust you with my life. I always have, and I always will".

Naoise nodded and the Mórrígan released her and smiled, but underneath she hid her relief from both Naoise and Cíanna.

Behind them, in the trees, the leaves stirred, but with no breeze blowing to shake the boughs. All three turned towards them, unsheathing knives they'd concealed about them.

From within the forest, a twig snapped.

Chapter 36

"Devlin tells me you two went through the prophesies this morning," Conor said to Seth as they sat eating a late lunch. "Had you read them before?" Conor asked.

"No," Seth admitted. "That was my first time to see them."

"What did you make of them?" Conor enquired.

"It's like reading any fantasy novel, you've got ambiguity about who the true heir is, a battle to be fought, and only one can be the winner," he answered.

"That's a very sceptical attitude."

"I'm a very sceptical person."

"About yesterday morning..." Conor began.

"What about it?" Seth challenged. Conor took a deep breath.

"Sometimes I have to be harsh, tough even. Too many would see me fail, see me fall," he said.

"Continue to treat those around you as you do, and you'll have more waiting to see that happen," Seth said.

"A King can't show any weaknesses," Conor said.

"Kindness is not a weakness," Seth threw back at him. "It can be a man's greatest strength."

Conor smirked.

"Too true, my friend."

"I'm not your friend. You never gave me the chance before compelling me."

"Forgive me."

"Sure. Release the geis, and we'll discuss terms and conditions."

"Ever the business man," Conor sighed. "But I'm sorry brother, I can't do that, I can't release you. I need you. Ulster needs you." He saw Seth's face hardened. "I can't help it. I'm bound by the constraints of my office, both as Premier in the political world, and as a King. Neither of us can escape our obligations, or our duty. I agree with you that the prophesies are ambiguous," he went on, smirking at Seth's look of surprise. "In fact, the major deciding factor will be the year the true heir was born."

"I don't get you," Seth replied, and a frown flittered across Conor's face at the Americanism.

"There are exactly six years between that little bitch and me. Six years," Conor answered. Seth shook his head.

"Nah. You've still lost me."

"The prophesies say the heir would be born on the eve of the sixth millennium. I've a contact in Queen's University in Belfast researching this for me, and his computer simulation puts the Celtic millennium as starting in 1990."

"You're pinning your hopes on this?" Seth asked. "I believe in computer simulations and models too, but hypothetical supposition, based on fairy tales and folklore, can't compare to proven statistical analysis. Your foundations for this belief are shaky at best." Fury flashed across Conor's face.

"The prophesies themselves are shaky, but it's all I got to work from," Conor growled.

"So why put yourself through all of this?" Seth asked.

"Because I believe in them, I believe it's my destiny," Conor answered. Seth sat back and played with his food, thinking back to Rían's reaction, just as passionate, and the complete opposite. Which one was correct? Ancient powers still existed, ancient rules still applied, the geis alone proved that. So who was the real heir, Rían or Conor? The Stone at Tara sounded declaring Rían. Was that enough to fulfil the prophesy?

"Will you stand with me, brother?" Conor asked, pulling Seth from his thoughts.

"Do I have a choice?" he asked.

"I'm not asking for you to swear allegiances," Conor answered. Seth remained quiet for a moment while he thought it through.

"I will stand in defence of Ulster, and if that means standing with you, then so be it," he answered. Not quite the answer Conor wanted, but it would have to do. The door opened and Devlin stood in the doorway.

"It's time," he said and Conor nodded, standing up. He paused and turned to Fleur.

"Thank you," he said to her. She acknowledged him with a tight smile, but Conor already turned away, exiting the room.

"What's time?" Seth asked. Conor turned back to him a smile playing at the edges of his mouth chilled Seth.

"A little ritual the Conclave is performing. Care to join me?" he said. Seth pushed his plate away and stood up.

"Sure," he answered, knowing this would somehow involve Rían and the Mórrígan.

As large and open as the attic was, so was the basement. In the centre of this vast space, a group of people stood, all hooded. The circle was cast and Seth stood beside Conor outside the circle as the misty scene in the centre of the circle came into focus, and he recognised the woods as Oughaval. The chanting from the Conclave, led by Devlin, began again, low and rhythmic, and figures began to form within the mist, hideous and malformed creatures, armed with fierce looking weapons. Beyond the trees, he made out the forms of three women, ready for an attack, and he instinctively knew who they were. He quickly glanced at Conor, but the King's attention was firmly fixed on the central scene.

He turned his own attention back to the centre, surprised to see a sphere of blue light surrounding the three women. Arrows rained upon them from the forest, but they burst into flames upon impacting with the sphere, and quickly burned away. Fury was etched on Rían's face but from the coldness of the glare, he knew it was the Mórrígan. The sphere must've been created by her, none of the others had that ability that he knew of, including Rían. The creatures created by the Conclave advanced on their intended prey, and the women took up a defensive position, as he had seen them do at Ardscull.

He glanced towards Devlin, the only one he could make out within the Conclave, and wondered if his presence here was by accident or by design. Were Conor and Devlin testing him, by having him watch this latest attack, when he could do nothing about it? Were they testing his allegiances? He could only look on, helpless, powerless to do anything, as the attack began on the three women.

"They're using magic against us," he heard Cíanna say, heard the disbelief in her voice.

"Then so can we," he heard Rían's voice reply, and a ball of fire appeared in her hand. She paused for a moment, not looking at her immediate attackers, but seeming instead to look beyond them, to be looking directly at the Conclave. She threw the ball with all her might, sending it over the heads of their assailants, towards the edges of the mist. Conor stood in its path and as Seth watched it coming closer, knowing Conor was in danger, the sensation of tightness in his chest grew, and light exploded in his head.

Instead of incapacitating him as it had the first time, it cleared his mind, made time slow down and he grabbed Conor by the shirt collar, pulling him out of the way, shielding him with his own body. The fireball burst through the circle, and Seth felt the searing heat on his back as it sailed passed them, impacting with the wall behind, and exploding into fiery fragments. Seth let Conor go, and turned back to the centre of the room. Within the circle he saw the three women transform into ravens, larger than normal birds, their cawing deafening to the ear, but despite the ear-splitting shrieking, the circle in the basement held.

As birds, they were far more nimble and manoeuvrable than their human forms, and in a series of dives, they disarmed their attackers, dropping the same weapons upon them from great heights, to devastating effect. Beaks and claws tore at flesh, large wings beat at bodies, delivering crushing blows, breaking bones. Glancing around the circle, Seth saw the effort of fighting the three taking its toll. At this rate, the circle wouldn't hold for much longer. Conor stepped forward towards Devlin.

"Let me talk to her," he said, and Devlin looked at him in horror.

"I can't let you do that," he answered.

"You can and you will," Conor told him. Seth grabbed him.

"Are you insane? I can't protect you if you step inside."

"You can if you come with me, brother," Conor answered but turned back to Devlin. "Let me speak to her."

Devlin created an opening in the circle, and the two men stepped through, but Conor held Seth back as he stepped into the mist. The misshapen army defeated, the three re-formed back into their human shapes, fury etched on the Mórrígan's face, as she stepped closer to the ethereal form of Conor.

"Give up the Ard Rí, bow to me as your rightful King," he demanded.

"Never," she hissed at him.

"Then face me in battle," he said.

"You, or the puppet you throw at me?" she demanded, knowing Seth would be listening. She unleashed a lightning strike at Conor, but Seth stepped in front of him and into her view, a short dagger in his hand that he used to deflect the lightning. "And there stands the puppet," she growled at him.

"Is that what you think I am?" Seth demanded.

"Isn't that what you are?" she countered. He said nothing in response, holding his tongue and his temper, reminding himself that these were the very ones who betrayed him, who dishonoured him. Conor came back into view from behind Seth.

"We will settle this once and for all," he said. "Choose your battleground."

With the circle undone and the mist dissipated, Devlin turned to leave but kept his head down. Anger burned within him, and he was reluctant to let anyone see it, angry at their defeat at the hands of the Mórrígan. In truth, he hadn't expected her to be so strong, but he knew she also drew on the will of the other two, Nemain and Badb. Not the names they used in this time, but them nonetheless. Seth tried to warn him, give the boy his due, and despite the boy's misguided loyalty towards them and the old man, he gave a fair account of himself in defence of his King, and he did so without hesitation. There would no longer be any doubt about where his allegiance lay.

"What's the significance of the ravens?" Conor asked Devlin as they left the chamber. Devlin turned to him but it was Seth who answered.

"The raven is the Mórrígan's symbol, her emblem, her talisman and what she turns herself into." Memories of Cúchulainn's death came back to him, the Mórrígan swooping around him he stood, dying.

"You sound like you have first-hand knowledge."

"Part of me does," Seth admitted. "I have some recollection, of being dive-bombed by a swarm of them, at some battle."

"But all three of them?" Conor asked.

"Maybe it was just an illusion, some conjuring by her," Seth said.

"It was no illusion," Devlin said, angrily. "What we saw was real, they transformed themselves somehow. I thought the ancient ritual to do that was lost, but it seems I was wrong."

He wavered a little and Seth caught him by the arm.

"How much effort did it take to fight her?" he asked. Devlin sighed.

"Too much," he answered. "My own fault, I shouldn't have underestimated her, but she's more powerful than I anticipated."

"I did warn you," Seth said, but Devlin shook his head.

"Even you couldn't have known how strong she is, not in this. Magical strength does not correspond to physical strength. Someone could be strong in magic, but not hold a sword," Devlin answered

"And if she's strong in both?" he asked. Devlin frowned at that.

"Then we're going to need every resource to face her," he admitted.

"You mean, I'm going to need all my resources," Seth growled.

"Would she use magic against you if you faced her on the battlefield?" Conor asked.

"That depends on whom exactly I'm facing, Rían or the Mórrígan," he answered.

"What if it's both?" Conor asked and Seth could only shrug. Devlin put his hand on Seth's shoulder.

"Don't worry lad. We'll figure something out to even the balance."

Chapter 37

Light began to fade as they returned to Ardscull, the door opening as they parked. The old man emerged, looking furious.

"What happened?" he bellowed to them as they climbed out of the car. All three bore cuts, scratches and bruises, but the Mórrígan seemed the most fatigued.

"They attacked again," Naoise was the only one who answered him, but not without an internal consultation with the others.

"Why didn't you allow me to come to you?" he demanded, rounding on her, the trio's weakest point. The Mórrígan sensed that from the old man and relayed it back to the others, feeling hurt and resentment in return from Naoise. Poor child, she thought, as Naoise's world crashed about her. Cíanna took her hand, and the Mórrígan gave her a comforting smile.

'You have your sisters', she sent to her in thought, 'and never forget, you are Nemain, you are Battle Fury. What need have you of this man's approval and validation?'

Naoise felt the strength of her sisters, and knew they were right, but it was hard not to feel hurt, or the loss of the only permanent presence in her life. Sure, she had Cíanna … and Seth, but when it came to vying for the old man's attentions, Seth invariably got most of it.

She and Cíanna met in boarding school, sharing a room in their first year, no doubt orchestrated by the old man. A friendship was slow to develop, Naoise considering Cíanna a rich, spoilt brat, not unlike Seth, and coming from a good and stable home, someone totally at odds with her own background. But unlike with Seth, her relationship with Cíanna grew into close friendship, their individual strengths complementing each other's weaknesses. Cíanna the academic one, Naoise more physical.

It was different with Seth. Everything with him turned into a competition, though he and Cíanna had a more amicable relationship. The three long summer months were only bearable by Cíanna's presence, often acting as an intermediary, keeping the peace, and in the process protecting them from the old man's wrath. He wasn't a patient, tolerant or forgiving man when it came to their childish squabbles.

Already feeling at a disadvantage because of her humble background, Naoise tried all she could to please the old man, to earn his approval, feeling obligated to him for having saved her from what could have been a tough and difficult life, a potentially short one. He never said it, but often implied as much as a means to quash any rebellious outbursts from her. She lived by his good grace.

Now, she found she missed Seth. Twenty years strengthened the bonds between them, competitions and rivalries aside. It mellowed them enough to even work together, compete together, support each other during mixed martial arts fights and tournaments.

From unstable beginnings, a mutual respect had grown between them, and she had to admit, she admired him, wishing she had his drive, and his confidence. And of course, it had to be said, he had great taste in women. The number of his girlfriends she'd enticed continued to be an ongoing bone of contention, and the only area where the competition remained intensely fierce.

Even in the business world, he continued to push her buttons, but positively, offering her a job in TOTAL, sending her off on a myriad of training courses, even funding her college education. Unlike the old man, Seth never held it over her. He just expected her to do her job well. He knew how to get the best out of people, was generous with his rewards, without resorting to fear or intimidation.

He was her brother, as much as Cíanna was her sister, and she missed him. It was going to be difficult to be on the opposite side of a battlefield to him, in a life and death struggle. At the mere thought of him, both Cíanna and the Mórrígan turned to look at her in surprise, but she felt comforted by them. They missed him too.

"I think we should go public," McCormac declared over dinner, deciding it was time to reveal part of his grand plan for her. "It would give us greater backing should Conor declare himself publicly as the Ulster King."

"I think we should remain as we are," the Mórrígan replied, and he glared at her.

"That sounded like Rían speaking," he accused.

"So the child and I agree on something," she commented. Beside her, Cíanna smirked. "From what I understand of recent history, there is no sovereignty here. To suddenly impose one after over a hundred years of independence would be foolhardy, not to mention unacceptable to the public. The world is not ready, nor is this country."

"But the prophesies say otherwise. They say you will be proclaimed," he argued.

"The prophesies be damned," she roared back. "A proclamation was already made, at the Lia Fáil. That is enough for now." He backed off, holding his tongue, but she saw anger burning in his eyes. "Besides, Conor can't go public, and make a grand declaration. He would be laughed out of his office, be stripped of whatever power he has within the province. *He* wouldn't be so foolish as to make this public." The last barb stung.

"And what of this latest attack, what of Conor's demand?"

"If Conor wants to fight for this, let him, I'm more than happy to oblige. I've seen how the boy fights, and Rían knows his style. I have nothing to fear," she answered. "I trust you can find a suitable place for that to happen." The old man threw his napkin onto the table and stormed out, much to the surprise of everyone except the Mórrígan.

Rían anticipated another visit, and wasn't disappointed as the flame-haired woman appeared.

"Why is the old man's suggestion, to declare ourselves to the world, so repugnant to you?" she asked. She'd sensed resistance from the girl as soon as the old man said it.

"Because this country no longer answers to any King," she answered. "To return to a monarchy would make a mockery of everyone who gave their lives for freedom."

"Was it a bloody war?" the Mórrígan asked.

"History records it as fairly vicious."

"Sorry I missed it."

"Do you think people's lives are for your amusement, and wars are for your entertainment?" Rían demanded. The Mórrígan regarded her coolly.

"Do you think I enjoy war?" she countered.

"Don't you?"

"You can sense me child. Is that what you really think? Open yourself to me and I will show you everything."

Rían shook her head, doubting the woman's motives, sensing a trap.

"Do you resist out of fear, or just stubbornness?"

"It's not out of fear," Rían answered, but the Mórrígan sensed something else.

"You fear me taking over, taking total control," she stated and saw Rían's jaw hardened. "Believe me child, whether I can or not, that is not my intent. I will open myself to you, and allow you to see for yourself."

Rían saw the nimbus of light surrounding the older woman and felt a prickling of static on her skin. She did likewise keeping all her defences and barriers in place, and reached out as she saw the other woman do, and as taught by Gráinne. The Mórrígan's power slammed into her as they connected and as memories slammed into her, she recoiled in horror.

"You were vicious," she gasped, but the Mórrígan shook her head.

"I did what I had to do, child," she answered, uncharacteristically quiet, but Rían could smell the bloodshed, taste the bitter metallic tang.

"How can you justify what you did, justify all that slaughter, as something you had to do?" she demanded.

"The fate of my people, my clan, rested in my hands. Your fate rested in my hands. Do you think me that cold-hearted and callous? And what of you? You have acted no differently. Despite only meeting your real mother for a brief moment, you were willing to defend her and protect her, to kill for her, if necessary. What then, makes you so different from me?" the Mórrígan's stare was firm, but without its usual cold harshness. Instead, Rían detected...not softness, but beneath the steely determination, lay compassion and understanding.

"There is no difference, child, only circumstance and timing," she concluded, standing up. She looked as though she was about to say more, but hesitated and disappeared, the connection between them severing abruptly.

The Mórrígan opened her eyes. Cíanna sat close by.

"Well?" she asked, seeing the frown on the Mórrígan's face.

"The child has learned a lot, much more than she could have from watching me alone and she is strong enough to resist any gentle probing from me. Someone is teaching her, and it is not I," she answered.

"Can she hear us now, know what we are talking about?" Cíanna asked, concerned, and the Mórrígan shook her head.

"No, there are some things I can still keep from her," she replied, but without any hint of triumph in that answer. To Cíanna's unease, there was a hint of resignation and weariness.

"What about Naoise?" she asked, and the Mórrígan sighed.

"She wears a mask of invulnerability and confidence, but beneath it..." she answered. "That's why I distrust him, he has broken her spirit. He would have done the same to Rían, and to me, if he had the chance. Glory and power. That's what it all comes down to, man's greed for glory and power."

"And Naoise?" Cíanna asked again.

"She may be broken, but he hasn't destroyed her. Nemain sleeps within her," the Mórrígan answered.

"Can she be healed?" Cíanna pressed, and she nodded, with a smile.

"Together we can do it. And now's as good a time as any."

In the Mórrígan's room, Naoise sat cross-legged on the floor, the other two sitting either side of her, all three with their eyes closed. The Mórrígan chanted, keeping her voice low, the language in ancient Gaelic. She opened herself to the elements, and the other two felt the forces of nature surrounding them. Creating a sphere, she made it large enough to surround them all, protecting them from any external force that could interfere, whether it be magical or human, and in this instance, also serving to contain the potentially dangerous forces the Mórrígan was about to unleash. Lightening streaked across the surface of the sphere, and cloud-like features swirled about as she chanted.

"Tá an Spíorad scaoilte *(The Spirit is freed)*

An eagla a lig amach *(The fear released)*

An Spíorad agus Corp aontaithe *(The Spirit and Body are one)*"

As she repeated these words twice more, her voice and the lightening grew in intensity. The sphere turned into a kaleidoscope of dark colours, swirls of deep reds, greens, so dark they almost seemed black.

She felt the struggle within Naoise, felt Nemain fighting the bonds of servitude the old man tied her to throughout the years. Cíanna saw them too, horrified at what the old man did to her sister, understanding the depth of the Mórrígan's rage against him, knowing it was what he planned to do to her. She directed this anger into freeing her sister, the restraints on Naoise so tight and heavy, it would require this much energy to release Nemain within her.

The lightening broke from the sphere confines, struck out at all three of them, but mostly directed at Naoise. Her body went rigid and her head shot back, her arms flung out either side of her. The Mórrígan caught one arm and gripped her, Cíanna catching hold on the other side. Naoise's back arched as her head fell further back, but her sisters kept their hold on her as lightening now struck her from every angle.

The Mórrígan repeated the last line, and Cíanna joined in. Lightning strikes hit Naoise at once, her body arching back at an almost impossible angle, the pain excruciating and, as the final strike shot through her, she screamed, blacking out for a moment. A moment was all Nemain needed to burst through in full force and fury. As they held onto her, her head fell forward, her red curls damp from perspiration stuck to her face and neck. Inside they could feel Nemain, feel her rage, her blood lust, and knew their sister had returned. The Mórrígan smiled and looked at Cíanna.

"Your turn," she said to her.

"My, what?" Cíanna said. "He's done the same to me?"

The Mórrígan nodded.

"Not as much as Nemain, but the bonds are there all the same. Something happened with you though."

Naoise looked at Cíanna with strange eyes.

"Oh yeah, now I see it," she said.

"See what?" Cíanna demanded.

"You already have power, but it's manifested itself in an unexpected direction," the Mórrígan answered.

"What are you talking about?" Cíanna sounded worried.

"You said it yourself not that long ago," Naoise answered, "you have the highest survival rate of patients admitted under your care in Accident & Emergency."

"Your power has manifested itself in your healing ability," the Mórrígan added. "Even our cuts and scratches from today are almost healed by your hands."

"You said Seth should've died in the old man's ritual chamber. In fact he did die, but you brought him back," Naoise said.

"An electrical charge restarted his heart," Cíanna argued.

"The last wound of Cúchulainn's was a fatal one, and should've been fatal for Seth too," Naoise argued back. Cíanna was about to disagree again, but stopped, sensing what her sisters were talking about.

"How?" she asked.

"You said it earlier, with both your parents as doctors, it was already in your blood, he just failed to see it for what it was, your innate ability to heal," the Mórrígan said. "Do you think releasing Nemain was all my doing? Whether you realise it or not, you found where the old man bound her Spirit."

"I did?" Cíanna sounded surprised. The Mórrígan nodded.

"Think you can find where he bound Badb?" she asked. The anger on Cíanna's face was more than answer enough for her, and Cíanna changed places with Naoise.

This time the bonds were looser, requiring less effort on the Mórrígan's part, but she also had Nemain's power to call on, and Cíanna's own power from within, and the break was less severe, less traumatic than with Nemain. Once completed, The Mórrígan's satisfied grin disappeared as she grunted in pain.

"What is it?" Cíanna asked.

"Headache," she answered through gritted teeth.

"The same as this morning?" Cíanna asked, and she nodded.

"At least I'm not losing consciousness this time," she muttered but pain sounded in her voice. Cíanna took her head in her hands and checked both eyes, felt the back of her neck for any obvious and physical signs of something wrong, using her newly realised skills to delve deeper, but found nothing to explain the pain.

"I can give you a pain-killer, maybe a sedative to help you sleep it off," she offered. "Maybe you're overexerting yourself."

"Maybe," the Mórrígan admitted, but in truth, she didn't think so. "Just give me something to stop this pain at least."

The old man sat in his study, brooding, sipping from a generous measure of scotch. Damn that infernal woman, he growled to himself, knowing it was entirely his own fault, but blamed timing and circumstance for conspiring against him over the years. If he'd returned the Mórrígan at the correct and appointed time, none of this would be happening.

The prophecies ordained this time to be hers, to achieve greatness, to obtain power. Now she seemed prepared to throw it all away, to walk away from the opportunity. Bloody woman, he thought, and bloody Gods. Would they ever grasp the notion that their whims and fancies impacted on and messed up the lives and plans of men? How they messed up his plans?

He needed to get her back on track. Already she started influencing Naoise into a rebellion, and that was the last thing he wanted. Having lost Seth already, he was damned if he was going to lose Naoise too. But her growing power was a worry. That shouldn't have happened, shouldn't have been possible. The child Rían never showed signs of having any ability before this. Perhaps it took the rituals to unlock that potential, but had he also unleashed something uncontrollable as well?

Now she only added to his difficulties in making him choose a battle site. This highlighted a problem, she had no champion. With Seth now under his geis, and on the other side, she had no one to stand for her, to fight for her and he was damned if he'd allow her to fight herself, no matter how good or strong she was.

As for the battleground, he needed somewhere historical, somewhere powerful, where old energies existed. He thought about it, knowing he also needed a battleground that unsettled Seth. He had no doubts the boy would be Conor's champion and as such, the old man wanted him off balance, wanted the Cúchulainn part off balance.

A location came to mind, but it would bring them close to the enemy. That brought with it another problem, the time he now lived in. Technology could be unforgiving, and in this technological era, having a battle in plain view of surveillance cameras, satellites and other detection equipment was undesirable.

No, this required privacy, not wanting it to become a public spectacle, and the only way to achieve that was to leave this Realm. That required a shift in time, in dimensions. In order to achieve that, he would need help, someone to aid him in that particular task. He had someone in mind, someone with a vested interest in this, and by engaging him, McCormac knew he couldn't be accused of trickery or deception.

He heard the scream from within the house, fearful of another attack, but he had no sense of power being used. In that moment he felt Naoise being wrenched from him, like a thread pulled to breaking point and beyond. The shock of the bond snapping caused him to cry out, a sharp pain exploding within him, which left him breathless, and he knew this was the Mórrígan's doing. How the hell did she manage to hide it from him? How had she concealed it? That worried him.

The second tear was less painful as Cíanna was ripped from him as well. His worry now grew to fear, knowing he now had no control over any of them.

Chapter 38

"Knockbridge?" Seth growled at Devlin. "What are they hoping to achieve? That it'll frighten me? Nice try."

"We won't be in this time either. McCormac proposes shifting to a different time," Devlin answered.

"Why?" Conor was about to ask, but Seth got there first.

"We need somewhere away from modern technology and prying eyes. Do you want the Gardaí, the Police Service of Northern Ireland or the army descending on us, which they would be likely to do at such a mass gathering," he answered.

"Mass gathering?" Seth demanded. "Just how many are you expecting to this circus event?"

"Everyone," Conor answered. "This will be the biggest event of the last two millennia. Do you think she will be there alone?"

"But just who is everyone?" Seth pressed for an answer.

"There are more interested in the outcome of this than you can imagine," Devlin answered.

"Like who?" Seth persisted.

"Other Druidic Sects for a start," Devlin began. "Those whom you met in the Conclave, are only representatives for their individual organisations, they all have a vested interest. There are other people working behind the scenes, with enough power to ensure everything turned out as it should, those who've helped Conor achieve what he has, and ensured that the prophesies will be fulfilled."

"By helped, you mean manipulated, made everything fit nice and neatly?" Seth demanded and Devlin frowned, not liking what the lad implied, wondering what put him into such bad form. He was far too surly and wondered if there was yet another clash between the two lads.

"What are you implying?" Conor growled at him and Seth turned to give him that cool look that Devlin now recognised as Fleur's, only Fleur's lacked any sign of malice. Seth bristled and seemed fit to kill Conor, if the geis would have allowed it. Since gaining the Kingship, Conor changed, and not for the better. He'd always been a bit of a spoilt child. Bright and clever, and quite amenable most of the time, but spoilt nonetheless. Kingship made him conceited, arrogant. Perhaps Conor's head was filled with his right to rule, took it too much to heart, and it corrupted him.

Devlin thought back on it. That corruption started long before the Rite of Kingship. Somewhere in the intervening years since college to now, Conor changed, losing his humanity, his sense of decency. He became selective in the knowledge he retained, holding onto the parts of the prophecies he believed referred to him. Devlin knew he should've been more vigilant. The signs were there after all. Subtle, but there nonetheless.

"I wasn't implying anything," Seth answered, barely concealing his sarcasm. Damn that lad, Devlin thought, he was too adversarial, and Conor didn't tolerate those who questioned or stood up to him like this. But then again, as much as the geis held Seth, Conor was in an equal bind. He couldn't risk losing Seth.

At the first opportunity, Seth quizzed Devlin on gessa, their restrictions and their limitations, and discovered he wasn't as confined as he'd thought. So long as Ulster and her King were in no immediate danger, he could go anywhere, whenever he wished. Seth disappeared a total of five times, evading security every time, but making a point of re-entering in a brazen and forthright fashion. Last night was his latest disappearing act. Was that the source of friction, he wondered?

The two lads continued to bicker and snipe at each other, but Devlin tuned them out. He had more immediate problems, such as preparing for this time ritual. He knew he needed to consult with Fleur on this one. Bending time had always been her strongest area. The room grew quiet and he snapped out of his thoughts in time to see Seth storming out.

"Push him too far, and he may not be there when you need him the most," he warned Conor. Conor turned to glare at him.

"And where can he go?" he demanded.

"Far enough away to be unable to reach you or save you in time."

Chapter 39

"Where did all these people come from?" the Mórrígan asked, both astounded and annoyed, as she surveyed the surrounding encampment below them. They journeyed to Knockbridge via helicopter, and she got a bird's eye view as they came into land. The old man pointed out Clochafarmore, visible from above, and a smile touched her lips as she remembered Cúchulainn's heroic last stand.

"Everywhere," the old man answered. "Your return has been anticipated for a very long time, and many have remained faithful to you, their faith and belief passed on down through generations."

She was escorted to her tent in the centre of the encampment and, at sensing her sisters, turned around to find them at the entrance. The old man approached and all three turned to regard him with cold stares, which unnerved him a bit, but he did his best to hide it.

"I'm meeting Devlin to create the time shift," he told them. "I thought perhaps you'd like to attend." She shook her head.

"I trust you don't need my help," she answered, and he bit back a retort as he left. She followed him at a discreet distance, looking on as he met with Devlin in the valley below, watching as both men faced each other and exchanged words, but she was too far away to make out their conversation. She was soon joined by Naoise and Cíanna who both watched on with unconcealed curiosity.

Down in the valley the two men faced each other.

"Any suggestions on when and where?" McCormac asked Devlin.

"The words 'go to hell' come to mind," Devlin shot back, and McCormac laughed at him.

"Now you grow a backbone?" he shot back and Devlin's jaw hardened at the insult. "Might I suggest we go back a few centuries," McCormac added. Devlin shrugged.

"Wouldn't there be a risk of some of the locals coming across the camps? Gatherings of this size would be enough to alert whatever militia controlled the area," Devlin replied, keeping his cool.

"A fair point," McCormac conceded. "What do you suggest?"

"We leave this realm completely, shift out of this timescape," Devlin answered. McCormac paused and considered it for a moment.

"I never thought I'd hear myself say this, but for once I think you're right," he muttered. "Ready?"

"Whenever you are old man," Devlin shot back. He connected to McCormac, as he did years ago when Devlin was under the other man's tutelage, and for a moment, McCormac regarded him with curiosity.

"You've actually studied since you left me?" he quizzed the younger man. It was Devlin's turn to give a sly grin. "Who's been teaching you?" McCormac demanded, but Devlin held his tongue, revelling in his former teacher's consternation. Devlin gave him a shrug.

"Perhaps you and I weren't compatible," he offered the old man by way of explanation. McCormac's eyes narrowed in anger.

The Mórrígan felt the shift in the energies surrounding them, felt the strength of both men as they performed the ritual to bend time, and from the corner of her eye, she noticed movement of sorts. She heard Cíanna softly gasp beside her as she watched houses and farm buildings disappear and forests replace them on the surrounding hilltops.

"What have they done?" Cíanna asked.

"They've brought us back in time," the Mórrígan answered. "But not too far, perhaps three or four hundred years, or so. We've also shifted out of …" she struggled for the right word. "Phase," she said. Both Naoise and Cíanna knew Rían supplied the technical word.

They watched as the men in the valley below them parted and the old man returned. The Mórrígan's attention wasn't on him as she spotted a familiar figure standing at the edge of the Ulster camp.

Seth stood at the edge of Conor's camp, having scanned the surrounding landscape, out of habit more than anything else, for any signs of impending foul play, almost hoping for something to be out of the ordinary. As if this, what was happening in the centre of the field, was an everyday occurrence.

The waiting ate at him, and he always hated this unnecessary hanging about. But he knew that this was all part of the ritual of battle. He stood instead and watched Devlin and the old man at work, but his gaze wandered up the opposite hill to the three figures that stood at the edge of the woods at the top. He instinctively knew who they were. Fleur stepped up behind him.

"How are they doing?" she asked, indicating the two men. Seth's eyes flickered to them before returning to the top of the hill.

"I think they've finished," he answered and Fleur followed the direction of his attention.

"Is that her? The one in the middle?" she asked, and he nodded. "She's pretty," Fleur commented and Seth turned to regard her.

"You can see her from here?" he asked surprised, and she grinned at him.

"No more than you can at this distance, but I've seen her on TV. She's quite striking," she answered. He smirked. "You still care about her though," she said and he continued to stare at the trio at the top of the hill, clenching his jaw, keeping his emotions in check. She squeezed his arm as she turned to go.

"Have faith boy, you'll get her back," she said, and walked away.

Chapter 40

"Concentrate," she said to Naoise as beads of sweat appeared on her forehead at the effort.

"I'm trying," she answered through gritted teeth as she tried to maintain the tiny sphere of blue light she held in her hand. Inside the sphere, there was movement, tiny figures moving about, talking, but so far, Naoise had only been able to conjure the scene. She needed to work on the sound. Suddenly the sphere winked out of existence. "I couldn't hold it any longer," she admitted. "I couldn't keep the connection to you." The Mórrígan laughed, one of those rare occasions when the mirth reached her eyes.

"You weren't drawing any power from me at all. I had no input. You did this on your own," she told her sister. "I told you, you had this ability." Naoise looked at her astounded, then glanced at Cíanna.

"I'm starting to feel left out," Cíanna commented.

"Yours is a different kind of magic," she reassured her. "Herbs, potions, medicines, that's powerful magic in itself, and I've no doubts I'll need it before this ends. I suspect Conor's Druid has set some sort of protection about their camp. Would explain why we can't hear anything."

"Agreed," Cíanna answered. "They've no doubt shielded their camp as we have ours." The Mórrígan nodded.

"But we need to know what is going on over there," she said and turned to Naoise. "Why don't you give it another try?"

"Why don't you try it with me?" Naoise hedged. "Together we could break through their defences." The Mórrígan shook her head.

"The idea is not to break through, that would only alert them to what we're doing. Besides, they'd know it was me, would know my signature. You're only learning so your probing would be a little more...delicate, more subtle than mine," she answered. She felt mirth from the others and narrowed her eyes, knowing she'd just stated the obvious.

"I'll give it another try," Naoise said and focused on her hand again, getting the sphere to spring back into life. A shadow fell upon them as someone entered the Mórrígan's tent. The old man stood at the entrance, disbelief and anger etched on his face. Naoise closed her hand, extinguishing the sphere she had just created on her own, and both she and Cíanna stood up, sensing from the Mórrígan that it would be best if they left. The Mórrígan also stood, and faced the old man. He stepped aside, allowing them to leave.

"What are you playing at?" he growled at her. "You're letting Naoise think she can do that, letting her think she can control energies."

She shrugged at him.

"She can," she simply answered.

"Naoise doesn't have the ability, I tested her as a child," he growled at her.

"The same way you tested Rían?" she countered, and without acknowledging the child had any capability, she confirmed the old man's suspicions. "Naoise has ability, but her fear of you suppressed whatever power she had. Nemain on the other hand, has ability, and the knowledge to use it."

"I restored Nemain years ago. Together they never showed any signs," he argued back.

"You may have restored her, but you kept her confined, subdued, and meek in order for you to control her, and Cíanna. Was that your plan for me?" she roared at him. He backed up a step, sensing and feeling her anger, her rage, but steeled himself and stepped forward again using his height to tower over her.

"I did what had to be done," he growled back at her. "You should not be here, fighting a usurper for the right to reign. You should already reign supreme."

She didn't succumb to his intimidation.

"With you by my side, no doubt," she growled back. "Is that how you'd have me, your puppet Queen?" She glared at him. "I warned you old man, you are only a Druid. Your purpose here is only to aid the Gods, not control them."

She brushed passed him, knocking him aside as she stormed out.

"That infernal man," she growled at her sisters as she entered Naoise's tent. Naoise closed her hand and the tiny sphere she had been holding disappeared

"We saw, and heard," Cíanna admitted.

"You were eavesdropping," she said, her hands clenching and unclenching, which the others noticed.

"I'd offer to spar with you, work some of that tension out of you," a new and more forthright Naoise said. "But I'm not taking the brunt of your temper right now. Do a kata, calm down."

She relaxed a little, and smirked.

"Sound advice sister, but since when did you ever walk away from a fight?" she retorted.

Naoise laughed.

"Never, but I'm not fighting you. Can't risk injuring you before your big day," she replied. "Have you told him you're going to fight?"

She shook her head.

"He's not going to be pleased when he does find out," Naoise added.

Chapter 41

Seth finished a run around the perimeter, satisfied by the level of security protecting the camp. If he wanted to disappear for a while, he'd find it somewhat difficult to escape from so many watchful eyes. Back at his own tent, which reminded him of the American Civil War re-enactments, large, square and white, he did a few katas to cool down and stretch, and knew he'd need to practice his sword-play later in the day. If he was the one who had to face the Mórrígan, he wasn't going to walk up to her unprepared. He had no doubts he would be facing her, and he guessed he'd known from the moment all this madness started. He took a cold shower, the only kind available in the camp, but at least he had room service, he smirked, as Fleur brought him breakfast. He caught her with one arm, and playfully landed a kiss on the top of her head, cold water dripping from his wet hair on to her. She shoved him off with a shriek as a drop landed on the back of her neck.

"There's something happening, up in the main tent. You should probably be there," she advised, and he nodded as he wolfed the food she'd brought him. He finished towelling off, dressed quickly, and made his way to the largest tent in the centre of the encampment.

"And I'm telling you, you're putting your men at risk," he heard Devlin say as he stepped into the tent, immediately putting his hands up in surrender as an automatic rifle pointed at him. God, how he hated guns, and Conor knew it, knew Seth regarded them with contempt. Conor gave a nod to the guard, and the gun was lowered, allowing Seth to step further into the tent.

"What's going on?" he asked and caught Conor glancing at Devlin. The older man did not look happy.

"Conor has decided to send a squad to deal with your friends," Devlin told him and received a glare from Conor in return. "Personally I think he's sending these men to a certain death." Seth glanced at Conor.

233

"I think you're right, they'll know as soon as your men get close to their camp," Seth agreed with Devlin and Conor scowled at him.

"And how are they going to know, brother? You planning on sneaking out of here tonight, to warn your girlfriend?" Conor shot at him. Seth sighed.

"Thought never crossed my mind," he answered, with a hint of sarcasm. "But she's already defeated a squadron sent by the Conclave."

"She also had you helping her that time," Conor threw back at him. Seth's face hardened and his eyes flickered for a brief moment towards Devlin. "She certainly didn't need my help," he answered.

"Both of your objections have been noted, but you're too late, they've already left. The attack is planned for tomorrow at dawn," Conor told them. "And you," he pointed at Seth, "you don't leave my sight until they return." Seth glared back, but said nothing.

Chapter 42

The Mórrígan stood at the edge of the forest, a cloak wrapped around her, keeping her warm against the dawn cold and dampness. A dense fog enclosed the valley below her, and she smiled to herself. She closed her eyes and opened herself to the elements around her, sensing the mist, its moisture, its energy. She inhaled and slowly exhaled her breath, and when she'd emptied the air in her lungs, she opened her eyes to see the last of the mist floating away. In the distance, she saw a lone figure standing, holding a staff in the air. She projected her spirit at the figure and found herself beside Devlin, Uí Neill's faithful Druid. Free for the moment from the confines of Rían's body, she stretched to her full height, as tall as Devlin himself, and her long red hair streamed out behind her. She playfully circled him, her ethereal hand stroking him. He seemed unfazed by her sudden presence.

"Foolish man," she said softly to him, "using my own tricks against me. Did you think you could hide them from me, your spies, your little band of assassins?" she asked of him and on cue, shouts and screams came from the hills. The sound of gunshots echoed about the valley. It shook Devlin's composure. He began another incantation but her hand flew up, grabbing the words as they materialised from his mouth. He stopped and gasped in shock.

"Witch," he hissed at her and she just smiled, but her eyes glinted like ice, and as ethereal as she was, her hand grabbed him by the throat.

"You dare speak to me in such a manner?" she whispered into his ear as he fought for breath. "I used the mist of concealment when we, of the Tuatha de Danann, landed on the shores of this isle. I led our armies into battle with the Fir Bolg, and defeated them, so that mere mortals like you could live and prosper here on this land. I am older than you can imagine, more powerful than you can ever know, do not try my patience with these childish tricks."

She let him go, propelling him backwards while he struggled to catch his breath. From the hills behind her roars and screams, mixed with gunfire, continued to echo as her forces found and killed Uí Neill's soldiers.

At hearing the shouting, Conor emerged from the largest tent behind the Druid, followed closely by Seth. They stopped short at seeing her standing there.

"Who the hell are you?" Conor demanded but the Cúchulainn part of Seth recognised her, and told Conor. "What are you doing here? What are you doing to my men?" Conor demanded, as the uproar continued. She stepped closer to him.

"Nothing more than you would have them do to me," she answered low and menacingly. She turned to Seth.

"Hello, lover," she said to him. He took a step back, feeling anger bubbling up inside him. "You keep dangerous company these days."

"No more dangerous than if I kept company with you," he retorted and she laughed at him.

"If you change your mind my love, you know where to find me," she said. With that, her ethereal form wavered, transforming into a raven, circling them, cawing loudly before climbing into the air. The raven flew towards the Mórrígan's camp, to the three cloaked figures standing at the edge of the forest, at the top of the hill. It landed on Cíanna's outstretched arm, before hopping across to Rían's inert body, slowly re-integrating itself. She looked to Cíanna and Naoise who stood either side of her.

"Having fun?" Naoise asked.

"Starting to," she answered. "What of Conor's men?"

"They've all been killed, or captured," Cíanna answered.

"Good. Return the bodies to him," she said, and returned to the camp.

"Does that mean I'm off your suspect list," Seth hissed at Conor, taking pleasure at seeing the King's confusion at this turn of events. "You wouldn't listen to us, and now you've gotten how many men killed?" Seth stalked off, knowing he'd be left alone for the first time in 24 hours.

Conor kept to his word about not letting Seth out of his sight and had either shadowed him everywhere about the camp, or, as was more often the case, insisted Seth stayed with him as he saw to the business of this war. From this vantage point, Seth sat back and watched the Ulster King in action, and concluded that he had very much underestimated this man. Conor, it seemed, liked to give the impression of being somewhat unintelligent, but it was all a ruse, a ploy, to make his opponent open up and reveal more than normal. Seth mentally kicked himself for falling into that trap. It wasn't like him to be so easily fooled, but damn, Conor was good.

As he sat in on one of the myriad of meetings Conor had, Seth lost himself in his thoughts, and he idly scratched at the largest scar on his torso. His fingers traced along the entire length of the scar, feeling it tingle, which started as soon as they arrived, and he knew it had to do with being this close to Clochafarmore. Power remained in the stone and he got a sense of it every time he wandered close. Now, released from Conor's watchful eyes, he stormed back to his own tent.

Later that evening he practiced his swordsmanship, calling on three of the better fighters to go up against him at one time, focusing all his anger into a single knot of rage. As with everything Seth seemed to do, it drew an audience to the clearing where he practiced. Armed with two wooden practice swords, he didn't give his three opponents a moment's respite as he fought them, losing himself in the rage, in the swords, knowing he was in ríastrad, but damn, it felt good. It felt clear and pure, and for the first time in days, his thoughts cleared and nothing weighed heavy on his mind.

The sun was near setting when his opponents could no longer stand, no longer face him or his fury. Seth's tee shirt clung to his body, damp with sweat. His muscles ached, but only as a result of exertion, he sustained no injuries, something that couldn't be said for his opponents. Even though the swords were wooden, they still caused damage, and bruises and welts showed on the other three men. If he fought like that on the appointed day, he would have no problems. But would he? Could he?

Cawing drew his attention away from his practice arena, towards the trees, and he spotted three ravens perched on a branch of a nearby tree. He looked about him at the ground and plucked decent-sized pebbles into his hand. Holding onto ríastrad for as long as he could, he took aim and fired one of the small stones at one of the three birds. To his annoyance wings flapped and the bird launched itself into the air before the stone could hit home, emitting a loud and angry caw. The other two birds flew into the air to join the first. Seth steadied his hand and let another stone fly, catching one of the birds in the wing. His aim was a little off, the pebble only caught it at the bottom of the wing feathers, but it was enough to produce angrier cawing, this time from all three. Without warning, one of the ravens dived at him, aiming for his head, but only managing to grab a clawful of his hair, which it yanked as he ducked. Furious, he hurled the remaining stones in his hand at his feathered assailant, but missed as the bird arose in the air, spiralling upwards.

"Bitch," he growled after it, as he rubbed his head.

Chapter 43

"His anger is going to beat us, little one," the Mórrígan told her. "I need your help in this coming battle. I need for us to work together." Rían glared at her.

"You want me to help you kill him," she accused the older woman.

"Believe me child, he'll have no qualms about killing us," she answered. "You saw how he fought, and that was only a practice."

"So you've decided you're going against him," Rían said, and she sadly smiled.

"Do we have a choice?" she asked. "Who else would stand as our Champion, who else could?"

"Naoise?" Rían threw back and the Mórrígan shook her head.

"Even with Nemain unleashed within her she couldn't," she replied. "They've grown up together, she wouldn't face him in battle. Besides her arm was badly bruised by that stone he threw at her. I wouldn't expect her to be battle-ready for a while."

"Not even if your life depended on it?" Rían shot back.

"But my life wouldn't depend on it," she answered, "only hers would. All it would mean to us, Naoise's senseless death aside, is that we surrender the title of Ard Rí, and march home with our tails between our legs. Is that what you want?" Rían gave her a sour look.

"I never wanted to be Ard Rí in the first place, so losing it doesn't bother me," she answered sharply.

"You would let Conor win, allow him to take the title? Seth would be the only one who could win it for him and Conor would likely have Seth killed, or worse, tie him to the Ard Rí forever. What better protector than a hero? If he made Cúchulainn stronger, using whatever means possible, we would lose Seth altogether. Is that what you want, child? As for us, Conor wouldn't allow us to live. So long as you remain alive, one of the true bloodline, you will always be a threat to him. As for me, I could never return again. With you dead, my bloodline would be wiped from the world."

"No, I don't want that," Rían admitted, "but there has to be another way. Can't we get Seth to step down as Conor's Champion?" she asked, before realising she now co-conspired with the Mórrígan, who gave her a little smirk.

"I'm open to suggestions, little one, but I can think of none," the Great Queen replied. "He is not Seth anymore, you know that, don't you?" she pressed, sensing Rían's conflicting emotions, and knew the younger woman was at a difficult juncture. All that was required was a gentle, delicate push in the right direction. "He's now Cúchulainn and yet he is the Seth that you knew. Unlike us, where we have remained two single entities, within him they've become one man." Rían seemed deep in thought.

"You have an idea?" the Mórrígan asked.

"It's just a thought, but..." she paused for a moment. "I'll need to do some research. Seeing as I have nothing better to do here, I may as well make myself useful and call up some books," she mused to herself before realising what she had said.

"So you have discovered how to use your power, little one," she commented with a hint of satisfaction. Rían coloured, but clenched her jaw.

"A little," she admitted.

"And shielded it from me. How?"

"From watching you," Rían answered. The Mórrígan's eyes narrowed at the lie, but to Rían's surprise, she let the matter drop.

"I'll leave you to your books then, little one," she said and left.

Rían stood by the windows of her room later in the day, watching with grim satisfaction as the Great Queen cried out in pain. The woman in control of her body held her head as another spasm hit. Using the same shielding she had in place to hide her growing power from the Mórrígan, the shield now protected Rían from any backlash from the headaches she created. After that first disastrous time, Rían learned her lesson well.

Gráinne told her that practice made perfect, and Rían practiced and perfected this move every evening, and for the past week or so, the Mórrígan now suffered with migraines. Rían suspected she wasn't fooled, and after that little pep talk from her, neither was Rían. The woman was trying now to win her over, to take over completely. Rían watched as Cíanna prepared and administered a powerful sedative to her body, knowing the shield also protected her from the drug's effects, but not so the Mórrígan.

These headaches began without warning, and without knowing the cause of them, the Mórrígan was powerless to withstand the agony, much less escape it. Cíanna eased her head back onto the pillows as the drug began to take hold, and her breathing slowed to a steady rhythm as she slipped into unconsciousness.

She shouldn't be susceptible to normal human afflictions such as headaches, or even migraines, and it worried her, wondering if it had anything to do with how she had been restored to this mortal world. The old man's methods had unbalanced the realms, throwing everything into chaos and disorder. Could that account for her suffering from these all-too-human ailments? Was it possible Rían's body just wasn't able for it? With her own new found abilities Cíanna held the other woman's head in her hands and concentrated, delving deep within the body to find a cause, but found herself blocked, found a barrier that she didn't know how to overcome. She let go and sat back, deep in thought, but she had a hunch.

Satisfied the Mórrígan no longer posed a threat to her, Rían willed herself into the Great One's room within her mind, just to confirm to herself that her scheme worked. She was a little shocked to discover that a room existed for the Mórrígan, but then again, Rían supposed the woman's spirit had to go somewhere. Rían cautiously stepped towards her with a sense of smug contentment, happy to know she had no defences against modern medicine.

At the start she hadn't been sure this would work, but with practice Rían honed this particular skill and so far, so good. Slowly dropping her shield, she opened herself to the elements around her, and immediately felt her energy, her power. So much power, Rían thought, not allowing herself to be intimidated by it, and set about putting the rest of her plan in place. In order not to drain herself, Rían needed to manipulate some of the Mórrígan's own energy, and she allowed herself to connect to the other woman, almost overwhelmed by that power. Rían physically took a step back and took a deep breath, blocking the Mórrígan's energy, stopping it from drowning her, and used it to build a cocoon about the sleeping woman, reversing the energy flows back onto her. When she eventually woke up, she should then only sense her own power reflected back on her, and not Rían's.

All of this was guesswork, but how else would she learn? As Gráinne told her repeatedly, only her dreams, imagination and fears limited her, fear the biggest hindrance, the most dangerous force in the realms. Fear caused doubts, caused energy flows to fail, caused the deaths of spirits caught in its grip.

Satisfied with her work so far, she stepped away, and as she had seen the other woman do, she completely opened herself and projected herself forward. She had a destination in mind and while she didn't have the exact location, she nonetheless knew where she wanted to be.

As with the first time she'd ever tried, she felt a rush of wind as she moved with lightning speed, and a juddering stop as she arrived. Idly she wondered if this was what it would be like to come out of space-travelled hyper-speed. At least with practicing this, she learned to anticipate the stops, and not land on her ass every time she came to a halt.

The figure before her stood with his back to her and she took a moment to look about his tent. When her gaze returned to him, she found herself looking into Seth's glowering eyes. She smiled at him, but something about his look made the smile falter.

"Do you think to tempt me by coming in her form?" he growled at her. Shocked, she took a step back, looking confused and perplexed.

"Seth, it's me," she said, stating the obvious. He sneered and took a threatening step towards her.

"You tricked me before using her, I won't fall for it again," he roared at her. Shocked and stunned, she just stood there and gasped as his hand grabbed her by the throat. As ethereal as she thought she would be, his grip caught hold and she struggled for breath, eyes widening in fear. She willed herself away from there and in a flash, she returned to the safety of her room, her hand going to her throat, still feeling his fingers there.

Trying to steady her breathing, she tried to figure out what happened, and it dawned on her. He assumed she was the Mórrígan, using her form. She found herself annoyed at him, that he hadn't realised it was really her. This was going to need a rethink, a serious revision of the plan and methodology.

She willed herself into Tír na mBéo. Gráinne already explained that this was the Land of Life, of the living. It was a positive realm, one where dreams could come true. A thought struck her. Dreams. The notion came to her in a flash of inspiration. If this was also a dream world, could Seth come here? Could he be brought here? Would he continue to think of her as his enemy, even in this world?

Only one way to find out she supposed, and reached out to the elements, trying to get a feel for him, a sense of him. It took a while, but she found him, and used her desire for him to try drawing him to her. It took more energy than she anticipated, but she felt his presence grow stronger. She heard the sound of gravel crunching underfoot as he walked across the lakeshore towards her.

"Now you're trying to trick me in my dreams?" he demanded.

She squared up to him.

"We're in place called Tír na mBéo, one of the other realms," she explained rather heatedly. "If I was her, I'd be a helluva lot taller, and have longer, redder hair. This is a spirit world, we appear as who and what we are."

It seemed to take a moment for her words to sink in.

"Rían?" his voice was a whisper. He hesitated a moment before grabbing her and embracing her, kissing her. She pulled away.

"Wow," she said, breathlessly. "I'd almost guess you missed me."

"How's this possible?" he asked.

"Magic, apparently," she answered, with a hint of sarcasm.

"But you don't believe in magic," he countered.

"I know."

He shook his head, but pulled her into his arms.

"I'm glad you're okay," he said, "I thought maybe…"

"She had taken over? Like I'd give in that easy."

He laughed.

"I thought maybe I'd lost you," he said.

"Oh yeah? Trying to choke me was a clever move then."

"That was really you?"

"Yeah. I didn't expect you to get such a good grip though." She rubbed her throat.

"How was I supposed to know it wasn't her playing games?" he defended himself. "You'd be the last person I'd have expected to appear before me, out of thin air, using magic. And what about the Mórrígan, what's to stop her from finding us here? How do I know she's not using you to get to me?" he asked.

"For starters, not everything is about you, or about attacking you, and she won't find us. I've already sorted that out."

"How?" he asked, and she gave him a sly little smile that made him wary. "So, who'd I hit this evening?" he asked, changing the subject.

"Naoise," she answered. "How'd you know it was them?"

"Three ravens in a tree, watching, spying, who else would it be? Who else could it be? One raven I might have overlooked, but not three. Is she badly hurt?"

"You put her arm out of action, but Cíanna's been trying to heal it."

"I guess she won't be standing as a Champion then," he said, leading the conversation to where he wanted.

"That was never the Mórrígan's intention. She plans to fight herself, or me or…both, I suppose. I don't want to," she told him. He stroked her face.

"Me neither, not if you're still in there," he admitted.

"I'm trying to find a way around it," she told him. She pulled away from his embrace. "But wait until you see what I can do," she said with almost child-like excitement. She turned away from him and he watched her with a mixture of unease and curiosity. The sky overhead turned dark and cloudy. Thunder crashed overhead and the wind whipped about them. Lightening appeared and streaked across the sky above them. Somewhat startled, he took a step back, away from her. She turned back around to face him, laughing, revelling in the mayhem of the elements, riding on the feeling of euphoria that it brought. His expression hardened, concerned that she was enjoying this too much, and he wondered how much of the Mórrígan she was turning into. Was she and the Mórrígan now becoming one as he and Cúchulainn had? She stopped and the storm ceased as though it never existed. She looked at him with unease.

"If you're not her, you're almost as powerful as she is," he told her. She shook her head.

"She's so much more powerful than I am," she answered. In this place she saw his thoughts, felt his emotions. "I'm not turning into her."

He looked surprised and shocked.

"How did you…" he started and she laughed at him.

"This place is all energy remember, and you, here, now, this is just your energy, your spirit, your soul. What you're thinking, especially if you've a strong emotion tied to it, creates an energy wave. Sometimes it appears as a flash of an image. It manifests itself here, and right now you're afraid I'm going to become her," she said.

"How have you been able to do it?"

"I found out by accident, but when I found myself here I met a woman, an elder. She's taught me a lot of things."

"So am I dreaming all of this?"

"To you it's a dream, but it's part of my reality," she answered. He smiled, growing more confident by the moment that Rían sat before him. She seemed to look past him and smirked, shaking her head.

"Glad to see you're starting to come around," she said with a hint of sarcasm. He shook his head.

"This is not good. I'm not going to like this place," he replied.

"Why not?" she asked puzzled.

"Now you know what's going on in my mind. My God, woman, is nothing sacred?"

Chapter 44

A weakened Mórrígan appeared the next morning, and Rían sensed the drugs affecting her. She watched the child flicking through pages of one of the numerous books strewn about on the floor. Conjuring books didn't require any degree of skill, but the vast array of them, all on Celtic mythology surprised the Mórrígan. The child also changed clothes and showered, judging by her damp hair and faint spicy scent in the room. Not that she needed it. In this place, the rules governing normal bodily functions ceased. A spirit didn't need to shower as a body did. Now what was the child hiding, she wondered.

She turned her attention back to the books, some stacked to one side, and she guessed Rían discarded those, others open, and arranged in a semi-circle.

"You going to sit down, or stand there staring at me?" Rían asked without looking up. The Mórrígan's anger flared, but she caught it, cooled it, and sat down.

"We've received word, Conor has declared Seth his champion."

"I know," Rían said, and when questioned, pointed to the windows. "I can still see what goes on," she added tartly.

"Have you found anything?" the Mórrígan asked, redirecting the conversation back to her original reason for coming. Rían's fingers tapped at the pages of one book, seemed lost in thought for a moment. the Mórrígan waited with uncharacteristic patience, and as a frown flittered across Rían's face, she sat forward. "What is it child?" she asked. Rían shook her head.

"Something, but … I'm not sure it would work," she muttered.

"Tell me," she pressed. Rían looked up at her.

"Macha's curse," she answered.

The Mórrígan laughed but shook her head.

"A clever idea, but impossible," she answered.

"Why?" Rían asked.

"The curse only lasted nine generations. Cúchulainn wasn't affected by it, he was partly immortal, and only just turned 17 years of age. He was barely a man then," she answered.

"Those are the questions I've been asking myself," Rían said, "but there are a lot of variances, a lot of different factors this time. For a start, that was Cúchulainn. We're not talking about him, we're talking about Seth, his descendant. Seth is mortal now, and not the son of a God, that we know of. And something else I found in these texts." Her hand pointed to a stack of about three or four books, all open, but laid one on top of the other. "These say Macha actually cursed them for nine times nine generations. That means the curse would last for 81 generations. Now, if we hypothesise that all this happened around the beginning of the AD calendar, say two thousand and twenty-five years ago, and going on the assumption that a new generation occurs maybe every 30 years, that means we are now up to the 67th generation," she said.

"You've given this serious thought," the Mórrígan said, trying to hide the proud smile that threatened to reveal itself.

"Of course," Rían answered.

"And if it's only every 25 years?" the Mórrígan asked. Rían looked apprehensive.

"Then we're up to the 81st generation and this the last time it will ever work," she answered. The Mórrígan sat, deep in thought, before a smile began to creep across her lips. "Is it possible that a remnant of the curse could exist? I think so," Rían went on, "Seth told me he sustained every injury, every wound Cúchulainn did, the scars manifested on his body as proof. I saw the before and after versions of the same body. If the old man was able to bring all that stuff back, then why not all the curses put on it as well? Surely if there's a trace of it…" she left the rest unsaid.

"Would you inflict such pain on him, this man you care so much about?" she asked her.

Rían shrugged.

"If it saves his life, or saves me from making the choice to kill him. Women have survived it for centuries, how bad could it be."

The Mórrígan smiled.

"You would condemn a man to suffer five nights and four days of labour pains?" she asked, laughing. "As for the pain child, it is the most brutal, and yet the most exquisite pain a woman can ever experience, because in the midst of that searing agony comes new life. Men do not understand this, nor do they have the will or strength to bear it. Do you still wish to put him through that?"

"If it saves his life," Rían repeated, her voice almost a whisper.

"Then I'll speak with the old man," the Mórrígan answered.

McCormac sat in silence after she asked him about the curse. Naoise and Cíanna knew better than to ask what she was up to, at least not in front of the old man. Whatever arguments they had amongst themselves, they showed a united front to the world. It was always that way with them. Besides, they could sense some of what she was thinking, and knew she was trying to give their little brother a chance of survival.

The continuing silence was suspicious. The old man sorely wanted to question her motives for coming up with this idea, wanted to question where the notion had come from. Macha's Curse? True, Macha had cursed all Ulstermen to be stricken down at the time of Ulster's greatest need. But that was almost two millennia ago.

He held his peace for a moment longer, hoping she would grow uncomfortable with the silence and divulge more information, but to his annoyance she also kept her own counsel and smiled at him, that cold, sly, knowing smile.

"It's possible," he conceded. "The Curse's power may be diminished after all this time, but if a remnant exists, and can be restored, then it can also be re-empowered. Are you that anxious to not face him on the battlefield?" he asked knowing this was aimed at Seth and she laughed.

"Not in the least. I just want to have some fun with him first," she answered, but he remained unconvinced.

Chapter 45

He awoke the next morning back in his tent in the Ulster camp. It seemed like he'd spent days in that other world, but in the cold light of day he paused to wonder. If it was only a dream why did he still feel her lips on his, her body against his? As he went for his morning run around the perimeter of the camp, he lost himself in the memory of it, finding Fleur arriving with his breakfast as he finished his routine.

"Conor sent a statement this morning, announcing you as his Champion," she told him. "Just thought you'd like to know." So it begins, he thought, and gave her a grunt in response. As he picked up a glass of juice, she looked at him askance. Something was off, different with him, she thought. This wasn't the same man she witnessed fighting yesterday. He caught her looking at him strangely.

"What?" he questioned with a defensive edge.

"Where have you been?" she asked, and he took a step back, wishing his grandmother had no special abilities.

"Just around the camp," he answered.

"That's not what I'm talking about boy, and you know it," she scolded him.

"There're guards all around the perimeter, where else could I've gotten to?" he countered.

"I'm not talking about physically leaving the camp," she snapped back, surprising him with the intensity of her growing anger.

"I think it was called Tír na mBéo," he answered, and after a moment, she nodded.

"I felt you leaving last night, and now today, you seem ... different, calmer," she said. "You obviously found something you were looking for, or someone." Seth almost choked on a mouthful of juice. "You found her, didn't you?" she asked and he paused for a moment before nodding. "Was it your girl or the Mórrígan?" she asked.

"Rían," he answered.

"You're sure?" she pressed, and he nodded. "And I'm guessing she was the one who brought you there," she added. He nodded again. "Tread carefully lad, Tír na mBéo may be the land of the living, the world of dreams, but even there, not everything is as it seems," she warned him.

"So was it just a dream or was I really there?" he asked. She put her hand to his chest and seemed to concentrate for a moment.

"You were definitely there," she answered, and gave him a motherly, 'I-know-what-you-were-up-to' look. "And she's strong, strong enough to pull you into that Realm, but at least she's learned to control it. Just be careful lad."

"But she said that who we are is how we appear in spirit in those worlds," he said. She thought about it.

"That is true, for the most part, but never forget, the Ancient Ones, such as the Mórrígan, are older than time itself. She knows more about the ways of the Universe, and all the Realms, than anyone else, what can and can't be done, but Tír na mBéo is one of the safer worlds," she lectured him.

"Safer? How?" he asked.

"In that place the rules are more or less set," she explained. "So much so, that even she would have difficulty bending them, much less break them. In these matters, where the Realms are concerned, a delicate equilibrium, a careful balance must be maintained. To break the rules in one, throws the others out of balance."

"But hasn't her return already done that?" he argued. She nodded.

"For once though, the Mórrígan is not to blame," she said.

"Then who is?" he asked.

"McCormac," she answered

It was mid-afternoon when Devlin received and opened the communiqué, taking his time reading it. He frowned and reread it.

"They have declared a war on Ulster," Devlin said, troubled. "Something is not quite right here." Conor snatched the thick paper from him and read the declaration.

"I don't see anything wrong," he said. Seth held out his hand and Conor handed it over. He saw the words, 'advancing on Ulster and her armies' and 'War on Ulster' and he agreed with Devlin.

"I think you're right," he said to Devlin, and Conor glared at him. "It's as if they're making a direct threat to Ulster, not to us."

"Exactly, and that's what troubling me," Devlin said. "We're kilometres away from the old border."

"But wouldn't declaring against Ulster, put me directly in their way?" Seth asked. "They know about the geis, they know how I'm tied to this, so why deliberately declare a war on Ulster?" Devlin shook his head.

"I honestly don't know lad," he answered.

"Oh for God's sake," Conor exploded at them. "You're both acting like old men frightened by a bunch of women. Can't you see things are falling into place, as ordained, as you said they would? We'll have our war, my Champion will kill that bitch, and then I'll be Ard Rí, as I should be." Seth glanced at Devlin, but neither man said anything. Conor threw his hands up in disgust at them. "You're a pair of doomsayers," he shot at them as he left the tent.

"I've created a tyrant, haven't I?" Devlin said to him.

"Yes, you have," Seth answered. "And thanks to the geis, I can't even kill him."

"Be careful boy," Devlin said. "I've a feeling something is about to happen, and this is directed at you somehow." Seth nodded before following Conor out.

He found Conor at the practice arena, already warming up as he arrived, and he gritted his teeth in annoyance. As Conor limbered up, Seth felt a twinge low in his stomach. He tried to put it out of his mind but the pain persisted and grew throughout the training session, and Seth struggled to keep his balance and concentration. He leaned on his staff, beads of sweat forming on his forehead from the effort. The searing pain came in waves, feeling as though he was being cut in two. He leaned over trying to catch his breath and ease the pain.

"What the hell is wrong with you?" Conor demanded, but Seth couldn't answer, he couldn't draw enough breath to speak.

The wording of the declaration troubled Devlin. It put Ulster in danger. Why Ulster, he wondered. He knew McCormac wouldn't attack the province. True, they were within travelling distance to the border, but why declare against Ulster. A thought came to him, a memory, something to do with Ulster's greatest need. What the hell was it? He wracked his brain trying to remember.

A wail arose, and grew in its intensity. As the moaning of men began to emanate from the encampment, the significance of the letter hit him. Clever, he thought admiringly, but trust a woman to find a woman's solution to the problem.

Chapter 46

Seth fell into an exhausted but fitful sleep. Even in his dreams the pains never subsided, and he found himself in an even stranger predicament. He was back in the little cabin in Tír na mBéo, and knew Rían was close by. He sat on the floor, his back braced against the wall as another pain hit. He gritted his teeth and tried not to scream. As Rían came through the door and saw him, she gasped, covering her mouth with her hand to hide her shock. He looked up at her, holding his swollen belly and gasped for air.

"Do you know anything about this?" he panted.

"Eh, yeah," she answered. "It's called the curse of Macha. You're in labour, which explains why you've dreamed yourself as having a big pregnant belly." She knelt down beside him.

"Whose bright idea was this?" he demanded, and she hesitated.

"Mine," she answered, and he looked at her, his eyes accusing her.

"Why the fuck would you do this to me?" he cried out. She caressed his face.

"To try to save you," she said.

"You call this saving?" he demanded, but another contraction hit and he cried again, grabbing her arm, almost breaking it. As it passed, he released her.

"Ow," she said rubbing her arm, and he glared at her.

"Ow... Doesn't... Even... Begin... to describe it," he growled.

"I'm sorry but it's all I could think of to keep you from the battlefield, to keep you from having to face us," she said and kissed him. As another one hit he sat forward and held his breath.

"This is going to sound corny, but breathe out and push against it, it'll help," she said into his ear and heard him groaning with the effort. He leaned back gasping for air, resting his head against her shoulder.

"Tell me about this curse."

"Don't you know? The Cúchulainn part of you must know it."

"I'm not exactly thinking straight at the moment," he snapped back, "I'm not remembering much of anything."

"There was this woman call Macha," she began, "whose husband went to a fair attended by the King, an Ulster King I might add, who boasted that his horses were the fastest in the land, nothing could beat them. Despite her warning him not to say anything about her, or even mention her, the husband pipes up that his wife is faster than the King's horses. So hubby drops her right in it, and for making such a wild accusation, the King put the husband under arrest while messengers were sent to bring Macha back and prove her husband's claim in order to save his life. She's a bit annoyed, to say the least, but she goes to the fair, very heavily pregnant. When she gets there, the King demands she proves her husband's claim to run faster than his champion horses. She tries to point out her obvious situation but he's adamant, and wants to see her prove it there and then. So, she runs the race and wins well ahead of the horses, but as she crosses the finishing line, she goes into labour. She gave birth to twins right there, but she cursed every man present, that when Ulster was in danger and in dire need of her warriors, they'd be struck down by labour pains for five nights and four days. And with that she died." He grunted.

"So I can thank Conor's ancestor for this unique experience?"

"Looks that way."

"He's getting worse," he said, "getting more paranoid and consumed by what he thinks is his destiny. He hates me but he's doing his best to keep me on side, keeps sending women to pleasure me."

"You're rejecting them all, of course," she said, mentally kicking herself for sounding like a jealous girlfriend.

"Oh God, no!" he exclaimed. "How do you think I got myself knocked up?" he joked. She thumped him then held him close as another contraction hit.

From the shadows a figure moved, stepping away from the couple. The Mórrígan had seen enough, satisfied Macha's Curse worked, and yet she marvelled at the cleverness of the child to have found this world, her cleverness at hiding it from her. The depth and strength of her power astonished her, as well as her ability to incapacitate her.

Cíanna figured the headaches out, stumbled upon the truth of their origin. In this matter, Rían acted in a cold and calculating manner, and the Mórrígan found she was both furious and proud. Rían was starting to display at lot of the same traits she, herself, was accused of. But just how strong was Rían, she wondered. She doubted the child's power stopped here, and if she could enter other worlds, then what else was she capable of? Jumping in and out of Realms was an ability only the strongest could control. Pulling someone else into one of these Realms required not only an unprecedented level of power, but also incredible control. More to the point, where had she learned this, and learned to conceal it?

She re-entered Rían's body and found both Cíanna and Naoise waiting for her, Naoise impatiently pacing the room, until the Mórrígan opened her eyes.

"Well?" Cíanna asked.

"You were right," she answered. "She's creating the headaches."

"The little bitch," Naoise growled, and Cíanna shook her head.

"How?" she asked.

"Somehow she's discovered how to inflict pain onto her body, like sending an electrical charge, a bolt of lightning."

"Does she know we're having this conversation? Can she hear what we're talking about?" Naoise asked, worried. The Mórrígan shook her head.

"She's not even in here," she answered. "She's ah, otherwise occupied." Both Naoise and Cíanna gave her a suspicious look. "No," she told them, annoyed at their lack of trust in this. "I haven't done anything to her, yet. She's in Tír na mBéo, with Seth and I can tell you the curse is working."

"Seth? But how?" Cíanna asked.

"Rían brought him in," she answered. Cíanna shook her head, incredulously.

"Is she really that strong?" she asked and her sister nodded.

"But the old man..." Naoise started.

"Never detected it, as he couldn't with either of you, for whatever reason," the Mórrígan finished.

"What are you going to do?" Cíanna asked, a hint of misgiving in her voice.

"That child is in for a rude awakening if she thinks she's going to get away with this," she answered, but they both heard the cold steel in her voice.

"And the curse is working? You're sure?" Cíanna queried.

"Oh yes, if Seth's swollen belly is anything to go by," she answered. They looked at her as though she'd lost her mind. "Even in Tír na mBéo he can't escape the contractions," she explained, "and he's dreamed himself as being about nine months pregnant."

They looked at her incredulously before bursting into laughter.

Chapter 47

Devlin and Conor looked up as the medic entered the tent, looking for them amongst the other advisers.

"How many affected now?" Devlin asked.

"Two hundred and fifty men so far," the doctor answered. "I'll confess, I'm at a loss as to what is causing it. It's not food poisoning and none have sustained any sort of an injury or infection."

"I know the cause, and it's a little outside your professional capacity and your help," Devlin told him.

"I can give them sedatives, painkillers to help," the doctor said but Devlin shook his head.

"Giving them drugs would only prolong their agony," he answered. "Best to let them suffer now than drag it out for weeks."

"Just what the hell is wrong with them?" Conor demanded. This mysterious illness shook him and Devlin was at a loss to explain how, or why the King remained unaffected. Conor put it down to the Gods sparing him, so he could take his rightful place, but Devlin doubted it.

"Macha's curse," Devlin said. "That's why they worded the note in that way. Macha's curse says that in a time of Ulster's greatest need, the men of Ulster would be struck down with birthing pains."

"Birthing pains?" the doctor asked incredulously. "You mean to tell me, all those men are going through labour?" Devlin nodded. Conor couldn't believe what he heard, the doctor even more sceptical. This went against every tenet of his training. True, he was a practitioner and believer of the old ways, but somewhere there was a point where pure science took over.

While medicine was a meeting of the ways between the two worlds, between the ancient, herbal, natural remedies and the modern surgical methods, what happened now was unheard of, unprecedented.

"Why isn't everyone affected then?" the doctor asked, glancing at Conor. Devlin frowned as he formulated his answer.

"I'm not sure," he confessed. "There are a number of possibilities. A lot of the men here are not descendants of the men who heard the original curse. Their families moved to Ulster after it happened. The curse itself has two conflicting stories about its life span, one account says the curse would only last for nine generations, the second account says nine times nine, and I'm now assuming the latter is true. One possibility is some of them are outside the generational limits and therefore remain unaffected."

"And Seth? How is it he's affected? He's American, it shouldn't have an effect on him," the doctor asked.

"His family, both original and fostered, were from Ulster," Devlin answered.

"But he's Cúchulainn," Conor said. "Cúchulainn wasn't affected before, why is he now?"

"Because he's only Cúchulainn in spirit, and he is also in a mortal body. He may be his descendant, but he is going to be affected like the rest of them," Devlin answered.

"All this witchcraft is outside my area of expertise," the doctor said, "but is there anything I can do?" Devlin shook his head.

"Not a damn thing. They just have to suffer through this for the next four days," he answered.

"Another four days? My God that's inhumane," the doctor exclaimed. Devlin nodded in agreement, watching a messenger enter and hand something to Conor.

"What do you expect? It's a woman's curse inflicted on them by another woman," he said watching Conor.

"Speaking of that pack of bitches..." Conor snarled, handing the paper to Devlin. "It says she'll meet us on the field tomorrow at dawn, and she's observing the old rules of single combat."

"With Seth incapacitated, who are you going to get to stand as Champion? She's certainly not going to allow you time for him to recover," Devlin said.

"I'll stand myself," he answered. Devlin couldn't believe his ears.

"Are you insane?" he bellowed at the King. "Do you think I have risked everything to get you to this point, to the verge of becoming Ard Rí, just to see you throw it all away?" Conor regarded him coldly.

"I'll be facing her. I think I can beat a woman," he retorted. Devlin shook his head in dismay.

"You are a fool, boy, to take this matter lightly. Perhaps you do deserve to die, out of stupidity, if for no other reason," Devlin said in a low tone to him, but all in the tent heard. Conor glowered at him before storming out.

How dare the old man speak to him like that, and in front of the others, his own men. He felt his control slipping. First with Seth and now with Devlin. How much longer before others followed? He knew he needed to win this battle with the girl to become Ard Rí, to hold onto that control. He made his way to Seth's tent.

Unlike the rest of the afflicted, Seth opted to remain alone. Conor sent one of the prettier girls earlier in the day to attend to Seth, but wasn't surprised to find Fleur there instead. She looked up as he entered and Conor tilted his head, indicating she leave. She did so, but only after a moment's hesitation. The woman showed no signs of fear of him. When all this was over and he was Ard Rí, this attitude would change. He stepped closer to Seth and hunkered down beside his bed. He grabbed a handful of hair, pulling Seth's head closer to him.

"How do I fight her?" Conor whispered in his ear as his Champion lay in pain.

"Who?" Seth asked, defiant to the end, despite the agony.

"Rían," Conor said, referring to her by name for the first time. It took effort but Seth laughed. "Tell me how to fight her," Conor snarled.

"She'll rip you to shreds," Seth hissed at him, gritting his teeth through another contraction

"Tell me how," Conor demanded and watched Seth gasp for air. In spite of the apparent agony, Seth looked at him with those piercing blue eyes and grinned at him.

"She'll use whatever she has to, but she'll fight with honour," he managed to say in between gasps for air.

Conor smirked.

"Good. If she fights with honour, than she can be beaten. I wouldn't be stupid enough to let any advantage slip by," he sneered, letting go of his hair. Seth grabbed him by the arm and Conor saw fury and pain in his eyes.

"If you fight with dishonour on the battlefield, and even if by some miracle you win, your men won't follow you," he warned him. Conor shook him off.

"She's only a woman," he said.

"You're a fool if you make that mistake."

Chapter 48

Sleep was a merciful release, but he was exhausted as she pulled him into that other Realm. She was waiting for him as he walked through the door of the cabin. Thankfully, his large belly from the previous night was gone, though the pain remained, albeit dulled. He wondered if that was Rían's doing, or the result of the herbs his grandmother gave him.

"We're meeting on the battlefield tomorrow. With you out of the picture, who's going to stand as Champion?" Rían asked.

"He's standing himself," Seth answered. "What about you? Is she still planning on fighting?" She nodded. Despite the herbs and the apparent dulling of the pain, another spasm hit, a mild one, and he gritted his teeth as he pushed against it.

"Be careful. He's a dirty fighter," he warned, regaining his breath.

"More than I am?" she asked surprised. He smirked.

"You fight with dirty tactics. Believe it or not, there's a difference," he said. "You wouldn't consider stabbing someone who was defenceless, nor had their back turned, would you?" She shook her head. "Well, don't leave your back exposed to him. Don't let your guard down, ever. And if you're not sure of your next move, step out of his reach until you figure it out."

"You do realise you're betraying your own side," she told him. He shook his head.

"It's not my side, and it's not my war, but both you and Conor have forced me into it," he answered. She looked at him, hurt and stunned.

"How have I forced you into it?" she demanded.

"You called a war on Ulster. The geis he put on me means I have to defend Ulster, defend it against you," he argued. She stepped away from him.

"That's not fair," she said angrily.

"And causing me labour pains is?" he retorted. "None of this is fair, but this is how it is. It's part of who we are now, and part of what we have to do."

"Hey, I never wanted any part of this, remember?" she threw back at him. "I'm doing the best I can, with what I have." She saw the muscles twitching as he clenched his jaw. Whether it was from gritting his teeth against the pain, or biting back a reply, she didn't know. In the space of a day, his face had grown gaunt and the Mórrígan's words came back to her. No man could bear this pain, this agony. 'Well, serves him right', Rían thought sourly, for getting himself geis'd, for getting her tangled up in this. If she hadn't met him, if he hadn't insisted on her as his interviewer.

"How the hell is this my fault?" he growled at her. Surprised, she glared back at him. "You know that image thing you were telling me about?" he asked, and she nodded. "Well, I'm not the only one it works on, sweetheart," he shot at her.

She clenched her jaw, biting back a response, knowing she'd regret saying it as soon as it was said. A smile slowly broke across his face as he looked past her. Damn, she thought angrily, she really needed to control her temper more, especially here.

"Fine," he conceded. "You kept your promise to keep me off the battlefield. While I don't agree with your method, or the result, there's nothing more we can do about it. And if you have to join forces with this woman, then do so. It might be your only chance." He saw her look of apprehension. "What is it?"

"She doesn't know what I can do, doesn't know how strong I am. If I open myself to her, there's nothing to stop her from taking over completely," she answered. He moved closer to her, put his hands on her shoulders and gently squeezed.

"You've held her off for this long. I know you can withstand her," he said, his voice growing softer and calmer, less combative. "You've never doubted yourself before, and the eve of a battle is neither the time nor place to start." She sighed and gave him a haunted smile.

"I'm just afraid I'm going to lose myself in this," she admitted.

"You won't. You haven't up to this point and you're stronger than you know," he reassured her.

"And how would you know?" she asked. He just grinned at her.

"You're not the only one with sources," he answered smartly.

Rían returned to her room, confused and exhausted by her meeting with Seth. She had never seen him so angry, and yes, she had to admit, the solution wasn't ideal, but it was all she could come up with. The start of the battle was only hours away now, at dawn. How archaic, she thought, but at least she wouldn't be facing Seth. True, she had faced him before, but not in a life or death situation. Would she have been able to kill him? She didn't have the answer to that, and at least now she didn't have to find out.

Deep in thought, she failed to notice the indistinct shift in energy from behind her. After all, what had she to guard against? The Mórrígan was out cold, but the apparent weakening state was now beginning to worry Rían. If the Mórrígan was that weak, if her own body was that weak, would she be capable of fighting in the morning. The blast of energy took her by surprise as she slammed into the wall, then fell to the floor. She looked up to find the other woman standing over her, fury and rage etched on her face.

"Did you really think you would get away with it," the older woman snarled at her. Rían stood and wiped the blood that dripped from her nose. First Seth, now this. A bad start to an impending battle, she thought.

"Get away with what?" Rían asked, only angering the Mórrígan even more.

"Your little headache trick," she said. "Childish and crude."

"It worked, didn't it?" Rían shot back.

"You insolent child," the Mórrígan growled at her, backhanding a slap across her face before grabbing her by the throat. Anger burned within Rían and, as she had some idea of what Rían was capable of, there was no point in playing games anymore. Rían slammed the heel of her palm into the Mórrígan's forearm, dislodging her hand from around her throat. In one fluid movement Rían rammed the heel of her other hand into the centre of the woman's chest, just below the breasts, sending her backwards.

Using the moment of distraction, she created her protective sphere, charging with everything she had, using anger to fuel it. The Mórrígan advanced upon her again, but stopped, sensing the protective shell. She reached out, her fingers touching the circumference of Rían's sphere. As she did, tiny darts of lightening danced about her fingertips, but she got no further. The strength of Rían's anger and fury held her at bay, and the Mórrígan stepped back, a cold grin appearing.

"You've learned well, little one," she said to the younger woman. "But you have yet to learn to control it."

"I can control it well enough," Rían snapped back, but the Mórrígan raised a questioning eyebrow. Her reaction was instantaneous. Rían sensed the shift in energies, but was too slow to react, and slammed against the wall again. Her sphere shattered into shards, scattering about the room like glass.

"You were saying?" the Mórrígan asked sarcastically as she stood over Rían's prone body. She leaned over and grabbed Rían's clothes, hauling her upright, pushing her against the wall again, with a little less force this time.

"You've been hopping across Realms you foolish girl, do you know how dangerous that is?" she roared at her.

"Any more dangerous than having a psychotic bitch in control of my body?" Rían shot back. The Mórrígan looked about to hit her again.

"You've behaved like a disobedient child, sneaking away in the night," she said.

"For starters, night-time was the only time I could do it and secondly, you're not my fucking mother," Rían roared back. The Mórrígan released her from the wall, and laughed.

"Tell me little one, how annoyed will you be to find you've finally turned into me?" she said, laughing harder at Rían's scowl. "Now, tell me what you've learned, everything you know about tomorrow's battle. Who are we facing?" she asked.

"We?" Rían demanded.

"Yes child, you and I. We will be fighting this together, if we've any hope of surviving," the Mórrígan answered. Rían's eyes narrowed in suspicion. It was Seth's suggestion, almost word for word. Had the woman been there, watching them, eavesdropping on them? How long had she known? How had she gotten past Rían's safeguards?

"Age and experience," the Mórrígan answered, sensing her thoughts. "I'll admit, you were cunning, using modern medicine to subdue me. As for your precautions, they were intricate, more complex than I would have given you credit for. But once I figured it out, there was no difficulty in finding a way around it. Now answer me child. Who are we facing tomorrow?"

"Conor."

The Mórrígan looked at her surprised.

"Well, this is a unique occasion, one for the history books, but I doubt there'll ever be a record of this battle," she said. "No Champions involved, just a King and a Queen facing each other. What else did your boy tell you?"

"He's a dirty fighter."

"Not unexpected from someone like him," she said. "So now will you join with me tomorrow, or do I have to force you? If I have to force you child, then we will both lose." Rían thought about it for a moment, knowing she hadn't much of a choice, and with Seth safely out of the fray... She looked to the Mórrígan, a tiny smile of triumph tugging at the corners of the other woman's mouth.

The Mórrígan already had her answer.

Chapter 49

Three figures stood at the edge of the battlefield, the Mórrígan in the middle, dressed for battle, her breastplate covering both her chest and back, looking grim and determined.

"Are you sure you know what you're doing?" Cíanna asked from her right hand side. The Mórrígan turned to her.

"How many battles have we fought together?" she countered. Cíanna shrugged.

"Too many to remember," she admitted, and the Mórrígan returned her gaze to the field and the approaching army. "But you're alone this time," Cíanna went on. The Mórrígan shook her head.

"I'm not alone, so long as I stay connected to the both of you," she answered. Cíanna knew what she was talking about. She herself felt the rage burning within Naoise, the rage Nemain held onto, and knew the Mórrígan could call upon that force, if needed, feeling the drawing of her own power, the healing part.

"And Uí Neill..." Naoise began.

"Is a dishonourable and dangerous oaf," she answered.

"So let me fight him. You shouldn't have to risk yourself like this," Naoise countered. She smiled at both of them.

"How's your arm?" she shot back and felt a flare of anger in response. Despite Cíanna's efforts, it still hurt. "Have faith my sisters. All will be well."

She stepped forward and missed the looks of concern that passed between Cíanna and Naoise. From the opposite side she saw Conor approaching from within his own ranks of men as he too stepped onto the field, his long and short swords at the ready. He continued until he reached the centre of the field.

"Tar anseo, bitseach mná *(Come here, bitch)*," he roared at her. She allowed herself a smirk as she unsheathed her claíomh mór, her large sword, and the sound of the metal rang in the dawn air. She glanced at the struggling form of Seth, who'd hauled himself out of his bed despite his agony, and felt guarded emotion from Rían at the sight of him.

"Táim ag teach, geadán, *(I'm coming, asshole)*," she replied, and heard a murmur of stifled laughs from both sides of the battleground.

"Ready little one?" she asked Rían.

"Yes," Rían answered and the Mórrígan felt her grim determination.

"Then let it begin," she said and felt Rían opening herself to her. Both energies fused together and the crackle of static energy could be heard throughout both camps. United, they stepped forward to meet the Ulster King.

"Tá an aon cinniúint deirneach a thabhairt do. Diúltaigh don Ard Rí agus dul amach i do bheathá *(I give you one last chance. Renounce the High Kingship and I'll let you live)*," he said as she approached, loud enough for all to hear. She laughed at him.

"An bhfuil seo do smaoineamh an comhrac, fear beag? Labhair tú go dti mo bás? *(Is this your idea of fighting, little man? Talking me to death)*," she sneered, producing more laughs from the side-lines.

She saw anger growing in Conor and smiled to herself. Both she and Rían understood that trading insults was an intrinsic part of the start of battle. Conor let out a roar and launched at her. She sidestepped him and as he passed her, she pushed him, using his momentum against him, knocking him off balance, and he fell to the ground. He turned over, fury etched on his face, but she noted a hint of a sneer. He knew she could have easily ended it there and then, but she didn't. Seth was correct. Honour was her weakness. Well, it wouldn't be his.

He jumped up and moved forward again, slower this time, and blade struck on blade. Sparks flew as their edges scraped off one another. He tried to undercut her with the short sword, but it hit the metal rings on the side of her leather breastplate, and she grunted at the impact. She brought her sword down, numbing his hand with a blow from the hilt. Dropping his concentration for a brief second, as he shook the numbness from his hand, she spun around and reverse elbowed him in the jaw, and then jumped out of his reach. In her state of heightened senses, she heard a stifled snigger, and risked a glance about at the lines of men, but it could have come from anywhere. Conor again issued a roar and thundered towards her, swords up. Her sword was longer than his, and she held hers in front of her, causing him to take action sooner than he'd planned, or else risk impaling himself. He parried with his long sword, but she swung around and his back was once again left exposed. She released one hand from her weapon and delivered a right hook to his kidney. He grunted in pain, but gritted his teeth and spun around to face her.

Throughout the day they attacked and parried each other's strokes, many of his attacks designed to open her defences, and with only one sword against his two, sometimes she found herself at the disadvantage. Other times its length gave her the advantage of delivering a cut from a greater distance without putting herself too much in harm's way. As the day grew into evening, she misread his intent in the growing darkness, and his blow struck home, cutting her and knocking her back. She fell to the ground and rolled over in time to see him about to plunge his sword down into her. She kicked out at the blade sending it sideways. She kicked up with the other foot, catching him in the groin, and he gasped for air as he fell to his knees, clutching his manhood in pain. She got herself out of harm's way and inspected the latest gash he'd inflicted on her. She picked up her weapon and stepped back, away from Conor.

A gong sounded and all looked towards Conor's camp, and at Devlin who approached the warriors.

"Nightfall has begun and this battle is ended until tomorrow, in accordance with the ancient rules." He looked to the Mórrígan. "Do you agree to this Great Queen?" he asked of her. Still breathless, she nodded, and turned back towards her own camp. She held her head high and her back straight, never once turning to look back at her opponent.

Within her tent, the story was different. As soon as the flaps closed behind her, she sagged, almost falling to her knees before Naoise caught her and helped her to her bed. Together with Cíanna, they unclipped the titanium fastenings from either side of the leather breastplate and lifted it away from her body. Underneath, bruises started forming. Cíanna opened her medi-kit and examined the wounds. None were fatal, but the last one Conor delivered could cause some trouble if left untreated. She grunted as

Cíanna cleaned it, stitched it then concentrated on accelerating the healing process. The tent flaps opened and she tried to sit up, but Cíanna pushed her back down, and wasn't gentle about it. The old man entered with a large cup.

"Are those the herbs I asked for?" Cíanna asked.

"As per your instructions," he answered as she took the cup. She lifted the Mórrígan's head and brought the cup to her lips.

"I can sit up," she answered.

"And risk bursting those stitches I've just put in? I don't think so," Cíanna said brusquely. Too tired to argue, she gave in, surprising the old man. He moved into the background and watched avidly, having never been privy to how the three behaved together when they thought no one was watching. Naoise stroked her hair, lifting strands from her face.

"You did well today sister," she said. "Nice touch with the last kick." The Mórrígan spluttered as she tried to swallow Cíanna's herbal concoction and not laugh at the same time.

"It was all I could think of doing at the time," she admitted.

"As well you did, or the extent of my services would have been to pronounce you dead," Cíanna commented, applying gel to her other wounds.

At a nod from Cíanna, Naoise helped roll her over, Cíanna jealously guarding the stitches she administered, and checked her back. Naoise then took over, her role and expertise as a sports therapist coming to the fore, and she massaged healing and restorative oils into her sister's body. Naoise barely started on her back when her breathing slowed and deepened as she fell into an exhausted sleep. Naoise didn't stop, knowing her sister was going to need all the help she could get for the battle's continuation in the morning.

Chapter 50

Devlin called men to the field to help Conor back to his camp. Sucking air, with an arm around a man either side of him, he staggered back to his own tent. Seth himself needed help to return to the tents as the contractions continued to come, but either they began to ease off, or else he was getting better at blocking them out, the pain became more endurable. By his calculations, he'd only one more day of this agony to go through, and he found himself enviously wondering what a normal life, one without curses, incantations and rituals, would be like. Boring he admitted as made his way towards Conor's tent. He heard Conor gasping and groaning to himself, and Seth allowed himself a smirk as he entered. Served the fool right, he thought.

"Well?" Conor asked him through gritted teeth as the doctor applied an ice pack to his groin.

"I lost count of the number of times you overreached yourself, where she could have stabbed you in the back," he started on Conor, feeling like one of his teachers delivering a lecture. "She could have killed you any time she wanted, but she gave you every opportunity to defend yourself, and you disrespected her by trying to stab her when she was down and defenceless. You deserved that kick in the nuts," he growled at the King. Conor's eyes blazed in fury.

"Whose side are you on?" he demanded. Seth looked a little surprised by the question.

"As per your geis, I'm on the side of Ulster," he answered giving him a look of sheer contempt. "It's only a kick to the bollocks," he said. "Get over it. At least we now know you have a pair."

He left, not caring if Conor retaliated or not, wondering if the labour pains were giving him this alternative perspective on things and more troubling, wondering how the man escaped them. No one could give him an adequate explanation, but the implication was ominous, implying Conor might not be from an original Ulster clan. While it remained unsaid,

Seth found himself pondering the possibility he was bound to a false King. Did Devlin promote the wrong man to Kingship? Conor claimed himself a descendant from Conchobar mac Nessa, but just how accurate was his entitlement? At least the old man's claim about Rían was correct, otherwise the Lia Fáil would never have sounded. Then there was the little matter of the Mórrígan being one of Rían's ancestors.

Conor lay there, gasping in shock at Seth's words as much as at the pain, not knowing what to think. He lay there while the doctor attended to the other wounds inflicted on him, some long and deep enough to require stitching, but at least he had the satisfaction of knowing he'd wounded her also. But damn, today was hard work, much harder than anticipated, and admittedly, Seth's words proved correct, she wasn't an easy opponent. Tomorrow would be better, he promised himself. Tomorrow he would put her out of her misery and put an end to this. Then he would be Ard Rí. Then the prophesy would be fulfilled.

Chapter 51

Day two of the battle began as day one had, three figures standing at the edge of the battlefield, their army standing behind them, awaiting the outcome of the day's battle. They were proud of their Queen. She fought with honour the day before and walked from the battle, head held high, and undefeated. Today they anticipated she would be victorious against the Ulster usurper. Within her, she felt Rían coming awake. Yesterday took its toll on the child, the Mórrígan knew this, felt Rían withdrawing from her as soon as she left the battlefield. That was the point where she fell into Naoise's arms, Rían's withdrawal coming as a complete surprise to her, the sudden realisation of the power the little one had given her throughout the day astounding her. What also worried her was the relative ease Rían had retreated without the Mórrígan first releasing that energy, and it worried her.

"Ready, little one?" she now asked of Rían. The rest seemed to have been good for Rían, and she felt the surge of power as she connected with her, again without invitation.

"We finish this today," she heard Rían growling inside her head. Having found herself at a disadvantage with only one sword the previous day, she opted for two today, finding she had strength enough for both her sword and a long dagger. Today she was first onto the field, and knowing the eyes of men were upon her, she sashayed to the centre of the field, no hint of injury or distress. Conor, on the other hand, limped forward. Whether it was a ploy to solicit sympathy from her, she neither knew nor cared.

"Deirim arís é. Diúltaigh don Ard Rí agus dul amach i do bheathá (*I say it again. Renounce the High Kingship and I'll let you live),*" he said. She was in no mood for this idle banter today. Today she didn't wait for him to attack.

"Mún as *(Piss off),*" she told him bluntly, and with cold and controlled fury, she launched her own assault on him. For most of the morning he found himself moving from one defensive form to another, but every time he was at a complete disadvantage, she allowed him leeway, a moment's respite, and every time he used it to launch an assault on her. Each time she rebuffed his attempts. By midday it was obvious to all around whom the victor was, but Conor refused to acknowledge her, refused to yield. Besides, the rules of single combat, as Seth had painstakingly laid out for him, were clear, only one could walk away from combat, and he was damned if he was going to let her be the one. He struggled with stroke after stroke, suddenly finding an opening and advancing forward on her. It was short-lived and her sword swept both of his weapons aside, leaving him momentarily exposed. Her dagger found its target, into his torso, his look one of surprise and outrage as he felt cold steel running through him. He dropped to his knees on the ground as his strength failed him, and he found he could no longer lift his swords.

"You are not even fit to die as a dog would," she quietly growled at him. "But you are a King, and you should die a King's death, made more honourable at the hands of the Ard Rí. Do you acknowledge me?" she asked. He raised his head and looked up at her.

"Shea, tá tu an Ard Rí *(Yes, you are the High King)*," he answered, his voice was a whisper, but all around heard his words. She nodded and stepped back, gripping the sword with both hands. With one powerful stroke, she removed his head from his shoulders, affording him the honour of a warrior's death and his body fell forward to the ground. About her, all was silent, no one dared breathe. From the ranks of Conor Uí Neill's men, movement came and Seth slowly stepped forward, sword in his hand.

"What do you think you are doing?" she demanded of him.

"Taking my place as Champion," he answered.

"Your King is dead, go home."

"Not while you stand at the threshold of Ulster, I cannot back down."

"You can barely stand, man."

"Let me worry about that.".

She stepped towards him, sword down.

"Are you that keen to join Conor?" she asked him incredulously.

"If it puts an end to this madness," he replied. She shook her head and threw a punch at him, easily knocking him to the ground. In the throes of another contraction, he was unable to get up.

Behind them, Devlin stepped onto the battlefield, hands held high and started reciting an incantation. Lightening began to fork across the sky and land on the ground close to her. She stood her ground, never flinching, as the bolts hit the earth. Furious at his actions, McCormac stepped forward, as did Cíanna and Naoise. With his staff held high, he also began an incantation to repulse Devlin's, but the Mórrígan held up her hand to stop him. Sensing Naoise and Cíanna behind her, she drew on their strength, the energy of their fury.

A wind grew, whipping at everyone, most of whom fled for shelter. In the midst of the tempest, Rían and the Mórrígan remained as one and undaunted. She looked up as a flock of ravens circled the field, cawing loudly, as they descended and swirled around her. She returned her gaze and attention to Devlin, and the churning feathered mass threw themselves at him. He reacted quickly, covering his head and face from their attack. He then conjured a sphere of silver light that grew from within him, until it became large enough to surround him, protecting him from the ravens, and he projected it outwards, repelling his feathered assailants. They scattered before him, cawing in defiance. The Mórrígan's face hardened. Before her a hound appeared, almost as tall as her, snarling, its vicious teeth bared. Seth, on seeing the mythical beast too close for comfort, scrambled away as fast as he could.

"I don't suppose you have your hurley and sliotar nearby?" she asked him.

"Forgot to pack it, sorry," he answered her. From behind her, she heard McCormac speaking again in a low voice and she held her hand up to forestall him.

"Come with me, little one," the Mórrígan said to Rían.

"Where?" she asked.

"To the skies," she answered. Rían felt the air, the streams of energy as the Mórrígan guided her, opening both of them to the elements and

Rían felt herself propelled upwards. A laugh escaped her from the sheer exhilaration and giddiness of the sensation of soaring. Rían allowed the Mórrígan total control and watched as she combined both their spirits into one form. The indistinct mass of black and iridescent blue shimmered and writhed until a raven became clear. Its size was immense, matching that of the hound and the remaining spectators of this fantastical battle gasped in awe and fear, moving out of the reach of both beasts.

"Men, forward to defend the Hound of Ulster," Devlin roared, struggling to be heard above the deafening cawing of the raven. The ferocious hound growled and leaped at the bird. With a single downward flap, the raven danced upwards into the air, moving out of the reaches of the hound's snapping jaw, the wind from its powerful wings buffeted those left remaining at the side-lines. The dog attacked again, but the raven circled around behind it, its beak stabbing at the animal.

Again and again, the dog lunged, and each time the raven danced out of the way, but not before delivering a scratch from its claws or a stab from its beak. Growing tired from leaping about, the dog resorted to snapping at the raven and sensing weakness in its opponent the raven now attacked with full force, its claws scoring the flesh on the dog's back. Enraged the hound renewed its attack, but it came too late. As it whipped around to snarl at the bird, the raven was waiting, and plunged its beak into an eye.

The dog howled in pain, but its rage grew into a frenzy. At a disadvantage and unable to see, the raven approached from its now blind side, and attacked its other eye. Completely blinded, but undeterred, it snapped around it at the sound of wings. The raven came from overhead, no flapping of wings to betray its approach, and landed on the hound, its claws grabbing the dog and sinking into its flesh. The dog howled in agony but the raven only tightened its grip, a talon plunging into the dog's heart.

The dog's dying whelp was a soul-destroying screech to all who heard it, putting fear into the hearts of the men who still stood there. Its legs gave way and it collapsed to the ground. Beyond it, Devlin looked stunned and paled in colour. As the hound exhaled its last breath, Devlin's body crumpled, and fell to the ground. The raven circled overhead but remained silent, tired from the struggle. As it formed, it now un-formed, and as the two spirits re-entered Rían's body she fell to one knee, resting her hands on the ground to steady herself while she caught her breath.

"The Hound of Ulster is dead, this war is over," she heard McCormac declare to all from behind her. From the corner of her eye, she saw movement and turned to watch as a furious Seth struggled to get back on his feet again.

"What are you doing?" she growled at him. He turned back towards his own forces, the army of Ulster.

"The Hound of Ulster stands," he told them before turning back to face her. "I am the Hound of Ulster," he told her, his voice flat and cold. Her eyes narrowed in anger and annoyance, but she too stood to face him, saw his face harden and his stance change. Around him she saw a shimmering of energy, shifting and swirling and recognised it for what it was. He'd entered ríastrad. In a slow and measured motion, he picked up his sword and swung at her. She ducked and rolled on the ground, grabbing her own sword as she passed it and stood upright again.

"Tell me lover, should I have my men find a suitable stone for you, or would your own do you again this time?" she taunted him. His eyes narrowed but he said nothing. Ríastrad blocked most of the pains from the curse out, but not all, and he grunted as yet another one hit. He didn't let it stop him though and he stepped forward in another attack. She deflected it with ease and counter-attacked, making him retreat a step.

"Perhaps I should rally around and find what belts and ropes I can, just to save you the bother later," she threw at him. Fury etched his face, but he said nothing as he attacked for the third time. Even with ríastrad, he wasn't up to full strength and while his attacks were powerful, she was more than able for his assault. She launched a counter-attack, making him give ground. They parried blow for blow, getting ever closer to each other until the cross-guards of both hilts connected and locked together. She aimed a knee at his groin, but he anticipated it and sidestepped her, locking his leg around hers, then followed through with a punch to her head. To his disgust, she laughed as she dropped into another roll, moving to just outside his reach.

"Poor Cúchulainn, you don't even have Emer to come to your aid this time, to hide you, to protect you," she mocked again and his anger grew at the mention of Cúchulainn's wife. He stepped forward taking a high guard stance. She blocked him with an upward stroke and stepped in, turning to stand alongside him and elbowed him in the jaw. He pushed her off with considerable force. He became predictable in his attacking strokes. This, she also knew from Rían's memories, which she had full access to, and she waited until his next over-cut. As his sword swung downwards and past her, she stepped in, reversing her grip on the hilt of her own sword. The sword's pommel impacted with the side of his head and she saw his eyes close before he hit the ground, unconscious. Such unseemly behaviour caused uproar.

"Enough," she roared over the din. "I have killed two already, more than enough to validate my claim. I will not kill a third unnecessarily," she told them all.

"What about him?" McCormac asked as she passed, referring to Seth.

"Take him, but bind him securely. I will not have him loose to wreak havoc when he wakes up," she answered and walked on.

"Well done little one," she said to Rían who remained quiet.

The old man watched on as the unconscious form of Seth was dragged from the field. Two soldiers, one either side, took him under the arms, his feet dragging through the grass. Behind him, the old man heard a faint movement, but sensed the person. Slowly he turned to face Fleur. She stood defiantly, a tall staff in her hand she used for support, the ends of her cloak rippling in the light breeze. Her expression wasn't a welcoming one.

"I was wondering when you'd show yourself," he said to her.

"You make it sound like I was hiding from you," she threw back at him.

"You've been hiding from the world, and hiding who you are, amongst these people," he replied. "You taught Devlin how to open the dimensions of time," he concluded. Her nod was almost imperceptible. "You sided with Devlin and Conor, knowing he was a false King?" he threw at her.

"It was better than staying with you, with your obsession, with your single-minded devotion to the prophesies," she retorted. "That obsession destroyed the lives of everyone I loved."

"Is this why you're here, now, to throw this back at me? You've waited over 30 years to get your revenge," he said coldly.

"A small price to pay for losing a child, and I've been waiting a lot longer than that," she retorted. "You drove her to her death. How could you do that to my child, to our child?" Her voice rose slightly but she held her anger in check. "Are you going to have our grandson suffer the same fate, at her hands?"

"I don't have the power to stop that from happening," he answered.

"But you're not powerless either," she shot back at him. "You restored her to this world. You can send her back, and leave the girl unharmed." He shook his head.

"You know as well as I that what is done, cannot be undone," he growled back. "No one will regret losing him more than I, but there is nothing I can do. He's out of my hands now and into hers."

"What kind of sadistic, unemotional bastard are you?" she demanded and he regarded her coldly. "You always said his part in the prophesies would be greater than all the others. His part has not yet been played out, so how can you allow him to die?"

"I see you haven't lost any of your passion," he commented dryly and her eyes lit up, fiery with anger. "He always did have your temper," he fired at her.

"Oh good," she retorted," at least I have the satisfaction of knowing he probably questioned you every step of the way, disrupted that smug, self-centred and arrogant attitude of yours." He gave her a long, cold, hard stare then turned to walk away.

"You destroyed our daughter, don't destroy her child," she shouted after him. "He's all I have left of her."

McCormac halted for a moment at her words, but didn't turn back to face her, and continued on his way back to his own camp.

Using the trees for concealment, both Naoise and Cíanna saw the old man standing on the battlefield. The Ulster side dispersed and only two figures stood alone. The Mórrígan turned to look at what held her sisters' attention having sensed their interest. She knew Naoise itched to try out her new skill, and the Mórrígan had to admit, curiosity got to her also and she gave approval to their eavesdropping. Now, they stood shocked by what they witnessed between the old man and that strange old woman. Naoise closed her hand and the little sphere she'd conjured winked out of existence. Seth was the old man's...

They looked at each other.

"No way," they said in unison.

Chapter 52

As Rían entered Tír na mBéo she found it dark and quiet, sensing something was out of kilter, but she couldn't explain it. Her thoughts returned to Seth as she tried to find him, wondering if he could dream if he was unconscious. She needed to talk with him, needed to find out what came over him on the battlefield. She understood his obligation to Ulster. She understood why he stood and faced her after Conor's death. But what she wanted to know, what she needed to understand, was the cause of his transformation after the battle with Devlin and his hound. He declared himself Hound of Ulster. While it was true Cúchulainn was called that, it wasn't Seth's title to take. Fear grew. Had Cúchulainn taken over within him? Was Seth lost to her?

From the doorway where she stood, Rían's sense of Seth grew stronger and she turned around, seeing him appear near the lake. She hadn't brought him here and he had no power to get here himself. So how did…? She opened herself, reaching out, but found herself blocked. Fear grew to terror as she realised what was happening. The Mórrígan was here, she had to be.

"Show yourself," Rían roared, startling Seth. The air between them shimmered and the Mórrígan materialised. Understanding the danger they were both in, Seth made a run, to confront her, to tackle her, but as she turned to him, she raised her hand knocking him to the ground with a force of air. Rían struggled with the block the other woman put on her, finding a way around it, and in an unexpected move, put her own block in place around the other woman. Rían had no doubts the Great Queen would blast it away in a matter of moments, but a moment was all she needed and she ran forward. Feeling a strong shift in energy, the Mórrígan turned back towards Rían, surprise and fury on her face.

"Do you think that will stop me, child?" she roared at her, and Rían felt buffeted by the force of the Mórrígan's power.

"Leave him alone," Rían bellowed back. "You've already defeated him once today." The Mórrígan gave her a sneer.

"I warned you, your feelings for him will get you both killed. It weakens our power," she growled at Rían. "And it was both of us who defeated him. You and I, child. I didn't work alone in that." Rían stood her ground.

"I had no control, you saw to that," Rían retorted and the Mórrígan laughed at her.

"Foolish child. Is that what you think? You could have withdrawn any time you wanted, but you chose to stay. You are not innocent in this," she replied stepping closer to Rían. Seth could only watch as the two women confronted each other. He saw a nimbus of soft blue light surrounding Rían and a similar but stronger one around the Mórrígan.

"You have no control, child," she sneered at the wind howling around them, and Rían knew the wind was only a manifestation of her own rage but it seemed to flow around the Mórrígan. "I could have taught you to control this, if you'd given me the chance," the Mórrígan went on.

"I don't need your help," Rían retorted, but felt pushed back by the Mórrígan's power. She retreated a couple of steps, back towards the cabin while the older woman continued to advance upon her. To Seth it seemed the two women entered the house and all went quiet for a moment. The Mórrígan re-emerged from the door, alone and walked away. Then the cabin exploded. From the ground, Seth roared and struggled with his invisible restraint, watching her as she approached him, flames rising to the sky behind her.

"Hello lover," she said to him as she lowered herself onto him, straddling him.

"Get away from me," he snarled, turning his head away from her, as she came to within mere centimetres from his face.

"Join with me. Together we could be a powerful force," she whispered into his ear, while she bit his earlobe. He grunted at the sharp pain.

"Never," he growled in return and pushed against her. His invisible bonds loosened and he fought against them. Getting an arm free, he swung and backhanded a slap to her face. Furious, she rolled off him and he felt free, but it was short-lived as she grabbed him by the throat. He grabbed her arm, trying to twist it from his neck, but he felt his strength leaving him before he blacked out.

He woke with a start, looking about him, finding himself severely restricted. His shoulders ached and he had cramps in his legs from the way they bound him, arms and legs outstretched, shackles at the wrists and ankles binding him to thick metal rods, one either side of him, with and no slack in the restraints, he found it impossible to get any sort of leverage, but it didn't stop him from pulling with all his might. Even controlling his fury and targeting one restraint at a time brought no success. Frustration and anger got the better of him and he struggled chaotically, without success.

Resigning himself to his situation, he looked around, assessing his surroundings, finding himself in a tent, not un-similar to Conor's, facing a throne like chair, and he guessed this to be the Mórrígan's main meeting or assembly tent. Dotted about at regular intervals were small wooden tables, upon which sat stone bowls, the burning liquid within, giving a soft glow. He wondered how long he had been out, also realising the cramps were gone. The pounding in his head where the blow landed continued to ache, but he ignored it. He felt weak, but at least the infernal curse was over.

He must have dozed for a while for it was light when he opened his eyes again and he was no longer alone. The body of Rían sat in the throne before him. She sat askance, her leg thrown over one arm of the throne, her elbow resting on the other, supporting her head. At seeing him awake, she smiled, a cold, hard smile and he knew for sure Rían was gone. The Mórrígan was all that was left. She stood and walked towards him, stroking him across the arms and chest. He attempted to shake her off, twisting his body as much as the restraints would allow.

"Poor Cúchulainn," she purred, her voice deep and enticing. "Always trying to be the hero." She leaned closer and whispered in his ear. "You always chose the lost cause."

"I recall you told me that before," he growled at her.

"So you do remember?" she answered, surprised.

"Some of it," he admitted, staring past her, not looking at her. She stroked him again. "Get away from me," he growled.

"You didn't mind when Rían touched you this way," she taunted him with a smile, looking up at him, pressing her body against his.

"You're not her," he answered.

"I could be," she said in a low and sultry tone.

"You could never be her," he growled and pushed her away with his body with as much force as he could. She stepped back and regarded him, her face hardening again.

"I'll offer it again, join with me," she said.

"Never."

"You can't stand against me forever," she said.

"I'll stand against you for as long as I can, as long as you stand at the edge of Ulster," he answered. She regarded him for a moment.

"Conor was clever to put that geis on you. And if I retreat? Then would you come to me?" she put to him.

"I'd rather die first," he retorted.

"That could be arranged, my love," she answered. "Or I could just keep you alive for my amusement."

He stared past her.

"Come back to us, Seth," she said, softening and manipulating her features to look so much like Rían that he looked at her. She stepped back towards him, reached out to touch him, her fingertips touching his chest. "You'd be safe with us."

He clenched his jaw and closed his eyes. It's not her, he told himself over and over again. Rían was dead. Only the Mórrígan remained, and he refused to give into her.

"Bitch," he spat at her. "Don't you dare pretend to be her," he roared, forcing himself against his restraints. "You can never be her, will never be her." Furious, she slapped him across the face, and his head rolled with the blow. She stepped back, fury etched on her face and he glowered at her. She knew she had lost him, knew she never had him in the first place, and wondered at the wisdom of letting him think Rían dead. She hoped to break his spirit, make him more pliable, but that appeared not to be the case. Had she underestimated the power of their feelings for each other? Love was one of the strongest emotions, one of the most powerful forces. This she knew, her love for Cúchulainn being a driving force behind her and these battles between them. But once again, he rejected her.

"You can have your wish and die, if you want," she told him coldly and walked around him. He heard the tent flap as she opened it and heard others enter. She reappeared back in front of him, accompanied by Naoise and Cíanna.

"Well, what do we do with him?" Naoise asked.

"He wishes to die," the Mórrígan answered.

"Any preferences to how we do this?" Naoise asked and a slow, cold smile played on the Mórrígan's lips.

"Take him to Clochafarmore, and tie him to it. Let him die like his heroic ancestor did, slowly, painfully and watching his guts slipping out," she answered coldly.

Seth watched her in fury, his jaw clenching, the muscles in his cheeks twitching furiously in raw anger, but he held his tongue. Soldiers appeared either side of him and he was released from his restraints. Despite the ache in his shoulders and four men holding onto the end of his chains, he surged forward, towards the Mórrígan. Naoise and Cíanna stepped in front of her, and he found the edge of Naoise's knife at his throat. But that wouldn't stop him if it meant a quicker death.

To his dismay, the pressure on the blade eased as his hands were secured behind him. He glared at the Mórrígan, every fibre of his being hating her, loathing her. He was dragged out of the tent and he resisted at every step with every gram of strength he had left in him, Naoise leading the way while Cíanna followed behind.

Inside her mind, she felt outrage from Rían. Of course she hadn't killed the child. She couldn't, not without killing herself, but she felt her testing the bonds of her confinement, feeling confident they were more than adequate to hold the child. The question now was what to do with her. Confining her was one option, but how long would that last. Within the cabin in Tír na mBéo, she ensnared Rían, trapped her, caged her and cut her access to all energy sources. She returned the child from the Realm before causing the house to explode. As for Seth, he hadn't given her any other choice.

"No other choice?" Rían demanded.

"There was none, child," she answered. "He thinks you are dead, he has no will left to live."

"Only because you destroyed that will," Rían accused her.

Within her confines, Rían's rage and fury grew to consume her, and she allowed the fury to take over, to fill her, feeling its power, feeling her whole body trembling with its force. She tested the constraints of the prison the Mórrígan put her into, testing for weaknesses, testing for an opening. There was none, but her rage shattered the Mórrígan's defenses. As the old man stepped into the tent, having witnessed Seth being dragged out, he saw the look of horror cross the Mórrígan's face as her body went rigid and she fell to the ground, unconscious

"Get Cíanna, quickly," he roared to the guard outside, but he had a feeling she needed more than just medical help. The soldier returned soon after, but without Cíanna.

"Well?" he demanded. The guard looked uncomfortable.

"I can't find her," he admitted.

"What the hell do you mean you can't find her?" McCormac roared.

"She's not in the camp. Neither is Naoise," the man hesitated and the old man noticed.

"What else?" he demanded.

"The prisoner, Seth, is also missing."

Fleur kept to the tree line as she moved closer to the enemy camp, the place where her grandson was held captive. She wanted to conceal herself from any potential watchful eyes, but the use of magic this close to the camp would alert those with any power or sensitivity to power. She already lost Devlin today, her rock, her refuge, she was damned if she was going to lose her only grandson, the child of her only child.

In this subtlety and subterfuge business, age went against her, no longer sprightly, she no longer had physical strength to count on. She had her own form of strength, and she was almost on a par with McCormac when she left him. She watched as they dragged the boy into the largest and most central tent in the camp, following at a short distance, but found herself peeking from around tents. That's right, she admonished herself, draw attention to yourself, acting the way you are, just walk around as if you had every right to be there. With so many people milling about the place, who'd look twice at a little old woman, making her way along.

The tent they brought him to was guarded. Not heavily, but there was no way she would have been able to overpower the soldiers standing outside, not without revealing her presence. The old man would sense her in moments. No, she would have to bide her time and wait for the right moment, the right opportunity.

She picked a vantage point, a spot where she could sit and watch, and where no one would ask questions. A little old woman sitting, resting, who would give her a moment's notice? She could sense Seth. She sensed the moment he awoke, came out of the depths of his unconsciousness before falling back into a lighter, more natural sleep.

She watched as the three women approached his tent closer to dawn, but only one entered, the one his heart belonged to. The other two remained outside, but they too entered after a brief while, and then Seth was dragged out. Fury etched his face, but that wasn't what she sensed from him. What she sensed bordered on despair and hopelessness. He had given up. She sensed his willingness to die.

She used her staff to pull herself up and followed them. No need to be discreet now, the boy's life lay in the balance. They went beyond the camp perimeter, but she failed to notice the figure approaching from behind her. As an arm closed about her neck, she cried out. The little procession ahead of her stopped and turned.

"Oh look," Naoise said, a hint of sarcasm creeping into her voice as her arm tightened around the old woman's throat. "Grandma's come to save you." Seth furiously struggled against his restraints and the soldiers holding him.

"If you harm her," he growled at her.

"You'll what?" she answered. "Kill me?"

"Either in this life or the next," he replied. She made a face.

"Seth, you were always so melodramatic," she retorted humorously. Naoise felt a familiar prickling on her skin and turned her attention back to the old woman. "Oh no you don't," she growled to her captive and slammed a protective shell about the woman, similar to what she saw the Mórrígan do. Cíanna brushed past him and held up a pressure syringe.

"I was going to use this to make your death quicker and a little less painful," she told him, "but I guess Grandma gets that honour now." She tossed it to Naoise, who caught it and emptied the contents into the old woman. Furious, Seth struggled with his captors, his size belying the strength he summoned from somewhere. From a pocket inside her cloak, Cíanna took out another pressure syringe as the soldiers wrestled Seth to the ground, face down.

"Say goodnight Seth," Cíanna said as she emptied the drugs into him, and the struggling stopped as he became unconscious and the soldiers stood up, backing away from him and looked to Cíanna for further instructions.

"We'll take it from here," she told them. "Go back to the camp. I think everyone will be preparing to leave soon." The two men nodded at her and gave Seth's inert body and the old woman's a final glance before following Cíanna's order.

Chapter 53

Rían soared, similar to when she and the Mórrígan took to the sky as a raven only this time she had control, but she felt no sense of triumph or supremacy at overcoming her opponent. All she felt was cold fury and rage. In truth, she didn't know where she was going until she landed there, but recognised it as soon as she landed. Dún Scáith, the Fortress of Shadows. How fitting for her mood, she thought, finding herself a little away from the fortress itself.

Inside the Fortress's defensive walls was a derelict looking structure, black towers that rose towards a dull and steely-grey sky, deserted battlements, with no evidence of any life, not a stir of wind, a chirp of a bird. Even the sky here was gloomy and forlorn, she thought as she surveyed her surroundings.

She stood in the open ground, facing the entrance to the fort, but the huge wooden doors were closed to her. She shuddered a little, thinking that as bad as her mood was, the Fortress was the last place she wanted to go, looking uninviting and forbidding. What a pity she couldn't have given the Mórrígan that same impression from the start. Perhaps none of this would ever have happened. Too late now, she told herself. What was done, was done.

She looked around the clearing where she stood. There was no life here, none that she could see, except for herself. Time to rectify that, she thought as she reached out, and sensed The Mórrígan. Within ríastrad, she discovered she had more control over this magic stuff, more reins on her ability, more clarity. Ríastrad always allowed her to think and see more clearly, helped her to fully focus.

The Mórrígan appeared before her as Rían pulled her into the realm, and stood, undaunted, as she felt the fury of the Great Queen who now stepped closer to her.

"How dare you," the older woman roared at her. "You think you can compel me, force me so easily?" She stopped within arm's reach of

Rían, not daring to step closer, truth be known. She felt pulled into this world, against her will, found she couldn't stop it from happening, which only served to anger her even more. Rían didn't respond but faced her with an air of quiet resolve, and the Mórrígan sensed that, also sensing her control of the power that surrounded them. Impossible, she thought. It took decades to learn that skill, that control. It was impossible the child could've mastered it so quickly.

Rían struck first, and a blast of energy slammed into the Mórrígan, knocking her to the ground. She rolled over, pushing long fiery red curls from her furious face. She stood up to face Rían and threw a punch at the younger woman, but Rían stepped back in time. As the Mórrígan's fist swung past Rían's head, Rían conjured up a quarterstaff and with lightning speed, struck at the Mórrígan's legs. Again, the Mórrígan fell to the ground, but she turned it into a roll and stood. She spun around, sword appearing in her hand, rage etched on her face. She thought about blasting the child to the ground, but when she tried, she found herself blocked, her access to the power diminished. Impossible, she felt a scream of pure rage welling within her, but she held it back, channelling it into an attack on the child.

Chapter 54

Fleur slowly opened her eyes, breathing deeply before sighing. Overhead, she saw sky. The clearest blue, with that odd twinkling of stars shining through, and instantly she knew where she was. She turned her head and found Gráinne sitting beside her.

"Am I dead?" Fleur softly asked her. Gráinne's laugh was gentle.

"I think it would take a lot more than two little girls to do that," she answered. Fleur slowly eased herself up and sat.

"You've grown old, dear friend," Gráinne said.

"You haven't," Fleur commented dryly.

"Oh, I have. It just doesn't show as much," Gráinne answered. "I may have found another. Someone with the same ability." Fleur looked at her in surprise.

"The girl," she guessed. Gráinne nodded in reply. "My grandson is in love with her," Fleur told her. Gráinne nodded again.

"As it was foretold. This was destined. But she will need a guide. She is strong and quite determined, a rich imagination and quite inventive. Not unlike someone else I know." She gave Fleur a knowing smirk. "I would as soon have you teach her than him," she added. Fleur gave her a puzzled look.

"Why? He is older, stronger than any of us," she said.

"You Mortals and Mystics," Gráinne began. "You live and die, plan and scheme in the mortal Realms according to how you see the prophesies, according to how you see the meanings in the words. Some things are just pre-ordained. Some things are destiny, and not all of it is known to you. In this matter it is not your place to question the nature of what will be, or what must be, or to question the wishes of the Tuatha."

"Is training the girl the wish of the Tuatha?" Fleur asked. Gráinne laughed, softly, in response. "But she is the Mórrígan, and one of her line. I wouldn't dare presume to teach a Goddess," Fleur went on.

"Not all is as it seems, a leanbh," Gráinne told her. "It's possible the Mórrígan is no match for her."

"Impossible," Fleur exclaimed.

"You think so? Then explain to me why two of the Goddesses of Battles and Fury could not kill you?" Gráinne put to her. Fleur's expression faded into that faraway look she always did when she gave serious thought to something. In that look, realms of possibilities, worlds of wonder and magic converged.

"They must have allowed me to live, whatever their reasons," Fleur said, but at a loss as to what those reasons could be.

"Well, there is also that," Gráinne admitted. "But in their mortal time and place now, they have little power, and Badb herself works as a healer." Fleur burst into laughter.

"The Vulture herself?" she asked incredulously. Gráinne laughed with her and nodded.

"The old man has played a dangerous game," she told Fleur. "You know as well as I that the best way for us to leave the Tír's is through what you call reincarnation, and should happen at the moment of conception." Fleur nodded.

"It is the only way," she said, but Gráinne shook her head.

"It's not the only way, but the safest for us and for the different Tír's. It maintains order and balance. But the old man has not worked within these rules. His meddling has had consequences, very serious ones."

"This is already known amongst us," Fleur said.

"Yes, of course," Gráinne agreed. "I forget you are not that fresh-faced, wide-eyed little girl anymore." Fleur laughed.

"Not fresh-faced, but still wide-eyed at times," Fleur told her.

"Well then, you'll also know four great Spirits were ripped from the Realms this time, before their time," Gráinne also told her. "The natural order of things has been disrupted."

"Nemain has power and ability, I can assure you of that," Fleur told her. "But it's limited. How is it then the Mórrígan has retained all of hers?"

"Timing," Gráinne answered. "This is a critical factor in these matters. Nemain and Badb were pulled into your world at the time of the two girls' births, not at conception. As for the Mórrígan, she returned much later than she was supposed to, and in doing so, he brought her spirit back into your world in full force. In fact, her return was destined to have been some two or three hundred years earlier, naturally, reborn into the mortal world, but something happened, and she wasn't conceived. Even then, the natural order of the Universe was thrown out of balance."

"The old man," Fleur guessed and Gráinne nodded.

"We suspect so, but we do not have sufficient evidence," she answered. "His actions have been most clandestine. He has concealed much from the Tuatha. While the Mystics, as you know, do not serve the Tuatha, he has broken ... protocol, between us."

"And what of the boy?" Fleur asked, concern creeping into her voice at the fate of her grandson.

"He has outlived Cúchulainn, and in many ways, has surpassed his ancestor in achievements. But his time has not yet come, his destiny not yet fulfilled."

"And Alana?" Fleur asked. Gráinne gave her a sad smile.

"You still grieve for her," she stated.

"Of course," Fleur answered. Gráinne reached out and gave Fleur's hand a gentle squeeze.

"She is at peace. Her purpose in the world has been fulfilled," she told her.

"How so?"

"She was the vessel for his return. That was her destiny," Gráinne told her old friend. "Take heart, my friend, she has joined her ancestors. She is with loved ones."

"That is good to know," Fleur said, her voice almost a whisper.

"Bear not the weight of her loss upon your heart," Gráinne comforted her.

"Tell me more about this girl my grandson cares so much for. What is to become of her? And what of the Mórrígan within her?"

"All is not what it seems. Do you feel strong enough for some travelling?" Gráinne asked.

Chapter 55

The Mórrígan knew she needed to get her temper and anger back in control. The bloodied lip was evidence enough that she acted out of pure rage and not thinking about what she was doing. Rían sustained some injuries, a few bruises, maybe a cracked rib or too, but nothing that caused her to bleed. The Mórrígan wiped her lip with the back of her hand, and spat out a mouthful of blood. The child continued to remain silent throughout this fight, but the other woman sensed the fury that burned inside her. Keep that rage going little one, she thought, and you will become me. Rían raised a questioning eyebrow at her, as though sensing her thoughts, and the Mórrígan's eyes narrowed in annoyance. A small smile played at the edges of Rían's lips, but she kept a tight rein on her emotions and her own thoughts.

Dark clouds rolled across the sky, and both Rían and the Mórrígan knew it was only an external manifestation of the turmoil raging within them. The Mórrígan stood facing Rían, and took a back guard stance, awaiting Rían's next move, sensing it would be elemental rather than physical. She wasn't disappointed, and a bolt of lightning struck at her sword. She dropped the weapon, crying out in fury and pain. She retaliated in an instant, directing a similar bolt at Rían, and faster than Rían anticipated, striking her in the chest, sending her backwards, to land her on her back.

The Mórrígan picked up her sword and ran forward, towards her young opponent, but Rían jumped up before the Mórrígan could strike her. Rían charged at the other woman, catching her around the waist, rugby tackled her to the ground. Once down, Rían delivered a few punches to her head, but not without receiving another blow to already distressed ribs. The Mórrígan grabbed her by the hair, pulling the younger woman off her, levering her knee up to push Rían off. Rían fell to the ground and rolled away to a safer distance, slowly standing, while she waited for the Mórrígan's next move.

From the shelter and relative safety of the trees, two figures stood quite still, watching the two women. Both had their cloaks wrapped about themselves, hoods pulled up, giving some protection from the elements.

"A precedent," Gráinne said.

"How so?" Fleur asked.

"It is the first time two great Queens have ever fought. The first time two of the same bloodline," Gráinne answered.

"The girl is the real Ard Rí then?" Fleur asked. Gráinne nodded.

"Descendant from the Great Queen herself. The child's ancestry was never in any doubt, nor was the High Kingship. What do you sense from them?" Gráinne asked. Somewhat surprised by the question Fleur gave her a questioning look, but Gráinne did not give her any reason or explanation. Fleur focused on the two women, concentrating hard on the pair of them. From both of them she felt their fury, felt the strength of their emotions and the control they both wielded on that emotion. Within the younger woman, she sensed something else. A loss. An emptiness. There was no hope, but unlike what she sensed from her grandson, this hopelessness she channelled into vengeance. This caught Fleur's attention even more, and she delved deeper.

"The girl thinks Seth is dead," she said to Gráinne, who nodded.

"Anything else?" the Tuathan elder asked. Fleur refocused on the girl again.

"You were right about her being a Mystic," she answered.

"And?" There was another pause as Fleur searched some more. She gave a gasp.

"I cannot teach her," she told Gráinne and the elder turned to look at her. For the first time since Fleur met the other woman, a cold, hard stare from Gráinne chilled her.

"Cannot, or will not?" Gráinne asked. Even though she spoke in her usual quiet tones, the steely hardness was unmistakable. Fleur involuntarily took a sharp intake of breath. The Tuatha de Danann could be difficult masters to please at times, but Gráinne never displayed their well-documented and hot temperaments.

"Cannot," she answered. "She'd outgrow my teachings, would probably outgrow the old man's." She gasped as realisation hit her. "She is stronger than he is, and as strong as the Mórrígan herself." Gráinne's face softened to her usual demeanour, and she nodded.

"They are evenly matched," Gráinne agreed, "but I think the Mórrígan has underestimated the child's reaction to thinking the boy is dead. The child has learned to control her emotions well, and while she does not care to live, she will do what she must to ensure the Mórrígan doesn't survive either."

"But if neither of them survive, won't the bloodline be destroyed?" Fleur asked. Gráinne nodded.

"In this battle, the Mórrígan cannot afford to lose, nor can she afford to win, and the child knows it," she answered. "If the Mórrígan wins here, the child's body will die, and the bloodline dies with her. If the Mórrígan loses, or the child kills her here, she will cease to exist forever and this will throw all the Realms into utter chaos, perhaps even destroy them." Fleur looked at her in alarm.

"Why would the girl do this?" she asked, frightened.

"For the same reasons as the Mórrígan," Gráinne answered cryptically, watching the Mórrígan and Rían, and said no more, trusting Fleur to figure it out for herself. Fleur turned her attention back to the two women who were again wrestling on the ground.

"Love," she answered. Gráinne nodded. "It was always said the Mórrígan lusted after Cúchulainn, but it was much more than that, wasn't it?" Gráinne nodded again, and gave her old student a sly smile. "And the girl," Fleur continued. "She's as much in love with Seth as he is with her, although he has tried to deny it to himself. Now though, she believes him to be dead, as he believes she is."

"Go an mhaith ar fád, *(very well done),*" Gráinne answered.

"Is there anything we can do?" Fleur asked. Gráinne shook her head.

"Nothing. Even this is out of destiny's hands. Night is falling and they will stop fighting soon. Perhaps during the night they can reason this out. For now, we must leave. Neither of them will be pleased to know they have been watched, and I for one, don't wish to be on the receiving end of either of their fury. Besides, the old man will figure out what has happened and will appear here soon. I can already sense just how anxious he is, and it's best he also doesn't find us here."

"He was never known for his patience, or his ability to await the outcome of an event that was beyond his control," Fleur commented.

"There's a danger in trying to control events," Gráinne told her. "No one person can ever truly know all the facts, and therefore can never be fully in control."

"I never knew you to be such a philosopher," Fleur said.

"It's the nature of the Universe," Gráinne answered. "Why fight it? Fighting only serves to create reactions and chaos, for every action there must be an opposite and equal reaction." She turned to Fleur. "It's time we left here," she continued. "You need to return to your world. Your grandson is going to want to talk to you, and when that is done, you must return to me." Fleur nodded, wondering what Gráinne meant, but she didn't get a chance to ask as the Fortress shifted out of focus and darkness overcame her.

Night grew to complete darkness, and in this place, the darkness was as gloomy and oppressive as the day. The Mórrígan roared at Rían to stop.

"You're yielding?" Rían asked, somewhat surprised. These were the first words she said to the older woman all day.

"Never," she hissed at her, "but it's night and we never do battle at night." Rían regarded her with suspicion. "It's no ploy child," she tried to assure her. "You know our laws as well as I. Once night falls, Hospitality must be observed."

To her relief Rían's stance relaxed, her sword and staff disappearing, as did the light of ríastrad, and overcome with exhaustion, Rían fell to the ground. The Mórrígan allowed herself a small smile of satisfaction at seeing her opponent so weakened.

"Can you manage a fire?" she asked her and Rían nodded. "Good, get it started and I'll find us something to eat." She started to walk away but Rían lashed out, restraining her, binding her with a force of air. The

Mórrígan stiffened and turned her head to look at her, the same furious look as she'd worn all day.

"Do you think I am without a shred of honour?" she growled at Rían. "That I would walk away and leave this place while this matter is not yet finished between us?" She felt the bonds disappear.

When she returned, Rían had a fire blazing, with enough firewood stacked close by to see them through the night. More surprising, Rían called into existence a kettle and was boiling water over the fire. The Mórrígan threw the carcass of a fawn onto the ground and Rían looked at it sickened. The Mórrígan laughed softly.

"I forgot about your disgust for meat," she said to Rían, "but you need to eat, or would you cause me dishonour by refusing food offered you?" Rían knew she was in a bind.

"Wasn't this how you tricked Cúchulainn into eating dog meat?" she growled back. "You made him break his geis." The Mórrígan shrugged.

"That was a very long time ago," she admitted. "It was his own fault, being foolhardy and too headstrong, not unlike your boy. I offered Cúchulainn the chance at greatness, but he turned it down."

"So you set about destroying him," Rían accused as she watched the woman cut chunks of flesh from the dead animal, wrap them in large leaves she'd also collected, and place them in the fire. She tossed a bundle of smaller leaves to Rían.

"Here. Make yourself useful child and brew a tea from these," she said. Rían reached out and picked them up.

"What are they?" she demanded.

"The leaves are from a small herb tree. One of the few things that grow in this place," she told her. "It's used as a restorative brew, by warriors after a battle." Rían continued to regard it suspiciously, but the Mórrígan ignored her as she continued to carve up her catch.

"In answer to your question child, I think your history books have a somewhat slanted view of what actually happened between Cúchulainn and me," she continued in a light and conversational tone. "Cúchulainn was adamant he would achieve greatness without the help from anyone, and especially not the help of a seemingly lowly woman. Do you understand the reason for appearing to him in disguises?"

"Sure. It's a common concept in most mythologies," Rían answered. "The hero must be great enough to see through the disguises, yet humble enough to know that only true greatness can ever be achieved through service to others. It is only in helping others, in defending them and their rights, in standing for justice, that a person can become a hero. But it's a double-edged sword. Only the most humble of men could ever be truly great, without seeking greatness for its own sake." For the first time the Mórrígan's smile reached her eyes and she looked on Rían with pride, as a mother would on a daughter.

"Well done, child," she answered and, much to Rían's surprise, she could hear the smile and pleasure in her voice. "Cúchulainn only wanted greatness for the sake of greatness, and while many of his deeds were heroic and noble, defending his province and his King and his friends, it was his arrogance that annoyed the gods, and in truth angered me," she admitted. "I didn't set about to destroy the man, but yes, to hinder him, to knock him down a peg or two. He needed a lesson in humility," she said.

"It's obviously a family trait," Rían commented dryly and the Mórrígan laughed.

"I take it the boy suffers from it too," she said.

"Greatly at times," Rían answered before remembering Seth no longer lived. Murdered on the orders of the woman sitting opposite her. As she watched the fire dancing, she drew her knees up to her chest and wrapped her arms about her legs, resting her head on her knees. Seth was dead and she found she now ached for that arrogant, self-assured manner.

She withdrew back into herself and thought about the whirlwind months since she met him, slept with him, fell in love with him. She surprised herself with that. Love him? Had she fallen for him? How could she love someone that overconfident, that pushy? If she didn't love him, then why did it hurt so much, why did it ache so much to think she would never see him again. She clenched her jaw, fighting back tears of frustration and grief, and anger flared again as she looked across at the murderous woman who'd caused of all of this.

When she fell asleep, the Mórrígan dared to venture around the fire to her, and hunkered beside her sleeping body. She was aware of the child's conflicting emotions towards her, but the rage returned, more than likely from thinking about the boy. She reached out to the girl and found her hand stopped. So, the child protected herself, even in sleep, and her hand felt along the outline of the shielding cocoon. Even more interesting the child's body was repairing itself as she slept. Visibly repairing itself. Bruises were fading, cuts were healing and she could sense bones mending. Was the child's anger at her that great? Did she love the boy that much, to want to avenge him this badly?

She returned to her own side of the fire, thinking she needed to do the same as Rían. While the Mórrígan never doubted her abilities or her powers before, never had cause to doubt them, she now began to worry. A novel concept for her, but then again, no other adversary had been this close in strength, skill or temper to her before. It was like fighting herself, and she found during the day, that when she could use her power, she could only use a conjured device, a method, once. The child learned too quickly, was able to replicate that method almost immediately. Even more disturbing, she had defence mechanisms capable of shattering most of what the Mórrígan threw at her. Had she underestimated the power of that love for him? She shifted on the ground to find a comfortable position, and willed herself into a healing sleep.

The old man stayed awake all night, watching and waiting for her to awaken, but knew he needed to delve in himself, to find out what happened. He stood by her bed, his hands held out over her inert body, sensing a ripple of energy surrounding her. He summoned up energy of his own to break the barrier, estimating it would only require a small amount of energy to break through, but as he tried the sound of static crackled in the air. He sent more energy and as the crackling grew louder, he felt it rebounding back into his hands, causing a tingling sensation, finding it annoying, and causing him concern enough to question why there were safeguards, and who had set them?

He drew on his reserves of strength and energy to overcome the barrier, directing it into her body. The reaction caught him by surprise and the force propelled him backwards. He hit the wall of the tent, and fell to the ground, his chest hurting from the blast, finding it hard to breathe. He struggled to his feet, sore and annoyed with himself for not realising the nature of the barrier surrounding her.

He stood over her and took his time to properly survey her. The energy surrounding her was alive, swirling and flowing about her. He tried a direct assault, making the mistake of thinking one or both women were incapacitated.

Taking his time allowed him to sense the battle that raged within. He reached out again, gentler this time, meeting resistance again, but instead of pushing against it, allowed it to flow through his fingers, getting a feel for the flow, the subtleties of the energies behind it, finding a tiny opening that allowed him to delve deeper. Patience, he told himself, knowing it was never his strongest trait, until he found them, found a sense of both of them. Now he needed to travel there, and put an end to this.

Chapter 56

The Mórrígan opened her eyes to a dull and grey morning. She stretched the stiffness from her joints and rolled over, glancing across the dead embers of the fire to where Rían lay, but found the ground empty. She jumped up and surveyed her surroundings, finding the child nearby, standing in front of the Fortress. She walked over and stood beside her.

"What is it?" she asked. Rían scanned the battlements.

"I thought I felt … something," she answered in a quiet voice.

"The Dún has always drawn people to it," the Mórrígan said. "Souls so tormented, that they cannot enter the other Tír's, but neither can they find solace in this one."

"I don't think that's what I sensed," Rían said. The Mórrígan scanned the Fortress and a small smile played on her lips.

"The old man found us, but he's put himself into the Fortress itself. That is what you are sensing child," she answered. "Foolish man. Doesn't he realise the Lost Ones will sense him, be drawn to him."

"What do you mean?"

"Within the Fortress, the Lost Ones will detect a living Soul, will seek it out in the hope of redemption and release from that place," The Mórrígan explained.

"So why didn't I end up in there?" Rían asked.

"You are not lost, child. You've found yourself, realised and accepted who and what you are," she answered with an amused tone. "Ready?" Rían walked away towards the battleground.

The old man made his way upwards until he came to the battlements. Down below him, outside the Fortress's perimeter, he found the two women, circling each other, swords at the ready. He reached out to get a better sense of both of them, and what he found stunned him. In power and ability they were evenly matched, Rían as strong in her ability to manipulate energy as the Mórrígan. How the hell had he missed that when she was a child? He was annoyed with himself for having missed such an important aspect of her. He could have trained her, refined her technique, and controlled that power of hers.

The Mórrígan struck the first blow, a punch to Rían's ribs, but she retaliated swiftly and he was shocked to see the Great Queen knocked to the ground, feeling the fury behind Rían's returning strike.

He watched throughout the day, as they attacked and parried each other's strokes, and at times simply circling each other, like panthers watching a dangerous prey, as both women caught their breath before the next strike. As night fell in the Fortress, he sensed other presences coming closer to him, using the darkness to hide their approach. Here, a living Soul was a beacon, a light drawing moths to its glow. He knew he had to leave, and leave the two women behind, without knowing the outcome. It did not sit well with him, not knowing, and he disappeared. Events were out of his hands now, and all he could do was wait.

Chapter 57

Seth came to, face down, and the tasselled edge of a cushion, beneath his head, tickled his nose. He moved, but felt stiff and his movements were limited, before realising his hands were still bound behind him. Swinging his legs down, he righted himself on the sofa, and glowered at Cíanna, sitting in the chair opposite.

"Where's Fleur?" he growled.

"She's still sleeping in the next room," Cíanna answered. "If I take your restraints off, do you promise not to hit me?" she asked, and he glared at her.

"You have to ask?" he growled.

"Yes," she replied, matter-of-fact. "You seem to forget we grew up together. I know what you're capable of when you're this angry."

He sighed, heavily.

"I promise," he answered through gritted teeth, standing up, and allowing her to release him. The door opened, and Naoise stood in the doorway.

"How's Fleur?" Cíanna asked.

"Sleeping, but she seems fine," Naoise answered stepping forward.

"What is this place?" he demanded. "Where are we?"

"It's a safe place and we're back in our own time. That's all you need to know for now," Naoise answered, leaning back against the door, arms folded.

"Safe place? Just what the hell is going on?" he asked, growing more aggressive as he closed in on Naoise.

"You've just been rescued, can't you accept that?" Naoise growled back at him, then turned to Cíanna. "And we rescued him, because...?"

"Because it's all part of the plan," Cíanna answered.

"What plan? Whose plan?" Seth demanded.

"The Mórrígan's," Cíanna answered.

"What?" he asked. "Why the hell would she do that? Leaving aside the fact she ordered me killed. Let me guess, she's just angry and misunderstood," he finished sarcastically.

"Yes," they replied in unison. Seth was taken aback.

"Remember the saying 'Hell hath no fury...'" Cíanna said.

"Like a woman scorned," he snapped.

"And how many times have you scorned her now, Cúchulainn?" Naoise countered, getting in his face, surprising him with her aggression. He never remembered her being this forceful before.

"Many times," Cíanna answered, "more than you can count." Anger consumed him at her accusation. Undeterred, Cíanna continued on. "Do you honestly believe this place and time are the only re-incarnations of Setanta, Nemain and Badb? The Sean Fhear brought us back countless times over the centuries."

"Impossible," he said. "I would have remembered... something."

"Really?" Naoise's tone matched his. He felt Cíanna's hand touch his lower arm.

"You were barely 10 years old when the old man performed the first ritual on you. Our first rituals occurred when we were born, and it should have happened that way with you, but it couldn't," she said.

"Meaning?" he demanded.

"When the old man performed the rituals on us, he brought our spirits into these chosen bodies at the appropriate age for these bodies. You were 10, so the spirit of a 10-year-old Setanta was instilled in you. The original Setanta became Cúchulainn at the age of seven. To you it's a vague and distant memory, you're not even sure if it's your memory or something you read years ago. As we grew older, more of the old memories were...uploaded, for the want of a better word, to correspond with our ages. By the time we got to the last ritual, the full integration of the Spirit, of the 'Becoming' as the old man calls it. We only remember the original Spirit, and it's brought into a body with a clean slate, free of all the ensuing incarnations. Also bear in mind you were not the one originally destined for this."

That took him by surprise.

"What?" he demanded.

"The old man doesn't know we know this, but the original heir would have been about the same age as you. Setanta was restored within him at birth, but he and his family were assassinated. He was killed before his ninth birthday, and from what I can gather, he was already a skilled warrior even at that age, the true heir of Cúchulainn. Or so everyone thought," she explained.

"Meaning?"

"You survived in the streets, despite the odds. Your mother was a junkie, and you overcame her addiction and lived. You had your own battles, different from the other boy's fights, but yours literally meant the difference between life and death. It took him about a year to find you and when he did, it became a matter of infusing your spirit with Setanta's."

"But with Rían and the Mórrígan it was different," Naoise butted in, and Cíanna sighed at the interruption.

"How?" he asked, trying to conceal his rapt fascination and failing.

"Rían is much older, too old for such a ritual to be performed and infuse the Mórrígan's spirit into her. She seemed to have a knack of disappearing at the right time, whenever the rituals were planned. With us, we were young and adaptable enough for the two spirits to merge into one, so that I'm both Badb and Cíanna; you're both Seth and Cúchulainn. The two spirits can't be separated; they are not separate. Death is the only solution. With Rían though, the Mórrígan's spirit was inserted into a body with a fully developed spirit of its own."

"So there are two separate spirits squeezed into Rían," Naoise concluded.

"When the old man said I was the living embodiment of Setanta..." he thought out loud.

"You are Setanta, in spirit at least," Cíanna finished. "We don't know any differently, from the time of the Becoming, we're complete, and we can't sense the two separate spirits. With you, it seems it took the touching of the stone, Clochafarmore, to make Seth and Cúchulainn integrate, make you one. As I said, we don't remember anything else, or any other times when the spirit was returned to this world, but the Mórrígan remembers."

"And man, is she pissed off with you," Naoise taunted.

"But why?" he demanded and Naoise rolled her eyes at him, but Cíanna answered.

"Unrequited love," she said. The answer shocked him and he stepped back, away from her and her words. "You broke her heart. Well, the Cúchulainn part of you did, every time she offered it to you, and you never realised it," Cíanna went on.

"She … loved him?" he asked. Cíanna nodded.

"And the only woman Cúchulainn ever completely rejected, just like you did back in her tent," she answered and he shook his head.

"But … I …" he began, but stalled. Cíanna laughed softly.

"Oh my, what a dilemma you've gotten yourself into this time Cúchulainn," she teased. His anger returned as his head whipped back around to face her, glaring at her.

"This time you are in love," Naoise answered. "You're in love with Rían. You are truly in love with her, but as the Mórrígan, she's your eternal mortal enemy." He glared at her and his jaw twitched as he clenched it in temper. "I think I can tell the difference in you between a mere interest and truly giving your heart away. Seth, I couldn't count the number of times I caught the two of you together before the Ceremony of Kings." This revelation only fuelled his anger even more. "I knew she was important to you."

"Didn't stop you from hitting on her?" he threw back at her, and much to his annoyance, she smirked at him.

"What, and pass up the opportunity to piss you off? I don't think so," she shot back. Controlling his temper, he turned away and walked to the end of the room. They both gave him a few moments to calm down. Cíanna took a step towards him.

"I think we can help you," she said. He turned to them.

"You'd betray her?" he said.

"Never," Cíanna answered, "we serve her with all our heart. But she is not comfortable with her… current situation." He said nothing so she continued. "It appears Rían's spirit is much stronger than the old man ever anticipated, and it has taken considerable effort on the Mórrígan's part to overcome Rían."

He frowned.

"But the Mórrígan killed her, I saw it happen," he said. Cíanna shook her head.

"It was made to look that way. If the Mórrígan killed Rían's spirit, then the body would have died also," she answered. His fury began to fade as her words sank in.

"She's alive?" he asked, almost in a whisper. Cíanna nodded, but he looked to Naoise, who also confirmed it with a nod. "You obviously have a plan to rectify this," he added.

"It's only an idea, and never really been tried before."

"What is it?" he asked. Cíanna looked to Naoise, the expert in all things to do with rituals. Medicine was Cíanna's forte, but the occult had always been Naoise's.

"We reverse the old man's ritual," Naoise answered.

"How?" he asked.

"You'll have to engage her in battle, and bring her to the point of death," Naoise confessed.

"You call that a reversal?" he demanded.

"It's the best I can come up with," she answered back. "But we need to talk to you about something else first," she added and held up her hand, a sphere growing, which she held in front of his face. He saw a tiny version of himself unceremoniously picked up and dragged from the field, then his grandmother making her way across to face the old man. He heard the words spoken between them, the heated argument, and both Naoise and Cíanna watched him, worried as the colour drained from his face. As the scene faded, Naoise closed her hand and it disappeared. Furious, Seth grabbed her by the wrist.

"This is not a trick on my part," Naoise told him. "It's exactly as it happened between them, word for word. Now, it doesn't take a genius to work it out. Even you should be able to manage it," she added, noting how well he held his temper in check. "The old man is your grandfather.

We thought you ought to know." He shook his head, as though trying to deny her words. He let her go, and she rubbed where he caught her.

"That's one of the reasons we took the old woman with us," Cíanna added. He remained scarily quiet, and from past experiences, they knew this much silence from him was a bad sign, meaning his anger reached boiling point.

"Who else knows about this?" he demanded.

"Just us three, we're not sure about Rían or the Mórrígan," Cíanna answered.

"What do you mean?" he shot back. Cíanna frowned and looked to Naoise.

"Just as we sedated you and your grandmother, we lost our connection to them," Naoise answered.

"And what does that mean?" he demanded.

"We've no idea where they are, or what's happened to them," she answered, but Seth could hear a faint trace of worry and fear in her voice.

Chapter 58

Fleur stirred and opened her eyes, finding Seth sitting in the chair opposite her and she smiled.

"At least we're both alive, lad. That's something, I suppose," she commented as she eased herself up, suspicious of his silence, and she noted the twitching muscles in his cheeks.

"Well, out with it. What's eating at you boy?" she asked.

"McCormac. Or whatever the hell his name is," he answered, and she heard anger in his voice. "He's my grandfather?"

She sighed.

"Found out, did you?" she said, "not one of my better decisions."

"And I wasn't supposed to be Cúchulainn?" he said, still keeping his anger in check.

"How did you know about that?" she asked.

"Does it matter?" he answered harshly. "Is Setanta even my real name?"

She shook her head.

"Believe me mo leanbh, it came as just as big a shock to me as I daresay it did for you, and no, Alana called you Orin when you were born, he renamed you when he found you."

"But why?" he demanded.

"It turned out that the great-grandmother of that boy's mother, and my own grandmother, your great-great-grandmother, were sisters." She sighed and eased herself to standing. "As soon as I realised, I knew I had to find Alana and you, but he got to you before I did. I couldn't let him know that I'd worked it out for myself. But then again he gave you a better life than I could have, and he never would have given up trying to find you, find us. Besides, what an accolade for him, his own grandchild having links to the past. He was a cold father, hard on Alana, and I don't imagine it was much better for you." She paused while he slowly shrugged and shook his head. "What else are you struggling with?" she asked of him. He stood up and paced the room, thinking.

"Rían," he admitted to her. "She's alive, I thought the Mórrígan killed her, and the other stuff..."

"What stuff?"

"Was she in love with Cúchulainn, or was it just lust, a conquest thing?" he put to her. She raised both eyebrows at him questioningly, and only then he realised what he'd asked. He leaned against the wall, arms folded across his chest, and tried not to laugh at himself.

"Well, you'd know all about the lust and conquest part boy, if the social columns are anything to go by," she said, "but women in those times weren't hindered by the rules of today's society, about how they should behave, and they had the freedom to be quite open and approach whoever caught their interest, and Cúchulainn caught hers. She offered Cúchulainn honour and greatness, and offered her love as well as her body. Now as you know, Cúchulainn was a bit of a philanderer, and it appears you inherited that particular trait from him." He gave her a flat look in response and she smirked at him before continuing. "Cúchulainn was only interested in being the greatest hero of all time. His motto being: 'better to die young and have a great heroic deed make you immortal, than live into an un-notable old age'." She tilted her head at him and he nodded in response. "The Mórrígan offered him help in battles, the means by which to achieve greatness, but he wanted, what you would call, 'the quick fix', and he also failed to see past her disguises, see her for who she truly was."

"That's the part I can't figure out," he admitted.

"Have you ever had a woman throw herself at you?" she asked and he searched her face for any hint of a joke at the question.

"One or two," he answered, economical with the truth.

"Yet, I'll bet it's the girl who made you work for her attention that you've given your heart to," she told him. "It's your girl, isn't it?" Fleur said and he nodded. "The only one to steal your heart, and the only one you couldn't conquer, the one you could never own, never possess."

"You make it sound like I'm a complete bastard towards women," he accused her. She sighed

"Seth, I've watched you grow, admittedly from a distance. I've read all about your exploits, the string of women you parade on your arm. I know you're no angel, and it's all a game to you, until you had to work for someone's attention, their affection, until they gave you a real run for your money," she said, and frowned at him as he burst out laughing. "And what's so funny?" she demanded.

"Rían," he answered in between chuckles. "She literarily gave me a run for my money," remembering their encounter at Oughaval Forest.

"So she became a challenge to you because you couldn't possess her, she wouldn't yield to you. Somewhere along the way, she became more than a potential conquest, became someone you admired, a real person, and you discovered an aspect of your life that was missing. In many ways you've mirrored Cúchulainn. When the Mórrígan offered herself to him, there was no challenge, no contest and therefore no conquest, no victory. But a woman such as her, no man can ever own her, could ever possess her. What she gives freely, she can also take away. Perhaps Cúchulainn sensed that, sensed he could never win with her, and in spurning her advances, in disrespecting her, he incurred her wrath."

"Hell hath no fury," Seth commented and Fleur nodded.

"And she's a dangerous one to scorn," she told him.

"What do I have to do?" he asked.

"The one and only time Cúchulainn and the Mórrígan fought, she didn't come out well, and so the love-hate relationship between the two has continued through the millennia. This time is no different, except perhaps because all the Realms are out of balance, the both of you are aware of what's going on, you can recognise that an ancient battle is still raging, but now have the opportunity to do something about it. Rectify it."

"How?" he asked.

"You have to battle the Mórrígan, if you hope to save your girl," she answered and he sighed.

"I've already had this conversation with Naoise," he told her. "I have to bring her to the point of death, without killing her. I don't know if I can do that to her," he admitted.

"You have to boy, or she, or both of them will destroy you, one way or the other," she said and he looked at her puzzled. "The girl is under a geis, one that's put on all Ard Rí, and that is of self-preservation. She can neither kill herself nor allow another to kill her so easily. Whether she wants to or not, she will find herself compelled to protect and defend herself, despite her attempts to the contrary, similar to yours to defend Ulster. The last time, with Cúchulainn, the Mórrígan was distracted by her passion for the man, but under the geis... Well, let's just say you or Cúchulainn won't find her an easy or gentle opponent this time."

She left him deep in thought and returned to Tír na mBéo where Gráinne led her towards the log cabin.

"The girl created this place from the mind of your grandson, I do not think either of them will object if we take shelter," Gráinne said. "You've spoken to the boy?" Fleur nodded.

"Somehow he found out about his grandfather," Fleur told her. "He's upset about it, more than he'd admit to."

"Understandable," Gráinne said, "the webs are breaking down, truths are being set free. Secrets long hidden are now coming to light." Fleur regarded her warily.

"Why do I get the feeling some of these uncovered truths have something to do with me?" Fleur asked. Gráinne gave her a cheeky grin.

"Sometimes you are too astute, my friend," she answered. "That is why I asked you to return here. Some truths need to be told, need to be revealed, in order to set those back on their correct path, to restore order and balance."

"But how does that involve me?" Fleur asked. Gráinne indicated for her to sit at the table, sitting across from her, and pointed to the centre of the table between them, where a three-dimensional image appeared on the wooden table top.

"What I am going to show you is what was meant to be," Gráinne answered. "There is no trickery on my part, no manipulation of the facts. What you see is what should have happened."

"Why do I get the feeling I'm not going to like it?" Fleur asked, as figures appeared in the scene between them. A tiny, younger version of Fleur stood on the table, a version of the old man facing her, and an argument ensued. Nothing new there, Fleur thought, arguments being the most stable part of their relationship, when they had a relationship. The scene before her seemed to be like looking at a 3d film on fast-forward as the characters moved rapidly about the place, and the scenes morphed from one to another. Fleur watched as she stormed out on the old man, went to Tír na mBéo and met Gráinne, much sooner than when she did. A doorway appeared and the tiny version of Gráinne pointed her towards it, through which the miniature version of Fleur had no hesitation in entering. The scene clouded over.

"What happened?" Fleur asked.

"You entered the Mystic World, we cannot see into their world. They, as you know, keep their affairs secret," Gráinne answered.

"But I never entered their world. A Mystic came here to teach me," Fleur said. Gráinne nodded.

"Remember, what you saw was originally destined, not how your life actually turned out to be," Gráinne told her and redirected her attention back to the scene on the table.

The doorway reappeared and Fleur stepped back out, more prominent streaks of white in her hair than she had now, and it was loose and long, trailing down her back, unlike the way she always kept it. The scene before them continued to fast-forward itself without missing any details, and Fleur watched herself travelling in and out of Realms with ease, met with the Tuathan, and formed alliances with them to battle a force threatening the Realms.

Within this alternative life the Mórrígan was still restored, and within the same girl. Seth's girl. What was her name again, Rían? So the girl was always destined for this, but the old man had so much more control over her in this version, manipulated her to his own end, causing even more chaos than he had to date. There was also no Seth in any of these scenes. In this version, the original boy also lived, surviving the assassination attempt on him, and was Cúchulainn from the very start. He was also the same arrogant little upstart as the original hero. There was also no Alana in this time, she noticed with a start, and said so to Gráinne, who nodded.

"You were never destined to have children," Gráinne admitted. "Your path was destined to be much different, and you were to be far more powerful than he was." The scene before them continued to unfold, and the Tuathan combined forces to face this new threat to the Realms. That of the Mórrígan, Nemain, Badb and Cúchulainn. All controlled by the old man. The scene concluded with Fleur facing the old man and vanquishing him. The characters faded from the table and Gráinne saw Fleur frowning.

"The old man saw the exact same version, many years ago."

"Meaning?" Fleur asked, puzzled but with an edge to her voice.

"He foresaw the ruination of his plans by your hand, and set about changing circumstances, changing events to ensure what you saw would not happen," Gráinne explained. She saw Fleur frowning. "Perhaps it would be explained better if you saw it from his view," Gráinne said.

Another scene unfolded before them, beginning with the same argument between her and the old man. The end of the argument was different. She did not storm off, she did not leave and the old man didn't allow her to anyway. He held onto her arm. This was what she remembered happening. The scene blended into a version of his study, in the house they'd moved into when they first arrived in the United States, and he always did have a knack for picking the smallest, darkest room for in which to cram his books. Probably by design, she thought, as she watched a version of herself rummaging through stacks of books, frustrated at not finding the one she needed. Was this a ploy on the old man's part, hiding the knowledge in plain sight, making it awkward to locate any information while not denying her access to it? The scene shifted to his ritual room, his kitchen, as she called it, and watched as he brewed potion after potion.

Even though these images also ran in fast-forward, the clarity was in no way diminished and Fleur watched, horrified as she saw him adding some of those potions to everything she ate and drank. She couldn't take her eyes off the image before her, and anger grew with every passing moment. She always thought she'd fallen in love with McCormac, but now that appeared not to be the case. She'd been poisoned, tricked and seduced by him. Nine months later, she gave birth to a little girl, but he'd already grown tired of her by then, and showed no interest in his daughter. She tore her eyes away and glared at Gráinne.

"Why?" she demanded.

"While you were with child, you left your studies, all your energy and power you devoted to raising and loving your child," Gráinne answered.

"He got me pregnant?" Fleur demanded, and Gráinne nodded.

"He did so to prevent you from achieving your destiny, to subdue you. He used your child as leverage against you. Uses your grandchild in the same way," she answered. Furious, Fleur pushed her chair back and stood up, stepping away from the table and paced the room, not unlike her grandson only a short while ago.

"I don't understand," Fleur began through gritted teeth. "If everything in my life was to deflect me from this other path, how is it my child became involved? How is it my grandson is now in the middle of it, if both he and Alana were never supposed to exist?"

"Need I remind you about one of the laws of the Universe?" Gráinne asked. "For every action, there is an opposite and equal reaction. Because of his meddling in the greater scheme, the old man caused this to happen. While there are endless possibilities, endless choices that can be made, multiple paths that lead in different directions arising from each choice made, some things are just destined to be. All choices eventually lead back to what was predestined. I believe that your path was disrupted, but as a result, you created alternatives in Alana and then Seth. I also believe that the boy will prove instrumental in correcting at least part of this imbalance. He is, after all, the grandson of two Mystics."

"But how is it he has no power himself, he is not a Mystic?" Fleur said gripping the back of her chair.

"It's a little peculiar he is without your power, but not unusual," Gráinne answered. "Perhaps it's part of his destiny. Had he any Mystic ability the old man would have usurped that power from him. As it is, the boy has other abilities and he has the will and strength to face the old man. He has the potential to undo all the old man's work. For every action... Besides, I saw the boy when Rían brought him here, and he shone, almost as if the light of Lugh himself was within the boy. The boy's power is different, something the old man couldn't see, nor foresee. The prophesies are attempting to correct themselves, trying to return to the right path. It is not too late for you either." Fleur frowned

"What do you mean?" she asked. Gráinne smiled.

"The door to the Mystic's world rarely opens, and only when someone is ready to step through," Gráinne answered.

"And?" Fleur asked.

"That door is almost ready to open, my friend. Are you ready to fulfil your destiny?" Gráinne asked. Fleur looked at her in surprise.

"I'm too old," she answered, trying to explain.

"Since when did age ever stop you?" she joked. "You tried to rescue your grandson against two of the fiercest Goddesses in the Celtic world."

Fleur laughed at her.

"That was rather foolhardy," she said

"Not foolhardy, it's a measure of your spirit," Gráinne answered, allowing her friend to think quietly, think on the opportunity to learn more, to fill the gap she'd always felt in her life, the sensation that she was meant for something more. Her grandson was safe for the moment, so what else held her back? Nothing, Fleur concluded, all arguments dying within her.

"Where do I go?" she asked of Gráinne.

Chapter 59

The Great Queen of the Tuatha de Danann called a stop, and a truce, to the fighting on the fourth day. Though exhausted, Rían mustered strength from somewhere, and was about to advance again on the Mórrígan. She halted at the Mórrígan's roar, but held her sword at the ready, anticipating this to be a trick of some sort by the older woman.

"You're surrendering?" she demanded of the Great Queen.

"I will never surrender, but we cannot keep this up," the Mórrígan answered. "Be reasonable child, what will we achieve? If you have your way and destroy us both, then only the old man will win. Would you allow that, allow him to continue destroying the balance between the Realms? And what of your boy, Seth? Would you abandon him so easily, forsake him, leave him alone to deal with the old man?"

"Seth is dead," Rían hissed back at her.

"No, he's not," the Mórrígan admitted to her. Furious, Rían swung her sword around, putting the point of her weapon to the Mórrígan's throat.

"You lie," she growled at her. The other woman shook her head and backed up a step, away from the sword's tip.

"He was taken from the encampment, alive. At least that was the plan," the Mórrígan answered.

"What do you mean? You sound like you don't know," Rían said.

"When you broke out of your confinement, you also shattered the connections to Nemain and Badb, to Naoise and Cíanna," she answered. "Our intention was never to kill him. Besides, the others grew up with him, they couldn't find it within themselves to do that, it was probably part of the old man's plan to ensure his survival. If necessary, who would make a better bodyguard for him than Nemain, Fury herself, despite having her spirit subdued?"

"But why?" Rían demanded.

"Seth, Cúchulainn… both were supposed to be our protector, our bodyguard, but you won Seth over, something I could never do with Cúchulainn. Unexpectedly, the old man's best-laid plans were disrupted, the direction he was pushing the prophesies were endangered. Through his actions, he caused chaos, disrupted the balance within the Realms. The death of the boy, Seth, would have had serious consequences, far more reaching than perhaps the old man could have foreseen. Were I to have the boy killed, I too would have been just as guilty of adding to that chaos."

"The old man can see the future?" Rían asked but the Mórrígan shook her head.

"No one can truly see the future. All they can do is gain a view of the outcomes of their actions, or their choices. But for every action…" the Mórrígan said.

"There is an opposite and equal reaction," Rían finished. the Mórrígan nodded.

"And the old man's actions have caused this chaos."

"For every action…" Rían repeated. "You called a truce. What do you have in mind? To stop the old man?"

"The old man is not my main concern," the Mórrígan replied. "That is a role for another. You wish to be free of me, have your body back, as it was before the Ceremony of Kings?" Rían nodded in response. "Well, there is only one way I can leave here child, and it is dangerous, potentially fatal. We must be taken to the point of death for our Spirits to be released," the Mórrígan said.

"We have to die," Rían answered.

"Yes," the Mórrígan admitted, "but Cíanna assures me, that in your world, you can be restored to life, and she is strong enough to save you from death. This wasn't how I wished to return to the world, nor do I wish to remain in this manner. This world is your world, of which I know nothing. I would much prefer to return in the proper manner, and my return to Tír na nÓg would restore some balance back to the Realms."

"Why would you do that?" Rían asked. The Mórrígan smirked.

"Child, I told you before, I will do what I must to protect my people. The Tuatha within these Realms are my people, and if releasing my Spirit will save them, then that is what must be done. If it means sacrificing my line to do so, then that is a sacrifice I am prepared to make. But, if there is a shred of hope to save my line, without destroying everything, then I would also take that chance."

"But I thought you said I couldn't kill myself," Rían put to her.

"You cannot," the Mórrígan answered. "When you were proclaimed Ard Rí by the Lia Fáil, a number of gessa were also placed on you. Some of them would seem foolish to your society now, but the rest are designed for self-preservation. Only in battle or by treachery can an Ard Rí be killed. Of course if the title of Ard Rí was challenged, and the challenger won, the gessa would transfer to the new King."

"So how am I supposed to die?" Rían demanded.

"You, or rather we, must do battle, child," the Mórrígan answered.

"Battle who?" Rían asked suspiciously.

"There is only one who has come close to defeating you, and only one who has ever bested me," the Mórrígan answered.

"You mean Seth and Cúchulainn," Rían said, and she nodded.

"It has to be them," she argued with her. "There can be no other. They are combined now within the one man, and perhaps the only force capable of carrying out the task."

"And if he won't do it, can't do it?" Rían put to her.

"A difficult task for him, to battle the one he loves, to kill her, so he can save her," the Mórrígan answered. "I think the boy will do what he must, will do what he can, to save you. It is his destiny."

Rían opened her eyes and groaned, feeling every bone in her body aching as she stretched. She found the old man sitting on the bed, beside her.

"Highness?" he asked and she glared at him. As part of the truce, both she and the Mórrígan returned from Dún Scáith, but the Mórrígan relinquished control back to Rían, trusting the younger woman to do what was necessary. The old man would need to be convinced the Great Queen remained in control. She was, the Mórrígan told her, content her descendant stepped into her role as Ard Rí. She sat up, realising she was back at Ardscull.

"I take it you were successful over Rían?" he asked. She gave him a hard glare.

"Nemain and Badb?" Rían demanded. He shifted position.

"They've disappeared," he admitted. "I think somehow Seth overpowered them, but all three are missing."

"So it begins," she muttered to herself.

"What begins?" he asked, and she gave him a cold, flat stare.

"I need to hunt him down, and put an end to this," she answered.

"I don't think that is a wise course of action for you right now," he said, and saw the blaze of fire in her eyes.

"You've interfered too much already," she snarled in response at him, and he involuntarily flinched, before catching himself.

"I only meant there are greater issues to be dealt with right now," he said and again she glared at him. "What happened in Dún Scáith?" he asked. Her eyes narrowed in anger.

"You were there," Rían stated, and he nodded but without his usual sureness, wondering how she knew. He had hidden his arrival. "You didn't stay very long," she commented with a derisory smirk. "Brave man."

"I've survived this long by knowing when to take my leave," he informed her, and then glared at her as she laughed derisively at him.

"What happened in Dún Scáith is between the child and me," she answered him.

"But you have overcome her?" he pushed.

"You dare to question me on this matter?" she answered, her voice low and menacing. She felt mirth coming from the Mórrígan and a hint of … pride.

"Now leave me," she ordered him, and hesitantly he did.

Chapter 60

Fleur's disappearance left Seth feeling a little lost. Strange, to have grown so close to someone so quickly, he thought. He thought of Rían too, when Fleur eventually told him about the battle raging between her and the Mórrígan, a fight he would have loved to witness, especially if the two women were as equally matched as Fleur indicated. It would have made for interesting watching.

Rían. Could he face her? She already whooped his ass at least twice, and if the two women were equally matched, would he be able for their combined force? Against Conor, together, they'd been a force to be reckoned with. Would he have stood a chance if Rían hadn't come up with Macha's curse? He honestly didn't know. Now he had to win, and yet not win. If he succeeded, he would lose Rían forever. If he failed, he would lose his own life, and Rían still wouldn't be free. He never felt this nervous before, this close to pure panic.

He stood watching Naoise working through her katas, flowing from one set into another, her movements far more graceful and confident than he remembered of her. Cíanna explained to him what the old man did to her, subduing Nemain. While he and Cíanna had a far more amiable relationship than the one between himself and Naoise, it was the first time they stayed up all night talking, aided by a few bottles of wine. At lot of truths came out, and he doubted Naoise would be pleased at how much he now knew about her, knew how much she needed to belong just as much as he did. So much for his psychology, when he failed to notice his 'big sister' was just as lost as he was. They were all lost, Cíanna told him.

The conversation turned to Rían, and he admitted his feelings for her, acknowledging the strength of them. Cíanna laughed at him, telling him it came as no surprise to anyone else except to him. With a little more alcohol in his system than he was used to, the lost little kid in him started to reveal himself, and all the imponderable questions in his head started to come out like; why was all of this happening? Why Rían? Why The

Mórrígan? Why? Cíanna laughed louder and he frowned at her. In between the giggles she explained, she wasn't laughing at him, but she'd had the exact same conversation with Naoise not that long ago. The only explanation she could give Naoise then, and give Seth now, was some things were just meant to be. But she also had a theory. He waited for her to elaborate. She took a deep breath, and another mouthful of wine.

"The prophesies," she started, beginning to feel the effects of the wine hit. He grimaced.

"Those damn things. The cause of all this mayhem," he announced, also a little drunk. Cíanna nodded.

"Too true, little brother, but while the prophesies may be the reason behind all of this, they are not the cause of it. Meddling with them, trying to twist them is," she answered.

"And that's where my dearest grandfather comes in," Seth answered, a strong trace of bitterness creeping into his voice. Cíanna sympathised with him. It took him by surprise, and while he was being strong and manly about it, it still shocked him to his core.

"His meddling upset everything," she said, "but why you and me and Naoise? Why Rían? Why the Mórrígan? Rían and the Mórrígan are one and the same person, ultimately. You love her, and she loves you."

Seth looked at her in surprise.

"Really?"

"Yeah, you dolt, of course she does," Cíanna answered. "My theory is, now that we are aware of the prophesies, we're all conscious of what's happening, and we're now in a position to right the wrongs, to restore the balance somehow."

"Fleur said the same thing," he admitted, "but in a lot less words." He became melancholic again, and she knew he was thinking about what he had to do.

"Just think about it," she said. "You get to save the world, more than one in fact, and you'll be saving Rían. What a hero." He looked at her, coming back from his brooding, and gave her a brief smile.

"Do I get a cape?" he asked.

"You can wear lycra tights for all I care," she shot back.

Now, in the cold light of morning, the pounding in his head started to subside. Naoise caught him watching her and stopped, stretched, and straightened herself up.

"How's the head?" she asked and he made a face.

"Haven't drunk that much since you ended up at that drinking contest in college," he admitted.

"You never could hold your drink," she shot back, and he laughed at the memory of it, and of her carrying him back to the dorms, but not before she chatted up his girlfriend at the time.

"I recall it wasn't the only thing you scored that night," he retorted, and she laughed.

"She was just curious, it didn't last," she admitted.

"Doesn't really matter now," he said, and she shook her head.

"Not really," she conceded. "How are you doing, now I mean?" He shrugged, knowing she asked about his latest shock.

"Still angry, I guess," he admitted to her. "I miss Fleur though." Naoise nodded.

"I kinda miss her too. I like her, she has balls. Could teach you a thing or two," she threw at him and he made a face at her. Some things didn't change, he thought, and thankfully so. But he liked this new Naoise. She was the same smart ass, but as he already observed, she was more confident, quietly so. She caught him watching her.

"What?" she demanded. He shrugged.

"I like this new you," he answered. She stepped towards him, swaying her hips as she did so, until they were face to face.

"It's still the same as the old me," she said lowering her voice so she almost purred. A little taken aback by her approach, he took a step back away from her, and she laughed at him.

"Nemain..." he began.

"Likes men. It's a little weird, but I might enjoy experimenting," Naoise admitted, and laughed at the look that crossed his face before he composed himself. "Don't worry, I wouldn't do that to Rían. Speaking of whom, she's all right. Just thought you'd like to know."

"What do you mean, she's all right. How do you know?" He caught hold of her by the shoulders, but she remained undaunted and unfazed by his aggressive action.

"She's back in the real world. The Mórrígan is with her, but the balance of power has shifted," she answered.

"Meaning?"

"The Mórrígan's taken a back seat, and Rían is in control, but the old man doesn't know it, yet," Naoise answered.

"How the hell do you know this?" he demanded. She smirked at him.

"I may only have limited power, but I sensed them when they re-entered this world last night, and Rían did a tentative search to find us," she answered.

"So why didn't Cíanna sense anything?" he asked.

"To be fair, Cíanna has a lot of strong points, but her sense of elemental power isn't one of them. She has a connection to that power, but it's different to what Rían and I have. So while the pair of you were getting sozzled last night, I was hard at work with my limited abilities," she replied. "You know the old man's probably going to be looking for us, especially if he finds out what we plan to do."

"We better get there before him then," he answered in a flat tone.

Screeching tyres in the drive, signalled Naoise's return later in the day, and she found him lounging out on the deck, that overlooked Carlingford Marina and lough. He grunted as the weight of the bag she dropped on him, landed on his stomach.

"What is it?" he asked.

"Take it out and look," she answered. He did so, and lifted out what seemed like a short wet suit, but more contoured, and made of heavier material, strategically reinforced in the chest, shoulders, ribs and groin.

"It's the Bat-suit," he commented sarcastically.

"It's body armour," she answered, sitting beside him. "It's used by mountain bikers and mountain boarders for body protection." Disgusted, he let it fall back into the box and threw it to her.

"I'm not wearing that," he said, angry with her for even suggesting such a thing. "It would be like ... cheating."

"You and your bloody honour," she threw back at him. "Rían has already beaten you at least twice, or have you forgotten? Have you forgotten how she fights? You said she uses dirty tactics, now combine that with the Mórrígan, and how do you think they'll fight. Do you honestly think you'll stand a chance? You'll be no use to anyone if you're dead, hero." He stood up.

"I don't need that kind of help," he retorted. "I can do this on my own. I know how she fights, I'll figure a way around her methods."

"You really think you're ready?" she shot back. In an instant, she was out of her seat and tackled him to the ground. A small blade appeared in her hand and the point of it dug through his shirt and into his skin over his heart. She sat on him, straddling him, leaning over him. He grunted in shock and surprise and glared at her only centimetres from his face. She pursed her lips together and made a kissing motion at him. Furious, he got his hands under her shoulders and pushed her off. She rolled into a crouch and laughed so hard her red curls bounced about her face.

"Still think you're ready for her?" she asked as she stood up. Seth glared at her. "There is no dishonour is wearing it. The Mórrígan herself wore her breastplate in that last battle, and I didn't hear you crying about dishonour then. There is no shame in protecting yourself against an enemy that you know will use every weakness of yours to their advantage." He stood, allowing her words to sink in, knowing she was right. "If you want to fight a woman, you have to start thinking like one," she went on. "We don't think about the niceties of a fight. We think about how to bring our enemy down, in the most expedient, and usually the most painful way possible," she told him.

"That's vicious," he threw back.

"That's life," she shot back. "The armour will at least give you a fighting chance, while you do the task required of you."

He thought about it.

"Fine," he gave in, and she gave him a small smug grin in return. He brushed past Cíanna on his way back into the house, and she kept her expression neutral as he went by, not wanting to annoy him any further, knowing it was the last thing he needed right now. Naoise was right. Rían knew his weak points, few that they were, and she'd already beaten him on her own before. She had the Mórrígan now as well, at least Cíanna assumed the Mórrígan was in there, somewhere. Naoise assured her as much, and Cíanna found herself experiencing … jealousy for the first time where Naoise was concerned. It was a unique and uncomfortable feeling for her. Naoise changed since Nemain's release from the restraints the old man placed on her. It was a little strange, watching your sister changing in front of your eyes.

"If I didn't know better, I'd almost guess you were coming onto him," she said as Naoise approached.

"I'm trying to prepare him for this battle," she answered.

"By wrecking his head? How is that going to help?" Cíanna asked.

"He's nowhere near ready to face what he has to, and he's scared," she told Cíanna. "He needs to be angry because only rage can have any hope of battling rage. As it is, there is only fear. Fear that he will fail and all will be lost, fear that he wins and he loses Rían anyway. This thing is so finely balanced the smallest error could be the undoing of everything." Cíanna listened to Naoise, noticing another new difference in her. She spoke more softly now, but her words carried, and with them the weight of authority. Cíanna smirked at her.

"I like this new you," she said and anger flashed in Naoise's eyes.

"Everyone keeps saying that," she growled. "What the hell was so wrong with the old me?"

"Nothing, but this new you is… stronger, more self-assured, more confident, and controlling her temper a little bit better." Naoise gave her a flat stare in response. "Will fighting her be so difficult for him?" Cíanna asked, redirecting the conversation. Naoise nodded.

"There is a geis on Rían, remember? Not something we ever talked about before, but it's there nonetheless. It was on her when she fought Conor. We thought with the Mórrígan in control, the geis might have been

restrained or less powerful, but it doesn't seem that way. She won't want to, but she'll be compelled to defend herself, to fight for her own life, just as Seth was compelled to fight when Ulster was under threat. He had no choice but to step into the fray."

"What if there was another threat made towards Ulster, would that help him?" Cíanna asked. Naoise shook her head.

"No good. He'd become just as consumed by his geis and we would lose any chance of this working out the way we want it to, any chance of saving Rían, the Mórrígan and the Realms," she answered.

"How do you know all of this?" Cíanna asked, and Naoise smiled.

"When you unleashed me, you also unlocked secrets and knowledge Nemain had access to, that was trapped with her," she answered.

"Like your elemental power?" Cíanna asked.

"Among other things," Naoise answered cryptically, stepping past Cíanna into the house.

Chapter 61

It took effort on Naoise's part, more energy than she anticipated, but she got herself to Tír na mBéo, the Nemain part disgusted at the effort and exertion required. The Mórrígan brought her here the previous night, and showed her how to make her own way back. She arrived at night, landing on her ass, by the lakeshore, and gritted her teeth against the jolt.

Reaching the cabin, Naoise didn't knock or hesitate before entering. They already knew she'd arrived and thankfully, no one saw her ungraceful landing. The Mórrígan embraced her.

"Mo deirfiúr, (sister)," she greeted her.

Naoise looked around the room, finding Rían sitting, facing the fire.

"The old man is searching for you," Rían told her.

"Not unexpected, and it's not like we're hiding," Naoise answered, sitting beside Rían.

"How is the boy?" the Mórrígan asked.

"Worried," Naoise answered. "Why didn't you bring him here?" she asked of Rían, who glanced at the Mórrígan.

"We didn't think it would be a good idea," she answered. "It's already hard enough to deal with, without having him here."

Naoise nodded.

"He misses you," she admitted to Rían. "Doesn't miss you," she told the Mórrígan.

"Can he do this?" Rían asked. Naoise stared at the fire for a few moments before answering.

"Physically there's not a problem," she began. "After all, we watched him in that other Realm against three men. He's going to be a tougher opponent than Conor."

"But?" Rían asked, and Naoise sighed.

"His head's not in the game, neither is his heart," she answered. "I got him some body armour today, but he's bitching about his honour again."

Rían laughed.

"Body armour? You reckon he's going to need it?" she said.

"Hey, you were one who elbowed him in the jaw, I'm just trying to give the poor boy a fighting chance," Naoise threw back.

"One thing has me worried," Rían confessed, and looked to the Mórrígan. "When we faced him the last time, he declared himself as the Hound of Ulster, became a different person. I thought that was Cúchulainn's title, not Seth's to take. What will stop that from happening again?" she asked.

"You forget, a leanbh, he is Cúchulainn," Gráinne answered her. "He took on that title and role because of his geis, he was compelled to fight, and the ancient part of him simply took over."

"So what's to stop that from happening again?" Rían asked again.

"We do not declare a war on Ulster this time," the Mórrígan answered her, with a gentle laugh.

Naoise watched Rían, saw her smirking and thought on what a difference a few days, and a drawn out fight had made. The animosity was gone. Perhaps it was the shared goal that now bound them together. Rían stiffened, and stared towards the door of the cabin.

"What is it child?" Gráinne asked, concerned.

"Did no one else feel that surge of energy?" Rían asked, incredulous that no one else sensed what she had. Rather than disbelieving her, a long dagger appeared in the Mórrígan's hand. Rían stood beside her, a similar weapon in her hand. A strong bond between them now, Naoise concluded and stood, weaponless. She didn't know how to create one, yet. Behind them all Gráinne reached out, and smiled.

"Be at peace. Rían's senses are true. I know who approaches," she told them. "Put your weapons away, I will not allow you to harm her, nor shall harm come to you."

Walking through the Gateway felt like walking through ice water. Maximum chill factor, without the soaking, and stepping back into Tír na mBéo seemed to take forever. The Gateway behind Fleur closed, and she pushed a strand of hair from her face tucked it into the clasp that bound her now long, white hair. She reached out with all her senses, something she learned to do in the Mystic Realm. How long had she been away? It felt like eons. In the Mystic world, it had been eons, with so much to learn, so much to see and within the Mystic world, mortality and death did not exist. Only learning, only new discoveries, but her time with the Mystics was over, for the moment

She sensed Gráinne and the Mórrígan, but was shocked to sense something else. Someone sensed her arrival here. Only another Mystic had that ability, she thought, and wondered who was also waiting for her. Could it be the girl, as she had seen in so many of the possible futures?

The cabin was awash with light from every window. She had no difficulty seeing the steps up to the door, that opened as she reached the top step, and she saw Gráinne's smiling face.

"Welcome back old friend," she said to her.

"I'd hoped to surprise you, but it seems someone knew of my return," Fleur answered, and stepped into the warmth from the fire. She stood before the Mórrígan.

"An Mór Ríon," she said, leaning on her staff to kneel before the Queen. The Mórrígan caught hold of her, gently pulled her back up. Naoise leaned in close to Rían.

"Seth's grandma," she explained, whispering into her ear.

"You have no need to bow before me, Sean Mná (old woman)," the Mórrígan spoke with gentle tones, surprising Rían with her almost meek approach. "One such as you has no need for subjection to the Tuatha. There is a treaty between our peoples."

"But broken by one," Fleur answered. The Mórrígan shook her head and smiled.

"An entire race cannot be held responsible for the actions of one man, nor can the treaty be broken, not while we work together to set those wrongs to right," she answered. Fleur gave her a deep nod.

"The Queen is great and gracious. I hope she can forgive me my original misconceptions of her," Fleur said. The Mórrígan laughed.

"The misconceptions of me have been well documented," she said. "And to be fair, not all untrue. I am guilty of actions I am not proud of, but actions that were required, nonetheless." She glanced to Naoise, and the Nemain part of her remembered some of those times, and actions. She gave the Mórrígan a slight nod. "You need no forgiveness from me, old woman, but I would ask one thing of you".

"The girl," Fleur answered and glanced at Rían. The Mórrígan nodded.

"As it was foretold," the Queen said.

"Whoa," Rían interrupted. "What was foretold? What has this to do with me?" The Mórrígan put her hand on Rían's shoulder.

"We've already seen, or sensed, who and what you truly are, child," she said.

"And what exactly is that?" Rían demanded. Fleur gave her a searching look, and knew why her grandson had fallen in love with her. Here was his challenge, and she shared the same fire and passion as he possessed.

"You sensed my arrival here, didn't you?" Fleur said to her.

"Yeah," she answered, cautiously.

"Only another Mystic, or potential Mystic, could have been aware of the Gateway opening," she answered. Rían sighed and rubbed her eyes with the heels of her palms.

"Great, just when I start to get to grips with one thing, life throws me another curveball," she answered.

"Now you're starting to sound like Seth," Naoise shot at her.

"Oh no!" Rían exclaimed. "Next I'll be crying about my honour, and I'll start brooding." Together she and Naoise burst out laughing.

"It appears they know my grandson quite well," Fleur commented to Gráinne and the Mórrígan.

"So it seems," the Mórrígan replied dryly, before turning back to Fleur. "You will teach her?" Fleur nodded.

"As it was foretold, it was destined we would come together," Fleur answered.

"But doesn't that create an anomaly?" Rían asked. "If the Tuatha and the Mystics are two different races, and I'm a descendant of the Tuatha, then how can I also be a Mystic?"

"I told you before," Gráinne took up the explanation. "It is rare, but not unique, happening every millennia or so. Many have the ability to move about the Realms, but you belong in our Realms and in your own world. In you lies the ability to live in, unite and connect with all the Realms."

"Even that is beyond my abilities," Fleur told her. "In you, the Prophesies come together. You are all things to all people, Ard Rí, descendant of the Tuathan, and a Mystic. A heavy burden child, and yet strangely, your fate rests in the hands of another."

"You have seen everything, have you not, Sean Mná?" the Mórrígan asked, and Fleur nodded. "You know what has to happen and why? You know the role your grandson plays in the scheme of things?" Again, Fleur nodded.

"But the outcome is not assured," Fleur answered. The Mórrígan and Gráinne both nodded.

"The burden weighs the boy down," Gráinne answered as the Mórrígan stood at the window of the cabin and stared out into the night.

"What a bitter twist of fate," she said, more to herself.

"That the one thing you wanted from Cúchulainn could be Seth's downfall, and puts all of this at risk," Rían answered. The Mórrígan turned to her, fire blazing in her eyes.

"So true, little one. His love for you could destroy everything," she answered.

"This dilemma is not lost on him either," Naoise informed them.

"Aren't we all forgetting one little thing?" Rían said. "With the exception of his attempt to defend Ulster, while he was under Macha's curse, I've never faced him when he and Cúchulainn were one. It isn't just Seth I'm going to be fighting."

"You won't be alone in this," the Mórrígan reminded her.

"But wouldn't it be easier if it was only me facing him?" Rían asked.

"Yes, it would, and it would make his part in this simpler too," the Mórrígan answered. "But unfortunately it will not work that way. While I reside within you, the power of the geis will affect me also. And, as you are my descendant, it is my duty to aid you, protect you as much as possible, and it is because he is also Cúchulainn that I will be with you."

"You just can't resist a fight with him, can you?" Rían smirked at her, and the Mórrígan laughed.

"It is our destiny," the Great Queen admitted. "We will be fighting two different fights, for two different reasons, but for one goal, to restore the balance to the Realms. With me joined to you, perhaps Cúchulainn, and his hatred of me, will help Seth overcome his crisis of faith."

"You know McCormac will try to stop you both," Fleur said, sensing a resolve of steel from both as they looked at her.

"Naturally," the Mórrígan answered, a hint of haughtiness creeping into her voice. "But I trust you've accepted your role in this?" A smile played at the corners of Fleur's mouth.

"Of course, Great Queen. I will do my part," the old woman answered. Rían and Naoise both glanced at each other, bewildered.

"I'm guessing there's more going on here than what's happening between Seth and me," Rían commented and the Mórrígan turned that haughty look towards her.

"And you wonder why I call you child all the time," she commented dryly.

Chapter 62

Rían arose at dawn, dressing quickly, and made her way out of the house before the security shift changed and a fresh, more alert crew came on duty. The old man grew more suspicious each day, increasing the number of guards dotted about the place, to prevent her from getting out as much as stopping anyone from getting in.

She had a choice of cars, Naoise's or Cíanna's, grabbing the keys to Naoise's sportier vehicle on her way out of the house. The engine sounded loud in the dawn silence, but it raised no alarm as she took a gentle speed down to the gates. They remained closed as she reached them. She looked about for the control panel, pouring all her concentration on it and by sheer will in sensing the power within it, she managed to override the locks. The gates began to open as she crawled closer to them and towards freedom, but movement from the tree line caught her attention and she looked on in anger, as the old man stepped out in front of her. From the Mórrígan within her she felt pure rage. Taking the car out of gear, but leaving the engine running, she opened the driver's door and stepped out.

"Rían, I presume," the old man said to her, his voice cold and barely containing his fury. "Where do you think you are going?" She remained silent but put all senses on alert. "Answer me," he roared at her.

"To put an end to this."

"An end to what?" he demanded. Rían felt the Mórrígan's strength surging through her, ready for a battle, itching for a fight, but she also sensed the power within the old man, felt it welling up. He lashed out at her, trying to contain her, but she saw what he attempted to do and instinctively put up a barrier, shattering his attack. Her retaliation was swift, and she blocked his access to the universal energy source, blocked his ability to manipulate the elements.

He looked at her in horror, but his fury replaced it. He watched her closely, seeing the faint shimmering outline about her, and knew she was in ríastrad, knew he couldn't overcome her in any way. No action against her could come quick enough to take her by surprise. And how did she become so powerful in controlling the elements? Who taught her? Time for a different tack.

"I made you what you are," he roared at her. She stood her ground against him.

"You had no part in making me who I am," she growled back at him. "You just abused what was there, manipulated it to your own end."

"I made you Ard Rí," he argued hotly. She shook her head.

"I was always Ard Rí, the Lia Fáil only proclaimed it."

"I brought the prophesies into line," he roared at her.

"With your own agenda," she roared back. "Have you no concept of the damage you've caused? If the Mórrígan and I didn't know better, we'd guess you were deliberately unbalancing the Realms, doing your best to destroy them."

He had no answer, and she didn't give him the opportunity. She pointed at him and he felt himself pulled away from the gates as she moved her hand, directing him where she wanted. Fury surged through him, but its power did nothing to help him break through her barrier around him. Without another word to him, she sat back into the car. No more need for deception or sneaking out as she slammed the car into gear and took off at speed, tyres spinning and screeching on the ground.

The barrier around him lifted moments later and he tried to lash out, to retaliate against her, but she was already out of his reach. It left a bitter taste in his mouth, to have been so easily overcome by her, but he knew where she was going. He'd walked the Mystical Paths again last night, seen what she planned to do. It was something the old man wouldn't allow to happen.

His blood or not, Seth was only a means to an end, and if his death meant saving the prophesies, then so be it. The boy was an anomaly anyhow. He was not supposed to be, and certainly not embroiled in the Prophesies as deeply as he was. Now, instead of defending the Ard Rí, he'd turned into her main threat, her foremost adversary. If he killed her, then all was lost.

The bloodline ended with her. There was no other, not without going back centuries, or further to find another thread, and even then, that line wouldn't be pure, would be too distilled when it reached this generation. If Rían died, then everything died with her. She and the Mórrígan accused him of throwing the Realms, the other Tír's out of balance. Such insolence, from the both of them.

The Prophesies were ambiguous at best, and open to a variety of interpretations. All he strived to do was give them direction and a clear path, and for that he was scorned, treated as an outlaw, a rebel, while the rest floundered with understanding the Prophesies, pulling them apart, analysing every nuance.

He took a stand with them, drew a route through them, and for that they accused him of creating disorder. It was a fruitless exercise, explaining his actions, they simply wouldn't understand, wouldn't listen, so he took matters into his own hands, and once again, he needed to protect and defend the fruits of his labours.

He returned to the house and grabbed his car keys. He thought about appearing there, using Mystic means to open a Gateway, but when he tried, he found his Mystical access and abilities restricted. How the hell had that happened? Damn that child. And damn him for being so easily fooled by her. Of the many Paths of the Mystics that he travelled, of all the different possible outcomes, the child never displayed so much power. She knew he'd been to Dún Scáith, but he'd used Mystic means to arrive there. How did the child know? Not even the Mórrígan had that ability, and it worried him.

Once out of the gates, he took off at speed, using the transponder signal of Naoise's car programmed into his sat nav to follow her, the module updating him with her location and his distance from her. Damn, that child was driving fast, he growled to himself as he pushed the accelerator pedal closer to the floor, ignoring the speed-limit warning beeping at him.

It took Rían two hours to get to Carlingford, and slowed to the appropriate speed going through the town, following the directions Naoise gave her the night before. Naoise already scoped out the nearby forest, close to where they were staying, and found the best location for her and Seth to meet.

While the woods were open to the public, access was via existing trails and fire roads, but Naoise hadn't stuck to those. She wandered throughout the entire place, hiked in the adjoining Cooley Mountains, and while she didn't know every square centimetre of the place, she built up an impressive amount of knowledge in such a short space of time.

What Naoise sought was privacy, a location that would allow them to fight in relative secrecy, with little chance of anyone else walking by or happening upon them. The last thing they needed was the Gardaí getting involved and any explanations involving the Mórrígan, Ard Rí and fighting to the death would end in a detention order, under Section 22 of the Mental Health Act. Detained, probably indefinitely, in a nice, warm, padded room.

Rían found the entrance to the forest and parked the car. She got out and stretched, stiff from the drive, but her mind slowly slipped into fight mode. Each step she took, the more she felt it taking over her, and she didn't fight it. From the boot, she retrieved the Mórrígan's large sword, the one used against Conor. Rían's now, she guessed, an inheritance from her ancient ancestor.

Strangely, there was no nagging in her head, no other voice, and when she analysed it, was surprised to simply feel the Mórrígan coursing through her, a part of her, at one with her. She paused and reached out with all her senses, feeling every tree, every leaf, every creature within the forest. Beyond that, she sensed Naoise and Cíanna and created a connection to them both as she saw the Mórrígan do. As she entered the woods, she allowed Naoise to guide her, to see through her eyes, as she made her way deeper and deeper through the trees.

When she got to the clearing at the edge of Carlingford Lough, she could go no further.

Chapter 63

Naoise tried her best with him, he knew that, knew her efforts to taunt him were ploys to get his 'head in the game', as she put it. He knew she was worried. She'd tried to talk to him, but he wasn't in a talking mood. She said it wasn't like him to lose this much hope. Then she slapped him across the back of his head, hard, and told him to snap out of it. Bloody woman, he growled to himself. Vicious creatures, but that was life Naoise said. That said, this new and improved Naoise proved to be a challenging opponent as they practiced and sparred together, and he wondered how much Rían told her about the weaknesses in his defences. Naoise honed in on them all, few that they were, and worked them out. He was sore and tired by the end of their practice session, but content. It meant a good workout, and he took his time under a hot shower, allowing the water to work out the kinks.

It was mid-morning and he now rested, sitting out on the decking, trying to read, but he found his concentration slipping and the words didn't make much sense to him. The two girls joined him in the sunshine, Cíanna sitting with her book, and Naoise just lying on the lounger, soaking up the autumn rays. He heard Cíanna's sharp intake of breath and he leaned forward to look past Naoise at her, as she sat upright and looked to be struggling with something. He looked to Naoise who remained lying back on the sun-lounger, her eyes closed beneath her shades and unperturbed. Cíanna composed herself when Naoise eventually stirred. She stood and put her hand on his shoulder.

"Time to get the Bat-suit on," she told him. He started to argue but she tilted her head, that slight angle of the head women did when they knew they were correct, and were not about to take any arguments to the contrary.

"She's here?" he asked.

"Close," Naoise answered.

A few times over the years, when he and Naoise competed at the same tournaments, they psyched each other up, mentally prepared each other, and gave each other objective views on their respective opponents. This time was no different. After changing out of his clothes, Naoise settled the body-armour about him, happy about the fit, but she was confident of the size, which she got a tad on the tight side. He put a close fitting tee shirt on over it, tighter for having to go over the armour. Against Naoise's advice, he opted for jeans. He had to admit though, that they limited his movement sometimes, but he argued with her that he wasn't entering a tournament.

"Don't expose your right side," she lectured him. "But the armour should give you some protection there. Watch Rían's elbows," and he smirked to himself. While he listened to Naoise, he ran through his own mental checklist, his techniques for getting his mind on track, of becoming focused. Naoise sensed this in him. The brooding was gone; no more second-guessing, no more doubts. There was a task to be done, a fight to be fought, a battle to be won.

"Don't become predictable," she said as a final warning. "Rían learns your rhythms very fast, she's quick to spot patterns. You need to keep her off-balance, and aim for the stomach. If you get the heart or the lungs, it's game over." She stopped, realising what she was doing. "I'm not helping, am I?" she asked. He gave her a quick flash of a smile, and she knew the old, super confident Seth was back. Took his damn time about it too, she thought.

"No, you are," he answered. "Just tell me where to find her." She gave him directions, then a gentle push to get him going. He had that look, she concluded, the one before every fight, when he blocked everything else out. It wasn't a cold or hard look, but one of peace and stillness. The Cúchulainn part felt stronger, much stronger than Seth ever sensed before, felt him flowing through his bones.

He made his way through the trees, and paused as he caught a glimpse of her through the trees. He quietly walked up behind her, but knew she already sensed him approaching. She stood with her back to him, and looked out over the water, her attention fixed on the opposite shoreline and the Mourne Mountains on the other peninsula. No words were exchanged, but he silently unsheathed his sword, and uncharacteristically made the first move, attacking her from behind.

She reacted in an instant, spinning around, and used the scabbard of her sword to avert his initial blow. He took a step back, and saw a shimmering around her, reminding him of when he was in Tír na mBéo, and knew she was in ríastrad. With her sword now unsheathed, she threw the scabbard aside, and counterattacked, using the move she made months ago to open his right side. To her surprise, he anticipated her, and his sword hilt cracked against her shoulder. She cried out in anger, and he saw her temper burning in her eyes, knowing her geis consumed her, and nothing short of death would end this now. Or her near-death, if he could achieve it.

He reached behind him, unsheathing a long dagger from under his shirt, and deflected another blow from her, then landed a back fist to her jaw. She rolled with the blow but spun around to face him again, her eyes narrowed in fury, but a brief smile played at the corners of her mouth. Naoise was right, he thought, he would to have to think like a woman to fight one.

Rían feigned to his right, but reversed at the last minute, simultaneously catching his left side with the blade, while releasing a hand from the hilt to deliver a right hook to his ribs. Both her sword and fist impacted with the reinforcements in the body armour. She grunted from both pain and anger at this latest development. In a counterattack, his fist caught her squarely in the midriff, and knocked her to the ground. She landed with a thump, but kicked out and caught his leg, also knocking him down. He got his arm up in time, blocking a reverse punch to his head, and rolled out of her reach. They both jumped up and faced each other.

"Any time you're ready to start," she taunted him.

"Ladies first," he shot back and she did. He shut everything else out from his mind, but her blade.

Inside ríastrad, time slowed down for him. This was how he always won his fights in tournaments. He could anticipate his opponent's next move. Now, for the first time ever in a fight, he was on an equal footing with his adversary. He couldn't anticipate her moves, couldn't pre-empt what she would do, but her attacks were swift, coming in waves of fluid motion. He deflected them all, searching for an opening, any opening to strike at her where he needed. She sensed his hesitation at one point, when he had the opportunity to strike at her, her heart exposed, and she kneed him in the groin. He merely grunted at the impact, the Kevlar padding saving him from that particular agony. She growled at him as her knee ached, and she stepped away, surveying the bulky bits about his body. She knew about the armour. Naoise already warned her, but she didn't think it would be this effective, damn it. No matter, she thought to herself. There were places the armour didn't cover, not as effective as striking the core areas, but damage could still be done.

Chapter 64

McCormac took guidance from the GPS tracker, and followed its directions to the woods not far outside the town, finding Naoise's car and parked beside her. He got out and walked sprightly to the tree line. He may have given the impression he was infirmed with age, encouraged that misconception in fact for his own advantage, but it was far from the truth. Yes, he was old, feeling ancient at times, but it was one of the advantages of being a Mystic, the usual infirmities of the mortal world were slow to manifest themselves. Age wasn't a disability, merely another step in the evolution of Mystics, for with age came wisdom, and patience, and understanding of all things within the Universe.

He stopped at the entrance to the woods, reaching out with his Spirit, searching for Rían within the forest. He found her, and yet she was different. Her signature, and that of the Mórrígan's had fused, and he grinned contently to himself. Rían and the Mórrígan had become one, finally. All he had to do now was ensure their survival, and he started walking, knowing she was ahead of him, somewhere. The deeper into the woods he went, the stronger his sense of her grew, but movement from the corner of his eye distracted him. He glanced around, but couldn't immediately find the cause of the disturbance. A twig snapped behind him, and he turned, his eyes searching the clearing ahead of him.

He reached out, surprised to find he was restricted again, knowing it wasn't Rían this time, he could sense her at the far edge of the forest. He frowned, puzzled and worried. Had she set some trap for him, knowing he would be following? A figure moved through the trees ahead of him and he moved his head to see past tree limbs, narrowing his eyes in an attempt to get a better view, a glimpse of who it was. The figure slowly stepped between the trees before coming into the clearing.

"You!" he growled at her.

"Expecting someone else?" Fleur asked.

"What are you doing here?" he demanded, growing worried with each passing moment. He had no sense of her, standing before him, and he was still blocked.

"To stop you," she answered.

"You wouldn't dare," he snapped back.

"Try me."

"Woman, don't try to meddle in things you know nothing about."

"And that differs from your meddling... how?"

"I haven't meddled, I've shaped destinies, guided the prophesies."

"Prophesy is only one person's version of events, snatches of possible futures, out of context most of the time, and rarely understood," she replied, keeping her calm and composure. If it was the only thing she'd learned in the Mystic Realm, it was that if she lost her cool, she lost the battle.

"Do you think it's that easy?" he said. "Prophesies have always been a guide, a roadmap within the mortal world. It is the purpose of a Mystic to interpret them, to understand them."

"And control them?" she asked. He shifted on his feet, working his way around the block, and was disgusted to discover a simple incantation stopped him. Simple, but a Mystic one. Only another full Mystic could carry it out, not a simple wizard, such as Fleur was. He banished the block, and a smile spread across Fleur's face, as the old man got a sense of her.

"Your control over the Prophesies is slipping, old man," she said. "It seems destiny is now reasserting itself, beginning with how you tried to divert mine. You purposely got me pregnant, you bastard, and now your grandson, your own blood, will be the one to cause all your scheming to fail. Ironic, wouldn't you say?"

"It'll never be over," he growled back. "There will always be some new twist, some kink in destiny. Sometimes it's a constant battle between destiny and prophesy. Something you have yet to learn. So you have become a Mystic now. Do you think that allows you to be so righteous with me, woman? I've seen what will be, what has to be, so get out of my way." Using another incantation, he tried to block her, but she rebuffed his efforts. She took a step towards him.

"I too have seen everything, what was and what was supposed to be," she answered. He was buffeted by a blast of air, but not knocked to the ground as she originally intended.

"Childish tricks, woman. Didn't they teach you anything else on the Isle of Mystics?" he snapped. "So you think you know of my treachery, but you would have ruined everything, been the cause of everything to fail." He shot a fireball at her and she recoiled as it hit, but the flames washed over her before extinguishing themselves. She straightened up.

"It's you and not I who've almost ruined everything," she answered. "You destroyed our child, and you're now prepared to destroy our grandchild. Your actions have unbalanced the Realms. Is it your plan to destroy them all, destroy the other worlds? What would that achieve?" she demanded.

"The Tír's will survive, they always have, and they always will, or haven't you seen that?" he shot back sarcastically. Her answering blast took him by surprise, and he landed flat on his back, but he jumped up to face her again. By the gods, if he got close enough to slap her, she'd land in the middle of next week.

"Just try it," she growled at him, sensing his thoughts.

"The boy is not going to survive," he told her, "I know you're sensing what's going on." She held her tongue, knowing Seth was under pressure at the other side of the forest.

Chapter 65

Seth ignored the gash on his thigh, it bled, but wasn't a life threatening cut. A few centimetres inwards and it would have been a different story. Rían paused for a moment to wipe blood away from the cut above her eye. If she wanted to fight dirty, he could too, and in stepping out of her way, he managed to elbow her. In truth, he aimed for her jaw, but it landed just above her eye instead. Enraged, she retaliated with a fierce attack, using short sweeping cuts at him, making him yield ground to her and opened up his defences, which is how he now sported a nasty wound on his leg. They circled each other for a moment while they caught their breath, looking for an opening, any opening.

Seth made the next move, coming in low from the left with his sword, and used the flat of his dagger to stop her sword from giving him another wound. His sword landed and cut her along her thigh, similar to, but not as deep, as the cut on his own leg. Ignoring the pain, she kicked out instead, the front of her boot impacting with his shin. He jumped back out of the way, but not far enough, and he winced in pain. The dagger spun in his hand as he made a lunge at her. She sidestepped him and the edge of her sword deflected his blade away from her midriff. He expected that, and reacted with a sidekick, catching her in the very spot his blade aimed for. She doubled up in pain as he spun around, stepping out of her reach, and waited for her to retaliate.

She paused to catch her breath, and wiped her eye with the sleeve of her shirt. Damn him, and damn that bloody armour, but she sensed hesitation within him. A weakness, she could use against him. The short sweeps caught him off guard, and she wondered if it would work again. Maybe a variation, she thought, as they circled each other again. She made the next move, starting out with short sweeps, but changed her third stroke, spinning around and reverse-elbowing him in the jaw. He roared at her in anger and she felt a smug grin bubble to the surface. She then reversed the hilt of her sword into his stomach and he grunted at the impact. So the centre had minimum reinforcements she thought, and calculated multiple variations of an attack. While he stepped out of arm's reach, he was within leg reach, and she spun around delivering a roundhouse kick to the spot where the hilt landed. The kick was strong enough to knock him to the ground. He landed flat on his back, knocking the wind out of him, leaving him exposed and prone. She made a lunge at him, but he raised his leg, just enough to sweep her legs from under her. She landed with a thump, and he pushed himself up from the ground, grabbing his dagger, making an aim for her midriff. She sensed his movement and rolled backwards to standing. She deflected his dagger and punched him in the face.

He staggered backwards, hand to his face, as he felt blood trickling. Bitch, he growled to himself. His sword was close by on the ground, and he caught his foot under it, kicking it into the air, where he caught it and attacked her.

Chapter 66

The trees around the clearing swayed violently. Both Fleur and McCormac created their own protective spheres, but were so close that they combined into one. The only element escaping the sphere was the wind that shook the trees. Fleur deflected another lightning bolt from him.

"How long have you been a Mystic?" he demanded of her. "You didn't have this power when we last met, on the battlefield."

"Didn't I?" she shot back as she combined air and earth, and the ground shook beneath him, but he retained his balance. "I got some basic training in the Tír's many years ago, after I left you. One of the Mystics left the Isle to come to train me."

His eyes widened in disbelief.

"Liar," he accused her and she laughed.

"Do you think you're so great, that these things couldn't be hidden from you?" she threw at him with a laugh. "You weren't looking for any Mystical power in me, so it was easy to hide. Just as it was easy to hide the girl's power from you."

He was about to launch another attack on her, but he paused.

"What?" he demanded. Fleur strengthened her barrier against any sneaky retaliation, but laughed at him.

"You silly old fool. For all your greatness you couldn't even see what was in front of your face. Some Mystic you turned out to be," she taunted him. "The Mystics on the Isle saw what you planned, travelled the road you set out on. Do you think it was such a difficult task to shield the girl from you, to shield her power from you? Yet she always knew when to run away from you, to run away from your plans. Strange that."

Fleur felt his fury, sensed the rage burning inside of him, and expected him to hit her with everything he had. She braced herself for the impact, and wasn't disappointed. She felt no fear of him or of his anger. She already travelled this Path, and knew she would survive. Did knowing the outcome strengthened her resolve against him? Sparks showered about them both, and Fleur heard a loud explosion, saw a flash of intense light, forceful enough to deafen her, and knock her to the ground. The last thing she saw was his outline in the light before everything went dark.

Naoise opened her eyes, and grinned at Cíanna.

"Grab your gear Doc, it's your turn now," she said.

"Who? Rían?" she demanded. Naoise shook her head.

"Fleur," she answered.

"But…" Cíanna began, but Naoise grabbed her by the arm, hoisting her out of the seat.

"No buts, move," Naoise growled at her, and Cíanna wasn't so sure she liked this new Naoise any more.

Spurned into action, she grabbed her medi-kit, and followed Naoise through the trees. Never fond of the great outdoors, she found the going difficult. Naoise paused, waiting for her to catch up, and eventually took her bag from her, slinging it across her own shoulders, in order to make the going easier.

They found the old woman lying unconscious in the clearing and while Cíanna examined the woman, Naoise circled the clearing, searching deep into the trees surrounding them. In the distance, she heard a car coming to life, and tried to reach out, but it was beyond her reach and abilities.

She heard groaning behind her, and turned finding the old woman easing herself up.

"What happened?" Naoise asked. "I saw a flash, and then nothing. "

"He disappeared," she said to them. "Seth?"

"They're still fighting," Naoise answered. While Cíanna continued to examine the old woman, Fleur closed her eyes and reached out, sighing at what she found.

Chapter 67

The day wore on, and Seth grew tired. So much for the legendary strength and endurance of Cúchulainn, he thought bitterly, as Rían began to get the better of him. As the sun sank lower in the sky, so did his stamina, and he found himself defending more than attacking. Ríastrad was slipping away from him, he was becoming predictable, and he knew it. Rían began to anticipate his moves, and that only meant one thing; he failed. No, he growled to himself, there was too much at stake for him to just give up. He leaned against a tree for balance, and to catch his breath, ducking his head out of the way of her strike that slammed into the tree. He wiped blood from both the cut on his jaw and the one above his eye. Time to get up close and personal, he thought, and rushed her in an unexpected move. She hadn't been ready for him, as he slammed into her, knocking them both to the ground. She groaned as she hit the dirt, Seth landing on top of her. Discarding his own sword, he pinned her sword arm down with his free hand.

"Hardly the time or place, lover," she taunted him, trying to move under his weight. He brought his dagger close to her, but she caught his arm, and it turned into a battle of wills. She got her legs out from under him and wrapped them about his waist. The body armour might be protecting him from blows, but it yielded under the pressure as she squeezed him with her thighs. His breath caught and he let the dagger fall, using his now free hand to push her leg away, but to no avail. Time to get nasty, he thought, and pushed his thumb into the wound on her leg. She roared in agony, and delivered a hook to his head, which he rolled with. She rolled him over and straddled him, grabbing his discarded dagger, and tried to stab him in the neck. He stopped her, and used his knees, coming up behind her, to throw her over his head while he jumped up.

She eased herself up and as she turned to face him again, he saw pure rage in her eyes, pure fury etched into her face and he wondered how much longer he could last against that force. She kicked his sword towards him, giving him a fighting chance. He stepped towards it, limping distinctly and favouring his injured leg, hoping she'd fall for it. She was wary of his motives, but relaxed her stance, and he used her brief moment of compassion to his advantage to get close and mustering all his energy, fury, frustration, he concentrated it all onto a final attack. If this didn't work, he knew it was game over for him. The old man would have won, and the Mórrígan would remain in this Realm until old age killed her, or another assassin succeeded where he failed.

Taken a little by surprise by his deception, having thought him too caught up in his honour to resort to such a tactic, she yielded ground to him, reserving her energy in defending against his short cuts. He learned not to over-extend himself, or leave himself open by using wide sweeping moves, and he now used short, slashing and stabbing motions, making it a little more difficult for her to anticipate the direction he would move in, but he was getting tired, and getting slower. All she had to do was let him tire himself out with this latest attack, and when she sensed his fatigue, she launched her own counter-attack on him.

He gave up more ground than she yielded to him, and he found himself pinned to a tree, wondering how the hell that happened. He should have been able to sense it behind him, and step around it, but in his exhaustion he failed to notice it. Pinned as he was against the tree, he had one more trick up his sleeve, or rather up his armour. Rían stepped in closer, picking up his dagger that lay nearby. Her intention was obvious. She was going to kill him, up close and personal, look into his eyes as the blade went in.

The knife that appeared in his hand was much shorter than his initial dagger, and he made sure Naoise hadn't known about it. It took Rían completely by surprise, as the blade sliced through her skin, as he stabbed her, just below her ribs.

Chapter 68

Rían fell into his arms, felt the body armour as she leaned against him for support, but her legs give way. He caught her, held her close.

"I'm sorry," he whispered into her ear as she gasped for breath. Exhausted, he fell to the ground, trying not to jar her. She cried out as they landed and lost unconsciousness. Limp in his arms, and in his exhausted state, panic starting to rise. Rían's body shuddered in his arms and she stopped breathing. He shielded his eyes from a blinding light him, but found Rían and the Mórrígan, as shimmering figures, before him.

"You see child, it worked as I promised you," the Mórrígan said, "but you need to return to your body, or you will die." She put her hand on Rían's shoulder. "Return and live as you were meant to. You are already becoming the Queen you were destined to be. Allow no one to take that from you, or take your power."

"As mad as this sounds, I think I'm going to miss you," Rían answered, and the Mórrígan laughed

"And I you. But remember that I am you, so I won't be far away," she said. To Seth, it seemed the shimmering form of Rían folded into the body lying in his arms. Rían opened her eyes and gasped for air, before falling back into unconsciousness, breathing again. The Mórrígan fixed him with an intense stare.

"You did well boy," she said to him.

"But you've sacrificed your chance to be in this world," he said.

"Have I?" she asked cryptically. "As Cúchulainn you will always only ever think, act and react on the spur of the moment, with very little thought to your actions, except for the glory they will bring you. But as Seth, the man of this modern world, you have the ability to understand and consider the consequences before you act. You are wise not to allow Cúchulainn to take over you completely"

"He didn't know," Seth told her. He felt a flash of anger from her as a hot breeze. "He didn't realise who you were, didn't know how you felt about him." She studied him for a moment before nodding to him, and looked down at Rían's body.

"Take care of her, as you were destined to, for she is of far greater importance than I dare say even the old man realised," she said. He nodded in response and she stepped away, turning her back to them, as she disappeared into the trees. Cradling Rían's body in his arms, he pulled his phone from his pocket and dialled Cíanna, who answered on the first ring.

"I need help," he said urgently.

"We know. We're on the way," she answered.

He opened his eyes on hearing a sound nearby, annoyed to realize he'd fallen asleep, but he was exhausted and fought to keep his eyes open. Hearing a rustling in the trees behind him, he gently placed Rían on the ground and stayed crouched beside her, dagger ready in his hand.

"You have about as much stealth as a rhino," he heard coming from the trees, recognising Naoise's voice. As the two women emerged from the trees, Cíanna's face was pure thunder.

"I'm a doctor, not a bloody stealth machine. Unlike you, I don't go skulking about in forests," she snapped back. To his surprise, Fleur also stepped out from the trees, looking a little battle-weary herself.

"Expecting someone else?" Naoise said eying his dagger, and he lowered the knife.

"Just in case," he replied. Cíanna stepped passed him to the unconscious Rían and kneeling beside her, carefully checked the wound. She looked up at them.

"I'm not going to risk moving her, but she should be in a hospital."

"She's going to be all right, isn't she?" Seth asked, trying not to sound as anxious as he felt.

"I'm sure as hell going to do my best," she said, taking her backpack from Naoise and opening it out beside her, pulling out all sorts of medical supplies.

"Anything I can do?" he asked.

"Get a fire started, and get it nice and hot," she answered.

"You get the firewood hero, I'll sort the fire out," Naoise told him.

Despite his injuries and exhaustion, he gathered an armful of wood and when he returned, found Naoise created a stone circle. She caught him smirking at her little girl-scout effort, and scowled back at him as he dropped the wood beside her. She set the wood in the circle and concentrating harder than he'd ever seen her in his life, holding her hands over the wood, sparks danced about and a flame erupted from the centre.

They sat, and watched as Cíanna worked. Taking a final pack from her medi-kit, she unfolded a foil blanket and covered Rían, before sitting back exhausted. Fleur took over, putting one hand on Rían's head and the other on her midriff, just above the wound. Cíanna stood and stretched, walking towards Naoise and Seth.

"She's going to be okay," she told them. "I'm going to leave her here for the night, and leave you something to give her for the pain when she wakes up. She's going to be very, very sore. Fleur's doing some Spirit thing, checking that part out. I suppose to make sure Rían is in there and is all right. Next, I want to take a look at you."

"I'll be fine," he answered, brushing her hand away, but she ignored him. While he suffered no fatal wounds, the cut on his leg was deep enough to require a number of stitches, as did the cut over his left eye. But for the most part, the body armour did the job in protecting him from anything more serious. The minor stuff Cíanna ignored other than to clean them up, rolling her eyes every time he winced or sucked in breath in pain.

"All done," she said, "though I doubt you'll be posing for photos in the Social and Personal columns anytime soon."

Fleur made her way to them.

"How is she?" he asked her.

"Well, it's only her in there, and at the moment she's using everything she's got to heal herself, so when she wakes up, she's going to be exhausted," she answered.

"She's certainly living up to her name," Cíanna commented.

"How so?" he asked.

"Breasel comes from an old Irish name that means brave or strong in battle, and she's just survived a fight for her life," she told him. "Don't move her until she wakes up, and let her come to on her own. The stitches should hold, so you should be able to carry her back to the house then."

"You're not staying? Not like you to leave a patient," he said.

"She's going to be fine, and she has you. Naoise and I are still connected to her, so if anything goes wrong, we'll know the instant it does," she answered. Seth knelt beside Rían, and gently brushed a strand of hair from her cheek. Naoise stood up and placed a hand on his shoulder.

"Keep her safe, hero," she said tenderly.

"And the old man?" he asked, watching the exchange of looks between the three woman.

"He disappeared," Fleur answered and Seth gave her a questioning look. "He was on his way here," she went on, "to stop you. To kill you, if he had to. I confronted him in the forest as you and your girl fought it out."

"You whooped his ass?" he asked, surprised.

"At one point we could sense you were about to give up, that she was getting the better of you," Fleur explained. "He didn't think there was a need to hang around. And I was whooping his ass. We'll talk about it tomorrow, boy. I don't know about you, but I'm exhausted. Naoise, be a dear and lead the way back. Let's leave these two to get re-acquainted."

He awoke with a start, surprised to find dawn light creeping over the mountains in the distance, and he eased himself up trying not to disturb her as she lay beside him. Beyond her, the fire had died out and he contemplated relighting it, when her eyes fluttered open. He stroked her hair and she gave a weak smile.

"Hi," he said softly.

"Hi," she echoed.

"How're you feeling?"

"Like I've had my insides almost ripped out," she whispered.

"Sounds about right," he said, and kissed her.

Epilogues

In yet another award-winning scoop, Rían Breasel uncovered, and reported on the mysterious disappearance of the Ulster Premier Conor Uí Neil, with the shock revelations of corruption and vote rigging now hampering the party who engineered and supported his meteoritic rise to the top. Other allegations also included using his position of leader to negotiate and bargain with leading business people for more support, status and monetary gain. In the end, it all came down to greed and the corruption of power.

Now, it seemed the man hid himself from public scrutiny along with his elderly assistant, their current location unknown to anyone. The story itself didn't last for long as those with potential connections to the disgraced leader now tried to distance themselves from the scandal, and the story eventually faded into obscurity.

All the information supporting her allegations arrived in a sealed envelope shortly after her return to work, her return to some semblance of normality. All she had to do was piece the story together, and as much as she hated taking credit for an invented tale, it was better and safer than telling the truth and neatly explained away Seth's presence in Ulster, removing him from any allegations of shady dealings.

IIM welcomed her back with open arms. Having already bound their allegiances to her as Ard Rí, they now found themselves bound to her conditions, that of anonymity. All she wanted was a normal life, a quiet one.

II

For months, Rían also found herself in the spotlight as the social columns speculated on her own brief disappearance from the public eye, jumping to conclusions and connecting her to the CEO of TOTAL, who, if the papers were to be believed also took a sojourn from the social scene about the same time.

Despite arriving separately to the same functions or social engagements, gossip columnists watched the pair with eagle eyes for any gesture, any hint of something between them. The biggest giveaway to fuel speculations was probably Seth Morand arriving at such functions alone, and it seemed he was no longer an eligible bachelor, much to the dismay of many. When pressed, each remained silent on the subject of the other, offering only general and non-committal comments.

However, their bubble of secrecy burst within months as rumours of Rían's pregnancy began to gain momentum, the rumours proving true as it grew harder to disguise her condition. Only then did they make a public announcement of their engagement, and confirmed the imminent birth of their first child.

Half a world away, the old man sighed and folded the paper, placing it on the small table of the sidewalk cafe. He picked up his espresso, allowing a small smile to play on his lips. After all, he was about to become a great-grandfather, and everything worked out nicely, and according to plan.

III

Every time the Mórrígan re-entered the world she remembered everything, remembered all the wars and battles she'd fought, remembered all the children she'd borne, remembered all the loves she'd lost, and all the times she'd died.

However, this time, it would be different.

This time, she would be born anew.

Made in the USA
Charleston, SC
19 October 2015